I0674695

William M. Baker

Colonel Dunwoddie

William M. Baker

Colonel Dunwoddie

ISBN/EAN: 9783743373419

Manufactured in Europe, USA, Canada, Australia, Japa

Cover: Foto ©Raphael Reischuk / pixelio.de

Manufactured and distributed by brebook publishing software (www.brebook.com)

William M. Baker

Colonel Dunwoddie

MILLIONAIRE.

A STORY OF TO-DAY.

NEW YORK:
HARPER & BROTHERS, PUBLISHERS,
FRANKLIN SQUARE.

Entered according to Act of Congress, in the year 1878, by

HARPER & BROTHERS,

In the Office of the Librarian of Congress, at Washington.

ONE WORD.

THE extraordinary circumstances of Col. Dunwoddie's case compel the author to present but one locality in the Southern States of the American Union, and to speak of but a household or two of the people there. If the measure of success should warrant, the writer hopes to portray more fully a region the varied interest of whose past and present is exceeded only by the abundant promise of its future.

CONTENTS.

COL. DUNWODDIE, MILLIONAIRE.

CHAPTER I.

CHARLES DUNWODDIE, COLONEL, C. S. A., OF CLAIRSVILLE, CLAIR COUNTY.

"One on the Maker's earliest plan,
A tall, primeval, Adam man,
Whose appetite hath preference nice;
A relish which discriminates
Pomegranates from the sugary dates
Among the fruits of Paradise:
Who mourns, at his tremendous cost,
An Eden but this morning lost."

CERTAIN remarkable events are herein to be related. The fact that they befell such a person as Col. Charles Dunwoddie makes the telling of the really wonderful story much the easier; the Colonel being a man whom to know at all was to know perfectly. There was a time when he was not a colonel. That was in the days—it now seems ages ago—before the war between the South and the North. In those Arcadian times he was simply a tall and talented young lawyer, who was known to write for the papers. Everybody said that it was his poetry, rather than his eloquence at the bar, which won him his wife. There was a great deal of talk about it at the time, because the lady, Miss Eliza Allen, the only daughter of Gen. Allen, was acknowledged to be not the most beautiful so much as the nicest and best young lady in all Clair County. He began his conflict with the world immediately on leaving college, at which he had taken the highest honor of his class, by fighting a duel—firing into the air himself, but being badly "winged." On pretty much the same impulsive principle, he had galloped out, during his courtship, twenty miles after supper to leave a bouquet upon the front porch of the lady's residence, informing her of his success in his first case at the bar that day, riding back in time for breakfast. The road through the post-oaks there and back was bad, and the night was stormy, but he went as upon wings, one of which was love and the other ambition, and little he cared. True, his horse was neither hippogriff nor Pegasus, and, therefore, was as dead as Julius Cæsar half an hour after he entered his stable, but his rider was never quite as alive before in his life.

Having married his only daughter to his satisfaction, the General died, leaving his plantation and a few dozen negroes to his two children, Eliza and her idle brother, Alexander. Then came secession. The young husband did not believe in such a remedy for acknowledged wrongs at all. He made powerful speeches against it: one in the brick court-house in Clairsville, where he lived, wherein he reached a pitch of eloquence which inspired him with the first hope he ever had that he really possessed genius. As to poetry, you cannot open any decent collection of the best authors which does not have at least one or two of his most stirring lyrics written at that date, he had so put his very soul into them.

But they did not prevent the war. With many others, from the St. Lawrence to the Gulf, he had abhorred the impending epidemic of civil strife; yet when it came, with all others from the Gulf to the St. Lawrence, he also took the terrible fever. Precisely two months after his great speech, he made, and in the same court-house, another speech, the reverse of the former and far more vehement; and on the strength of it a company was raised, of which he was unanimously elected captain. He had been a Whig of the school of Henry Clay—of Washington, rather. During the war he carefully enshrouded himself in the smoke and deafened himself with the cannon to everything like deliberate thought or theory, making the fighting the exclusive business of his head as well as his hands.

The end of the war saw him back again in Clairsville. He was a colonel indeed, but of a regiment which he had so led that, with some severe scars himself, he was almost the sole survivor. The instant he became his own man again by the arrival of peace, as he had leaped into the war from a point dozens of years previous to it, so he forsook as in an instant his temporary sojourn in the strife of the time, and all that was to follow immediately upon it, and passed into the days that were to be, say twenty years after.

Practically speaking, however, he was glad to get back to his family—the more especially as it was about all that was left him. His slaves had vanished like a flock of blackbirds. To save his life he could not have got five dollars per acre for his lands. His wife had a genius for economy more wonderful in results than even his for poetry; and Horace, their oldest child, the manliest of boys, had been of the greatest help to her. None the less it did seem as if the Colonel and his household had reached the utmost edge and end of the world. It did not matter so much that the Federals had burned his law-office, and every law-book he had, during a raid into Clair County; the whole state was too poor, as well as too sick to death of strife for a while, for any one to go to law with anybody as to anything whatever.

His wife had been, so to speak, the good sense, and for years before his death, of her father, Gen. Allen, and she suggested that the Colonel should establish a paper. He did so, and named it the *Clair County Clarion*. By sheer force of vigorous writing, he

made it the ablest journal in the state. This led him into active politics. Only for a brief and bitter time, however. Upon the whole, he preferred camp-life at its worst and guerrilla fighting at its deadliest to the sort of things he found at the capitol of the state. He published meanwhile a valuable book or two upon the resources of the state, which had quite a circulation, and entered again, in addition to editing his paper, upon the practice of the law, as people became rested enough from war to quarrel once more in the old-fashioned way of which they never grow weary. Clairsville was still his home.

But all his life Col. Charles Dunwoddie had one serious trouble. His social standing was of the highest, there being, as all the world knows, no better blood in the South than that of the Dunwoddies. Nor was his affliction in bodily health, his being the wiry vigor which belongs to men of dark complexion and spare build. No man could desire a better wife, girls nicer than his Alice and May, or four finer boys than his Horace and George, Harry and little Charlie—this last gentleman, of two years old, having already seated himself, in the estimation of the household at least, upon the supreme bench, and being always addressed, by reason of his sobriety of demeanor, as "Judge." Col. Dunwoddie was a person of commanding presence and ardent temperament, and his trouble did not lie in any physical defect. By reason of the restless energy, as well as the ability of the man, no one was, in certain senses, quite as well known as he, in his own state especially, and throughout the South. Not that he was ever thought of as a possible governor or member of Congress. In addition to his well-known detestation of the politics of the day, he was considered as altogether too conservative as well as independent. At the bar he was successful by reason of his personal magnetism with the jury, but chiefly on account of his reputation for integrity and an almost Quixotical sense of honor. No one in the South stood higher as orator and editor, and no name even competed with that of Col. Charles Dunwoddie as author and poet. Upon the whole, he was considered as a somewhat impracticable gentleman, whose talent, however, amounted to genius: even his bitterest enemies were proud of him. He was somewhat lofty in manner as well as in stature, rocky and angular in fact. This made it that much more natural that he should be volcanic at times, and more than one eruption in the past revealed reserves of force in the man, and fire. Never at rest for a moment, neither he nor any one else could tell what might happen next.

The supreme trouble with Col. Dunwoddie was that he was so poor—so "*dead poor*," as the current phrase ran in that section. It was very remarkable. No man could have a more keen and even passionate liking for books, pictures, foreign travel, handsome house and furniture, the leisurely society of the refined, as well as all that is generally associated with the idea of wealth. The richest of men, with generations behind him of the wealthiest of ancestors, could not have missed his money had he been suddenly stripped of it more than did this gentleman who had never really had any. That he was not rich was, in his estimation, a sort of absurd disaster. It was an outrage as foolish as it was wicked. Yet he would always have been poor had there been no war. He was one of those talented men who, however free from bad habits, can no more make money than the untalented rich man can make poems. It was not that he did not want money. He wanted it to gratify his own refined tastes; wanted it still more to enable him to aid the many excellent people in his knowledge who needed instant help and needed it sorely; wanted money, most of all, for the sake of his family, which he loved to infatuation. He went into the making of money as impetuously as he had gone into the duel, yet, somehow, all of his firing was into air still, while every shot in return hurt badly, if it did not kill. No man could work harder, yet, in some way, the very intensity of his anxiety to be richer seemed itself to defeat him at every step.

That was his one trouble, he was so poor. There are myriads of the race who take their being poor as matter of course; but not so Col. Dunwoddie; he never consented to it for an instant. Other people take poverty as they do their daily air; not so with him. Far from accepting it as one does the atmosphere of the world common to all, the Colonel took it as one does the ague. He had never been rich—there was not the smallest probability that he ever would be; none the less did his poverty strike into his blood and bone, into his marrow and his soul—it poisoned the whole man. If ever a husband had a wife who was the living and loving antidote to the miasmatic despondency produced in him by being poor, the Colonel was that man. That was one reason he gave way to it. It was with him as it is with people who persist in breathing the atmosphere of a swamp because they have a sovereign cure for ague in easy reach at home upon a cupboard shelf. What made it worse for the Colonel was that, being orator, poet, author, lawyer, editor, he was in the unceasing habit of uttering what he thought and felt. Of course he never opened his lips in regard to his private affairs to any one else, but he certainly did, and that much the more, to his wife. She was so silent herself, as well as sympathizing, and the sound of his own voice in talking to her excited him to say more than he intended. Her husband was so eloquent as well as pathetic that it was impossible she should not have listened. In everything else the manliest of men, Col. Dunwoddie had poured into her ears whole Iliads of his woes. That, however, was part of the schooling which made her, having sufficient substance in herself in addition, the woman she was, as will be abundantly explained.

It was some years after the war, and when the Colonel was deepest down in one of his most trying times, that the extraordinary series of events befell which is now to be told, and told as simply, as truthfully, and as briefly as possible.

———◆———

CHAPTER II.

THE RETURN OF THE PRODIGAL, AND WHAT WAS SLAIN THEREAT.

> "The man supplies the woman's needs,
> But where he fails 'tis she succeeds,
> Like brain and heart; this understood,
> If brain gives man his masterhood,
> The heart supplies the brain with blood."

COL. DUNWODDIE was in public one of the most reserved and dignified of men. Writing at his desk in the *Clarion* office, pleading at the bar, making a speech upon platform or stump—even when he paused on a street corner to talk with a knot of friends—wherever he was, the drill of the war held him erect in a bodily sense, and the yet sterner discipline of that strife with men and things which never ends made him courteously yet decidedly distant in manner. He was, however, like one who consoles himself for enduring the most elaborate of uniforms while in public by indulging in the loosest of dressing-gowns and slippers in private. If he seemed to be older than the oldest of his associates abroad, he appeared to be, in certain senses, younger than little Charlie when at home. There was a reserve of manner even in riding to circuit courts with his fellow-lawyers, but his children would rather go fishing with him than with any schoolmate.

After the war, and for some time before it, Alec Allen, his brother-in-law, had been a burden to Col. Dunwoddie; how heavy a burden no one could imagine who had not known the size and weight of that relative. Some time before this the Colonel had induced Mr. Allen to go West, yet the night this story begins he returned and took a seat at the supper-table very much as if he had never been away at all. When he had left it was all that the Colonel could do to lift the large and lazy man out of his contented indolence and start him westward; now that, like an enormous boulder, he had rolled back again, the Colonel knew that it was for life. Had any one questioned him in regard to his returned brother-in-law, the person asking would never have suspected from anything in his words or manner what a heavy affliction poor Alec really was. He was that much more unreserved in speaking about him to his wife. At her request he had suppressed his feelings and gone to bed on the evening in question. He has tucked the cover closely around his chin; he will forget his years of useless efforts in behalf of his shiftless relative; he will try and hope; he will at least go to sleep.

But his annoyance is too much for him. He thrusts the bed-cover down from beneath his chin with both hands, and begins—

"Great—!" and draws breath to express himself with, if possible, an energy equal to the emergency. His wife's sweetness of disposition is swifter than his wrath.

"Patience! Great patience, Charles," she interposes, completing the sentence for him. "It is very hard, dear, but that is the only way to express it."

As she says it, standing beside him lifted up into a sitting posture in bed by his indignation, she places her forefinger upon her husband's lips. It is a busy, an exceedingly useful forefinger. It mends many a household rent, but none of them are so serious as that which now employs it. There was no telling to what extent the rip and tear would go if she was not, and very often, so prompt.

"Well, great patience! then," her husband yields; "but you know, Eliza, how peculiarly unfortunate it is just now—how very inconvenient—"

"—It is at this time." He had begun the sentence with the rising inflection of one who is entering upon an inexhaustible theme, but she completes it for him with the downward accent of one who closes a subject. In regard to his sentences, too, his wife was, as in everything else, his other and better half. "Not so loud, dear," she adds. "Alec, poor fellow, is in the next room, you know, and your whisper is as sharp as a knife. He has just gone to bed, and will hear every word you say. I am ashamed of my brother, but I will be that much better to you, being his only sister. All the way back from Nevada, just to add to your cares. It is too bad! But the best thing is to be patient—patient."

"Patient?" Her husband, who had laid himself down, sits up again to ask it as a question, but his wife smothers at the source all that is following the word with her lips pressed upon his. Now the Colonel had a habit of clothing his arrested feelings in whatever dead language from his old college days came handiest, and so letting them also die. "*Patientia vincit omnia*," he therefore adds, and lies down again. In this, as in many an instance, English is wholly inadequate to the annoyance. Besides, it is a way of at once expressing and also suppressing feelings too vigorous for him to smother.

"It must be midnight; and now, Charles, do go to sleep," Mrs. Dunwoddie pleads, in the lowest of tones, lest her brother should overhear. She need have no apprehension. His coming back has never struck that brother for a moment in the light in which the others regard it. Although by no means a fool, Alec Allen is exceedingly slow. He falls asleep the moment he lies down, and, as if under the weight of his huge bulk, in a way which would have awakened the envy of his brother-in-law, who, being of spare frame, alert, and anxious, finds the task of going to sleep the hardest of a good deal of hard work he has to do. It is not that Alec Allen is unusually wearied with travel, for he is under thirty, in perfect health, apparently, and has not hurried himself at all on his journey. The fact is, he is always tired, constitutionally fatigued. The one thing, even more than eating, which he does with the most energy as well as promptness, is to sleep. To him slumber comes by nature —is an idiosyncrasy. Not so with Col. Dunwoddie, who has long ago learned that, next to his wife, sleep is his best friend; and well she knows that, in dealing with her husband, sleep is her surest ally.

"But I tell you what it is, Eliza," he resumes the instant he awakes the next morning, "I do tell—"

"Sh! sh!" she interrupts him, having arisen before him; and, turning from the glass at which she is dressing her hair, she makes a warning gesture with her brush towards the next room.

"I really do not see how we can," he says, in a lower but that much more determined voice. "It is impossible to respect such a man. You know how lazy he was before he was induced to go to Nevada. And now, here he is again upon our hands, worse off than he was before. What is this?"

The question had reference to Col. Dunwoddie's singular employment. He was seated, as he spoke, upon the side of his bed untying knots made, since he lay down, in his clothing. He has a great many things to think of as a lawyer, the leading man of a church—although by no means a member thereof, far from it—editor of a paper, author occasionally of a book or so. Valuable thoughts come into his mind after he goes to bed and before he can get to sleep. Quite often an idea will break like a midnight burglar into his deepest slumber, and he will find himself wide awake and so thoroughly in the grasp of the assassin of his rest that the only way to be rid of it is to tie a knot in the clothing left on the floor beside him. He would rather lie awake all night than disturb his wife. She sleeps like a lynx, awakened by his least motion; but he has learned to steal his hand cautiously out and knot the fleeting thought into his clothes. A knot in his stockings will recall a brilliant idea for that poem he has in hand; another in his drawers will serve to remind him of the sick family of a man killed in his regiment upon whom he must call the next day; yet another in his suspenders will secure that otherwise missing link in his last case in court. He repeats his queer rosary to himself now as he sits, but Alec in the other room is too much for him.

"You know, Eliza," he says, "how hard it is now.—What did *this* knot mean?—And Alec has ten times my physical strength. He must see that we are even poorer than when he left us. I dare say I will have to refund the money somebody out West loaned him to get here upon. One half the race have to carry the other half upon their backs. I tell you, I for one am broken down in the doing of it. No, sir," for Col. Dunwoddie always said *sir* when getting warm, even if it was with little Charlie— "No, *sir*," he repeated.

"Charles!" it was all his wife said. The interruption fell like a dam across the stream of his talk, but it rose higher on that account.

"If I was not so *very* poor, Eliza! I can conjecture why gnats, houseflies, mosquitos were made," he proceeds, "but not why he was created. There was a providence in the creation of Alexander the Great, but why—I tied this knot," surprised to find one in his neckcloth; "Oh, it refers to that butcher's bill—why, I mean, *this* Alexander was created, I solemnly declare—"

"Hot pot!" breaks in little Charlie, of two years old, from his crib—"Hot pot! hot pot!" louder and louder as he emerges out of sleep into broad day and hearty hunger; for "hot pot" means warm milk, and is Charlie's entire knowledge of the languages so far.

"Yes, darling," says his mother; "and I know you too well, darling"—this to the larger of the two of that name—"not to know that you are too true a gentleman,

to say nothing else, to show any unkindness to poor Alec. Especially at breakfast, dear. You'll see! It *is* a providence, a puzzling one, I know, but it is one.— Come, you precious treasure." This last to Charlie.

Charlie is ten pounds too heavy for his mother, who is a frail little woman; but she will persist in rating the strength of her hands according to that of her love, and bears the child down-stairs. She is a woman whose nerves have been severely strung during and since the war. To live in a state of apprehension, quick and keen, has become her nature, and yet she is ignorant this morning of the amazing change about to befall them. There is, however, a dawn which goes before the rising of every sun, and, before that change befalls, there will be a struggle, in their instance also, of the darkness and the light. The supreme event of their lives is hastening towards them; but it will send its messenger in advance, a terrible forerunner it is, and this very day its footstep is upon their threshold.

CHAPTER III.

BROTHER AND SISTER, AND THE LACK OF LIKENESS THERE MAY BE BETWEEN THEM.

"Sir Reynard passed where grazed the flocks;
  'O fleecy, foolish folk,' he mocks,
  'Ye are so stupid!' said the fox.
  'We fatten here,' they met his scorn,
  'Not fearing trap or huntsman's horn;
  Besides, we are what we were born.
  You, too, are stupid when asleep,
  And very soon one slumber deep
  Your wit and ours alike shall steep,
  And we be equal,' said the sheep."

IT was rather a dull breakfast. Mrs. Dunwoddie was singularly silent. Her husband was reducing to system for the day's work, as he ate, all the knots he had tied the night before, and was occupied, most of all, with a particularly tough knot, a Gordian one, in fact, in reference to the small-farming scheme so much discussed at that time throughout the South. As he rose to hurr down to the *Clarion* office and put his ideas into imperishable type, he was stopped by his brother-in-law, whose existence he had forgotten.

"I say, Colonel," the other remarked, with a face unusually broad and beaming, "I would like, when I get rested and you are not in such a hurry, to talk to you a little."

"At any time, Alec," Col. Dunwoddie replied, and hastened away. He had too long and thorough an experience of the other to attach the smallest importance to his conferences.

Horace, the eldest son of the family, a youth over twenty, had eaten his breakfast before the rest were up, and hurried off to the railway office. Being a specially energetic young man of the new era, Horace had an almost painful aversion to his Uncle Alec, whom he regarded as a perfect type of a period past, when even young men could rest contented, their hands in their pockets, while somebody else, black or white, worked for them. More than that, the young man had long entertained hopes in regard to a certain Emmeline Anderson which he had never breathed as yet hardly to himself, and this portly uncle of his had suddenly come upon his ardent wishes like an avalanche, burying them, for the moment, out of sight. Alice was answering the many questions of May, her younger and prettier sister, in regard to a picnic to be held as soon as the spring fairly opened. Harry, the bookworm of the family, had hurried through his meal, in order to finish a book he was reading before school began. George was the wit of the household, and, after vain attempts to engage his uncle in conversation about the bears of Nevada, he was occupied in slyly teasing Charlie, the youngest of all, who sat beside him at table. Charlie was the gravest and most dignified member of the circle, and, solemnly eating his bread and milk, the Judge, as they called him, refused to be tickled by the fingers of his brother

in his fat legs which hung down under the tablecloth.

Mrs. Dunwoddie had a sense of relief when all were gone at last but her brother and herself. She sat at the table, washing the cups and saucers, wondering how that brother could seem so hearty and happy, so unusually free from care, when he was without a plan or a penny in the world. As to Alec, having finished a hearty breakfast, he stood, his hands deep in his pockets, supporting himself against the mantel; for Mr. Allen rarely sat when he could lie down, or stood up when he could lean. He was a large-limbed, broad-chested, square-headed man, and, as he leans near his sister, he slowly strokes his yellow beard, which reaches almost to his lowest vest-button. He is dressed in that thread-bare broadcloth which is so much more suggestive of poverty than is the coarsest jeans. It is only too plain that his trip West has been, like all his life heretofore, a failure. There is an aspect of ox-like goodness about the man, an acceptance in his broad face of things as they are, a satisfaction even in being a passive verb through all his inflections, which would have rested his over-eager brother-in-law to contemplate could the Colonel have thought so. Evidently there is little of the man beyond his outer self. He does not drink or swear, gamble, lie, or steal; the trouble is that he is as stationary in regard to any actual goodness as in reference to any positive wickedness. "There never was a man more admirably adapted," Col. Dunwoddie had often remarked of him, "to saying and doing, thinking, feeling, and being just nothing whatever."

And yet a close observer would have imagined that there was some unusual purpose in him as he stood there. Unless he was actually a fool, there was no sense in his laughing lazily to himself over the head of his sister, bowed down at her work as she sat. It may not have been so, but he seemed to be holding something in indolent reserve as he said at last very slowly:

"I wanted to say something to you, now they are all gone, Eliza. But I'm in no hurry. Besides, once or twice this morning I've had the queerest feeling in my head. I had one or two attacks of it out West. The solemn fact is, I'm too fat. How can I help it? I never do anything to make myself fat. What a pity it is that the Colonel works himself to an edge like a razor; he's a good deal thinner than when I left. What does he weigh?"

"What did you want to tell me, Alec?" asked his sister, her head still bent over her cups and saucers, for her brother's very presence seemed to press her down.

"Oh, well, it does not matter. We will talk about what I wanted to say when I get rested a little;" and the man seemed greatly amused, his face one broad smile in singular contradiction to the indifferent tones with which he spoke.

"Have you made any plans, Alec?" his sister asked at length, looking up anxiously. "Plans, I mean, about business?"

"Plans? Well, no," her brother replied in a leisurely way. "No, Eliza, I cannot say that I have, any settled ones I mean. But I'm in no hurry. I intended to talk things over with you and the Colonel if I was not so bothered, this morning, with my head;" and he holds his hand to his forehead, which is very full and red, and then puts it deeper into his pocket again as he stands. "My head is dizzy as you please. Oh, as to plans, we'll talk over matters when the Colonel comes home to-night. I do believe I will go up to my room and lie down."

His sister looks up at him, and fairly colors with mortification. To think that Alec, who is so vigorous, should depend upon her husband, already tasked as he is beyond his strength. She grows pale as she resolves to speak to her brother on the spot, and as she has never done before. Mrs. Dunwoddie is but a small woman, and she is worn with many years of terrible anxiety and care. Alec Allen's experiences have merely fattened him. Hers have had a very different effect: they have developed in her a singular amount of silent will, and the first exercise of her will is to control herself; the second is to sustain her husband. Before marriage she had been, as has been said, the "nicest girl" in the county; comely, that is, and quiet, modest and sweet and good. In women of her blonde and gentle sort severe trials generally either kill outright or leave their victim a sort of living corpse, limp and maudlin, slatternly and helpless; all the sugar in their blood not turned into gall simply because it is diluted into a watery worthlessness. But Mrs. Dunwoddie had experienced in herself a miracle as great as in the case of the poor woman who had touched the hem of a certain garment, and she was that much the stronger and truer woman for every trouble she had endured; retaining, too, in a wonderful degree, her youth and comeliness, it was almost impossible to believe her to be the mother of a youth so well grown as her son Horace. In virtue of this it was that she asked now, and it was something wholly different from what she intended to say—

"Have you seen Emmeline yet, Alec?"

"Yes," he replied; "you know it was only on her account I took all the trouble of going West. I went to Judge Anderson's straight from the depot."

"And what did Emmeline say?" the other asked.

"Say?" her brother, who had again put his hand to his forehead, replied—"say? Oh, she said—I do feel so queerly in my head. Oh, what—what she said? I suppose I ought to have dropped in on the barber first, ought to have changed my linen if any of the Colonel's shirts are large enough for me. But I wanted to see her. I went straight to their house just as I was. I don't think it was right in her, Eliza—I declare I don't! She was at home, and came in. I suppose I did look a little rough. Yes, she came in where I was, grown from a girl into a—a queen is the word, isn't it? I suppose I did look like a bear; but I never once thought she could, would, have changed into such a splendid woman. Although," he explained, "I ought to have known it; I always knew she would be that, you know."

"Well?" his sister asked, at length.

"You cannot think how od ""·· I do feel," he said; "but never mind, that . all right; it's passing off."

"And what did Emmeline say?" Mrs. Dunwoddie asked, but she did not look up. Brave as she was, the tears were running down her cheeks as she spoke.

"Emmeline Anderson?" her brother replied, in a perplexed way. "That is what I don't know; I wish I did. She did not come running in and throw herself in my arms—not by any manner of means," Mr. Allen said, with emphasis; "on the contrary, quite the reverse."

There was a long pause.

"I was an enormous fool to do it," Alec Allen said at length, "but I did love her. I put more force into loving that young girl than I ever did into anything in my life. She never gave me the least encouragement. Of course, I kept on loving her all the time I was gone—how could a man help it? Do you suppose," Mr. Allen continued, taking an easier angle with the mantel-piece against which he was leaning, and putting his hands deeper in his pockets, "that I do not see how foolish it is in me to hope such a lady as she has grown to be can ever care for *me?* Not much! But I could no more help loving her—" any illustration sufficiently strong is beyond the speaker's power, and he says nothing more.

"Did you see her mother?" his sister asked.

"Yes, she came in. They must be tremendously poor, I do suppose," he said again, with what seemed to be almost satisfaction.

"Of course," his sister replied. "You know that the war left all of us poor here in the South. We had very few negroes to lose. I am glad they are gone, Alec. If," Mrs. Dunwoddie said, with energy, "you had not had them to depend on when you were born, and had been trained to hard work, it would have been better for *you*, Alec—much better! Look at our Horace. He has to get up early, so as to be at his desk by seven every morning; and he has to work hard, and is held to responsibility all day. It is making a man of him. So of all our boys, they are healthier and manlier, purer and happier, in every sense for it. I do wish, Alec, that you had been compelled to earn *your* bread —but—" here Mrs. Dunwoddie slackened and ceased.

"Think so, Eliza? Humph, maybe so," the other remarked. "I don't. I am not built to do hard work. It's easy for other people to talk about handling an axe or a hoe, a pen or a spade; but, you see, I've to handle myself to begin with, and you have no idea how much I weigh. People who try to handle me always give it up, I'm too heavy, and I know my weight so well I never even try. And so they are poor still?" he added, with such complacent repetition that his sister replied with energy—

"You know that they lost everything by the war, Alec. Not their slaves only, all the money they had was invested in Confederate bonds, as you well know. Judge Anderson regarded it as his duty to do so. Being the leading man of Clair County, he must set the example of confidence in the Confederacy. Long before the end came, having been so much in politics, he knew what the result must be, and he was too old to endure it. You remember, Alec, that the news of the killing of his last son at the battle of Five Forks was his own death. He knew that there was nothing left for his family. It was the very thing which should have determined him to live," added the energetic little lady.

"I say," her brother added, in a singularly good-humor, "that is the way you are so determined—you have got all the energy of the Allens in your blood. That's the reason I have so little—you've got my share too. But it don't matter, I'm willing," and, after slowly considering matters, he went on—

"Yes, Miss Anderson was such a child, and yet she seemed out of my reach even then, and I was so poor. It is a wonder I was never hit during the war. I am sure I did not hurry out of the way of the bullets. When I got back from fighting I was flat broke, as well as dead tired. Who could even plan to do anything those days? And the Andersons have plenty of lands they can't sell, plenty of debts, and are — poor." It was with a kind of relish he said the words, meditating over it in his slow way, and as if he was feeding himself upon the thought. "And I am such a lazy fellow, that's a fact—ain't I, Eliza?"

To his sister's astonishment he broke into a sudden peal of laughter. It would have exasperated her beyond endurance if it had not alarmed her.

"You must have a fever, Alec," she said; and then added, "Poor? Of course. They had lived in abundance all their lives; but, since their negroes left them, no slave they ever owned has worked as they have done. A good many of us, Alec, are as poor as when you left, some of us poorer — much, much poorer." She was afraid that she had allowed a flavor of bitterness in her tones, it was so unmanly in Alec to be indolent when those he should have died for, if necessity was, were so hard pressed. She need not have feared, however, that her brother would have noticed any reproach in her language.

"Mrs. Anderson came into the room," he said. "She talked with me a little in her cold and stately way. They never did care anything for me except for your sake and the Colonel's. She said to me, 'And, so, Mr. Allen, you are the same man you were when you left us?' 'Certainly I am, madam,' I said, 'the same man exactly.' It was curious. Emmeline—Miss Emmeline, I should say—excused herself and went out. Her mother said again, 'You have not changed indeed, as I see,' and she looked at me in such a way; it was as if she did not think I was worth being angry with, which was curious. 'I am exactly the same man I was when I went away,' was what I replied once more, very slowly and solemnly," he said, with lazy iteration. "She looked at me with a lingering kind of hope as I began, but," added the speaker, "it all died out of her eyes as I finished; and she went out while I was resting a little in their parlor. I didn't care, I could wait, you know. Presently a mite of a yellow girl not as high as that came into the room—not as high as *that*," Mr. Allen repeated, with his hand a yard from the floor —"all that is left them of two hundred as likely negroes as you ever saw, and *it* does not belong to them!—came into the parlor and said, 'Please excuse de ladies for to-day.' Of course, I did excuse them, and then took up my valise where I had left it in the front porch and came on over here. That is all. When I left, their black boy Parker was foreman of the crop on their place. He was a sensible fellow. I hope he is with them still."

He said it not merely with complacency, but with a sort of sluggish enjoyment, which again angered and distressed his sister. Beyond measure was she mortified and disheartened. For years she had cultivated the power of hoping as other people cultivate a talent for music. She had needed to do it in connection with her husband; but he had afforded her soil, so to speak, for it, in his desperate struggles to realize by hard work all that she was hoping. In regard to this barren brother of hers, it was like cultivating hope without either seed or soil; but, with a woman's angelic unreasonableness, she had gone on hoping from the moment he had left them that Alec would, somehow, change his nature with his location when he went West. He was much older than Emmeline Anderson, and was too evidently of a coarser grain and a lower grade of character than the girl at the time of leaving. But who could say what might happen? His sister had hoped that he might have earned some capital to begin upon when away. She had even dared to think that he might come back, having undergone some impossible transformation which would have brought him in the range, at least, of hope in connection with such a woman as Judge Anderson's daughter. Mrs. Dunwoddie now saw how absurd such an expectation had been. The girl had grown into a young woman who was superior even to Mrs. Dunwoddie's expectations. And Alec? He had fattened, as it were, into a grossness of soul, as of body, worse than his sister had dared to fear.

She looked at him. He was big enough to knock an ox down, hearty enough to eat it up afterwards, and there he was! Not a penny did he have in the world, not a purpose; and he evidently cared nothing about it, was positively happy. He was actually beaming upon her as if he were a hero instead.

Mrs. Dunwoddie had been silently crying; now her tears dried up. She felt so savage that she was frightened at herself. Never in her life had she been so prompted to express herself bitterly.

"Alec Allen—" she began, with dry lips.

"Well, Eliza," he said, looking down on her, both hands in his pockets, with a good-natured indolence which was aggravating.

"Alexander Allen—" she began, once more.

But a tremendous event was impending. Her brother did not know it. Such an idea had never come into her mind. From long habit, she paused a moment. The event was known only to her Maker, and yet she trembled in the pause, weak and willing as a little child, knowing nothing except to be silent where she would have spoken severely.

"Never mind now, Alec," she said, in lower and softer tones, with even a smile upon her face; "I wanted to say something, but not now. We will talk of it some other time."

"Why, Eliza, how pretty you look," he replied. "I feared you were going to scold me. What about? About my not writing to her? Why she wouldn't promise to write to me when I left. And how could I write? There was nothing in camp to write on, unless it was the bottom of a skillet, and its legs were in the way; not even a stove-pipe hat. Besides, we had no paper. Moreover, I was always used up when I got into camp of nights. But I feel that old sleepy feeling coming back again. I believe I'll go up to my room and lie down. Don't get up, Eliza, I can spread up the bed so as to do. We will make another call at Mrs. Anderson's house in a few days. The fact is, I didn't feel well when I was there yesterday." He went to the door, and, pondering for a few moments, came back to his sister, and laid his hand on her shoulder as she sat.

"Eliza!" he said, in such tones as made her look up with surprise. But he seemed to have changed his mind. "Oh, never mind," he added, "not to-day. I'm afraid you are working too hard, Eliza, and the Colonel, too. Hard work makes you thin and pale, although you look as young as ever. I never did believe in hard work, and see how hearty I am. But you are a lady, Eliza—a genuine lady," and, to her astonishment, her brother stooped down and kissed her before he went out. She was so annoyed about him that she almost shuddered as his beard swept her face. She seized upon her tea-towel to wipe the spot where he had kissed her; then laid it down. She was glad, ah, how glad afterwards, that she had not said a bitter word; had not made a gesture, even, of impatience.

She heard his heavy step up-stairs, heard him as he cast himself upon the bed. Then, being all alone, she leaned her head weeping upon the edge of the table at which she sat until her tears had ceased to flow. It was the darkest hour in her life. Her tired heart was beating in her as if against the future, and as if that future was a darkness so dark as to be felt. She never forgot the past; to her it was but a little less vivid than the present. As to the future, it was to her as a stone wall; the utmost she could do was to lie prostrate at its base, she was so tired, tired.

CHAPTER IV.

DISASTER UPON DISASTER.

" Each morn repeats creation's dawn,
　Each eve creation's fate :
　Forever alternate
Inflowing life and life withdrawn.
　For Nature's blood
　Hath ebb and flood,
　The systole, diastole
　Of ever-pulsing Deity."

ALTHOUGH Col. Dunwoddie groaned over his poverty a good deal, while his wife never alluded to it, it was she who felt it most keenly. It was not merely because she made all the purchases for the family —her husband having no more to do with it than if he were a boarder—but all the bills came in to her. Who but a woman knows the thousand-and-one little things needing to be replaced constantly in the household? Not for herself; she had learned during such a long time to do without small matters of personal use, not to say adornment, that like another Robinson Crusoe, and upon an island more desert, she had grown into doing without almost all she desired as into a second nature. Her distress was not at all about the boys. She would not have changed matters as to Horace if she could; and so of George and Harry who were at school, as well as of little Charlie. It was a pity,

however, that her husband should be galled by the harness of unceasing labor.

"If I could but get one month of rest," he often said—"rest not from work which I delight in ; but if, for a single month, I could be freed from this unceasing anxiety, I do believe I could do more work and better for a year after. Give me one round month of appetite, of sleep, of perfect *rest*, and see if I did not write some poem, publish some book, make some speech, which would insure my success in the future."

It was her girls that troubled the mother most. Alice was eighteen and May sixteen, and they wanted certain things so naturally and so keenly. Some small article of dress, perhaps, with the changing season, for which they shed many a tear. How heartily did their mother sympathize with while she rebuked them; for it was in vain that they tried, after such a night and by sisterly agreement, to scoff at the very idea of caring for such things. It was little they could hide from those loving eyes.

Mrs. Dunwoddie never in her life had her burden press so heavy as the morning after her brother's return. "He might at least have contrived to bring his nieces some little gift—a ring or a dress," she said to herself as she went the round of her duties. "If I was only a strong man, young and healthful, with all the world open before me, it does seem to me 'that I would succeed, if I had to take it by storm ; other men have done so !" And then Mrs. Dunwoddie, the strongest person under that roof, almost bewailed the fact that she was nothing but a woman—a poor, weak woman.

When the bell rang for dinner her brother did not come down. The wife anticipated the impatience of her husband, who was sharpening the carving-knife at the head of the table, by excusing herself for a moment as she went up-stairs to see. Although she was merely, as she thought, a weak woman, she had vigor enough on her return to let her husband eat his dinner before she said a word. Next to sleep, a hearty dinner made a world of difference in him, as she had long ago learned.

"Charles, dear," she said, as soon as the children had left the room, "I want you to clothe yourself with patience. Poor Alec is sick up-stairs—very sick. I have sent Harry for the doctor."

"Great heavens!" It was all that her husband said. Dinner or no dinner, the tidings were too terrible. Such a man seriously sick! How could his sickness fail to be on the same large scale as himself, and as slow! It was not merely the drop too much for the household cup, already filled to overflowing—it was an ocean too much.

Col. Dunwoddie hastened up-stairs. There could be no doubt of the fact. Both remember that Alec Allen had spoken the night before about sickness in camp as one reason why he had come back from the West. It is only too plain that he who had seemed so well had brought it home with him. If the small-pox had broken out instead, it could not have been more sudden, nor the threatened results more disastrous. As Col. Dunwoddie looks upon the unwelcome arrival, already delirious under a burning fever, he stands at the death-bed, in imagination, of his wife, of Horace and Alice, May, George, Charlie, and of his wife again, and worst of all.

But Mrs. Dunwoddie had thought of that already. Harry had gone on, after sending the doctor, to Mrs. Anderson's, with a message from his mother, in answer to which a servant had come for little Charlie, with a cordial invitation for all of the young people to make Mrs. Anderson's house their home during the sickness of their uncle, so that they were out of the way; Horace, their eldest, making his home for the time at the hotel, which was but a step from the depot where he worked. Meanwhile poor Alec had been brought to a room down-stairs. Before the end of the week Mrs. Anderson and daughter drove up to the gate, fastening the horse themselves for fear of disturbing any one, and went in.

During the days of prosperity before the war the closest intimacy had existed between the two families, and the fact that Alec Allen was the brother of Mrs. Dunwoddie was the sole reason why any engagement between Emmeline Anderson and himself could ever have been possible. Nothing was more natural than that mutual affliction should have drawn the households still closer together. Col. Dunwoddie had not been merely the friend as well as legal adviser of Mrs. Anderson, he had sympathized with the mother and her daughter as only a man of his temperament can. No one more radiant than he was when he consoled and prophesied prosperity for them in the future; no one less so when, at home, he spoke about his own affairs. In a word, Col. Dunwoddie was, their foreman, Parker excepted, the one person besides his wife, upon whom Mrs. Anderson and her daughter had leaned in their distress.

As the two ladies stood in the hall conversing with Mrs. Dunwoddie they could not help hearing the sick man groaning in the next room. Mrs. Anderson was anxious to get away.

"I am glad you sent your children to our house, dear Mrs. Dunwoddie," she said, "and that they seem to be so contented with us. If we can be of any further assistance—" But here she was interrupted by a cry from the chamber of the patient.

"Oh, so poor, poor, *poor!*" he said, with increasing emphasis upon each repetition of the word. Besides incoherent sentences seeming to refer to the war, or to camp-life in the West, the poverty he had left in Clairsville, and had found there on his return, appeared to be his only thought. But now he added one word—"Emmeline!"

Mrs. Anderson, who was as cold as she

was sorrowful, colored violently, and laid her hand upon her daughter, who had started at the pitiful cry.

Before the war Judge Anderson was not merely the richest man in all the region of which Clairsville was the centre, his plantation the largest, his house the handsomest, his slaves the most numerous, his hospitality the most lavish. He had once been, governor of the state, then a senator in Congress. During the last twenty years he had been chief-justice upon the Supreme Bench of the state. When the war began the family was regarded as the proudest in the county. All men lifted their hats to the white-headed old Judge, whenever he was seen along the streets— the coldest in his bearing, as well as the most commanding of men. His wife, although the soul of kindness to her slaves, to all who appealed to her protection, was well mated with her husband in stateliness of bearing: her years at the head of her circle when her husband was governor, and in Washington, to say nothing of their long residence in Clairsville, during which he had been upon the Bench, had habituated her to that. If her two sons were the most popular of persons, handsome, liberal, dashing young men, it was only what was natural. The ending of the war was like the very ending of the world to these parents, as to so many. One of the sons had been killed at the battle of Five Forks; the other had come home from Gettysburg wounded to death. A month before the negroes became free the Judge died, too old to bear up under, as it were, the very universe crashing into ruins around him. With that it seemed to his wife and daughter as if the end of the world had come. Hardly was he buried before almost every negro had abandoned the place. Of the dozen house-servants, only one old cook, who had been the mammy, or nurse, of Emmeline, was left. Even old Isaac, of an age so great that it could only be guessed at, who had done nothing in the memory of any then

alive but sun himself in front of his cabin and eat clabber and hominy — even poor old Isaac had departed. The only one left to the ladies, and who could be of any real assistance, was Parker, a very black man, young, strong, and unusually sensible, who had risen, before emancipation came, to be what was called "Foreman of the Crop." Parker was himself paralyzed for the hour by the universal breaking up; but he had both heart and judgment enough to stay where he was, at least for the present, and upon him they had to rely. In a state of bewilderment, mother and daughter went with Parker over the stables, where hitherto all sorts of vehicles had awaited their use. The carriages still remained, to be covered with dust and cobwebs from long disuse, for the departing slaves had ridden off every horse. The smoke-house stood open, with not a ham left. All the poultry, except a few Guinea-fowls which could not be caught, had been taken. Two hundred hands had once worked in the fields, and now the gin and cotton-press stood as in the centre of a desert. It was almost with terror that they went from cabin to cabin among the negro quarters—even women whose babies were but a few days old had gone; and the well in the centre, with its long pole, the old and thoroughly worked steel mill near by, at which "the people" ground their allowance of corn — the whole once-crowded space was as desolate as if a plague had raged there.

Of course there were many of the slaves who were glad to come back after a while as from a debauch of freedom. But when they did it was under very different auspices. Mrs. Anderson and her daughter had not the least knowledge of business, and the neighbors were too much occupied with their own troubles to help. It was then that Alec Allen, just back from the war, could have stepped in and made himself master of the situation; but, almost as little trained to business as the ladies, it never even occurred to him to offer his assistance. In the end the plantation was rented to a shrewd overseer from East Tennessee, with Parker as his headman among the blacks. This overseer made an enormous crop, went with it to the city to sell it, and, the proceeds in his pocket, was never seen or heard from again. In this way the estate passed into the control of Parker himself as chief manager—the first time a negro had come into such a charge in the knowledge of mortal man, in that region at least.

And thus we come back again to Mrs. Anderson and her daughter conversing with Mrs. Dunwoddie in the hall adjoining the room of the sick man. When the young girl started forward at his cry the mother laid her hand upon her arm, nor did she release it until they were out of the house.

"You need have no fear for me, mother," she said. "Even if I had not been too young to do so when he left, I never loved him. While he was gone I tried to make a hero of him. Now that he has come back it is—impossible. Impossible! But I must help Mrs. Dunwoddie."

And so it befell that, the day following upon the visit, that lady was greatly surprised as she was busy in her kitchen to see Emmeline Anderson walk in. The married lady was a light-haired, blue-eyed, lovable woman, who, if her husband had been rich and at leisure enough to have petted her, would have been as weak and dependent as such women generally are. That husband was, however, so dependent upon her instead, in his despairing moods at least, that she was made thereby into a very different person. Her nature was the same. She could no more cease to be of a loving and utterly dependent disposition than she could change her eyes from being blue, or her tones from being low and soft, and her hair into locks as black as those of Emmeline Anderson. The difference was that, compelled to rest on some one

else, she had cast herself wholly upon a stronger than he.

Emmeline Anderson was two or three years younger than Mrs. Dunwoddie's oldest son, Horace. She was a mere child at the beginning of the war. Had there been prosperity, she would have grown into a woman as haughty as she was beautiful. With her dark eyes and hair, she had also a force, an audacity, almost, of character, very unlike that of Mrs. Dunwoddie, or her own mother. The long, long expectation in which she and so many others were held during the war, and in an almost breathless attitude of suspense, had turned her, as it were, in and upon herself; and the disasters since the war had not arrested, but only intensified the growing energies of the young girl, making them the more determined in that they were the more repressed. It was as if a spring of the finest steel had been coiled closer upon itself, and compressed into a space far smaller than that for which it was intended; her mother trembling at times for the result—she dared not conjecture what—which must come of it some day. She was not eighteen as yet, in vigorous health, and poor Alec Allen had found it wholly impossible to express to his sister, the morning he had spoken of their meeting, the emotions stirred even in his dull nature by the improvement he had found in her. In fact, it was the sudden revelation to him then of a beauty, as well as a passion and power, in the woman which had so dazed and daunted him. Nor was it to be wondered that Horace Dunwoddie had fallen desperately as well as hopelessly in love with the young girl. He at least had the sense so to conceal it that none but his own mother suspected anything of the kind.

"I am come to help you, Mrs. Dunwoddie," she said as she came in. "After we were here yesterday two more of our old servants came back to us. Do you remember Sally and Jane, our house-girls? Their husbands have gone into drinking and politics and gambling, and have beaten and abused and then abandoned them. There is no telling how long they will stay, but while they are there mamma can spare me. She does not wish me to go into his room, of course," the young girl added with a blush, "but I can help you. Your children are the best that ever lived. They are helping mamma so much at our house that I must help you. You will be glad to know how excellently Parker is managing things for us," she added. " You must let me stay."

"My dear child," Mrs. Dunwoddie said, "I wonder if you think I would allow it. When I will not suffer my own girls to remain for fear of the fever, do you suppose I will for a moment—"

It was impossible not to hear what was going on in the next room, now converted into a chamber, and as Mrs. Dunwoddie spoke the voice of the sick man rang out loud and clear, "Poor, poor, *poor!*" and then the same peal of laughter, harshly out of place. In all his sickness there was nothing more than that. Instead of finding anything in this to confirm her friend's view, the young lady, even while she crimsoned in a manner painful to see, merely continued—

" Mrs. Dunwoddie," and she said it in a way which caused the other to look at her in amazement, there was so much of suppressed purpose in her eyes, "if my own mother cannot prevent my coming, do you suppose that you can ? I will not go into his room, but I will stay. That will do, Zady," she said, taking a carpet-bag from a little yellow girl who had accompanied her; " you can come to the front gate to-morrow to see if I need anything. Go back. I believe this is the way to your spare room," she added, turning to her astonished friend, and she had gone up-stairs before Mrs. Dunwoddie knew what to do.

But her visit was not to be a long one. When a man of the heavy build of Alec Allen does come down, it is with a crash. A lean and spare man, like intellectual Col. Dunwoddie, would never have caught on fire with fever, or, having taken it, would have endured it like asbestos—not hurt, merely whitened by the burning. Not so with Alec Allen. He seemed to be only a heap of inflammable fuel for the conflagration. There did not appear to be sufficient will in him, which is merely another name for the principle of life, the soul, to rally itself against and put out the fire which was consuming the poor fellow.

Meanwhile it was a terrible trial to those who waited upon him. There was such a horror upon the negroes of the fever, which they insisted upon believing to be the dreaded yellow-fever, that it was impossible to get more than the occasional help of the most stupid among them, and that at large pay. Even with the energetic help of their young neighbor, the days reminded Col. Dunwoddie of the darkest he had ever known in the hospitals during the war. He was obliged to launch deeper into an indebtedness which it already terrified him to think of; writing his editorials and preparing his law-cases, in view of the court soon to meet, in the few intervals of nursing. There had been a time when more than enough of Alec Allen's associates would have helped, but now, alas, those who had not been killed in the war had scattered abroad in the breaking up which had followed upon it.

"And how I am to watch night after night, and yet be able to write, I cannot see," the Colonel said to himself very often, as he waited upon the sick man. "And to think of the burden it is to *her*, even with Emmeline's aid. That she must slave herself for this—animal!"

His brother-in-law would not have looked at him with such aversion had he not been already overtasked, and for so long—so very long. Poor Alec! He was like some wild beast, lying in bed with uncombed hair and a wilderness of beard, his hairy bosom all bare as he continually threw down the cover with his brawny arms faster than his brother-in-law could replace it. He seemed to be twice as large as ever, the bedstead creaking and groaning under him as he turned and rolled. From head to foot he was crimson with his disease, reminding his attendant of some great back-log in a Christmas fire.

Mrs. Dunwoddie came and went continually, helped more than she had thought possible by the presence of Emmeline. For there was small romance in the matter as far as this young lady was concerned. Before the sick man went West, his well-known devotion to her had been only a matter of vexation and anger when it was not one of amusement. Whenever she had thought of him at all during his absence it was to wonder if, in case he ever came back, he would be still so absurd as to persist in loving her. It was not Alec Allen that drew her there, beyond her pity for him. Nor was it merely her sympathy for Mrs. Dunwoddie. She hardly understood herself why she was in the house. Really, it was the struggling of forces in her which were outgrowing her power of repression; the longing to do and to be more in all womanly senses than she had ever had opportunity for before. She soon ceased to start at the occasional moan of the sick man coming to her ears, as she assisted Mrs. Dunwoddie outside in a thousand thoughtful ways, of— "Poor, poor, *poor!*" followed by an insane laughter as at the best of jokes. It simply disgusted her. If the poverty in Clairsville since the war had so imprinted itself upon his sluggish nature, why had he not tried harder to remove it? The circumstances of her later days had not been favorable to sentiment; and Horace Dunwoddie, for instance, working like a man, was far nobler than this sodden fragment, so to speak, of a wrecked world.

"If this poor fellow," Col. Dunwoddie would say to himself, "was ever of any use on earth, beyond having fought for the Confederacy, what is it? I do not want to be hard upon him, Heaven knows; but what good did he ever do anybody in his life?" After saying which, already tired out, the Colonel would have to hold his kinsman down again by sheer force upon the gridiron of his fever.

"And to think," he would continue to himself, at the next interval of rest, "that it took all my authority to keep Horace from working all night with this man after toiling, as he must do, at the depot through the day. Why could not the poor fellow have stayed West? have been sick there as much as he pleased, and have been waited upon and—yes—and nursed by men as strong and with as little to do as himself? To think of his casting himself like an enormous baby upon these two weak women—" but at this juncture the weary nurse would be compelled to arise and again hold the sick man down.

The physician came and went, and did all he could. But the end drew near. The fever was rapidly consuming its victim. At last the poor fellow lay in his pitiful weakness dying. He had never known a sane moment. It was midnight, and Col. Dunwoddie and his wife stood over his pillow. They were utterly worn out by weeks of severe watching. The husband, with his finger upon the fluttering pulse, held up his hand, and Mrs. Dunwoddie leaned over, checking her tears in order to listen.

"Poor, poor—*very* poor!" and then followed the first variation in his monotonous iteration since he had been stricken down. "Poor—so poor! Isn't it the *best* joke you ever heard? Good for you, Alec! Bully for you, old fellow!" The dying man seemed to be shaken out of his unconsciousness as by the force of the words. He was sadly emaciated, and in pitiful weakness he beckoned to Col. Dunwoddie to bend down. It was plain that he was, and for the first time since he was stricken, in his right mind again. He was eager to say something. It was as if he had fallen over the edge of a precipice, but was making desperate efforts to climb up again, to hold on, at least, to the crumbling verge until he could say what was on his mind.

"There's a man named Gamaliel Middleton," he struggled to utter. "I ought to have told you the first thing when I came. It is very important! Middleton—Virginia City—O God!" He tried to hold on to Col. Dunwoddie's face as with his agonizing eyes, even after his fingers had lost their hold upon the edge of life. His soul slipped its last grasp in his darkening gaze, and, with a shudder through all his frame as he fell into the abysm, the man was gone.

CHAPTER V.

THE DARKNESS DEEPENS.

"Th' electric flash which strikes and kills
Is not the only fire which fills
All clouds and clods, all stars and hills.
To every man who lives there flies
Or soon, or late, as from the skies,
The thunderbolt of some surprise."

HARDLY three months had fled since Alec Allen had come back from Nevada, but it seemed to the family a much longer time. It was an absurd figure of speech to apply to such an easy-going individual as poor Alec; but in one of his bitter moments Col. Dunwoddie had said to his wife, "His coming was like the breaking upon us of a storm, and, heaven knows, we had endured tempest enough before!"

And it had been a terrible time. Col. Dunwoddie had broken down the day after the funeral, and had lain sick — his affairs in the utmost confusion—for weeks. Then little Charlie had taken his turn. Mrs. Dunwoddie would have been ill herself from the outset, but her love for first her husband and then her child had so reinforced her will that she refused to give way. The child would have died had not the mother held to it, night and day,

with a grasp which death itself seemed unable to break. As soon as she was able to let it go, by reason of its recovery, she herself, and as if by the very act of relaxing her hold, fell sick. For a month she lay utterly exhausted at the gates of the grave. Her husband was greatly assisted in nursing her by Emmeline Anderson, who had said to her mother—

"You need have no fear for me, mamma. Had poor Alec been more of a man I dare say I would have grieved myself into an attack of sickness. As it is, I feel younger and stronger than I ever did. I want to be—yes—stronger than he ever could be, more of a man even than Col. Dunwoddie ever was. Both were as brave as lions in battle, but my idea is to be strong in everyday life, the harder things get to be all the *stronger;*" and she said it quietly, but with her hands clinching themselves into fists, her color deepening, her eyes growing darker. Certainly the young girl had never seemed so full of healthful energy before. She had been born to social pre-eminence, to great wealth, to be petted at home and admired abroad, to be waited upon by multitudes of people who seemed to be, in all social senses, at least, as much her slaves as those who worked in her father's fields. But all that was gone. The last illusion left her, as it was the least, had been poor Alec Allen. He had once been, before he too was stripped by the war and its results, as gallant a suitor as any. During all his absence West he had held her—although she did not know it—passive and waiting; but he was utterly gone now, with all the rest of her old world. All that was left her except her mother was—herself. Her mother looked at her with almost fear, and vague but grave apprehension; she was so unlike what she had been.

And thus it came to pass that one Saturday night Mrs. Dunwoddie sat up for the first time since her sickness in her easy-chair, the household grouped around her. During all the illness her husband

had at least tried to be as much of a soldier on a forced march as possible; but
now the colonel was giving place in him
to the mere man. As his wife grew better
he began to relax into his old despondency. He lay at length upon the lounge,
and if ever a man was prostrated he was.
Deeply in debt before Alec came, he dared
not calculate how much deeper he was now.
Moreover, the first of the year had come
during his troubles, and the subscription
to his paper had fallen off astonishingly.
There was a serious difficulty, also, in the
church of which he was—as has been said
—the leading person, although not a member. A case in court, upon which he had
been preparing himself for many long
months, had gone against him, and with it
the large fees made conditional upon his
success. There was a mortgage, too, upon
his house, in regard to which he had never
dared to speak to his wife, overburdened
with care as she already was, and which
could no longer be put off.

The man was desperate. To divert his
mind he recalled the line of thought in his
last editorial, and, his brain being so sharp-
ened, he suddenly saw how he had laid
himself open in it to be criticised with se-
verity by the men whom he knew to be
eagerly lying in wait to do so. Never
mind, there was his Poem. In the fever
of his sickness it had raged in his brain—
that poem — like a conflagration. It was
by far the best he had ever written. No
doubt every paper in the South would
quote from it; possibly it would get into
the circulation of the Northern press. But
now? In the coolness of recovery it seemed to be nothing but miserable doggerel;
he groaned over it as over a dead child.
"I should have known better," he said to
himself, "than ▮▮▮ave put that illustration
of the 'Arctic Pole' at the beginning of
the thing instead of the end."

The very children, down to little Charlie
in his mother's lap, knew how depressed
their father was; but with faint conception

of the depth of his distress as he lay motionless on the lounge, his hands clasped over
his eyes.

"Father ought to take the practical view
we railway people do," Horace remarks.
"I used to indulge in sentiment until I
went to work as clerk at the depot. It is
amazing how solid it makes a man having
to deal with iron; how sharp as well as
cool a man gets to be who knows that
a train must come and go to a certain
minute. As for me, I intend to drop all
feeling, and become as much of a clock as
I can. Sentiment and poetry is a thing I
abhor."

The young man speaks with such energy
that all the group look up at him as he
sits, pencil in hand, at the table. He said
he was making calculations. If he was, it
must have been in algebra, for, if not x and
y, at least a capital E and A, perpetually
repeated, made up the largest part of his
estimates. His uncle was dead. He was
sorry, of course, but the avalanche had disappeared almost as suddenly as it had fall-
en. It was almost too absurd to think of,
but who knows? Emmeline Anderson had
become as if in a week more beautiful than
he had ever imagined she could be. And
was not he a man? Yes, and he would be
a thousand times more of a man than ever.
He detested sentiment, and yet it would
have been out of the power of any poet to
have put into words the unspeakable love
which filled his heart. Not for Emmeline
Anderson alone, at least not then, as its
chief object. No son could have loved a
mother more, and yet his largest love was
for his father. That father had made an
intimate companion of him since he could
remember; he regarded him as by far the
most perfect gentleman he had ever known.
He knew more than his mother of the terrible struggles his father was enduring, and
even the dark locks of the girl he was beginning to love so ardently were as nothing
to him compared to the rapidly silvering
hair of his father. Except in all dutiful

obedience, and in every respectful attention in his power, he said nothing of this love, and yet it gushed deep and pure, and with the vigor, as it were, of the manliest strength, from the depths of his heart. His very scribbling of other initials was, in part, to divert his mind from a trouble in regard to his father which was almost more than he could bear; it was so great, and he was so powerless.

"My dear," Mrs. Dunwoddie said at last, laying her hand, wasted by illness, on her husband's forehead, "I wouldn't—wouldn't."

"I won't," he answered; and, rising to a sitting posture, he says cheerfully, "Well, George, how are you coming on at school?"

"As fairly as a fellow can," George replies, "who won't cheat in his exercises, and would rather die than taddle. You see, papa, it is just in this way—"

But his father does not hear a word he says, for he is trying to heave up the North Pole, misplaced in the poem, so as to shift it aright. Then he is conscious that George is eagerly talking, conscious only far enough to cease composing his poem, and go to constructing George's future instead. Shall he be a lawyer? Lawyers are generally such wretched politicians. A physician? Doctors have to wait so long for practice—and the father remembers with terror what a heavy bill he must be owing their doctor.

The best thing George can do is to become a merchant. A merchant? Where is the capital to come from? Which brings him back again to the old, old, *old* question—money—and he lies down again at full length, and covers his face with his hands. Horace sets his teeth, and scribbles savagely with his pencil. His mother sees it all, or thinks she does.

"I would not bother to-night about money, either," she whispers softly in his ear as he lies. But he lies still this time, does not rise, hardly hears.

"Oh, ma! it would be such a change if we only had money—if it was but a *little*

money." It is Alice, the eldest daughter, who says it, because she resembles her father so much.

"I don't want it," May breaks in. "But, oh, if the Confederacy had only succeeded!" There is a general hushing of May; it is as if she had been speaking of the dead. "I am not rich," May adds, "but all the world knows I am pretty."

"Hush!" Mrs. Dunwoddie said, "listen!" and she proceeds to read a very laudatory editorial from some paper in regard to her husband's poetry. She had a singular success in finding and bringing out such sugar-plums. "It gives this specimen. I never saw it before. Hush, all of you!" and she read aloud—

"The Alps! the Alps! I sprang from rock to rock,
    Glad as the chamois, o'er the chasmed flow;
With heart tough-fibred as my alpenstock,
    Adown the glaciers joyously to go,
    Outjourneying in an hour their centuries' flow;
To scale with eager steps those summits where,
    On highest peaks poised like an eagle there,
As if, on mighty wings in central air,
    I owned the whole wide world. Now, done with all
The world below, not more than with the skies,
With men, and with my vain attempts to rise
    To God, I cease to climb and hope! I fall
In death's deep snow, like him who wearied lies
Down in the drift and sleeps, and, sleeping, dies."

"Wait," Col. Dunwoddie said before anybody could applaud, and with a grim smile he read, producing a paper from his pocket, a ferocious assault upon himself, the venom of its sarcasm being that the Colonel's poetry and politics were equally detestable; he read as much as the outcries of his household would allow, and then lay down again more prostrate than before.

"If I owned money," said Alice, who had a sock on her hand, "I w . l never darn any more for these boys as long as I live. What is the use? I mended this very hole week before last, and here Harry has worn it through again."

The wish was like the first note of a familiar chorus, and all followed—

"I would buy, if I had money," May said, "a beautiful set of jet jewelry—mourning, you know, for poor Uncle Alec. With," she added, "a black silk to match. Oh, how I do wish I had a silk. A girl never is a lady until she wears a silk, never!"

"And I would buy a library full of books," cries Harry, who is reading at the centre-table as usual. "I would get a full set of Dickens, and Scott, and"—a long list follows, to which nobody listens, for Alice is saying—

"I would have a superb piano," and the tears come into her eyes as she says it. Her instrument had been destroyed during a raid of the Federal troops while the war was raging, and what remained of the broken case was full of bran for the cow out in the stable that moment.

"Don't cry, Alice," her brother Horace says. "I intend, when I get money, to buy up enough of our railway stock to be a director; on the way, you know, to being president of the road at a salary of twenty-five thousand dollars a year. I will get a piano for you, and not charge a penny for freight either." It is said lightly. In fact, the effort of all is but to amuse their father.

"I would get your father an encyclopædia," Mrs. Dunwoddie says in the same strain. "Ever since the Federals burned his books, whenever he sits down to write he has to remember what he once read. It was so long ago, no wonder it strains his brain so. He told me so," she added, smiling. "It is time for you to go to bed, Charlie," she continues, and as she puts aside the fair hair from the forehead and blue eyes of the little boy, who lifts them to her as he sits in her lap, she adds, but by no means to any but herself—

"He is so perfectly beautiful since his sickness. Oh, how becoming velvet would be!" It was a foolish thing, but for months she had set her heart upon a little suit of black velvet as she had never done since she had dressed her doll when a child. In imagination she had unrolled the velvet and made the dress over and over again—now in this way and now in that—with far more loving labor than her husband had

ever given to his most elaborate writing. When sick she had been foolish enough to cry over the utter hopelessness of ever being able to do so in reality. It was very foolish; but, then, nobody but God ever knew of it.

"What would you do, Col. Dunwoddie?" It was George, who thought it quite witty thus to address his father. "Do, if you had money?"

"Do?" his father said, trying to enter into the somewhat dolorous joke of the moment. "Well, I would buy a home of about thirty acres on the bank of a river, with a hedge twenty feet high all around, and a dense grove inside. And I would never write another line, or plead another case at bar, or see a soul except ourselves, and we would love each other and raise strawberries, and — rest, rest, rest!"

"With a spare bed far away to go to and sleep when Charlie cries at night," May suggested.

"And enough closets for ma, at least once in her life; not less than five hundred," suggested George.

"Oh yes, and not a hencoop but exactly as your mother wished it; and a watch for Alice and May, and a grand piano, and—all the new books and magazines," said Col. Dunwoddie. At this moment his wife had Horace take Charlie up to bed, following him herself, after bearing him around for everybody to kiss good-night, and her husband lay back again. Lay back on his lounge to sink down, down, down into the deepest depths. A hush fell upon the young people, and they read or talked as quietly as possible.

Down, down, down!

"I have tried all my life," he went over the ritual of this worship of the Prince of Darkness as he had done so often before, "to be a true man and a good man. I have worked as hard as it is possible for mortal man to work. If there is any poor fellow I have refused to help I don't know it. I don't drink, or gamble, or lie, or steal. Other people waste money—but I don't—on billiards or horses—not even using tobacco. God knows there would be no church here if I had not kept it up with my money. And all for what? If I had been a drunkard, a loafer, an adulterer, a murderer, I could not have been pursued more steadily by the avenging Furies. Everything I touch fails. Look at my poor wife. There is not an angel in heaven worthier some little favor, at least, than she is. And here I am, a man—a strong man—and cannot even afford her a little trip after all our terrible sickness, nor a spring dress or bonnet for her and the girls; and at my age, too, after so long and so hard a life."

. Only the soul itself knows how deep down it can descend into the darkness! The man got up with a face so set and pale that it terrified his children. He went into the hall, took his hat, and went softly out. A whole lifetime of cruel injustice to him on the part of his Maker, if, indeed, there was a Maker, maddened him — as he looked at it. Walking rapidly through the darkness to a distant corner of the garden, he threw himself upon a bench under an old peach-tree, cold and wet as the night was.

Was it really wrong to do it? The insurance upon his life would pay his debts, and leave a tolerable balance for Horace to support them, his own little salary added to it. Some insurance companies would not pay in case of suicide. But it could be arranged. Surely there were ways by which no one, even of his own family, would ever suspect it. As to God—God?—

*   *   *   *   *   *   *

Who that saw the man fallen on the ground, with set teeth and fingers digging convulsively into the earth — with words that sounded like blasphemy—would have imagined that this was the Col. Dunwoddie who was universally regarded in all Clair County, and many counties around, as one of the most thoroughly excellent gentle-

men there, the best of citizens, and a model man in every sense!

"Utterly abandoned!" The miserable man repeated that clause in his devil's rubric over and over again. "So long! So severe! So curiously complicated! Not a variation upon the unceasing succession of disasters for so very long!" * * * * * And he subsides exhausted at last into the old refrain—"Abandoned, abandoned!"

*   *   *   *   *   *   *

He would have thought otherwise could he have known that Horace had followed him out, had stood in the distance seeing him as he lay in his despair. But the youth could not imagine the depths of his father's anguish. Nor did he weep as he stood. Only the Being who made it could understand the affection which filled the heart of Horace Dunwoddie. He turned upon himself savagely—

"That I should have been thinking of her, and my father in such agony!" and stole away with reverent footsteps, whole months added, so to speak, to his growth.

It was an hour after the Colonel had left the room when he came back. He had washed his face and hands, and lay down again on the lounge. He had been exhausted by his violence of feeling into an utter weariness, the sole expression of which would have been—"I know absolutely nothing. Providence, Justice, God? I know nothing whatever. Maybe so. Maybe not. All I do know is that I know, or can know, nothing whatever."

There was a sense almost of relief in this blankness of utter ignorance; and as he lay he said aloud, at last, very quietly, "Harry, I fear your devotion to books is ruining your memory. Was there anything in the post-office?"

"It is only as it always is, pa," Harry looks up from his book to say; "nothing of any value," and hands his father a letter, and plunges back again into the pages before him.

"You are just like me when I go to my

trap, pa," George, who is building one with laths upon the carpet, remarks. "Every day you go to your box at the post-office you wonder what you have caught to-day, and it never is anything half so grand as a fellow expects."

Col. Dunwoddie takes the letter in his hand as he lies, and glances languidly at it. A circular he supposes. He gets them by the basketful. Circulars about subscription-books; patent furnaces; desperate appeals for money by charitable societies; remedies for rheumatism; cures for cancer and all deformities, horribly illustrated — no end to them. He winces: it may be a bill. Possibly it is another of those many letters of late telling him to stop the *Clarion.* Perhaps—and he tears it open because he has nothing else to do just then. He reads the first line, and his lips suddenly become dry with wrath. As he reads he grows dazed. Horace has returned to the room, and his keen eye is upon his father. Col. Dunwoddie reads the letter rapidly over again. Then over once more. As he finishes it—governing himself by a powerful effort—he lifts his eyes and meets the gaze of his son. That son has not the faintest idea of who the letter is from or what it is about, but he almost recoils from the eyes that meet his. Not that the elder of the two says anything, but it is as if an electric flash had passed between them. The father gets up again very slowly and quietly and passes out of the room — out of the house. He goes to the bench beneath the peach-tree, falls upon it in a revulsion of feeling, weeping—Colonel though he was, editor and lawyer as he is—like a babe.

As his father left the room, Horace Dunwoddie turns away from the young people, walks across the room, and, standing before a window, looks out into the darkness— not in the direction his father has gone; he knows there is no need to do that. It is strange, not a syllable has been said, an exclamation made; and yet even Harry looks up from his book, George from his trap, the girls from their sewing—all know that something wonderful has happened.

CHAPTER VI.

" 'I make Minerva,' Phidias said,
   'I carve her curves, I poise her head,
   To reign a queen when Greece is dead.
   I leave Apelles every hue;
   No colors hers—black, red, or blue—
   Only the purest white will do,
   Only the ivory's finest grain
   Such sovereign beauty can retain,
   Such soul which Time assaults in vain.
   Her lips are silent, yet, ye Greeks,
   Through them eternal beauty speaks.' "

WHEN Col. Dunwoddie returned to the house, he found that all the younger children had gone to bed, wondering but saying little. On entering his wife's room upstairs, it was to find that his eldest son was just bidding his mother good-night, for she had lain down, being still very weak. Horace lingered for a moment, as if he expected his father to say something; but he only remarked as he drew off his neckcloth —"Good-night, my dear boy; I am anxious that your mother should have a good night's rest. Be as quiet as you can in getting up in the morning." And then to his wife, "Go to sleep, my dear; there is no medicine for you like plenty of sleep."

Mrs. Dunwoddie was greatly exhausted, but she felt that there was something restful in her husband's tones, and fell that much the more sweetly asleep, to slumber soundly all night. It had required an effort upon Col. Dunwoddie's part to restrain himself from speaking of the letter. He was surprised to find, however, that with its amazing information had come a sudden broadening and deepening, a quieting and strengthening power, in itself almost as wonderful. Although he lay as still as possible for fear of disturbing his wife, whose regular breathing was like music to

C

him, knowing how much she needed rest, it was very little sleep that he himself got. It was as if he had taken just enough opium to make him wide awake, and yet with a wakefulness which, for the time, exhilarated more than sleep.

As a lawyer and writer, it had become the habit of his life to put his thoughts into forms of expression; and he said to himself as he lay, "How still and silent are the awful forces which revolutionize the world. To think of the inconceivable power lodged in a little half-sheet of letter-paper like that, and lodged from it in me, too, and I have not as yet breathed a syllable of it, or stirred! Poor Horace! I am afraid he will not sleep to-night for wondering what is the matter. He knows it is nothing painful, at least." And then the wakeful man went off into a hundred plans, which went on forming themselves in his brain as he sank asleep, and so until he woke up suddenly. It was as if a mocking voice said in his ear with sarcastic sharpness, "You fool! Not to see that it is all a hoax." It was like a dagger. Lying broad awake, he went over the letter in his mind; and then, stealing softly out of bed, he began to dress, for morning had come. As he came to knot after knot in his clothing, the record of his exceedingly varied ideas during the night, he untied them in a spirit very different from that in which they had been made, derisively even; for his broken rest was telling upon him, as it always did. But it was plain that it was the best way to treat the letter as a foolish trick of some one. Yet it would be too terrible if it were so. As his wife awoke at Charlie's cry of "Hot pot, hot pot!" he recoiled at the possibility of having to go back to all that was their life before; but that was the best plan, it was a nonsensical attempt to humbug him which should *not* succeed. Perhaps there would be people about his office or along the streets that week watching. They would see what a botch they

had made of it. He was sorry, when he went down-stairs, that Horace should linger so after his breakfast in hope that his father would say something. Poor fellow!

The next day was Sunday. Of one thing Col. Dunwoddie was very sure, and that was that his letter ran as directly counter to the day as anything possibly could. No man at church wore an aspect of more respectful attention than he; and yet, had the sermon been in Sanscrit, the Colonel would have understood it as little — his mind being in the letter, and in the extraordinary possibilities it opened before him. But it was not until night, and after all but his wife and Horace had gone to bed, that he alluded to it.

"By the bye," he said, in an indifferent manner, as he rose to help his wife upstairs, "I had a foolish letter Saturday night. Some scamp is trying to play me a trick. It made me angry at first. It won't prevent you from sleeping, Eliza. Would you like to hear it?" And, placing the lamp upon the mantel, the Colonel produced the letter. Hoax or not, he had kept it, with his watch, under his pillow the night before, and he now read it:

"'*Bigthing, Slag County, Nevada.*
"'*You beloved, blundering old Booby*—'

"I should have said," Col. Dunwoddie remarked, "that this choice epistle was addressed to Hon. Alexander Allen, to my care, of course. As there was no one else to do so, I opened and read it. I was very much amused. Listen—

"'*You beloved, blundering old Booby:*
"'*You always did remind me of an enormous pumpkin, with your yellow beard and your big, lazy body. You can spell the pumpkin with a b, and it will do just as well. You said you would write when you got to Clairsville. Of course you did not. I never expected you would. The utmost you can do is to ripen in the sun, too sluggish except to eat and drink, and grow bigger and bigger. If I did not know that you are too indolent even to get*

sick, I would suppose you were dead. In that case I am writing to your ghost, and, if that were so, what a ghost you WOULD *make! Excuse me, my dear Alec, for I love you, especially since you got so rich. I suppose I love you, big as you are, by force of contrast: you are so dull, and I am so—the reverse of dull, and you know it!*

"'*Joking aside, why don't you draw? Is it because you are too desperately in love with Miss Anderson? The lode pans out better and better every day, old fellow. Your corner lots, too, have gone up like a kite. In six months they will go down with a rush—better authorize your broker to sell soon. Ten per cent. is tremendous interest to get on that gold on deposit, and it does seem a shame not to be enjoying at least your interest in some way; it will get so enormously large that you will find it harder to handle than you do yourself.*

"'*But you need not write, for I know you won't. I am out for our people to see about the lands in your state. Oh, if you people would only let emigration and capital come in! I wonder if you Southerners do suppose people will go where they are not as free to talk as they are to feel and think, and as free to print as they are to talk, and as free to talk as—they please? No, sir; at least not until there is nowhere else to go. Upon the whole, if everybody, North and South, was as quiet in regard to disputed matters as you are in regard to everything, what a happy world it would be. Especially if they always had a friend to advise them as sharp as—*

"'*Your Nevada brother, Gam.*

"'*P. S.—Be with you almost as soon as this letter. I am bringing that blessed Paper you wrote for with me. There never was as much wrapped up in a sheet of paper since paper was first invented. What a Big fellow you are, Alec!*'"

Col. Dunwoddie laughs as he folds the letter, and says to his wife, "Quite a clever hoax, my dear. I don't think I have an enemy, except Tom Terrell, in the world, and it is only done as a joke. It was merc-

ly to amuse you that I read it at all;" but he does not look at Horace, who has risen to his feet. Mrs. Dunwoddie had been growing paler and paler as she sat; and now, her lips apart, looks—she is so reduced by her long and serious sickness—from her husband to her son without speaking.

"Will you let me see the letter, sir?" Horace asks; and, taking it, he examines the envelope carefully, then reads the letter over without a word, then examines the postmark again. "Col. Dunwoddie," he says—beginning, as a business man should, clear and calm, but his face ablaze—"dear father," he goes on, "no man would try to hoax you all the way from Nevada. Besides, men who hoax do not write a copperplate-hand like that. I ought to know a business-letter when I read it. You see how perfectly cool I am—not at all excited"—his handsome face glowing with pleasure, and his eyes sparkling. "Col. Dunwoddie—dear father—I congratulate you with all my soul!" and as he takes his father's hands in both of his that father thinks there never was a nobler-looking young man in the world.

"Mother, darling mother!" the son adds, falling on his knees before her as she sits; "thank God, you will have no more care as long as the world lasts. It is all your money—yours, yours!"

Mrs. Dunwoddie looks at her son with dry eyes, looks up at her husband bending over her, tries to rise, tries to speak, tries to kiss her son, and falls upon Horace's bosom in a dead faint. There is an exclamation behind them at the same moment. It is Emmeline Anderson, who has just entered with flowers for Mrs. Dunwoddie, and who drops them and springs forward at the sight.

"Not one word, Horace," the husband says in the ear of his son.

"Certainly not, sir," he replies; and lingers, blaming himself that he should have forgotten in his impulsiveness how feeble his mother was, as his father and their visitor do hurriedly all that is necessary.

"I never knew her to faint in my life," Col. Dunwoddie says. "She is so very weak, you know. We ought not to have allowed her to sit up so late. I am glad you happened to come in."

"So am I," the young lady said, never pausing a moment in her care of her friend. "Horace, please go for the doctor immediately. I was practising with the choir after church to-night," she explained, "and brought Mrs. Dunwoddie the pulpit-flowers on my way home. You need not be alarmed, Colonel, she is recovering already."

But it was an hour after the doctor had come and gone before the young lady would leave her. Meanwhile Horace had, at her request, sent home the servant who had accompanied her, lest Mrs. Anderson should be anxious about her. Mrs. Dunwoddie had ¹anced eagerly, when she had come to herself, first at her son and then at her husband; but she had said nothing except to kiss her visitor and thank her.

"I am very foolish," she said. "It is because I have been sick so long. Can you not stay all night, dear?" and all present were conscious, as well as the one addressed, that there was in the tones and manner of Mrs. Dunwoddie a certain childlike clinging to her visitor which no one had ever observed before. But she could not stay.

"Mamma is far from well," she said; "all you need, dear Mrs. Dunwoddie, is sleep. I would only trouble you. Early in the morning I will be in to see you. Good-night," and there was a striking contrast between the elder lady and the young girl who bent down, dark and strong, to kiss her. It was in vain the family insisted upon her allowing Horace to procure a carriage. "I took a servant and walked to church to-night," she said with a smile, "far and dark as it was. I preferred it. Who would not rather walk?" she added

to Horace, who gladly went with her, as he had done very often of late during her attendance upon his sick mother. "I am almost glad—yes, glad, that the illness in your house all these months," she added still more brightly, "has given me so much to do. What I hate most of all is to sit still, to do nothing, to be nothing. But I won't speak of myself. There is one thing I want to say to you, Mr. Dunwoddie," the young lady added, as she walked—"you must be very careful with your mother."

"We intend to be, Miss Emmeline," he replied. "It has been a long and hard winter with us all. With her most of all, because the strain has been severest on her. It always has been," he added. "But the spring has come—"

"Mr. Dunwoddie," the other said, as if she had hardly heard him, "I am glad to have this opportunity to talk to you. We understand some things better than men. The Colonel is busy about his affairs all day, and so are you, and then only a woman can understand a woman. Listen," she said gravely. "Your mother is the best woman I ever knew. My own mother I love and respect, but she is different entirely. Her situation has been different, her temperament, her reading—everything. You know how cold and reserved she is in manner. Well, she told me only this morning — we happened to be speaking about Mrs. Dunwoddie, but we are often doing so for that matter—and I will tell you what she said, for I have a special object—'Emmeline,' she said, 'I have never felt myself inferior to any other person since I can remember except one, and that is—' 'Mrs. Dunwoddie,' I said for her, and she said, 'Yes.'"

"Thank you, thank you"—her companion began eagerly, but the young lady went on.

"What I have said is not only true, but all this is for a purpose. Men do not understand things. You must take more care of your mother. She has had too great a strain upon her, how I do not understand, except that the better people are the more we look to and depend on them. Take care of her—care—better care of her, that is all."

"Thank you, Miss Emmeline," the young man said, with a new light breaking in upon him, not unmingled with self-reproaches, "we are going to do so. Spring is just opening, you know. We are going to give her the longest and best rest she has ever had. You will see."

"Your uncle's sickness was a severe addition to her cares," she added, to break the sudden silence which followed.

"Uncle Alec—I mean Uncle Alexander's? Yes, so it was," and the young man paused. He was almost hurt that the other should have spoken so slightingly, it seemed to him, of their dead relative. In the last hour or two that uncle had become a wholly different person from what he had ever seemed before. "Uncle Alexander was a noble man in some respects," he added; "he was somewhat slow in his way, but he was a—a—I may say a very large—large-hearted man. He did not say much, you know."

The young man hesitated, more embarrassed than his companion dreamed. He was alarmed at her hints in regard to his mother's condition. All his life he had loved his mother as one loves the very sunshine, essential as it is, indispensable, matter of course. She had often been sick, but she had always got well, and had never complained, always speaking of any ailment as a something but of the moment and soon to be over. And, now, his companion's words awoke vague but terrible alarm, and for the first time. Then there was this new matter of the letter. Suddenly relieved of his anxiety thereby in regard to his father, he was as suddenly left free to think of his companion with a boldness he had never felt before. He could not remember the day when he did not worship this young lady as his ideal of all loveliness. The way in which his uncle had made a fool of himself in regard to her

had caused him to hide his one great secret the more carefully. But things were changing now, and had he not become old enough to assert himself? All these things embarrassed him as he ventured in regard to his uncle—"He did not say so very much, you know—"

"Very little," the young girl replied, somewhat dryly; "but," she added, as they reached her house, "I never heard any of you speak of him as your 'Uncle Alexander' before." She had taken off her hat as she said it, and stood facing him—her large serious eyes fastened inquiringly on his. There was something so searching in their gaze that the young man colored under them in the brilliant moonlight.

"I am very much obliged to you," she said. "Good-night. Please give my love to your mother, remember, the first thing when she awakes. Thank you. Good-night."

Horace Dunwoddie was living, while she spoke, in his eyes and not in his ears. Was it that she had changed? Could it be that he had suddenly grown into clearer and bolder seeing under the stimulus of the Nevada news? He had known her so long; none the less it was as if he had come on the instant upon the master-work of some great sculptor. He had never really seen her before. Never again could he cease to see her.

She stood at the moment framed like a picture in the gateway of her home. It was a large mansion—quite a grove of pines and oaks between it and the road. Winter was drawing to a close, and the midnight air, for it was now very late, seemed almost congealed in the dense silence and darkness of the house and trees behind her, making a background against which the young girl stood out, the moon shining full upon her, in strong relief. Besides her mother, she was the last of a family which had been, and such a short time before, the centre and, largely, the source of the social life of all that region. Now, with the slaves and the wealth, the stately father, the spirited brothers were gone. In her lingered the soul, so to speak, of all that was departed; but her seriousness was not that of sorrow, it was the dignity rather of strength. Growing up in such a family, she, like her companion, was better educated than their troubled times would seem to have allowed; their knowledge making up in depth for what it lacked in breadth, in substance for what it failed of in sparkle. Horace could not have been his father's son as well as, since the war, his close companion, not to have learned much in addition to his schooling.

"Do you know," he said, compelled to utter in some way his sense of her beauty as she stood, "I was reading about Zenobia last week, and you remind me of her."

"Do I?" she said, her face the brighter in contrast with its usual gravity. "I am glad of it; I am not content to be less than a queen."

"It was an emperor who conquered her—Aurelian," he added.

"I remember," she replied; "but there are no emperors in these days."

"Are you sure?" he asked slowly.

"Certainly," she answered, her large eyes opening with surprise; "they were all killed fighting for the Confederacy. Who is left?"

"We will see," he said, simply. "You will not let me go with you to the house? Then, good-night."

"I am nearly three years older than she," Horace Dunwoddie said to himself as he walked home; "and I wish she would seem a little more as if she knew it. Oh, how strong she is—as strong as she is beautiful. What excellent sense, too, to know my mother so well. She saw through you instantly, you snob," he added, turning savagely upon himself. "Because you have found out that he has got — had got — money, he has become Alexander, has he? Alexander the Great. Bah, you puppy! That poor uncle of mine made himself a laughing-stock about her—not that he did not love her, but that he was so ridiculously unworthy of her. I happen to be, I hope, a different man. She will love me when I make her do so—and I will."

———————

CHAPTER VII.

MR. GAMALIEL MIDDLETON ARRIVES.

"Letters are already mailed
  Which will change your life for you;
Ships for you have weighed and sailed,
  Freighted deep, and nearly due.
Comes the end with rapid pace,
Patience is the chiefest grace."

"Even if it is not a foolish trick of some one," Col. Dunwoddie demonstrated to his wife as she reclined in her easy-chair the next day, "it is plain from the reckless manner of the writer of the letter that it is a great exaggeration. My dear wife," he insisted, anxiously, "I am fearful lest you should think that your poor brother has left us thousands where it may be merely hundreds, even if it is anything at all."

"My dear Charles," his wife said with a serene smile, "I have never even thought upon the question. The anxiety is all on your part. I do believe you have had more solicitude since you got the letter than before; I never knew you to be so nervous."

"Heaven knows I have had enough to make me so, Eliza. There is the *Clarion*, upon which I have spent so much money and toil. Would you believe—" and the husband entered into quite a long and minute detail of all the many serious annoyances he had endured in connection therewith.

From time to time as the Colonel spoke he rubbed the side of his nose with the long forefinger of his right hand, the rubbing growing harder and more frequent as he waxed more and more excited in the detail of his trials.

"But you have been very successful at the bar," his wife said, as cheerfully as she could for her weakness.

"My *dear* Eliza, how little you know," he said with a pitying smile, and proceeded to give her an account of the loss of his great case after all his many months of severe preparation. That led to a detail of the rascality of Tom Terrell, the opposing counsel, the perjury of witnesses, the astounding stupidity of juries—most of all, the ingratitude of clients; the lawyer pleading the cause of his manifold wrongs as if his sick wife were a court to act upon them. In this case the court was too partial, as well as too deeply bribed beforehand, to do other than listen with greatest interest to the eloquent statement, her color rising as she sat.

"Well," she urged at last, "we have at least our home, a nest for our brood—"

"My dear, I would not pain you for the world," Col. Dunwoddie began. "You have been very ill, you are still weak. When you are strong enough there is a terrible trouble— But let us talk of something else. When does Miss Anderson visit you again?"

"Charles," poor Mrs. Dunwoddie said, holding firmly to the arms of her chair, "what is it? Why has it been concealed from me? I know by your manner of late that something has been almost killing you. Do you think I am always asleep when I lie so still at night? When you are thinking, thinking with your eyes wide open, however quiet you are, do you suppose I do not know it? I am almost well, I am quite strong now. Better tell me everything."

And, after some further protest, the husband did tell her all, down to the smallest item, of the dismal story. So absorbed was he in its painful details that he did not think for a moment how severely he was trying the woman already tried beyond her utmost strength.

"But why have you compelled me to distress you, Eliza?" he said. "It is only because you have such excellent judgment, have been so steady in your faith and hope, and because I have never hidden anything from you, that I have spoken." The poor martyr sat quite still. Her brows were very hollow, her cheeks pale and thin, her every nerve strung to its tensest under the dealing of her husband, who never for a moment imagined that no familiar of the Inquisition was ever so cunning in cruelty as he had been in his love.

"At least," she said—"at least we have One upon whom we can rely—" But the Colonel hardly heard the words of faith and hope which she was trying to utter, her heart stronger than her voice.

"My dear Eliza," he said at last, "if you were one of the swarms of foolish wives, do you think I would talk so freely to you? I never knew you to utter a syllable of complaint in my life. It is because you are so sensible, have so much faith. Well, then, listen," and he entered into a full detail of the sad trouble then going on in the church which they attended. It was very sad in every respect; and, as the Colonel dilated upon the certain disastrous consequences to the church and to the whole community, he became excited—although he was no member—beyond all control of himself, for he had lost a good deal of sleep of late.

"I tell you, Eliza, I begin to doubt," he said at last, allowing to escape in words what had been merely the passing despair of his thoughts in their darkest depths—"to doubt whether there is a particle of truth in Christianity. The theory is beautiful, very beautiful; but I tell you solemnly I know no more as to its truth than if I were an earthworm writhing in the mire under the tread of—"

"Charles, *dear* Charles," his wife said through her tears, "please, please—"

"And here is this wretched letter," he continued; "have I not had experience of hopes excited only to be darkened? In all probability it will prove to have been but the worst of our many bitter disappointments. In all things there seems an infinite malig—" '

"If you *will* talk so, Charles, at least let me go to my room," the poor woman said, attempting to rise.

"My darling wife," Col. Dunwoddie hastened to her side, "surely you know that it is because I love you so dearly that I feel as if we were cruelly wronged. When I know how worthy *you* are of everything, and then see how overtaxed you are every day! It is because I love you so. To think that you—"

But at this instant there was a ring at the door, and soon after Emmeline Anderson entered the room. She had walked rapidly from her mother's, and was in the full glow of health and high spirits.

"What is the matter, dear Mrs. Dunwoddie?" she said, as she laid aside her hat and wrappings and leaned over and kissed her friend. "You look weaker and more exhausted than you did last night. I do hope you have not been talking—nor listening," she added, looking around upon Col. Dunwoddie.

"Mamma is better, and sent these flowers with her love, and says you must rest—rest. We do love you so, dear Mrs. Dunwoddie." And again she stooped and gently kissed her friend, who seemed to cling to her. No wonder, she seemed so fresh beside the other, who was wearied with many years, now, of toil and care.

But the strength of the visitor did not lie merely in her health. The dark hair clustered thickly around a face which was being set into the mould of power by something apart from herself. But a few days before Col. Dunwoddie had been quoting Byron, to the effect that the powers of nature, though "wondrous strong," are less than is

"The light of a dark eye in woman."

To illustrate this he had cited, with the intense though silent approval of his son Horace, the power of Emmeline Anderson's eyes. Certainly, he had a new sense thereof when she turned them upon him now as he drew on his overcoat before leaving for his office.

"Col. Dunwoddie," she said, "I intend staying all day. I am family physician, and I will have no talking with my patient. I will not allow anything that can excite her. She is too weak."

"My dear Miss Emmeline,! as if we did not love and value her beyond all the world beside," the husband said, smoothing his hat upon his sleeve before he went out. "Do you not suppose *I* know? There was a case in my own knowledge which I can never forget. A distinguished clergyman married a lovely lady of my acquaintance. There never was a rosier or happier bride. He had a theory—it was in regard to the millennium. The man had read and written upon the subject until he could think of nothing else. His people had got so wearied of the topic that he had no one but his wife to talk to about it. And he *did* talk to her, morning, noon, and often deep into the night. For his sake she tried to interest herself in it, to argue against him, because she saw how it delighted him. Miss Emmeline," Col. Dunwoddie added, "that man argued his wife into a decline. He so demonstrated his position from books and history, from reason and Scriptures and the daily newspapers, that he succeeded in accomplishing the end of the world in her case, at least. I attended her funeral, and that man never dreams to this day that he killed his wife."

"I have no doubt of it," the visitor replied, looking at the speaker in a way which he could not fully understand, "not the least. We are shocked when a drunken brute does the same, and yet men who are as blind to the fact as your minister are doing like things to-day. Please go. I will take care of Mrs. Dunwoddie."

"What a magnificent woman she will make," the Colonel said to himself as he walked down town. "I never knew a more perfect type of Southern beauty, *but*— Oh well," he added, "it is the terrible change in her circumstances. So far as young men are concerned, I know that having to depend on themselves will do them good, make stronger men of them. But it is a dreadful thing for our young girls, accustomed, as they are, to such gentle nurture. And then, poor Alec. I am afraid his sluggishness had an unhappy effect upon her. It would be bad if Judge Anderson's daughter should become—become too independent, too self-reliant—unwomanly. But what an astounding revolution the South is passing through! God save our women!"

Neither the lady referred to nor Mrs. Dunwoddie were particularly cheered by his return to dinner; they were getting on so quietly together, and he had never seemed quite so tall, so spare in frame, so nervous as on that day. He asked anxiously if any one had called, seeming depressed when told that no one except certain neighbors had done so. The fact is, he had been expecting the arrival of the writer of the momentous letter, and when he was not in the excess of hope he was apt to be in the extreme of doubt.

"I feared so," he said to his wife as he helped Miss Anderson at table. "Feared so!"

"My dear," his wife began brightly, "Mrs. Levison was here this morning. Mr. Levison is, you know, president of Horace's railway. It would have delighted you to hear what she said of her husband's opinion of Horace. He said that he regarded him as one of the manliest and most reliable young men he has ever known. He is sure he will succeed. You know," the fond mother continued, "how many of our noblest young men have fallen into bad habits, given up in despair. I am so glad about our boy!" And as she said it Horace himself came in. He was a noble fellow to look at, with broad shoulders, sturdy arms, a bold yet modest way of looking every man in the eyes, and of speaking confidently and to the point, which secured the respect of every one. He had the aspect of having taken a cold bath that morning, of having had the handling of men and of money, of being ready, able, and willing for whatever should come up next—as much the aspect at least of this as can lie in manner.

"I wanted to see how you are, mother," he said, hat in hand, his face in a glow, after saluting all.

"Of course you did not expect Miss Emmeline would be here," his father asked, a little maliciously.

"No, I did not," he said frankly. "I am glad to see you, Miss Emmeline, but I could not, or rather I would not have left business for that." Although he flushed as he said it, nothing was plainer than that he preferred truth to compliment. "I cannot stay a moment — good-by!" and he was gone.

"It may do—all this revolution, now that the slaves are freed—for our young men. I was thinking of it this morning," Col. Dunwoddie remarked; "but for our young women I fear not. If there is a thing I like in woman it is softness, gentleness, the down upon the peach, the dew upon the rose. There is an almost infantile dependence in woman, according to my idea, an utter trust and leaning upon the sterner sex, which has heretofore aroused all the chivalry in our men. A woman likes a man to be a *man*."

"You are right, sir — a man," their visitor added with quiet emphasis.

"And," the Colonel continued, "we men do like a woman to be a—well, a *woman;* one to be gently cared for, shielded, relieved of every burden. Now," began the speaker afresh as he saw himself under the full and questioning eyes of Miss Anderson— "I belong to the Old School. Before the war—"

But at this moment his younger daughter May came into the room in more than her usual eager way.

"Oh, ma! oh, pa!—good-morning, Miss

Emmeline," she said. "A gentleman is waiting to see pa in the parlor. I was hurrying back from school to know how ma was, and he took off his hat and asked me the way here. You don't know how dreadfully mortified I was. I had on my old school-suit, and all my hair needed fixing. Because he is such a very nice gentleman"—the young lady lowered her voice before the uplifted hand of her mother, but continued just above a whisper—"He has such dark hair, all curly about his forehead, and a lovely moustache. His clothes fit him so beautifully, and he wears kid gloves buttoned up, and his boots are as bright as can be. Then he has such a heavenly smile, and lovely teeth, and a black cane, and the pleasantest voice. He says he is from Nevada, and his name is Mr. Middleton. Do go, pa!"

———————◆———————

CHAPTER VIII.

MR. MIDDLETON HAS A SUDDEN INSPIRATION.

"Milton did not always know
 He would write his epic grand;
Long did Shakespeare have to go
 Ere his Hamlet he had planned.
Sudden in your grasp they stand,
Things you got not with your hand.

"Saul did not intend to kneel
 Just before the vision blazed;
Nero did not plunge the steel
 Till his steps pursuers grazed:
When you are most blamed, most praised,
You of all are most amazed."

AN hour or so before May Dunwoddie burst upon the household in the manner just described, a gentleman had stepped off from a train arriving at the depot from the West. It was evident that he was a stranger, from the neat valise which he carried in his hand. It was not a very large valise, yet in five minutes' notice its bearer—and in whatever part of the land he chanced to be at the moment—could, and very often did, pack up in it the entire universe, so far as he was concerned, and catch the next stage or train, never to return. A

trunk accompanied him on this trip, but it was wholly exceptional, and was itself the highest compliment he could pay Clair County. The new-comer wore an overcoat and hat, to say nothing of his boots and gloves and cane, which would have made him a marked man. There was a certain slouchiness in the drooping rims of the felt hats and loose attire in general of people in Clair County, which, in the languid leaves of the ailanthus and oleander trees, too, was alike owing to the climate. The truth is, Clairsville was a small and somewhat dull place, and the best citizens there felt so thoroughly at home with everybody that they showed it in their dress. There was a lassitude not more in the arms and legs of the people than in the tones of their voice—and the new-comer walked the platform of the depot in a brisk manner, asking a question or two in sharp and decided tones, which showed the most stupid negro lounging on the spot that the man was from a different latitude; and no lady, at least, in the town but would have pronounced him to be one of the handsomest of men.

With a quick, keen eye, the stranger had studied his surroundings as he stepped off the train, unconscious that he himself had been seen by eyes as sharp as his own. When Horace Dunwoddie had listened the night before to the letter read by his father, every word of it seemed to come as naturally as could be into the swelling current of his life hitherto. The night before that, when he had caught the glance of his father's eyes, as the Colonel had read the letter for the first time lying upon the lounge, the meaning of the document, however ignorant he was of its contents, had flashed upon him as does fire upon tinder long made ready for the spark. He was like his father in being tall, sinewy, and of that peculiar nervous organization which makes the possessor at once exceedingly sensitive, and yet tenacious in prejudices as in purposes to the last degree.

It is that temperament which is ridiculed as high-toned, high-strung, and which is a mental and moral peculiarity because it is first a physical. You admire precisely the same characteristics in the long legs, spare body, small ears, bright eyes, deep chest, lean flanks of a race-horse or a greyhound, when they are of the purest blood and highest breeding; and in the dog, the horse, and the man you have the greatest speed and tenacity of which flesh and blood is capable. Had Col. Dunwoddie or his son Horace dropped into a shoemaker's shop— say in Vermont—to be measured for a pair of boots, the worthy mechanic would have regarded the small foot, with its instep excessively high above and arched below, as almost a deformity; yet there is no more personal merit or demerit in this than in the case of the negro at the other end of the scale, the sole of whose foot is level with the earth.

The stranger waited until the train which had brought him was gone, and then looked eagerly around. As he did so his eye fell upon Horace Dunwoddie, and he stepped up to him as the one person of the many there to whom he should speak. With Horace's father it would have been different. Any one would have been struck in an assembly with the appearance of Col. Dunwoddie, but you would not have been in a hurry to speak to him. That, you instinctively felt, required an introduction, as he was evidently a person of some distinction. Besides, there was, in the case of the Colonel, an air of preoccupation, of anxiety which might express itself in irritability. And Horace was becoming the duplicate of his father, but with the happy addition thereto of his other parent. He was broad-chested as well as tall; his eyes were not merely piercing and quick, like those of his father, but they were calm, also, and steady like those of his mother. Like her, he could be silent and quiet for long periods, which was impossible to his father. There was that in-definable something in him, the milk as of his mother in the refined and almost womanly expression of his eyes, which made the new-comer sure that, whoever his father was, his mother must be a superior woman.

There was this, however, which the new arrival could not know of the young man; this that, having been born in and saturated with the spirit of the old era in the South, of the days before the war, he was determining, as far as he could, to understand and enter manfully upon and possess the new era which lay before him. There was that which was as much the inevitable effect in him of the new times in which he was beginning to live as a blossom is the effect of the coming on of summer; and he comprehended it all little more, even while he yielded to it, than the blossom does the ripening season. To Horace Dunwoddie his father was the pattern of all gentlemen, even while he felt that there was a good deal in his father's noblest qualities which were obsolete and becoming every day more and more so; and he loved him and was keenly jealous in regard to him because of this very thing. Having been thrown since the war more with his father than with his mother, he had keener sympathies for the one than for the other, his likeness to his mother, soul as well as body, lying in this silent but passionate devotion to Col. Dunwoddie as the chiefest of men. Yet, although he would have been himself the first to deny and resent the imputation, Horace knew that there was a something in father and mother which was forever past and gone in comparison with the days which were before him. From as long as he could remember there had been an ever-increasing expectation, as vague as it was great, in regard to the future; and the tidings contained in the letter had fallen naturally, as it were, into the current of his hopes, making that current both clearer and stronger. Ever since he had watched for the coming of the writer of it, because he felt that the new era came in the person of the writer, and came to him rather than to his parents. To him instead of them because, in some way he knew not how, it was a change which he could both understand and master better than either. For that was the way the entire event had impressed itself upon the mind of the young man — it was a vast and powerful something, not so much to be enjoyed as to be grasped and controlled. Therefore it was that Horace Dunwoddie was on the lookout for the stranger, anxious yet eager to meet him. He had supposed he would be, perhaps, merely a variation upon Hiddikel Queasy, a Clairsville character whom he abhorred.

"Will you be so kind as to tell me," the new-comer asked of him, "where in your town I can find a Mr. Alec Allen?"

"Excuse me," the young man replied, "you are from Nevada, are you not?"

"Yes, sir. But why do you ask?" the other said with an uneasy sense of the fact that the one who asked the question was controlling himself to do so.

"Come into my office—it is here in the depot—and I will explain," Horace Dunwoddie said in a lower tone; and having seated the other therein, standing before him he said in a sympathetic manner—

"I am sorry, sir — your name, if you please. Ah, Mr. Middleton—Mr. Gamaliel Middleton—I am happy to know you, sir. But I am very unhappy to have bad news for you;" and he waited a little while the other changed countenance as he looked up at him.

Mr. Middleton was not much, if any, over thirty. He was an under-sized man, but extremely well-formed, with regular features, beautiful eyes, hair and moustache singularly silken and curly as well as dark; and he seemed as if just out of the hands of the most skilful of barbers as well as of tailors. Horace had never seen in his out-of-the-way Southern home so admirable

appearing a gentleman; but he observed that the face of the other seemed to become discolored rather than pallid as he spoke—it was as if his new acquaintance had suddenly become much older.

"I am sorry to say your friend has been very ill indeed." He spoke slowly, but was surprised that the face of the other brightened rather than darkened as he went on. "It is very painful," he added, "but I am obliged to tell you that your friend is—dead."

"Is it possible!" Mr. Middleton said with consternation; and yet, as if suddenly relieved of some other apprehension—"Is it possible! Can it be!—is it *possible!*" in tones and manner of deepest affliction.

The young man turned respectfully away, walked across the room, and stood looking out of the window, until the other said, at last,

"Poor Alec! poor, poor Alec! And he was the last man I would have expected to die. What a villainous world it is! Just as he had become so very—had become— While he was so young, I mean. Do you know the circumstances, sir?"

"I should have introduced myself. I am Horace Dunwoddie," the other replied, "Col. Dunwoddie is my father. The speaker said it with a certain flush of pride, as he always did, since no man was better known in the state than the Colonel; and the son, like his mother, exaggerated his father's standing beyond the wont of most sons. "Uncle Alec died at my father's house, sir."

As he said it the stranger arose, nor did he take his seat again. "And you are Col. Dunwoddie's son," he said, extending his small white hand, which he had ungloved for the purpose, "and the nephew poor Alec has told me so much about. I am glad to make your acquaintance, sir." Horace Dunwoddie felt almost thrilled with what seemed to him a species of magnetism in the tones and cordial eyes, as well as in the close and clinging grasp.

Melting more and more towards him as he proceeded, he gave his uncle's old companion a full detail of his sudden sickness and death. Meanwhile the other listened with an intensity as if in regard to something which remained to be told beyond that. And when all was said, after a considerable silence, his handkerchief to his eyes now and then, Mr. Middleton asked at length—

"Did he say much in regard to his life in Nevada?"

But the other was wondering a little, not so much at the fineness and whiteness of Mr. Middleton's handkerchief as at the diamond ring upon the hand that held it, for he had rarely before seen a diamond upon the hand of any but a lady, nor any as large as that. There was a certain perfume, too, on the air, which he had supposed was used by none but ladies.

"Anything in regard to his success out West?" Mr. Middleton varied his question, his moistened eyes now bent upon the floor.

"Hardly a word," Horace replied; and added, "You know that Uncle Alec was unusually slow in talking as in everything. He mentioned you once by name."

"You are right," the other said promptly; and, looking up, "Remarkably slow. I am glad he had not forgotten me. I loved him like a brother, was the most intimate friend he had; I may say I was the only friend he had, for there was a rough lot of people out there, I assure you—very rough. But Alec was very slow, very indeed. The last man in the world to succeed, the last man living. He said nothing about it then? Nothing at all, did he? I only ask."

"Nothing whatever."

"He was struck down, you tell me, the morning after his arrival. Possibly he may have talked during his sickness. Wildly, foolishly, I dare say. The fever, you know. Did he say anything of any—any interest?" the stranger inquired.

"No, sir," Horace Dunwoddie replied. "He was unconscious during his whole ill-ness. My mother says that he spoke to her just before he was taken sick of something he was intending to tell her, intending to consult my father about, but all that he did say was, 'Poor, poor, poor,' and—"

"Anything else?" Mr. Middleton asked.

"I think," the other replied, with rising color, "that—that he repeated the name of a young lady."

"Miss Emmeline Anderson," the stranger added for him gravely. "No wonder. Alec, poor fellow, told me all about it one night. Ah, yes! He hoped to marry her. That is, some day; for Alec was exceedingly indefinite in his plans—poor fellow! poor fellow! And nothing else?" he asked, with anxious yet brightening face; and added, as Horace shook his head—

"I intend to call upon her at the earliest moment. That is," he added in his most polished manner, "if it is thought proper I should do so. She is the daughter, I learn, of Judge Anderson, with whom the whole Union is so well acquainted. We at the North, you know—prejudiced, I dare say, as to our way of thinking—deplored his going into secession, after holding out against it so long, more than we did that of almost any other leader of the South. His character, as well as position, was so national, you know. Not that I am a politician, Mr. Middleton added hastily, "it is not at all in my line—politics I detest," with an almost lady-like shudder. "We were speaking of your uncle. If ever a man was unfitted to succeed among those rough-and-tumble people, Alec was that man. And then," Mr. Middleton added, "you have no idea sir, what rascals we have out there. I do suppose that we are blessed with the most atrocious scoundrels, the most consummate villains, the very pick of the ruffianism of the universe. Why, sir," he continued, "there are men there who would no more hesitate to murder you if you had money, no more hesitate—"

"I am glad, judging from your letter, that Uncle Alec had the sense to invest as well as he did." The young man was almost surprised to hear himself say it, and in so calm a tone. It was as if he spoke in virtue of an influence upon him apart from himself—of summer upon the blossom, let us say.

"Ah, that letter of mine came to hand, did it? I was going to ask you about it," Mr. Middleton exclaimed, with his eyes full upon those of the other. "Glad? So am I, very glad, very glad indeed. I intend to talk it all over with your father. But it was sad about Miss Emmeline Anderson—very sad. I suppose she is plunged in the deepest grief. I fear she will not be able to see me."

"Mr. Middleton," the other said, "you are laboring under a mistake. Miss Anderson was never engaged to my uncle. She is an exceedingly superior lady. I am sure she never—never—actually— Uncle Alec was very different from her." And Horace Dunwoddie announced to himself as he ceased speaking that he was a fool, registering a vow to hold his tongue hereafter, if possible, which, with a flash of his father's despondency, he greatly doubted. But the new-comer broke in upon his self-reproaches.

"I see," he said eagerly. "Certainly. Of course. In which direction, by the by, does she live? Ah, over there? I have never seen her, of course, but I knew your uncle well; he was a good fellow—in some respects a splendid man—but I often wondered—"

At this moment the roar and bell of an incoming train was heard, and Horace Dunwoddie had to excuse himself. He paused outside the door to look at his watch. As he did so he heard a sound within as if Mr. Middleton had smitten his hands together, and then the exclamation—

"I'll be shot!"

The truth is, the new-comer had been struck, almost on the instant of learning that Alec Allen was dead, with the most brilliant idea of his life. He had stumbled

upon it as upon a nugget of gold. Rather it was a jewel upon which the whole machinery of his life would turn thereafter, only they never put jewels of such enormous value into time-pieces. The exclamation had been smitten from him as by a blow; but, as if it had been a nugget or a diamond which he had found, henceforth his anxiety was intense to conceal until he could use it. That one exclamation had broken from his lips in the urgency of the moment, and he cursed himself even for that in the same instant; no man was to hear another, not in a whisper even, in regard to the matter.

Horace Dunwoddie stood for an instant, watch in hand, listening to the noise of the incoming train, and conscious that the new era in his life was coming upon him as speedily and surely, and that it was a something which was much more apt to crush him under its revolving wheels, rushing upon him, as it was, with a force simply incalculable. He knew that he did not comprehend all that was coming, but this he did know, that he could come to understand it better than his father. The one thing which was clear to him as he hastened about his duties was that, in some way wholly unknown to him as yet, the fortunes of his own household, possibly that of Emmeline Anderson, would devolve upon him. It was all very vague. What he knew was that he could not be too calm if he was to be strong — that was all. And somehow the depot, and the noisy train, and the crowd of idlers which came in with it as floating trash comes in with the tide, and his business which had once seemed so important—all things had suddenly become smaller and much more manageable.

When Mr. Gamaliel Middleton walked away at last, having had directions how to find Col. Dunwoddie's house, he seemed to have suddenly relaxed. The instant he parted with Horace Dunwoddie he was another man—it must be said, very inferior—to what he was the moment before. His new friend had insisted upon sending his valise after him by a negro, who, as is always the case, was not to be found on the instant; and Mr. Middleton, cutting as he walked with cool precision at the mullenstalks, cane in hand, was safe to think matters over.

"Shot?" he said to himself as he went. "Shot? I'll be consigned to perdition!—Oh, Gamaliel, my son, it will be the richest lode *you* ever struck!—What a sleepy old town this is.—The grandest idea!—No gas nor water works, I suppose.—I wonder if they know how to read.—What a splendid chap this young fellow is!—That is, if he only knew anything.—Gamaliel, my little boy, he is in love with her.—Isn't it the grandest idea!—A million, man, a round million, round and glorious as the rolling sun.—You double-distilled fool, what did you clap your hands for where that young Dunwoddie might have heard you?—Never mind.—But won't it throw this town into convulsions.—Nitro-glycerine is nothing to it!—Hold on, let me plan a little, and it will be the making of myself and my sister Clara."—But at this moment he was aware of a school-girl hastening along upon the other side of the street.

"A native, I suppose," he continued to himself. "What a charming dairy-maid! You will be a beauty one day, my darling, if you only knew it. I wonder if *she* is like her."

But nothing could be more respectful than the way in which he lifted his hat, crossing the street for the purpose, as he said—

"Pardon me, miss; will you be so kind as to show me the way to Col. Dunwoddie's?"

"Certainly, sir," she replied, with a flush of pleasure. "I am Col. Dunwoddie's daughter. We live in that house just beyond the China-trees. I am going there now." d y

And thus it was that Miss May, leaving her companion in the parlor, broke in upon the household in the way already mentioned.

CHAPTER IX.

HORACE DUNWODDIE MAKES A DISCOVERY.

"The laborer digging in the mould
Right rarely strikes on pots of gold;
Yet, toiling on with might and main,
He comes at last on golden grain.
There is connection strong and clear
Between the deer-hound and the deer,
A subtle something closely binds
The seeker and the thing he finds:
An ownership in what is sought
More vital than in what is bought."

"ONE can hardly realize it," Col. Dunwoddie said to his wife and Horace, seated together in the parlor after the rest of the family had gone to bed. "It was only last Saturday night the letter came to hand; Sunday night I read it to you both; Monday afternoon Mr. Middleton arrived at the depot; met you there, Horace; was shown the way to the house by May; here we are this same Monday night. It is only a few score hours from the first, and yet years seem to have passed."

"Why did you not have Mr. Middleton to tea, my dear?" Mrs. Dunwoddie asked. "We would have been glad to receive him as our guest while he is in Clairsville."

"That is one thing that troubles me," Col. Dunwoddie said, rubbing the side of his nose with his forefinger, as he did when composing a leader for his paper, a line of argument for a case in court, a poem for the press—when harassed by these or any other forms of trouble. For that was a peculiarity of the Colonel—anything requiring special thought was an affliction; the more special the thought, that much the more severe the affliction. Not that he was at all indolent—it was impossible for a man to be in motion more incessant. The beating of his heart, the heaving of his lungs was not more essential to his existence than was an unceasing activity of some sort; and every instant the particular occupation of that moment was an affliction in proportion to its interest, because exactly in the degree of its interest was it, and from first to last, an anxiety.

"That is the trouble," he repeated. "At the close of my conversation with Mr. Middleton, I urged him to stay. His valise had arrived, but he would not. When he pleaded fatigue, I offered to show him to his room immediately. I wonder what could have been the reason? In any case, he begged that we would excuse him for the night, and he is now at the hotel. I confess I do not like it at all," he said anxiously.

An explanation of this may be found in the fact that the instant the gentleman reached the hotel he had his trunk up to his room. Then he locked his door, unlocked his trunk, with hands trembling—from the rapidity of his walk, perhaps—took out a large envelope, apparently full of papers, and hurriedly glanced it over, eagerness in every line of his face. After this he replaced the bundle and sat down to think—think!

"You have not told us how you like him, my dear," Mrs. Dunwoddie said.

"Very much, indeed," her husband replied, plainly in a humor to talk. "He is a handsome little man, very well dressed, and his manner as well as voice is in strict keeping with the rest. Like all Eastern people, for he is originally from the East, he is guarded in his manner. We are what God made us, without any care what people may think of us. I dare say we do lounge about, stretch our long legs in the finest parlors, say what we think, wear what we please, resent insults on the spot, and all with too little reference to our own interest. Now Mr. Middleton wears his manners as he does his clothes; he selects and uses certain tones of voice and little engaging ways as he does his shirt-studs and cuff-buttons. I know enough of him already to know that. He is a gentleman of what is called culture. If there is a word I hate, it is that. Culture! You take a pig and fatten him for show; you pick out a tulip and manure it with certain chemicals until all its petals and colors are different; you work with a watermelon-vine or a peach-tree until it produces exaggerated fruits—and it is exactly so with people. It isn't that you make a person different from what he was—that may be all right—but you make him different from what he is. He is two men, and the inside man is the real one. The instant the strain comes he drops his culture as easily as he does his gloves or his coat. Upset one of those fine gentlemen in a stage, shipwreck one of those exquisite ladies on a desert island—"

"Excuse me, father," Horace interrupted, but you have not told us yet—"

"About what Mr. Middleton said?" Col. Dunwoddie interrupted his son in his turn. "I did not because I am far from being satisfied. Of course we had a great deal to say about your uncle's illness. Then he told me of several instances in which he was of great service to poor Alec. Had your uncle lived, I dare say he would have told us about the singular way in which he was rescued from the claws of a grizzly bear by this friend of his. I was greatly annoyed," Col. Dunwoddie continued, "at something Mr. Middleton hinted, rather than told me, as to the way in which men squandered all they made among the infamous people of Virginia City. I asked him what paper it was which he spoke of in the postscript of his letter. He was startled when I mentioned it; but when I showed it to him he said it was only a joke, a something he would explain some day. He hesitated so," the Colonel added, "that I fear it is a jest which it will hardly do to tell a lady. He was more or less swindled out there—your poor brother—my dear. But we will not talk about it now." And Col. Dunwoddie arose and walked to and fro from one end of the room to the other, as was also his wont when in the agonies of authorship or any like anxiety.

"But surely he said something, father," Horace insisted.

"I wonder at you, my son," his father said, with some irritation. "You see how feeble your mother is, and how anxious I am not to distress her. Besides, it was hardly to be expected that I would show undue eagerness at our first interview, in regard to any small property Alec may have left. I have never for an instant," Col. Dunwoddie added with considerable vehemence, "attached the slightest expectation to any notion of the kind. I have had to work very hard — work against unceasing disappointment. Long ago I learned to expect nothing—nothing whatever—from any source. It is in that way I have been trained to patience and calmness. It would be a pity if by this time I was not hardened into cheerful endurance. All my life I have been a poor man — a very poor man, and," Col. Dunwoddie added, "I am certain of but one thing, that I will be a poor man till I die."

"But we are happy in our children, Charles," Mrs. Dunwoddie said, smiling bravely in her easy-chair. "Here is Horace, our mother's-boy as we used to call him. He is a strength for us now, and he is more of a man every day;" and she lifted her loving eyes to her son, who stooped down as he stood over her and kissed her pale cheek with that purest and manliest of all affection on earth, that which a noble young man has for his mother whom he thoroughly respects as well as loves.

"Horace may die any day," Col. Dunwoddie said, "or he may—I wouldn't excite your mother in that way, Horace—be killed at the depot any hour. Sentiment is excellent in its way, but what I want is certainty. Why do you suppose," he suddenly turned upon his wife and demanded, "Mr. Middleton asked so particularly about Alec's baggage? I did not like it at all."

"We were compelled to burn it," his wife replied. The doctor ordered that the day he first came. But I examined it myself, dear. I assure you, besides a few dollars and an old newspaper or two, there was nothing whatever of value. I believe the poor fellow had not bought an article, hardly, since I fitted him out when he went West."

"It does seem *peculiarly* unfortunate, none the less," her husband replied. "The older I live the less faith I have in men; and, do you know, I imagined Mr. Middleton seemed pleased when he learned that Alec's baggage had been destroyed. Such people are so thoroughly buttoned up, so to speak, to the very chin in their—culture, that it is not possible to know what they really think and feel. The misery of the matter," he added, as he resumed his rapid walk back and forward, "is the suspense. If we only knew! You know I warned you both. I am glad I never entertained the least expectation. Never was I so pressed for money—terribly pressed; but I never did indulge any confident hope in my life which was not disappointed. The greater the hope the greater the disappointment. Don't worry your mother, Horace;" for his son had again stooped to kiss her, and with a face as bright and hopeful as that of his father was dark and desponding.

"You darling mother, you ought to have been in bed two hours ago," Horace said, in his hearty way. "Please let me;" and, slipping one strong arm under his mother as she sat, the vigorous son lifted her, laughing and protesting, to his bosom. "You have done it often enough for me, mother, it is a pity I cannot do it for you," he said, as he bore her in triumph out of the room and up-stairs.

"Dear mother," he said, as he laid her upon her bed there, "go sound asleep. Father is worried a little to-night. Men of genius could not write if they were not strung as tight as a harp-string all the time. As sure as you live it will all be right. Do you think I would have congratulated you so if I did not know that. I will give you this to sleep on to-night—I *know* that it is all right." But the soporific soothing was still more in the tones of her son's voice.

"I don't trust in your knowing, my boy," his mother said, "but I do in your loving. Remember one thing, Horace. Your father is right in saying that we can rely on nothing, and in nobody perfectly. I cannot rest either in him or in you, any more than in myself. I rarely talk to you, my son, about such things; but remember, there is no rest in this world except in God, and the instant you separate yourself from Him the inflowing faith ceases. That's all. I have special reasons, dear — reasons you know nothing about now, for saying this to you. Good-night."

"Father," Horace said, when he had returned to the parlor, "I wanted to tell you something." He spoke in a low voice. Col. Dunwoddie was still walking to and fro anxiously, and he stopped and looked his son full in the face.

"What is it, Horace?" he said, nervously. "Any new trouble? Something wrong at the depot? Have you heard anything more about that mortgage? Can any of those church people—"

The young man had taken a paper out of his breast-pocket when he spoke. As he saw the haggard face of his father, he paused and then replaced it. He was the stronger man. With all the more devotion to his father on that account, he grew calmer as he stood with a new manhood pouring into his veins.

"There is no trouble," he said cheerily; "none whatever. All I want to say is, that I congratulate you now as I did at first. Please do not allow yourself to be worried. All will be right as sure as you live. I told mother so, and she is going to sleep soundly. Dear father, we all love you both so much. Two girls, sir, and four boys! See what a man I am getting to be. Six of us,

Col. Dunwoddie. Our future is as bright as day. I do hope nothing will disturb mother or you from sleep. Good-night."

It is amazing how much there is in the mere tones of the voice. Col. Dunwoddie would come home and find all his family in a gale of glee about nothing at all, around his wife; and by the sadness of his brow, the quality of his silence as he ate his dinner or supper, much more by the despondency of his words, he could chill and still the gladness like a sudden cloud. Often his densest tribulation had vanished at the singing of his daughters or wife, at the mere music of May's school-girl laughter, or the steadier charm of his wife's voice in conversation. So now, Horace had said nothing in particular, but there was a substance in his manner, a subtle fibre and force in his tones, which reassured him.

An hour later and the household was buried in profound sleep—all except Horace. With his shoes drawn off, so as not to make the least noise, he was in his room writing. Evidently it was work of which he was making a deliberate business, for he did it with great care. When it was completed, he read it over, then folded and placed it in his pocket. After that he sat leaning back in his chair, his hands clasped over his head, his eyes on the ceiling. He saw as distinctly as if they were there in person, considering each of them gravely and thoroughly in turn, the faces of his father, his mother, Alice, May, George, Harry, little Charlie. Then came Mr. Gamaliel Middleton, whom he contemplated very steadily indeed. Then his father stood before him again—tall, lean, anxious, a genius and a gentleman. Last, Emmeline Anderson closed, as she had begun, the procession.

"It is not," the young man thought to this spectral visitor, "that I love you. I cannot remember when I did not. But the world is opening before me, with a vast work to do, and you are the strongest human being I know. You will have to help me. You do not know this or me, but you will."

Then he went to bed and to sleep.

----◆----

CHAPTER X.

A FAMILY COUNCIL.

"I base on rock my homestead halls,
Of granite build my household walls—
Therein with wife and child I bide;
Who will may have all earth outside.
This world to me is cold and rough,
To me my home is world enough."

"WELL, Horace, what is it?" Col. Dunwoddie demanded of his son the next morning. "You insisted upon bringing your mother down-stairs in your arms, and I have an idea that you would have brought me in the same way if you had dared to propose it. We have eaten a hearty breakfast, as you suggested. Here we are, Alice and May, Harry and George, your mother and myself. What is it? Make haste, for I am in a hurry to get to my office."

"Is it not a glorious day, father?" Horace replied, standing by the window of the breakfast-room. "Spring has come at last. How bright and clear it is! I heard the birds sing before day. All the trees will be in full leaf in a week. You can smell the flowers upon the air."

"I think one of them has bloomed already," his mother said, looking fondly at him. Even his father was struck with the appearance of his son. He seemed to have become a man as in a week. All present looked at him with new interest.

"Father," he said, keeping himself calm as by a settled purpose, "I wanted to tell you last night, but I was afraid it might break mother's rest in some way. You do feel strong, mother? You will pardon my not telling you sooner, father?"

"Certainly, Horace, what is it?" And he arose in some astonishment.

"I know you will approve afterwards. Won't you tell the children all about the letter from the first? I thought it was due them. Besides," Horace urged, "we have loved each other so much. And they will have to learn to be strong and silent. The only way is to trust them. Please, father."

Col. Dunwoddie glanced at his wife, who was pale, but quiet and smiling. She nodded with a laugh.

"I show great confidence in your judgment, my boy," he said, and then read aloud the letter, at which the children were more puzzled than ever, while their father explained that Mr. Middleton was the writer, adding somewhat irritably to Charlie, who came in at the moment, "Run away, boy, run away!"

"Please, father, let the Judge come in too," Horace pleaded. "He won't talk much. Besides, he is such a solemn old chap." And the young man cleared the plates aside and sat his little brother before him on the table, his mother holding him on the other side by his belt.

"Pardon my nonsense, dear father," Horace added. "And now to business. After Mr. Middleton left me yesterday afternoon at the depot, I thought very fast and very hard. Of course, all I could do was to go over everything that happened from the hour Uncle Alec came back. I remembered mother's telling me that his clothing was burned. But did you ever see that before?" And he held up a money-belt.

"Certainly," his father replied. "I unbuckled it myself from around his body the morning your uncle was struck down. There was a gold piece in it, which I gave your mother; the belt I threw into the closet, and have never thought of it since. It is well to tell you, my children, that I have never attached any confidence to the letter I have read you. Even now that I have seen the writer of it, I have nothing certain to say. In fact, I greatly doubt whether anything will come to us.

Horace does not show his usual sense," the Colonel added almost angrily.

The one referred to glanced at his mother, and his eyes grew brighter as he read in hers, so like his own, the same unfaltering trust as before, and he said—

"Nothing was more natural, father, than what you did and what you say. But the first thing I did when I came home last night was to get that old belt from where it lay in a corner of the closet. Sure enough, there seemed to be nothing in it. But—but—"

The young man walked across to the window and stood looking out for a time upon the glorious weather. He was strung to such a pitch of excitement, none the less intense because he was holding himself firmly in hand, that he was keenly sensitive to everything. He heard the distant tinkle of cow-bells, and the neighing of a horse somewhere. Even then he could distinguish the clink upon the anvil of a blacksmith's hammer, and the rolling sound of what he knew was a hand-car passing upon the railway. With the weight of his discovery upon him, he smiled, the belt held in his hand, at the intolerable pomp of an old turkey-cock ruffling its plumes outside under the inspiration of the same spring which was touching the fields with green and hastening the flowing of his own blood in brain as in heart.

"Well, I do declare!" exclaimed Alice.

"Oh, there is a secret," cried her sister May, and if there is a thing I do love, it is that."

Horace turned at the words. He loved and admired his father to an exaggerated degree, as a Bayard of all chivalry, but his closest relation at last was with his mother; between these two was a perfect understanding. Turning from the window he walked slowly back and stood by her. Col. Dunwoddie could not help remarking even then how much the two were alike, especially in the smooth wide brow and in the eyes, large and steady. It was this which was giving the young man his increasing influence over the father as well as over the household—an assurance that Horace was doing exactly as Mrs. Dunwoddie would have done in his place; it was as if she were acting in and by him. He now spoke—

"Father," he said, looking steadily at him, "you have been in battle often. Besides, you are a strong man, and a gentleman. I know you can stand it. Dear mother," he said, "do you think you slept enough, ate breakfast enough to bear a little strain? You know," he said playfully, "what a big piece of beefsteak you ate, and six eggs — wasn't it? Please, don't frighten us again." And Horace told, and was a long time in doing so on purpose, how he had been so foolish before as to make his mother faint.

"Well, Horace," was all she said, a little paler, but still more wonderfully like her boy in the steadfast strength of her eyes.

"See," he continued, "the belt is double," holding it up. "Observe how I ripped it down one edge. See? Well, and I found that in it." And taking a folded paper from his breast-pocket, he handed it to his father.

"What do you mean, sir?" the Colonel said sharply, as he glanced his eye over the paper. "Here is a list of what seems investments, in your handwriting."

"Oh," his son said hastily, "that is a copy I made. This is the original. You see, it is written on copying-paper. Compare the hand with Mr. Middleton's letter. It is the same, you observe. If you will read aloud, I will check you from my copy."

Col. Dunwoddie did so almost mechanically. The list was an inventory of property, belonging, as the heading specified, to Alexander Allen, Esq., of Clairsville, Clair County, of such and such a Southern State, made under oath before a notary, in Bigthing, Slag County, Nevada. The date must have been about the time Alec Allen had left Nevada, and the document was signed by Gamaliel Middleton. Attaching, in his dazed condition, almost as little meaning to what he recited as if it had been in a language unknown to him, he read a statement of so much gold in this bank and that, in Nevada, California, New York. Then followed amounts of shares in well-known mines in Nevada and Oregon as well as California. Next came estimates of bullion at specified quartz-mills. There was a full page of it, beautifully written out. As Col. Dunwoddie reached the sum total, the hand of his son was ready, and promptly covered it. The older man caught the amount and looked at his son in stupefied silence. He was not aware that Horace had taken his hand and pressed it to his lips, did not hear Horace when he fell on his knees before his mother, and said—

"Wasn't it a dozen eggs you ate, mother, and at least two beefsteaks?"

But Mrs. Dunwoddie seemed not at all inclined to faint. She placed a hand upon each of the sturdy shoulders of her son, calmer than he was a good deal, smiled through her tears, and simply said—

"Ah, my boy, you need not fear. It was so sudden on Sunday night that I had no time to think. I do not give it the value you do, dear. My only feeling is — is — Never mind. You exaggerate the value of money, Horace. It cannot—cannot—"

As the young man looked in his mother's face his own grew suddenly pale, his lips parted, a glance of instant intelligence passed between them, and kissing her, he was about to say something eagerly, when she smiled, laid her finger on her lip, with a warning gesture, so to speak, in her eyes, as to his father and the rest.

"Well, Charlie, what do you think of it all?" he said, as if by a sudden effort, to the little boy, whose fat legs hung down as he sat on the table beside him. "Hey, Judge?"

The sober-visaged child looked seriously in his brother's eyes, removed his chubby finger from between his lips, and said very solemnly—

"Hot pot!" and restored his finger to his mouth amid the almost hysterical laughter of the other children. Col. Dunwoddie was the first to speak. He was leaning against the mantle-piece, and was slowly rubbing his forehead with his hand. He spoke as if mechanically—

"Dr. Livingstone says that he learned a curious fact when a lion sprang upon him one day in Africa. You read everything, Harry, what was it?"

"Oh, that was when he was under the paws of the lion," Harry explained. "He had his great claws on the Doctor's bosom as he lay, and he felt the breath hot on his face. He says that he was not a bit miserable. He was so stunned that he had a kind of stupid pleasure in it, even. The beast was like a big dose of opium. And that's the way I feel now," the boy added. "I don't understand—I am bewildered."

"That is the way with me. What is it all about?" George exclaimed. "Don't be such an owl, Horace; tell a fellow."

"There is one thing that I know father wants to tell you all," Horace remarked. "You see, I thought it over last night after I had made out the copy. That is, that none of us are to say a syllable to a soul about the matter."

"Oh, Horace!" May protested, "what was the use of telling us if we can't tell? The only thing I care about it is to tell the girls at school. Who wants to know a secret if you can't at least let people know that you have got one and won't tell them. Pshaw! what a pity!"

"Your brother is right," her father hastened to say. "You are not, one soul of you, to give the least hint to anybody as to this matter. That is, as Horace says, the reason we trust you, since you know that Mr. Middleton is here. The reason why—"

"Why, pa," George broke in, "Mr. Middleton is at the hotel; he will tell—he has told everybody already."

"No, he has not," Horace said. "Depend upon it, sir," he added, turning to his father, "Mr. Middleton has inquired thereabout us and Uncle Alec, but he has not said one word about Uncle Alec's fortune."

"Uncle Alec!" Alice said with indignation. "You ought to be ashamed of yourself, Horace. He is our Uncle Alexander. I always thought we did not appreciate him as we should. He was silent, and deep, like all truly great men. If he had been a light and trifling person he would have blurted it all out the instant he entered the door."

"You should not interrupt me, children," Col. Dunwoddie resumed. "But there is a good deal in what you say, Alice," he continued gravely. "I wish you all to speak of him hereafter more respectfully. He was undoubtedly more of a man than was generally supposed. You are right, Alice." And Mrs. Dunwoddie was struck, but not for the first time, at the increasing likeness between Alice and her father. She was two or three years older than her sister May, and was inclined to be tall and spare. Like the Colonel, too, she was apt to be greatly elated or profoundly depressed, living for a larger part of the time, like her father, upon the uneasy edge between the two; liable to be thrown in either direction any moment, and by causes so much internal as well as external that, as George worded it, "A fellow can't tell where to find Alice. If," he would urge, "she cannot be jolly all the time like May, I do wish she would settle down to be out of sorts, then, all the time, for then a fellow would know what to count on, you see."

The fact is, although an excellent girl, as well educated as was usual at that depressing date among Clairsville girls, Alice Dunwoddie was not pretty—she was almost homely. Keenly conscious of it, she had thought it was owing to the sorrowful times the family had endured, although her younger sister had seemed but to bloom

the more brightly on that account. The poor girl, by reason of her lack of beauty, had pined the more for greater opportunities of dress as well as of society, while May, who loved fine clothes as much as her sister did, rarely did more than laugh at her wardrobe where her sister wept. It would have been well for all the rest, as well as Alice, if she could have been less like her father in some things. "For," as George argued when aggrieved, "she is so anxious now while she is young, what *will* she be if ever she should get to be an old maid!"

Mrs. Dunwoddie sat in her easy-chair, the least-excited person there, unless it was Charlie. Either she was able to place herself, as it were, apart from her family as never before, and to look at them as from the outside, or there was something suddenly new in them as she looked—certainly she had never before seen her household in so clear a light. It may have been owing to the passing away that morning, as in a moment, of the long and weary winter. Never had there been so severe a season in their memory, and the pressing troubles of Col. Dunwoddie, which had come to a climax in the sickness and death of poor Alec, and in the long illness of the rest following upon it, had made the season seem the longest and darkest they had ever known. But to-day summer had come as at a bound. The air was as balmy as it was brilliant. It was not the turkey-cock alone which was inspired thereby—the whole orchestra of nature seemed to herald the beginning of a new act of the drama. Dogs were barking, birds singing, cocks crowing, hens cackling, children laughing on their way to school, the negroes ploughing in the fields varying their importunate appeals to mules or oxen with snatches of camp-meeting songs; even the oldest person, black or white, was strongly inclined at least to whistle as he went with new hope about his business. It was impossible for any one in the room not to be lifted as upon the new tide of life which was coming in. And then this wonderful wealth! It was all very bewildering, but it was like the sudden coming of a more glorious summer still. To the mother's eye every individual present had developed as on the instant, but as by a ripening merely of what each one had been before. Even Charlie's cheeks, which had been thin from his sickness, seemed fuller than yesterday, and, sensible woman as she was, Mrs. Dunwoddie said to herself as she clasped his plump leg dangling from the table—

"I know it is silly, but the first thing I will buy, if Alec has left us anything, shall be the velvet. He will soon be a boy—a big boy—and I must see how he will look in it before—before—" and she caught the eyes of Horace fastened without a smile upon her face, and laughed at him instead of giving way to any weakness, shaking her head at him as she did so.

"I must insist upon it," Col. Dunwoddie said, after all had left the room, with renewed injunctions to be silent, except his wife and eldest son. 'Yes, I must and do insist upon it that we remain perfectly calm. Let us have no excitement," the Colonel repeated as he walked the room nervously. "I do hope, my dear Eliza, that you will not allow yourself to be agitated. As to myself, even if there is anything in it, which I continue to doubt—greatly to doubt—I can see only increased care and anxiety. The people will annoy us terribly. As sure as the rumor gets abroad, I will be urged to pay the heavy debt on our church, which I will not do. I want to let it be distinctly understood from the outset that, while the church is managed as it now is, I cannot and I will not do anything for it. Just to think, Eliza—" and the Colonel entered again upon the story, very wearisome to his wife long ago, of the peculiarly exasperating way in which the church troubles had got worse and worse. "If I had the writing out, not of the creed, but of the creed *and*

practice of most of the membership of that church," the Colonel said at last, " it should be, and written out in letters a foot long over the pulpit—"

"Well?" said his wife, with a smile.

"*Video meleora proboque*," quoted the irate man.

"I beg your pardon?" asked Horace. "What?"

"—*Pejora sequor!*" he added, with emphasis, and went into still larger details of the unhappy affair.

"Money!" he exclaimed at last. "I do know that it would be, as things are, an unmitigated curse to that church. No, sir! Not one cent. Never! And it is easy to imagine," he continued, "what a stir *that* will make—my refusal. I will be expected, also, to complete the monument to the soldiers, of course, since I was their colonel. But it is unreasonable to suppose that I should give as much as will be expected. And there is the cemetery. I am chairman of the committee upon fencing it. As the idea originated with me, of course I must be liberal; but I cannot be as liberal as may be demanded. In case Alec has left us anything, we must erect a handsome tombstone, a monument in fact, to him. With all deference to you, Eliza, with all possible respect for his memory, it will puzzle me beyond measure to know what sort of an epitaph to write. I dare say we did not appreciate your brother, my dear, as Alice says. He had noble traits — noble traits; but it is easy to see how people will view anything which, under the circumstances, may be said or not said of him."

"My dear Charles," Mrs. Dunwoddie began gently, "why should you distress yourself?"

"Distress myself, Eliza?" the Colonel broke in; "that is the one thing I am guarding you against. I merely suggest these things that you may keep yourself perfectly quiet when they come, as come they will. Are you not staying too long from the depot, Horace? I am anx-

ious to keep your mother very quiet indeed. I remember reading what a perfect
fool William the Fourth made of himself
when he came unexpectedly to the throne
of England. He was a fat and foolish old
man whom nobody regarded before. It
turned his brain. There never was such a
laughing-stock as he made of himself, fuss-
ing and fretting. If Alec has left us money, which I greatly doubt, let us be and remain perfectly cool. You had better go,
my dear boy, that your mother may rest;
for I fear that, notwithstanding all I have
urged upon the children, this matter will
get out. The number of curious callers
will be appalling. But what annoys me,"
he added, rumpling his iron-gray hair with
his hand, and then rubbing his nose harder than ever, " is what to make of this Mr.
Middleton. I never met a man who has
more the exterior of a gentleman; he is
very pleasing indeed. But why has he
been so silent? We are, as I distinctly
told him, the only relatives Alec had; and
yet, although he made out that list himself,
he never alluded to it. I am afraid—I am
much afraid—"

———◆———

CHAPTER XI.

MR. MIDDLETON MAKES THE ACQUAINTANCE
OF A WHOLLY NEW VARIETY OF MAN.

"The wild geese flying north or back
Fly on some feathered leader's track.
Bees have their queen, and on the plains
The strongest stallion king remains.
If but two men escape a wreck,
The one is at the other's beck;
Cast on a rock, the dripping pair
Find ruled and ruler even there."

It could not have been more than two
weeks after the family council just spoken
of that Mr. Gamaliel Middleton, sauntering
slowly in the suburbs of Clairsville, on his
way to Mrs. Judge Anderson's, yawned fear-
fully; so hearty a yawn was it that he had
to stop to do it justice. Nor is there any
denying that Col. Dunwoddie's town was

a dull little village. It was in the heart of
what is known as a "post-oak country,"
the soil of which was as level as it was
sandy, a small river washing one side of
the town. The original seed at the plant-
ing of the place was the court-house of
Clair County, a huge building of red brick,
square, severe, substantial, in the centre
of the public square, around which were
ranged the brick blocks containing the
principal stores, lawyers' and doctors' of-
fices, apothecary establishments, livery-sta-
bles, and, alas, drinking-saloons. Upon a
second range of streets, lying behind the
business buildings, were the churches,
blacksmith-shops, school-houses, hotels at
almost every corner, the number of pho-
tographic rooms being as much in excess
of the needs of the region as were the of-
fices of the lawyers, dentists, and doctors.
Except during elections and court weeks,
Clairsville was dull—very dull indeed.

"Not a public library in five hundred
miles," Mr. Middleton yawned yet again.
"A city paper is yellow with age before it
gets here. There is nothing to shoot in
the woods but crows and squirrels, nor
anything to catch in the river but sun and
cat fish. Not a theatre; nor a museum.
Only two barbers, Leonidas Dunwoddie
and Yellow Jessamine, to vibrate between.
I had hoped they would have had some
negro riot, or one of the awful family-
feud fights we read about. Nobody gets
drunker than they do in the East; and
a real gambler is, I suppose, utterly unknown. Everybody rides on horseback.
No wonder, when the roads are too sandy
for any but the slowest going with wheels.
As to the depot, one cannot be there to see
the trains passing all the time. If I did
not have such a tremendous affair on hand
I would die."

"Let me see," the lounger continues:
"there is Squire Stevens, who keeps my
hotel; and Ferdinand Clarke, who plays
billiards all the morning and gets drunk
every night; and Tom Perkins and Harry

Chalmers, who lend him a hand at it. Hiddikel Queasy, too—rascal! Then there is Mr. Robinson, who keeps the provision-store; Mr. Jenkins, the Methodist parson; Mr. Potter, the Baptist; and Gen. Atchison, as they call him, the Presbyterian pastor who fought like the mischief during the war. Who else? Oh, yes—Charlie Marston, the horse-jockey; Major Clarke, who owns about a million of acres—plenty of dull, good people besides—I am getting to know them all. As to that old Major Clarke, con—" but Mr. Middleton glanced around before completing the sentence even to himself; —"*found* him!" he went on. "The fat and ignorant fool lashed the North for an hour yesterday over my shoulders. 'They are all that is knavish,' he says, 'and mean.' He has lost his negroes. 'All he has left,' he says, 'is his wild land, and Ferdinand, his wilder and more worthless son. Any Southern man,' he told me, 'who married a Yankee woman, ought to be tarred and feathered, and he would help do it.' I only wish," Mr. Middleton added, "that I had a fair crack at him somewhere outside the South, with a horsewhip."

At this moment the new-comer sees a man riding towards him along the sandy road. He knows at a glance that it is Tom Terrell. He is a large man, coarse in his appearance; and Mr. Middleton has been in Clairsville long enough to know that he is vindictive in his hatred of Col. Dunwoddie, and of himself as under the protection of that gentleman. The fact is, Mr. Terrell is the chief rival of the Colonel at the bar, and is the more intense in his hatred to everything not Southern because the other is disposed to be tolerant, making a patriotism of being a ruffian because the Colonel is a gentleman. Full of oaths, habitually under the influence of bad whiskey, he glories in the large amount of his indebtedness. In some complicated fashion he had never been in battle during the war, but ugly things were said of him in regard to the killing of negroes since.

Certain it is that he plunged, from the earliest moment after the war, into politics, and furiously. No one who heard him in the Legislature, on the stump, along the streets, could doubt what he would do if the war should begin again, "which," he says with terrible adjurations, "I hope it may." Apart from this, the aversion between himself and Middleton is as instinctive as that between a mastiff and a cat.

As Tom Terrell sees the latter approaching he reins in his horse and sits still to look at the new-comer as if at some strange but contemptible vermin. The feline rage is aroused thereby in the other, but he walks steadily along, desperately unconcerned, yet feeling the unspoken because unspeakable scorn of the horseman bestowed upon him as he walks slowly past him, as if it had been the blows instead of the cowhide the man held in his hand. As he passes, Tom Terrell touches his horse on the off side with his spur so as to make him swerve almost upon the pedestrian, and then rides on, breaking into loud and contemptuous laughter. Mr. Middleton is armed, and could have shot him with his whole heart. But if there were no other reasons to prevent, he has matters in hand too important for that.

"You are a greater fool than — bully," he says to himself of the other, when his wrath had time to cool; and his eyes brighten at some thought which comes to him on the instant, and which is, in fact, never out of his mind.

"I suppose," he says to himself—"I suppose it is because not a soul in the state knows who I am, or dreams of my secret, that they seem so stupid. Oh, Middleton, Middleton, you rascal, you never had so grand an idea before! It is as stately as St. Peter's; it's gorgeous — superlative! Bless you for dying, Alec! and bless you over and over again for what you did before you died. And to think that I own the thing as one does a diamond. It is so immensely valuable, and yet it is a thing I can carry hidden in my hand—never even suspected; but here comes the very prince of darkness. How are you to-day?"

Mr. Middleton directed the question to a man who overtook him at this moment, and who was more exactly the opposite of himself than if he had been a Chinese from the other side of the globe. No person could have been dressed more admirably as to fabric and fit than was Mr. Middleton; and no man could have been clothed more coarsely, or with less reference to the curves of his person, than the negro to whom he spoke. Moreover, Middleton's manner and tones were, when he wished, accurately correct as were the words he used, while the language could not have been spoken with fewer verbs to the number of its nouns than in the case of the other, whose complexion was as jetty black, and whose hair was as unmistakably wool, as Mr. Middleton's skin was fair, and his hair and moustache soft and silken. When it is added that the features of the negro were as purely African as those of the white man were Grecian, what more can be said? This may be added: that although it was impossible, so far as the outer person was concerned, to conceive of a greater unlikeness between two men, that unlikeness, marked as it was, did not suffice to express a more radical diversity between them still; a diversity not so great in body as in heart and mind, soul and spirit; a diversity as of the original essence of the two, and lasting as eternity.

"How do you do?" Mr. Middleton asked again.

"Well, sir," the other—who seemed more sparing of words than was common to his race—replied, lifting his hand reluctantly to his old hat.

"Do you live here?"

"Yes, sir," very respectfully, yet unwillingly.

"How long has it been? Did any of these people ever own you? Were you born here?"

"Yes, sir." The black man covered all the questions with the words. He was walking the same way, and the white man slackened his pace for the moment to that of the other.

"What is your name?"

"Anderson Parker, sir."

"Anderson?—Anderson? Why," Mr. Middleton said, with a light laugh, "you are not a relation of the Anderson family out there, are you?"

"Judge Anderson was my master, sir," the other replied, but without seeing any joke.

"You do not live on their place now?"

"Yes, sir; I am manager for them."

"Oh—foreman of the crop. I remember hearing Col. Dunwoddie speak of you, my man. Mrs. Dunwoddie, too. She spoke in the highest terms of you. From all I heard, you must be an exception to your people. They had a great deal to tell me of your energy, integrity, good sense, and the like, Mr.—Mr.—"

"Not Mr. at all. Anderson Parker, sir," the negro said, and ceased.

"Ah! I am from the North, and do not understand exactly what they call their former slaves here. But I wonder," Middleton said, "that a man of your standing is not in the Legislature of the state, at least. After that you can get to be anything, or have everything you want. You can read and write?—can cipher a little? I would think a man as sensible as you are would 'want to take a part in politics, in elevating your race, in proving to your former owners that you are men as well as they. If I were in your place—"

But at this moment they were passing a large red gate which opened into a field on their left, a cotton-gin and press in the distance; and the man, opening the gate by its long wooden latch, merely said,

"Thank you, sir; I go this way. Good-morning," and passed through.

Mr. Middleton was amazed and angry. There was a sort of square solidity in the face and slow aspect of the black man, an intent yet self-possessed way about him, as he carefully saw that the latch was in its wooden catch after he had got in, which struck him. It was as if the other had deliberately separated himself from him—was barring himself against him, and after his condescension, too! Mr. Middleton grew angrier. There sprung up in him an aversion to the negro. He was but a child in size in comparison to the powerful frame of the other man, and he felt as if he had been treated as a child. And this, notwithstanding his unspeakable superiority to the freedman.

But he had visited at Judge Anderson's plantation before, and he knew that he had reached the place. A hundred yards beyond the gate, the rail fence, staked and ridered, gave place to one of plank neatly painted. Another hundred yards, and he had reached the front gate. He opened it, and entered upon a large lawn set out in spruce and pine trees, with ample post-oaks extending their boughs over the breadths of grass beneath; beds of flowers being disposed here and there where the shadows were lightest. Full one hundred yards back from the fence stood the mansion, an imposing but irregular structure two stories high, surrounded on all sides, and for both stories, with broad piazzas. The visitor paused to wipe his forehead, and to pass his hand over his hair and face. Then he thought deeply, his eyes upon the ground. A gladiolus in full bloom caught his glance to one side. Looking around to see if he were observed, he stepped towards it, and was in the act of deliberately breaking it down under his lifted foot when he thought better of it, and passed slowly and smilingly on. A few moments afterwards he was seated in the parlor, full of old-fashioned furniture, and in a short time Mrs. Anderson came in. Mr. Middleton was not, in spite of all his endeavor, at ease with the lady, and after some other conversation he laid hold has-

tily upon the first topic which came to hand.

"I fell in, madam, with one of your people a moment ago," he said, in what he intended to be a conciliating manner. Now Mrs. Judge Anderson was, as has been said, a stately dame of other days than those upon which she had been wrecked, so to speak—pale and sad and cold. Very evidently the world to which she belonged was gone forever—buried out of sight with her husband, her sons, her former wealth and large circle of friends; and never did a grave hold more that was good and noble as well as dearly loved. With the existing order of things she had nothing whatever to do, except that, in Heaven's mysterious providence, she continued to live when, but for her daughter's sake, she would have preferred to die. She would not have seen Mr. Middleton but that Col. Dunwoddie had brought him on the occasion of a former visit, a week or so before.

"One of my people?" She lifted her eyes to his face with surprise.

"Yes, madam. A fine-looking colored man. He said his name was Anderson Parker," the other said hastily.

"Oh, Parker! yes, he was one of our favorite servants before the war. He is a valuable one still," the lady said; "he manages the place for me."

"He seems to be a silent but substantial man; not very bright I would think," the other remarked, merely in order to say something.

"Do you think so?" Mrs. Anderson said. "We consider him the most sensible man of all his people in this region. Against his wishes he was elected by the negroes to the Legislature, as they call it. I am told that he was chosen Speaker of the House, so called, and was regarded as the ablest of their color."

"Is it possible?" the visitor exclaimed. "And he is still with you? I would have thought that he would have found a field in political life, which would have intoxicated him. I have known white men, madam, who found it impossible to escape the fascination, the vortex of political success. To a man of his color, I would have imagined that the opportunities would have been exceedingly attractive. Pardon me," the visitor added, for the lady was becoming colder and apparently paler than before.

"I have never conversed with him upon the subject, of course. Nor has he ever alluded to the matter with me. I learn, however, from Col. Dunwoddie," Mrs. Anderson replied, "that he resigned and left the capital before the close of the session. He was succeeded by a miserable white named Hiddikel Queasy. The Colonel is familiar with political affairs, and tells me that Parker is their most powerful speaker upon what is called the stump. He has preached very acceptably, also, I learn. My personal knowledge is limited to his management of my place, and I have learned by many years of experience to trust entirely to his honesty and excellent sense."

"It is remarkable," the other replied. "I wonder Col. Dunwoddie, in speaking of him as your foreman, never told me of his political experience."

"It is not a pleasant theme to any of us," the lady remarked dryly, and with a bitterness in her manner as well as her tones. "My sons taught him to read when they were children together. He must have studied a good deal since."

"It is very remarkable," the visitor repeated. "His opportunities were wonderful —in the Legislature, I mean—wonderful."

"Col. Dunwoddie informs me," Mrs. Anderson continued, "that he could have been elected, monstrous as it sounds, to the United States Senate. It was that which caused him to abandon the capital in disgust."

"Disgust?" Middleton could not refrain from asking; "but I cannot understand—?"

"Nor do I," said the lady. "The depth of corruption is something so entirely new in our annals that none of us attempt to comprehend it. Our negroes we know, we can even sympathize with them in the dreadful position into which they have been degraded as the unfortunate result of the war. We know they are not to blame; we pity them heartily. But their white leaders are of a species wholly unknown to us—except those of them who belonged to the class of poor whites before the war, and for whom our slaves had the profoundest contempt. My impression is that, in this case, even if Parker could have consented to such companionship, the horrible greed, dishonesty, avowed and unlimited corruption of all kinds was more than he could endure. Col. Dunwoddie thinks that the man had the sense to see that a reaction must come, and to escape the miserable business as soon as possible. With my full consent, he will not allow a political meeting on the place. He is giving all his attention to my plantation, and, I would judge, is rapidly and honestly accumulating property by his exertions. Now that the blacks have lost their natural protectors, they need a leader. Poor creatures! they have made a sad change for owners who make slaves of them by buying up their very consciences. I had not intended to speak upon such matters, but Parker is the only one of them at all capable of being their leader. And yet I am told they hate him." Then, as if seeking to change the subject, she added, "I am glad to know that Mrs. Dunwoddie seems, as you say, to be much stronger. It is impossible not to be well in this sudden coming of spring and summer. This is my daughter, sir," she added, as the young lady came into the room. "I believe you have met before. My dear," Mrs. Anderson added to her daughter, "I must ask you to entertain Mr. Middleton; I have an engagement. If you will excuse me, sir?"

"Perhaps you intended going with your mother?" the gentleman added as he bowed to Mrs. Anderson, leaving the room. "Do not allow me to prevent."

"I have just returned from Clairsville," the young lady said, motioning him to a seat and herself sitting down. "I walked. It was warmer than I expected, and I am glad to rest."

CHAPTER XII.

MISS EMMELINE ANDERSON HAS TWO VISITORS.

"Between some men and others whence
    Is there such utter difference?
    Where else is such unlikeness found?
This lion, like all lions, roars;
This eagle, like all eagles, soars;
    One lark sings shrill the world around.
But men from men are so diverse,
Because our range from best to worse
Is the unbounded universe."

Mr. GAMALIEL MIDDLETON and Miss Emmeline Anderson felt themselves drawn together by the attraction of a mutual interest. In some senses it was the strongest either of the two had ever felt in regard to any other person. The young lady came of a line of ancestors who, upon the side both of father and mother, had been in some instances distinguished for generations. Through all her childhood she had lived on the plantation surrounded by slaves, and she had taken the fact that her father was highly honored of men, and her family a leading one in the state, as she took the landscape and the climate. During the war, although but a young girl, she grew up as in the atmosphere of a universal belief that henceforth the South, throwing off the North as a burdensome section of the continent, which had hitherto cramped as well as oppressed it, would rise to a glorious prosperity and supremacy, in which her father and her family would be more prominent than heretofore. No one born outside such a belief can imagine to what degree all this was an absolute certainty to them. Who can imagine, then, the stunning effect of the overthrow of the Confederacy!

It was a merciful thing that the death of her brothers, the failure of the South, the emancipation of the slaves, the funeral of her father all came together, nearly as one blow. The force of the stroke made the stunning effect more complete. Mrs. Anderson never rallied, her world had been too grand a world, its destruction had been too sudden and wholly unexpected for that. Besides, she was too old, and she consented to live, when all else was dead, merely by force of the maternal instinct. How *could* she die with no one to protect her daughter, who would be left alone in a howling wilderness of free negroes and insolent poor whites, her income as exposed and uncertain as she herself was!

It was well that Emmeline Anderson was so young when the old world came to an end; she might come to forget it, at least in some degree. Still better was it, however, that the girl inherited something more than the traditions of her family. Something more, even, than what had been the beauty of her mother and the high spirit of her father. Or was it the breaking down of almost all of her surroundings which had broadened her mind in widening her field of vision? Views yet wider would come, but the original depth and strength of character was in her already. Her parents had cared for her education only less than they had for her health. From her childhood she had learned to ride, and had beaten her brothers in many a race along the sandy roads; and since the war hardly a day passed but gave her a good walk, at least, if it was only to Col. Dunwoddie's, to the post-office, or to the cemetery where her father was buried, and in which her dead brothers had been laid. The disasters which prostrated her mother seemed to have spent their force in developing her. Thrown utterly upon herself, she was that much the stronger for it, with that subtle sort of strength which takes the curves and colors of beauty as well as its fire and force.

As Middleton lifted his eyes to her face upon the departure of her mother, he found, as in his previous interviews, only this hindrance to his entire admiration of the young lady, that he could not understand her. He had seen hair as dark before. Among the Spanish ladies of San Francisco he had seen forms as slight and supple, if not eyes as large, as black, and as full of a certain life which seemed to have its springs in the depths of the soul itself. He had heard tones of voice as beautifully modulated among Mexican *señoritas*, but in this case there was nothing whatever of the unrestrained flow of speech which he had observed in the olive - complexioned beauties. Their lips were not rosier, nor were their teeth more like ivory; but they talked and laughed and sang so unceasingly that one had greater opportunities of admiring them. Would longer acquaintance ever make him know this girl? What was it that she held in such reserve? He was at that moment the man in all that region who had enjoyed the largest and most varied association with his kind, and he said to himself as he sat- -

"This young girl holds hidden within herself a good deal that does not appear on the surface. It is, in fact, much the largest part of what she is and what she will one day show herself to be. One comfort is, she is almost as ignorant of herself as I am."

Which was a fact. But this also was true, that, ignorant of herself as she was, Emmeline Anderson was even better aware than her visitor of holding in herself a reserve of power. She had not estimated it definitely, any more than a capitalist may have counted to a cent all his coin; but a capitalist feels strong to the tip of his fingers, in virtue, none the less, of his gold; and so did she by reason of what she felt herself to be. The advantage with the lady was that her wealth was a something of which no defaulting cashier could deprive her, and she was slowly coming to resolve that no heedless expenditure, much less rash speculation, of her own should rob her of it. So that while the collapse of the Confederacy was death to the mother, it was a new measure of life to the daughter.

"It is a delightful day," Miss Anderson, Middleton remarked; but his thought at the moment was, "I wonder how this singular country-girl likes me."

"We could hardly wish for a more pleasant," the lady replied. But she was saying to herself, "I wonder just who and what you are."

For the lady was not a newer experience to the gentleman than he was to her. She had never been outside of Clair County in her life — the war and its results had prevented that. All the men under forty-five had been conscripted into the Confederate service while she was very young. The small fraction of these who had come back at the end of the fighting had scattered off to make a living elsewhere, or had taken to drinking while waiting to see what they had better do next, or had' been made suddenly into old men by battle, prison, hospital, prostrating disappointment, and, worse than all, the same grinding poverty which had crushed Col. Dunwoddie. The hopelessness of political affairs, too, had paralyzed the men of Clair County, until it was beginning to seem to them their normal condition. Even Middleton himself had no idea what a contrast he seemed to men in general in Clairsville. He would have been a marked man, so far as good looks and admirable clothes and polished manners go, anywhere. It was not the hilarity of his aspect in contrast with the depression around him, nor even the energy of his tone and bearing telling of a more bracing climate, but an undefined breadth about the man as of one who had been everywhere, which gave him a charm of which he was himself unaware, and to none more than to the lady he was visiting. She had read about a wider world than her own; there were growing powers within her prompting her to something beyond the sandy level and post-oak openings which had hemmed her in all her life. Moreover, the war and its result hung darkly over the whole area of her home and her experience, and she yearned passionately for something brighter and happier as well as broader. And now this amazing news in regard to the Nevada inheritance had quickened her pulses to a degree of which she was herself unconscious. Nothing was more natural than that the conversation should speedily turn to that. After some discussion of the weather, so dull was Clair County there was really nothing else to talk about.

"I am glad of it, and am glad to have been the messenger of it," Middleton said at last. "You will pardon me, Miss Anderson, but I have been in the East a great deal among the cities and manufactories, the crowded streets and exchanges and banks, and people in this state are not so prosperous as could be wished. In the West, too, we have our harbors and rivers covered with vessels, the railways creating new towns as they are being built, to say nothing of the mines, yielding literally hundreds of millions of gold and silver. I never was in the South before, and I never before met people whom I more highly respect for their noble qualities; but, if you will allow me, many of the best persons in Clairsville seem to be poor, very poor. We have poverty, bitter poverty, elsewhere, but it is a new sight to me to see people of the highest refinement so poor. And, from all I can learn, Col. Dunwoddie was perhaps more pressed than almost any gentleman in the place. I am very frank."

Miss Emmeline colored. The gentleman certainly was sufficiently frank in speaking of what was a painful fact of her region and of herself. The truth is, Middleton's wardrobe held more than his different suits of clothes, being a wardrobe from which he changed his appearance according to place or season. Among brokers in Wall Street he had the aspect in every respect of an experienced broker. Thrown among the roughest set of miners gambling around a camp-fire in Nevada, his corduroy and jeans and buckskin were not more in harmony with theirs than was his whole style and bearing in every other sense. Invite him to a ball or to a funeral, to a small tea-party or to a ward-room caucus; to a ceremonious dining, a picnic, a duel, a fandango among the Mexicans of California, an interview with the President of the United States in regard to some appointment, a cock-fight, or a board of railway directors — whenever and whithersoever this versatile gentleman was summoned, in much less time than it took him to change his linen could he address himself, and perfectly, to the part. Never was there an actor who could throw himself more completely into his role, whatever it was; but, through all his transformations, and they were as varied as humanity allows, and very frequent, he never for an instant ceased to be Gamaliel Middleton. To-day, at Mrs. Anderson's, he wears the garb of a frank and warm-hearted man. Not that he is unacquainted with the proprieties, but that he is too full of joyous frankness to be restrained by them. If the young lady only knew it, there was under it all an eagerness to please her which was surpassed only by an almost trembling uncertainty as to whether he knew how to do it or not. She was a kind of lady so new to him.

"What excellent people the Colonel and his household are," he adds. "The poorer they were the gladder I am at their good fortune."

"So are we, sincerely glad. I believe my mother and myself," the young lady continued with a brightening color, "were the first outside of the family to hear the news."

"Mrs. Dunwoddie told you, I presume?" Middleton asked.

"No, sir," she said, somewhat reluctantly. "We are very intimate friends, indeed, but I think Mrs. Dunwoddie rather shrinks from the subject. She seems to me to attach less importance to it than I would have supposed. I have even been tempted to think that she almost — yes, shrinks from it as from a something to be feared. She has been sorely tried with years of cruel anxiety. The death of her brother, and the sickness following upon it, was too much for her. I have almost feared that these tidings, coming so unexpectedly to her too, will be but as another strain upon her weakness. Mrs. Dunwoddie is," the lady said, with her serious eyes upon his, "the loveliest, the most estimable woman I ever knew. My mother, of course, excepted," she added.

"I have no doubt of it, none whatever. She reminds me," the visitor added gravely, "of my own mother. All that I am I owe to her, and I am said to be her living image. My life has been an adventurous one. I have been cast into circumstances of singular trial. My father was an excellent man, a leading officer of a church as well as mayor of the city in which we lived. His large business prevented that care over me which he would have desired. So that it is to my mother I owe everything."

"She is no longer living?" the lady asked.

"No," Middleton said, with eyes and tones lowered. "My father died suddenly, and my mother was unable to survive the loss. I have but one relative on earth, my sister Clara. She is at school in the East. In fact, I have had no other settled home for her, and she has been a pupil or teacher, in one city or another, all her life. She is all I have, and I hope I may be excused for saying that I am proud of her. I have some hope of bringing her here."

The lady looked at him with increased interest, little imagining that he was saying to himself, "What a horrible thing it would be if she knew that my mother eloped with a negro-minstrel before I was out of school, and that my father, if he *is* my father, is a broken-down billiard-saloon keeper, to whom I would not lend a cent to save his soul;" although in this, as in every like case, merely the mildest paraphrase of either the thoughts or words of the gentleman can be given. There is a shade of blackness so much beyond that of printer's ink that it cannot well be used in these pages.

"And Mrs. Dunwoddie seemed to shrink from speaking even to you in relation to the fortune," Middleton remarked after some silence, and as if to divert his mind from too mournful a topic.

She has hardly alluded to the matter," Miss Anderson said, with the color coming again to her cheeks. "I learned it from others. It was unexpected, quite unexpected by them."

"Very naturally, Miss Anderson. Mr. Alec Allen was an intimate friend of mine. A better man I never knew. He took large and deliberate views of things. My impression is that he was better adapted to planning than carrying out his plans in person. He was strong, but—"

At this point there was a slight motion in the pose of the lady's head, a closer attention of her eyes. Middleton was aware that he was suspected of sarcasm, and hastened to resume his frank manner.

"You knew him," he said, "and you will allow me to say that, at last, it was all the merest good luck, as they say in the mines. One man has good luck, another has very bad luck. A man may have the sharpest intellect, may spend thousands of dollars upon geologists, and all for nothing. He may devote years to prospecting, as it is called, toiling night and day. Mr. Alec Allen had luck, just as he had light hair and blue eyes, just as he was of a portly build, and could eat and sleep heartily. He did not go after it, and therefore luck came after him. It always does. It was like falling off a log, if you will excuse the camp-slang. He hit upon a lode in a spot that no other man ever thought of, and it happened to be the richest in Nevada — immensely rich."

"I would have thought Mr. Allen would have lost it as easily as he found it," the lady said, not without a spice of aloes in her tones. She had, when very young, tried hard to make a hero of Alec. It was beyond her powers—she had not imagination enough—and the effort had been an utter failure.

"No, Miss Anderson," her guest replied, "it was in that my friend's strength lay. No sooner was it known what a *bonanza* he had struck than he was surrounded by a swarm of scoundrels who tried to get it from him — speculators, gamblers, confidence men, lawyers, landsharks of all sorts. I used to wonder how he would come out. They cajoled him, bullied him, argued with him, lied to him, promised, threatened. There was one thing — they mutually neutralized each other — half-a-dozen of them were killed in trying who should plunder him first. But there, if you will excuse the slang, was where Alec Allen had them. He did nothing at all. He would eat and smoke and sleep and let thi gs slide—excuse me. By doing nothing whatever, his lode did everything for him. Miss Anderson," Middleton said with utmost sincerity, "his luck was wonderful. After he had come to own the whole ledge, everybody saw that any fool could have told them it would pan out the richest ore in the Sierras. It seemed to have waited until that one man should come, everybody else stumbling over it as blind as bats; and everything he has done with it, and with every dollar he has got out of it, has prospered in the same astonishing way."

"It does seem strange," the lady said thoughtfully; and no wonder. Money was a very scarce commodity indeed in Clairsville. The most desirable plantations could not sell for enough to meet the taxes. Articles which had once seemed the necessaries of life had long been luxuries almost as much out of reach as the stars.

"People speak of grinding poverty," the gentleman continued, divining her very thought, "but the want of money which hurts most is that which is felt by people who were once rich: people of refinement—"

"Excuse my interrupting you, sir," the lady said; "we prefer to be poor. For any one to be rich now is almost a proof that he has been plundering in some way. But, it does seem as if there was something extraordinary in Mr. Allen's good-fortune, although he was merely the accidental means by which it was secured for others. There must be some object to be answered by it. It was not for his sake. He merely got it and died. Beyond fighting for his country and being a kind-hearted and inoffensive man, it was not easy to understand," the lady added under the influence of the other's frankness, "what end in life Mr. Allen accomplished. It is plain now —that is, it is becoming plain; and he will perhaps have answered a great end."

"Very great indeed," Middleton assented with energy. "Over a million of dollars! The amazing thing about a pile— a fortune, I mean—like that is the way it grows of itself. While you are smoking a cigar—excuse me, while you are—are knitting a stock — no, not that — while you are—"

"Crocheting a pattern," the lady kindly suggested.

"Precisely; while you are doing whatever that is, your money goes on increasing by thousands. Allen was a much richer man when he died than when he was taken sick; and he doing nothing all the time but being sick. All you have to do is to do nothing at all, and your million keeps turning itself over and over again under

E

your feet like the globe. Not making any noise, without any help from you, while you are eating and sleeping. It is perfectly wonderful to think of," the gentleman continued with the utmost zest. "While you are making a joke, or laughing at what some one else says, all the time you are becoming richer and richer."

For the instant the young lady felt with Mrs. Dunwoddie as if there was an unpleasant something in the whole affair; but her visitor continued eagerly—

"A million of dollars, Miss Anderson! Can you estimate it?" And he proceeded to tell her of the inventory, which he had himself made out, of the Nevada wealth, although he did not think it necessary to speak of the way in which Horace Dunwoddie had discovered it.

"Do you know, Miss Anderson," he said at last, "that I hesitated for some days after arriving, to give Col. Dunwoddie a full and final statement of what seems now to be his property through his wife? My consternation at finding my friend dead, my unspeakable grief, indeed, prevented. And I could not but respect theirs also. Besides, I shrank from telling such astounding news in full, almost as I would have done had it been something terrible."

Mr. Middleton *had* hesitated. During one or two days and nights at the Clairsville Hotel, and before he had spoken with the Dunwoddies after Horace's discovery of the inventory in his uncle's belt, he had done, perhaps, the deepest, steadiest thinking of his life. So intense was his anxiety to know and to do, as well as to say, only what was best under the sudden circumstances, that he came as near praying for help to get out of his "tight place," so he phrased it to himself, as he would have done had he fallen, instead, into the deepest cañon in the Nevada mountains without food or outlet. Not that Middleton had not had an inspiration as of genius from the first; but he had hesitated—hesitated. It was the emergency of his life,

and he was justly slow in deciding. When, however, he had decided, his decision was clear; so clear and final that he entered upon what was to be done with the utmost alacrity as well as energy.

He now recurs to the delightful theme. "A million of dollars in gold, Miss Anderson. It is over a million, but that basis will do. A million! You can travel over Europe, buy pictures, diamonds, yachts, fast horses, fine houses! Have you ever been North, or East? You have no idea what splendid hotels they have." And he entered with the eloquence of sincerity into a description of the operas and theatres, the parks and stupendous dry-goods establishments, the concerts, ice-cream saloons, race-courses, and magnificent jewelry establishments of the chief cities. Middleton had an exquisite taste, as well as passion, for millinery in every sense of the word, and he dwelt with real artistic power, as well as zest, upon the furnishing of the houses as also upon the matter of dress, with reference both to ladies and gentlemen, so far as he had studied the subject, in London as well as Vienna and Paris. The young lady had, as yet, only such vague intuitions of all this as Eve may have had—rather as some queen dethroned and imprisoned while yet a child may have felt. It was impossible not to be interested. Clairsville had been very wearisome; she had known only disaster and sadness so long! The bright face and joyous tones of Middleton were in such strong contrast, too, to her mother's cold, sad countenance; and that of Col. Dunwoddie had not been much more inspiring. She herself was so strong and well, so full of vague but passionate wishes. Middleton could not but feel that he was making a successful visit. The heightened color, the kindling eyes, the evident pleasure of the inexperienced girl swept him beyond his own control.

"I trust you will pardon me for saying it," he remarked as he arose to leave, "but

I have rarely—very rarely—known a lady who—" and there he stopped, as if his frankness was carrying him too far, in the expression of his admiration. "I am afraid of unintentionally offending— I will bid you good-day." Nothing could be more smoothly deferential. There was a respectful flattery in his manner which had an effect beyond words. The same wind which howls and wrecks can gentle itself down into a zephyr which is timid as to the disturbance of the lightest tress of a lady's hair; but nothing in nature was more versatile than Middleton. The whole cosmic force in his case was simplified, however, into the briefest of axioms, and that axiom was contained in the neat inscription upon his card — "Gamaliel Middleton" — that and nothing else. He loved his sister Clara so far, at least, as to support her generously. But she had never lived with him. It would have been out of the question in the roving life he had led. He rarely thought of her except when making a remittance and receiving her acknowledgment. So rapid were his changes in life, so brief was his association with any set of persons, that society, in his estimation, was but as the fellowship upon the billiard-table of the ivory balls; the essence of the game lying in his striking against and driving his next neighbor before him, under penalty, if he did not, of being driven himself. Nor, having a single eye to his own success, did he spare himself any more than he did any other.

"If you blunder in this thing," he said to himself as he walked away, "I will cut your throat. The prize is too big to lose. If you lose it, you fool, I will kill you."

For he felt that he had talked too much. And so did the lady. She, too, could enjoy life keenly; and yet there was that to her in her visitor's conversation, interesting as it was, which had a certain taint of greediness, even of gluttony. A handsomer or more pleasing gentleman Miss Anderson had never met, certainly none quite as in-

teresting. And yet there was, under all his eager description, a certain unpleasant sound, as of the swinish crunching of acorns, which was offensive. When she herself was alluded to, however refinedly, in that connection, there was an instinctive recoil from being classed with the swine which fared so sumptuously, or the acorns upon which they fed. Although she was ignorant of the world, her visitor's attempt at compliment was so distasteful to her that it somewhat spoiled the flavor of the whole visit.

She was the more sensitive by reason of a visit on the part of Horace Dunwoddie a few days before. His father had commissioned him to tell Mrs. Anderson and her daughter of their good-fortune.

"Please, my dear—" Mrs. Dunwoddie had said the instant the suggestion was made. "Dear Charles, do you think it wisest? I would a little rather not. The ladies have not been here since they knew I was better. Suppose we wait till they call. Do you not think it will seem a little, a little—?" she said with a smile and a color in her pale cheek.

"As if we were intoxicated?" the Colonel said. "Perhaps so, my dear, but not with friends so intimate. They might feel hurt if we did not speak soon, and they may not call for many days. Besides," Col. Dunwoddie added with a malicious glance at his son, "Horace is—desirous of doing so."

The poor youth colored up to the roots of his hair; he felt a tingling to his finger-tips as his father spoke. It had been very great news indeed for him to hold in so long, for not a syllable had as yet been told any one outside of the family. There had been a full conversation with Middleton, who had cordially congratulated them on their wealth. To a young man like Horace the wonderful event, fully confirmed by Middleton at last, was new wine, and the fermentation was very great in the new bottle. It was natural he should desire to tell somebody. The one person next to him, besides his own family, in all the world was Emmeline Anderson, and he was eager to speak.

"I wouldn't if I were you," his mother said, with her forefinger uplifted in warning as her son approached her. His wholesome face was all tremulous with the flickering flame of a first love, fully kindled only of late. The light and color of her own girlhood came back to his mother's face as if in reflection of his as he said with a kiss—

"Please, mother?"

"I wouldn't," she said ominously, her wisdom holding its own against her admiration and love for her boy.

"Please?" he persisted as unreasoningly as Charlie would have done when he knew he was asking for what he ought not to have.

"No," she said, even if she smiled yes. For there is this in a woman's intuitions which proves that they are instincts, they never falter or change; you might as well ask a skylark to soar under water, or a fish to swim singing to the stars. "No!" And she would have said it had she or her son been dying. "No, my boy, don't do it!"

"Your mother is merely teasing you, Horace," Col. Dunwoddie exclaimed in high good-humor. "Oh, go and be done with it. Horace has reasons, my dear. He has not told us, but they are reasons we will cordially approve. Besides, I want to consult with you. Mr. Middleton tells me that I can draw for any amount very soon. Do you not agree that I ought not to give, largely at least, to the debt of the church with those persons in power? I would gladly clear off every cent if I did not believe the weight of debt is the only thing which restrains them—"

But Horace was eager to go, and at once.

"Please, mother?" he begged, with his hands put piteously together in supplication, and was gone.

Col. Dunwoddie drew a frightful description of the condition of the church, especially if relieved of debt, but it was very little his wife cared just then. It may be an eternal ordinance of nature and all that, but it is very hard for a mother to see her son love another woman. She may get used to it in the case of other sons, but with the first it is terribly hard. And Horace had persisted in going. It was plain that he loved another more than herself, and that when he knew a certain secret which Mrs. Dunwoddie had confided to him alone of the whole family. It was very hard. Her husband, walking up and down the room, was full of his church grievance, and did not notice that, paler than before, she had sunk deeper into her easy-chair, as if another prop had just plucked itself from beneath her.

And this was the reason Emmeline had evaded the question as to how she first heard of the Nevada matter in her conversation with Middleton just recorded, a conversation which took place a few days after Horace had carried out his intention of calling upon her. She had reasons. Her father, Judge Anderson, had considered Col. Dunwoddie as one of the first of men, a gentleman after his own old-fashioned sort, the only person in Clair County upon his own level. In consequence of this the two households had been quite intimate, in spite of Alec Allen's infatuation for the young girl, since that was an absurdity merely to be laughed at. And Emmeline Anderson was aware of the hidden devotion to her all along of Horace Dunwoddie merely as that of a manly boy. But her nature was too much the slow unfolding within her of a large future for her to be particularly yielding, even as a child, to a school-boy's love. Then came the disasters which absorbed every thought. And now Horace Dunwoddie had shot up into a young man of fine person and quiet manners, giving assurance of being a superior man even to his father. Being the younger of the two, she had looked up to him as one who seemed resolved not only not to be crushed by his times, as so many were, but to master them. Although there had been a constant coming and going between the two houses, Horace Dunwoddie had never made her a set visit. When she came into the parlor on the occasion of his call, a few days before that of Middleton, she supposed it was some message from Mrs. Dunwoddie, and became embarrassed from the moment of entering the room by reason of the evident embarrassment of her visitor.

The fact is, notwithstanding his manifold resolves to keep cool, Horace Dunwoddie had a pressure upon him too sudden as well as too great for him to endure. His love for his fair neighbor had been the guarded treasure of his life, the most precious of all. Even if his Uncle Alec had not, in a lumbering fashion, stood in his way, he was too much like his mother, as well as chivalrous like his father, not to have hidden his secret. Of late his love had greatly increased. His uncle was gone. He had himself become a man. Emmeline had shown long and devoted attention to his mother while sick. She had emerged out of her trials with a defiant energy which had given a vigor to her loveliness beyond all his calculations. He had looked forward to long years of hard and patient toil in behalf of his own household before he could be in a situation to approach her with his love, for his own family had great and pressing need of him first. And now? This sudden wealth had annihilated time and toil and weary waiting. More than a million of dollars! What was there to hinder? There was no one his father and mother admired or loved so much as she. And he had loved her, it seemed to him, for ages.

All this pressure was too much for the poor fellow. Naturally strong, he had banded his strength, as one does an oaken chest, with iron resolutions to be calm and silent. But he was not as strong as he had supposed. Besides, he had been too long under a strain. He managed to get through the usual salutations, as well as the proper inquiries in reference to Mrs. Anderson. Very coolly he replied to all inquiries in regard to the health of his own mother. He was calm enough in telling her the story of the Nevada fortune. As Emmeline Anderson listened with breathless interest she saw that the glow in his cheeks, the glitter in his eyes, the impossibility of sitting down while he spoke, was because of what he knew the money would be to his father first, then to his mother, then to his sisters; it was plain he had not thought of himself.

There was nothing that was not manly enough in all that. Like his father, however, the sound of his own voice deepened his excitement. There sat the lady whom he had loved long and silently, and who had seemed to be whole years beyond his reach. Her lips were slightly apart, her color was coming and going with intense interest in all he said, her eyes were lifted to his like those of a child. He had not intended anything of the kind, never dreamed of doing it when he came, but, having begun to talk, he could not stop. Having long ago lost his heart, the process had undermined, so to speak, his head. To his own surprise and terror he suddenly found himself telling her passionately how he had loved her, how he had loved her all his life, how he had never loved, never could love, any one else if he lived forever. How he had not dared to think that he could say all this for years to come, but that *now* he hoped—

When he had first begun to speak of his love the young girl had risen to her feet, bewildered, but at these last words her bewilderment changed into wrath. He was not so intoxicated by his passion now that she seemed, and so suddenly, in his reach as not to feel, even before he saw it in her eyes, that he had made a disastrous mistake. And so he supposed because he was rich he had only to speak! She had heard how a sudden fortune could turn a person's brain, and here was an instance with a vengeance! Suddenly rich, very rich indeed, although with money he had never earned, he could all at once own her as he could a negro! He was launching out as a fast young man, and she was to be his first extravagance.

He had never before seen her angry. She had been sorely tried by the disasters which had befallen her household, and no woman could have seemed more gentle and subdued as she ministered to poor Mrs. Dunwoddie. He had forgotten that this was Judge Anderson's daughter when the word Anderson stood for all that signified pride as well as wealth and influence. Her stern old white-haired father, her dashing and high-spirited brothers, her cold and stately mother, all were blended on the instant, to his eyes, in the woman who stood before him. She had never before been so angry. Her wrath terrified her, it was so deep as well as so hot. Horace Dunwoddie was daunted, but only for the instant, and not so much at her wrath as at his own folly. Was he not Col. Dunwoddie's son? And she had utterly mistaken him! After the first moment he faced her as cold and strong as she was strong and hot. Neither could recall afterwards what the other said, it was like a tropical gust, too violent to be coherent.

He found himself walking away from the house very slowly, as if from a pleasant and leisurely visit. Inwardly he was mortified at himself, exasperated at her, at his unoffending uncle sleeping so soundly in his grave, chiefly at himself. The first effect of his hard lesson was to make him, outwardly at least, quiet and firm. In the coolness of his outer frame of mind he took a species of artistic pleasure in hav-ing seen her when she was so much more beautiful, when she was revealing more fire and force of character than he had suspected in her.

"My mother was right," he said to himself at last; "she always is, and I knew so at the time. I can see it now. I ought not to have gone. It was low bred. But I don't think I am likely to make the same mistake again. Very well, I did go. There never was a man more honest and sincere. Did I intend to say anything? When she comes to think she must see that I never thought of her in connection with money. Hang the money! I hope we will not get one cent. Henceforth I intend giving myself to my mother." As it was, events were making him a man very rapidly.

All this took place, as has been said, a few days before Mr. Middleton's visit to the young lady just recorded, and explains her hesitation in reference to the way in which the Nevada matter had first been told her. Middleton had observed it at the time, and although he had been thinking quite vigorously before, it set him to thinking more energetically than ever. As the result of it all, he said to himself before he fell asleep that night—

"There is something I do not fully understand as to young Dunwoddie and herself. But I am more than his match or hers, and I will risk it. Such a girl and a million of dollars! I am not afraid. The whole set of them, Dunwoddies and Andersons, are as completely in my hand as a man could wish. Poor things! they know as little of me, or of my plans, as if I were God. The only thing I hate is, that matters are too sure and certain for me. There is one of two things to do — no, there are two of three things for me to do, and nothing easier. If you fail this time, old fellow, I'll cut your throat *and* blow out your brains."

CHAPTER XIII.

A BIT OF CIVIL WAR IS THREATENED.

"'An infant's tear,' the savans say, 'conceals
Electric storms with bellowing thunder-peals.
A hailstone holds a fire which would suffice
To whelm a London in its sphere of ice.
Like spark to powder, but one thing is lacked,
To wake the sleeping force to instant act.'"

ONE afternoon, a few days after the events last recorded, Emmeline Anderson came out of her house, and stood for a moment upon the steps leading up to the ample veranda which ran around the entire mansion. She had risen that morning, as she always did of late, while her mother was still sleeping, and had done through the day all that the household needed at her hands. The week before she had a houseful of their old servants to help her, but, except little Zady, who was too young to understand emancipation, almost all of them were gone again. Their new freedom was to them the liberty of perpetual motion; the instant they settled down to work the fear began that they were sinking back into slavery, and no wages withheld them at last from realizing their freedom by putting it in exercise. The young girl had never known, till emancipation came, what exertion meant, genuine exertion of mind and body, and she throve upon and enjoyed it.

It was natural she should. Her mother, wandering aimlessly about the house, or sewing from force of habit, was growing whiter of hair, colder, more silent every day, living wholly in the ashes of the past; but the growing life of the young girl refused to stagnate, and recoiled from inaction as from death. It was by the irrepressible instinct of her youth that she now came out of the gloomy house into the open air. It was like escaping, if only for the moment, from the narrow coffin of an era that was dead into a broader and happier time.

As she stood she observed through the trees between her and the road a man riding by towards Clairsville. His horse was an unusually fine animal, but the rider was gaunt, awkward, and so taken up with controlling his steed that he could do no more than glance in passing at the house. An exclamation of disgust rose to her lips as she saw who it was, but she suppressed all except a shudder of loathing. The moment after she had forgotten him, for, with a glance at the clear sky, she went into the house, and soon came out again dressed for walking. During her father's life she had rarely walked to Clairsville; but times were changed. Parker had every horse at the plough for the spring work. Besides, there would have been no one on the spot to curry, saddle, or harness a horse if there had been one in the stables. And so she took her way towards town on foot, there being an independence in it which gave zest to the walk. The winter had disappeared as if it had never been. Nature had forgotten the dark periods of the past, was clothing itself in the verdure and bloom of a universal gladness, and why should she be sad? With increasing enjoyment she walked, now alongside of the post-oaks on her left, and then by the long stretch of the stake and ridered fence of the plantation upon her right, until, with a bend of the road, she came in sight of an old warehouse, used by the negroes as a church, where the plantation ended; but there she stopped. The man who had ridden by had been halted, she saw, opposite the building, and by two horsemen, one on each side. She knew the men in the distance, and was so terrified that, glancing about, she was relieved to see Parker mending the fence near by, his gangs of negroes ploughing upon the level field nearly half a mile away.

"Parker," she said, hastening to him, "was not that Hiddikel Queasy that rode by just now?"

"Yes, Miss Emmeline," he said; and he had taken off his old hat, a respect he showed to none besides her mother and herself.

"Look, Parker," she asked, "isn't that Tom Terrell and Ferdinand Clarke with him?"

"Miss Emmeline," the black man said, respectfully but doggedly, "I wouldn't bother myself about it." He had his back to the group in question, and it was plain he intended to see nothing.

"Parker," she said, "lay down that rail, get over the fence, and come with me this instant. You know what may happen."

"Miss Emmeline," the man replied, if possible more respectfully still, "I can't. Dey ain't goin' to hurt him. It's Hiddikel Queasy"—the name was an epithet as the man used it—"and I know dey ain't goin' to hurt *you*. Must go to de hands, miss;" and, replacing his hat, the negro slowly walked away.

The girl would have spoken, but it had occurred to her that the presence of any negro might make matters worse, and she paused a moment, her hand upon a projecting rail, to think.

The men coming from town were indeed Tom Terrell and Ferdinand Clarke.

The former was more than usually intoxicated; he was too intelligent, however, to have done more than cast a contemptuous curse at the Yankee politician in passing, knowing the disastrous consequences if the freedmen should be stirred up by any assault upon their leader. But the other was a different character entirely. The only child of old Major Clarke, what habitual spoiling at home had not accomplished in him had been effected in the army, in which he had fought like a tiger, going in as a mere boy. He was one of those thoroughly worthless youths whom it is impossible not to like. Almost emaciated in consequence of excesses of all sorts, he dressed well, and under the rim of his olive-colored felt-hat he had a fine frank eye and a winning smile, which, together with his profuse generosity, made

him a favorite even with mothers who would rather their sons should have died than taken to his courses. He was intoxicated as well as the burly lawyer with whom he rode, but liquor inspired him like laughing-gas — made him an overflowing fountain of fun, feather-headed as he always was.

"Halloo, Hiddikel!" he cried out when he saw that individual riding towards them; "what have you done with that last ten thousand you stole in the Legislature? Sing out, scallawag!"

The person addressed did all that he could do under the circumstances. Not daring to joke in return, he put on an aspect of the utmost dignity, and endeavored to ride gravely by the men he dreaded.

"Great heavens, how grand we are! Hold up, let's contemplate you," the wild young fellow exclaimed, putting his horse across the path of the other. "You do make a beautiful Speaker of the House, don't you? And they say you will be elected United States Senator. Look at him, Terrell—just look at him!"

It is but the truth to say, Hiddikel Queasy did not present a dignified appearance. His face and body were too frail for that, his eyes too weak, close together, and watery, his hair too long and scanty. It was all that he could do, moreover, to keep upon his horse, which was backing before the blockade of his enemy, or starting forward under the spur of its rider. Besides, the man was mortally afraid, and showed it—that was worst of all; his homely face, always pale, had become livid. In his eagerness to escape he spurred his horse at last so severely that the animal reared upon young Clarke. With a loud laugh that adversary struck the animal with his whip, and, recoiling from that, Hiddikel and horse came in violent collision with Tom Terrell upon the other side, knocking him from his saddle, he was so drunk.

"You scoundrel!" the exasperated lawyer roared; and in a moment he had torn the other from his horse, which went flying down the road, Ferdinand Clarke having given him a cut with his whip, accompanying it with a yell of laughter. Meanwhile Tom Terrell grasped his victim firmly with his right hand, while he held his left over his mouth to prevent his crying out.

"For these many years, Ferdy, my boy," he said to his accomplice gravely, almost solemnly, for Hiddikel was as a babe in his grasp, "have I wanted to thrash one of these vermin. I have been dying to do it. When Providence throws the worst of them into my hands, shall I refrain? It were gross ingratitude to Heaven. Tie our horses, Ferdinand; we will take him in this old house. He has held many a midnight meeting here with his niggers. The very place!"

"All right, Terrell, anything for fun;" and, as he said it, hastily fastening the horses to the fence, the young man was following his friend when he found Emmeline Anderson standing in his way.

"Mr. Ferdinand Clarke, I believe?" the lady said, a little out of breath.

"Miss Anderson!" the other replied, his hat in his hand, and considerably astonished. "Delightful afternoon we have. I feared we should have had rain. I trust Mrs. Anderson is well." And no gentleman could have been more respectful in his bearing.

"What is Mr. Terrell going to do with that man, Mr. Clarke?" she asked.

"Not hurt him, Miss Anderson, I assure you, not at all. It is Hiddikel Queasy, and we have learned with pain," the young fellow said with an engaging smile, "that the rod was omitted from his early education. Mr. Terrell is merely intending, in the very gentlest way—"

"Mr. Clarke," the young girl said, "it is on our land, and I will not allow it."

"Pardon me, Miss Anderson, I will see to it that only the mildest chastisement is administered. It is Hiddikel Queasy," he added, as if it were necessary to say nothing beyond that. "Don't go in, miss!"

There was, at the moment, a sudden outcry from within instantly checked. Entering the old house, Emmeline understood it. The captive had cried out during the brief moment in which his foe had taken his hand from his mouth to get out his handkerchief. The next instant Tom Terrell had thrown it around the man's head, and was drawing the ends as hard as he could, the handkerchief being over his mouth, holding the struggling wretch by it as he did so.

"Mr. Terrell, are you not ashamed of yourself?" she said, going up to him, the sickening of her heart overmastered by her indignation. "You pretend to be a gentleman, and do such a thing! Let him go instantly!"

But the lawyer was almost insane with drink and wrath long nursed against his victim. Moreover, he had been the lifelong foe of Judge Anderson—a bitter enemy in politics and at the bar, as everywhere else —and the Judge had not concealed his contempt for him in return.

"I am sorry not to be able to oblige you, Miss Anderson," he said, after he had looked at her for a moment, surprised at her sudden appearance; "but this is no place for a lady. Perhaps you don't see that it is Hiddikel Queasy! Without any seeking of mine, I've got the rascal at last, and I intend to cowhide him. May I beg that you will leave us."

"Mr. Terrell, *please* let him go!" she said, coming nearer to him, laying her hand upon his arm in entreaty.

"No, miss," he replied. The eyes of the man were bloodshot; his head was lowered like that of an infuriated bull.

"I beg of you, sir!"

"No," he replied, brutally.

"Why, bless you, Miss Anderson," Ferdinand Clarke interposed, "we won't hurt the scamp. It just happened so, and all we want is a little fun. Won't you allow me?" and with a beaming smile he offered to escort her to the door.

"Gentlemen," she said, "you know as well as I do—better—that for every blow you strike this man some one will be killed."

"Let 'em be killed. Who objects?" growled the lawyer. "Mighty few of the dead after it is over will be white. Who cares?"

"Shame upon you!" she exclaimed, seizing upon the arms of the man who was in peril, and whose ferret-like eyes were glancing eagerly and entreatingly at her. "Let him go!"

"I won't," the ruffian replied. "Go away."

"Mr. Clarke," she said, turning to the other, "you were in the war. I am told that you fought gallantly. In what battles"—pointing with scorn at the lawyer—"did Mr. Terrell learn to beat a helpless prisoner?"

"Battles? He? Tom Terrell? He never was in a battle," was the reply.

"I thought so!" she exclaimed. "As a lady to a gentleman and a soldier, I appeal to you, sir. But you will let him—" she begged again of the brawny lawyer—"let him go."

"I won't!" he replied more violently than ever.

"You won't!" Ferdinand Clarke roared, as if his amazement at the insolence of the other had paralyzed him till then. "Won't? Drop that man instantly!" he yelled, advancing upon him.

The lawyer glanced at him from his overhanging brows like a mastiff who has his paws upon a bone, growling curses.

"Miss Anderson," Ferdinand said to the lady with a light laugh, "I will attend to this if you will be kind enough to retire. I pledge you my honor—"

But the lawyer saw the hand of his former accomplice steal towards his bosom, and in attempting to get his hand upon his own revolver, his victim made a sudden effort, broke from his grasp, and, the handkerchief still tied about his head, sprang through the door, and leaping the rail fence, sped towards the freedmen ploughing in the distance. The lady had heard of too many like events not to know what was impending, and, as the men drew their weapons, she stood between them.

"Make haste!" she said, "get your horses and go. They will be here in five minutes. Go!"

"Miss Anderson," Ferdinand Clarke remarked, "you are right—we had better go. Especially as what would happen here wouldn't be a priming to what would come of it." And both of the men moved to the door, the lawyer putting up his revolver and hastening out in advance.

"Miss Anderson," the younger of them said, returning and removing his hat, "before I go allow me to say that I wish to apologize for all this. We only wanted a little fun, you know, and on my honor as a gentleman I will give Tom Terrell the soundest thrashing he ever heard of for presuming— Halloo! hold up!"

He snatched his weapon as he exclaimed from his bosom, for Anderson Parker had, on the instant, sprung into the room through a window, the fragment of a fence-rail in his hands. Small wonder that the dissipated youth recoiled. The negro stood confronting him like an enraged animal. He seemed to have grown blacker and bigger in his wrath, the sweat pouring down his broad face, his hairy bosom open, the teeth gleaming between his lips.

"You dar to say one word to her!" he said, his club uplifted in his hands.

"You! boy!" his mistress said, the language of other days coming back to her. "You are mistaken. Go, Mr. Clarke— make haste."

But it was too late. There was the rush as of a crowd outside, and, hastening out, they saw that the escaped man had given the alarm, and the negroes, abandoning their ploughs, were swarming towards the spot. In his alarm, the lawyer had been less expert in unfastening his horse than with the handkerchief, and in a moment both of the white men were encompassed by the angry negroes, who kept at a little distance, however, aware of their revolvers.

"Look here, men," Ferdinand Clarke called out, clambering upon the fence as if it were a frolic, "we've got two revolvers each. You don't know your multiplication-table, but twice two is four, and four times six is twenty-four. I see your razors and hoes; but, sure as you live, twenty-four of you will get sent to heaven. What do you care for Hiddikel Queasy, honest boys like you? Hiddikel Queasy! Coward. He sent you, and did not dare to come back. Bah!" and he laughed in a way which was infectious; for, dissolute as he was, the reckless young scatter-brain—his felt-hat to one side on his head, his eyes glancing brightly upon them—was as devoid of any malice as a bluejay.

But Parker, standing on the steps of the house—Emmeline Anderson beside him—interposed. "Go back to your mules, folks. What you doin' here?" And in a lower tone to the white men, "You get on your horses an' break for it, right away. Fust thing you people know," he added to the crowd, "dat Hiddikel Queasy will hab roused all de niggers in de county. Do you fool folks s'pose de white people won't come too? You know what *dat* means! G'lang wid you. Mules gettin' dere traces tangled all dis time;" and, climbing the fence, he went towards the abandoned ploughs, the hands slowly following after him.

Standing upon the steps, Emmeline Anderson observed the two horsemen halt after they had ridden a little distance. Evidently a violent dispute was going on between them, but suddenly they parted, spurring in opposite directions. As they did so, the laughter of the younger of them rang loud and clear upon the air. In a moment he seemed to be aware of the im-

propriety of his levity, for he curbed in his horse, took off his hat, made a respectful bow to the lady, and then rode soberly away.

———◆———

CHAPTER XIV.

MR. GAMALIEL MIDDLETON MAKES HIMSELF AT HOME.

"'Your household cat that coucheth snug
Upon your thickest fireside rug,
Intends not with its tiger's fur
Your hearth's adornment, nor with purr
A thanks in music for your ear;
Nor rubs itself against your foot,
Yours but its own content to suit;
Nor for your pleasure in your lap
It coils into a sweeter nap.
'Twould eat you, were it not afeared,
As once it did your singing-bird.
Its law, and simpler cannot be—
'The universe exists for me.'"

As Middleton had intimated in his letter to Alec Allen, he was visiting the South in the interests of an Eastern company which had been organized for the purchase of land.

"It may surprise you, Col. Dunwoddie," he remarked to that gentleman a short time after his call upon Miss Anderson, "that we should put money into this. I have been telling you of brilliant operations in mining stocks, of railway shares and land speculations, in San Francisco and New York. But all that is simply gambling. Alec Allen secured an immense fortune where thousands are ruined. Lands in the South are a safe speculation — *safe*, you see. We select them with care, pay almost nothing for them, and rely upon the heavy emigration certain to come when political affairs are quieted down, and that is as sure as is calm weather after every storm. Here is a letter I got to-day. Our people authorize me to secure your services as their legal adviser. You can go in with us, or be compensated in fees, as you see fit. We have heavy capital, and we employ men of the highest standing at the bar as well as those who are most thoroughly acquainted with the South. After the fullest inquiries, I learn," he added pleasantly, "that no one in this section has such a reputation as yourself. If you accept our business, of course you will keep matters quiet, as we have no wish to throw up the price of land. But as sure as you live, sir," Middleton continued with enthusiasm, "there will be a large emigration here some day. There are richer lands elsewhere, but you cannot induce people to go where it is unhealthy. For climate, fertility, convenience to market—we will not say so to anybody, at least not until we have made our purchases—I consider Clair County unsurpassed."

In this way it came to pass that Middleton grew to be quite at home in Clairsville. He was continually coming and going in examination of lands, and the fact that Col. Dunwoddie was his lawyer and friend gave him a currency among the best people, without which he would have been looked upon with an aversion stronger than mere suspicion. Almost immediately after his coming he had adopted a dress and manner in keeping with his surroundings. Aided somewhat by the heat of the weather, he had adjusted himself to Clair County in everything, down to a lounge in his gait and a more leisurely mode of talking.

And so it came quite naturally that he should be a good deal at Col. Dunwoddie's house. He was always ready for a ride with George and Harry, a hunting trip or a fishing excursion. On returning from one of his business absences he brought a small Indian pony, which he had picked up, he explained, for almost nothing, and he had himself superintended the making of a little Mexican saddle for Charlie. Some of his associates elsewhere would have been astonished could they have seen him in the yard leading the animal about with Charlie strapped upon it, as happy as the sedatest of children could be. He was fond also of

telling stories about Nevada on the piazza of an afternoon. It interested their parents to see how absorbed all, Alice especially, became, as he told of the original pioneers of 1849, and the silver "grizzlies" which they were privileged to wear upon their coats, of the plains and the sierras, of Lake Tahoe, nearly seven thousand feet above the level of the Pacific. Many a twenty-pound trout had Middleton to catch over again in its waters for the benefit of his hearers, and they were never weary of being told of his success in shooting ducks and wild turkeys, deer and bears. He had not been without his adventures, too, among the Piute and other Indians, Chinamen and Mexicans.

"I would like to tell you about Virginia City," he said one moonlight night, as he sat upon the steps of the piazza, Charlie between his knees, Harry and George on either side, Alice and May looking on near by, their mother in her easy-chair, "but I do not like to either. It is all well enough to say that it is built on the side of a mountain, and is one of the most romantic places in the world, but I cannot think of it without remembering the horrible state of society there. Nor is it the gambling, robbing, murdering I mean, for they hang people for that. It would be better for you, boys, to die than to live there," he said with energy. "No modest women, except the wives of some of the miners, would enter the place any more than if small-pox was raging there. I always think, when I speak of such things, of my mother, especially of my sister Clara. I want you to know her, and hope you will some day. But, talking about Virginia City, it is built upon a foundation of silver. The mines honeycomb the mountain two thousand feet under it, but, for wickedness, that whole Sodom and Gomorrah of twenty-thousand people rests on the very crust of —excuse me—hell itself."

The moon shone full in his upturned face, and the ladies could not help seeing the shudder with which he said it, closing his eyes a moment to shut out the very memory.

"Bigthing, Slag County, was Allen's headquarters; coarse names they are. But I will tell you," he said, "about the discovery of the Comstock Lode;" and with genuine gusto he told them about the two Grosch brothers who made it, and how one died from the blow of a pickaxe in his foot, and the other was frozen to death before getting the least good therefrom. "Which shows what a vain, vain world it is," he added. He went on, however, to tell how the first miners, searching only for gold, used to curse the bluish stuff which was so abundant, and which they never dreamed was silver-ore; of how "Old Pancake," as everybody called Comstock, gave his name to the lode; of how people were at that moment digging out of it one tenth of all the silver produced on the globe. "Just to think of it, when your uncle and I were there, twenty-two millions of silver, boys, were dug out—twenty-two millions! *Millions!*" There was an omnipotence of power and sweetness in the syllables, in comparison with which other words were tame and insipid.

To Mrs. Dunwoddie there seemed to be an almost aggressive force in the words, an hostility in this mention of money as of something wolfish; but then she was nothing but a woman, and an invalid at that. It was late that night before Middleton had done describing the wonderful shafts, the heaps of bullion, the processes of getting out the clean, pure, precious ore. "Millions on millions!" Who could fail to share the appetite of the one who spoke for all that was contained in the words? And this was but one instance of many similar conversations.

May Dunwoddie, however, as the days rolled by, appreciated matters the least of all.

"What is the use of having a secret if you cannot tell it to a single girl," she complained every day. "Pa says, 'Be sure and hold your tongue to - day, my child.' Ma says, 'Remember, May!' the last thing every morning when I go out. Horace is always saying, 'Be careful, May.' And to think that I could have a silk dress right off if pa didn't think it was wisest not to make any display. I'm sure the girls suspect something, they keep looking at me and whispering together so. One of them gave me a whole pickle at lunch yesterday, and then took me off and whispered, 'You'll tell *me*, won't you, May ?' And I had to be just as brazen, and look her in the face and say, 'Tell you what, you foolish thing ?' with my face all in a blaze. And you needn't look so demure, Miss Alice," she would add, "all the girls are dying to know who Mr. Middleton is, and how it happens that he always comes with *you* to church. Aha, miss! it is your turn is it ?" the lively girl added, for it was her sister that was blushing now.

Alice was very properly offended—her sister, being a mere school-girl, to talk to her so ! And yet she did not seem to be. Her face was the brighter for it; and she shared a little purse of gold, which her father had given her for the rarity and not the spending of it, with her sister that night.

"He did not suppose *I* would be prudent enough," May remarked, when she was through with hugging and kissing her sister in her usual ardent and impulsive way. "Who knows," she said, "but it may turn out that, if I am not quite a young lady yet, I am the most *prudent* of his girls, at last ?" and her sister's face glowed again under her laughing eyes.

The blush seemed to be always coming and going in Alice's face these last days. Until of late, the mourning she wore had made her homelier than ever, but it was impossible not to see the improvement in her since Mr. Middleton came. She did not seem to be too tall and spare, as she had done before. The sullen dullness was gone from her eyes; a bloom was coming to her cheeks; a girlish laughter to her lips. Even George noticed it.

"What is coming over you, Alice?" he said. "You have not scolded a fellow for a week, and, if you can't laugh out loud and strong like May, you are beginning to smile, at least, like thunder. If you'll only keep it up! The bother is, first thing a fellow knows you'll be all down again."

Mrs. Dunwoddie ventured a motherly word of caution at last, but in her wise way.

"Mr. Middleton is at Mrs. Anderson's a good deal," she said to Alice when they were alone one day on a shaded corner of the piazza. "Emmeline does not come here as often as she used to. I suppose it is because of that Nevada matter. She is very much delighted on our account; but, unconsciously to herself, she feels more keenly the circumstances in which she is placed, and shrinks, since Alec's money came, from what may be a contrast with us. It is strange; although I have known her since she was born, I do not understand her, and less every day. Her mother's heart is in the grave with her sons and husband, and Emmeline is growing up alone in the world. I almost tremble for her, she is so deep and determined. But I was going to tell you, that when she was here yesterday, I took occasion to speak of Mr. Middleton. He is a remarkably pleasing gentleman," she added, adjusting the honeysuckle vines near by her as she sat, with her face from Alice as she spoke; "and I thought Emmeline ought to be told that we know nothing about him beyond his connection with your uncle."

"Pa read me a letter from his land company in New York," Alice ventured, "in which they speak highly of him."

"As their business agent, yes," Mrs. Dunwoddie proceeded; "and I told Emmeline of it. But what do we really know about him? We have had too many adventurers among us, my dear, to trust any one entire-

ly. I told her that the most plausible and pleasing of them sometimes turn out—"

"Oh, mother!" Alice interrupted, "I do hope you do not mean that he is a—carpet-bagger! He was telling me yesterday about his mother. She was like you, he said. And he said that the only relative he had living was his sister Clara. He educated her until she could teach; and he said he hoped that we would come to know her and to like her, she was so accomplished. Yes—and I had forgotten it —he said then that it was a great mistake if any one supposed, because he had been associated with Uncle Alexander, that he was rich. He told me that he was not so at all; that he had often made money, but had always been swindled out of it by others. He said that he was working hard, and hoped to be, at least, independent."

"He told you a good deal, my dear," Mrs. Dunwoddie said; "but I was speaking of Emmeline."

"Why should you talk to her about him?" Alice asked.

The mother winced at the tone of the question, her eyes still upon the honeysuckles, and said quietly—

"Because, my dear, Emmeline Anderson has seen a great deal of sorrow, and she yearns to be happy. She is young, of an ardent and impetuous nature, and has been closely shut up in what may seem to her a dull life. Mr. Middleton is attractive, has seen a great deal of the world, is of a bright and joyous temperament, and can make himself very pleasing."

"Yes—but, ma, what has all that to do with her?" Alice persisted.

"Everything," Mrs. Dunwoddie said, turning gravely to her daughter. "She is a beautiful girl, and Mr. Middleton may fall in love with her — that is, if he is not already engaged. Before she knows it, she may become attached to him; nothing could be more natural. But we ought to know much more about the gentleman first." The mother knew the pain she was inflicting; but in surgical cases the hand of love is stronger as well as wiser than that of the coldest science—and steadier, too, although it is the surgeon, not the patient, who suffers most.

"I had as frank a talk with Emmeline as if I were her own mother," she went on. "I do not understand her. She looked at me with her large eyes, and had not a word to say. Do you know, Alice," Mrs. Dunwoddie said, conscious of her daughter's silence, "that your father has just found out how much poor Horace has loved Emmeline all these years? How blind men are! I was sorry Horace insisted on telling Emmeline about the Nevada matter; and I think she was annoyed about it. It may prove to be a groundless fear, but I feel as if she were suddenly removed farther away from us. But she is a thoroughly sensible girl, and I am glad I had that conversation with her about Mr. Middleton."

"You spoke about Horace and Emmeline," Alice said, after quite a silence, and as if to divert her mind from something else. "Do you think he has spoken to her?"

"Horace is taken up with other things just now," the mother replied. "He has a plan as to something he hopes to do that I will tell you about before long. If he loves her, he must wait. We must all learn to do that, Alice. Your father is becoming very impatient; but I am not well enough yet to break up our home, and I am persuading him to wait before taking any decided step. I find it hard to hold him," she added, with a smile; "but we were very poor, and it will take us some time to become accustomed to our—millions!"

CHAPTER XV.

THE FIRST LUXURIES OF THE NEW WEALTH.

"Flute, cornet, harp—hark! loud and clear!
The sackbut, psaltery, dulcimer!
Prostrate with all the world I bow—
What other god, O Gold, than thou!
As worship, Give, O give, I cry;
Thy gospel but, Eat, drink, and die!"

UPON the day following this conversation, George Dunwoddie remarked at dinner, and somewhat sourly, as to their new affairs—

"I don't see any good it does a man. Except that Alice isn't so cross, what fun has it been, say? Every morning I pinch myself before I get wide awake, and say to myself, Roust out, old chap, don't you know your father is—" and the boy added the words in a low and sepulchral whisper—"is *rich?* But after I've bounced out of bed in a hurry and looked around, *I* can't see anything of it. If Harry, here, has got so much as a new book, he hasn't told me. I can't see that Charlie—hi, old Solemn!—eats a spoonful more of bread-and-milk if he is— *rich*"—again in accents of awe. "And it's got out in school, like—like a house on fire. Before school, at recess, after school, all the fellows are around, like bumble-bees bothering me. One says, 'Give us a dollar, old fel.' Another jerks at my elbow, and bows and scrapes, and says, 'Please, Mars George, gimme chew of 'bacco now you's rich.' Bob Smithers pitched my hat on top of the school, and said, 'It isn't the correct thing for an af-fluent individual to wear,' and I had to go for him."

"Silence, sir!" Col. Dunwoddie said, and added, "I have been annoyed myself of late. The Clairsville people, wherever I go, stand looking at me as if I were a curiosity. I believe some of them wait for me on the sidewalks and doorways, knowing I must go that way to my office. Everybody salutes me deferentially. This morning when I went down to my office, I found a man waiting to borrow money to meet a mortgage due at noon. I hardly knew him by sight, and he said he had got up at daybreak to be sure and catch me. Poor fellow, I believe if he had not been in the army he would have gone down on his knees to me, he was so desperate."

The news of the fortune certainly had got out. May Dunwoddie came in from school a few days after, overflowing with her experiences.

"Oh, ma! oh, pa!" she said at the tea-table, "it's all over town that Uncle Alec has left you ten millions of dollars. Susie Robinson told me that Jane Bronson had told her that Maria Nelson's father's black Sam saw the wagons unloading great bags and bags of silver and gold at our front gate at midnight. Mary Ann Tomlinson asked me please to let her see some, and she wanted to feel my pockets. All the girls insisted on being introduced to me; and it was — 'Allow me to make known to you Miss May Dunwoddie, ahem!' until I was mad enough to box their ears. Clucy Smith and I haven't spoken — oh, for months on months — and she said to me, 'Ah, yes, I perceive now,' as sarcastic as she could, 'why you refused to go with me, madam; you are so extremely wealthy —hem, yes!' It was because," the excited young lady exclaimed, "she said I had put mullen-leaves on my cheeks to make them red, and she knows it. And all the girls begged me to beg pa to give a picnic, and asked how many horses I would drive in my carriage, and whether I would dress in my silk every day, and if I would wear three-buttoned gloves, and all that, until I broke down and had a cry. I knew it was only their fun, but I never saw any good Uncle Alec's fortune did *me*. What is the use of money if you can't spend it? The idea of Uncle Alec! He's the funniest god-mother!"

"He isn't a fairy at all," Harry corrected her, "he is the Slave of the Lamp—Aladdin's Lamp—a sort of ghost;" but Harry saw the impropriety of his illustration, and stopped.

"I thought we would be harassed," Col. Dunwoddie said to his wife and Horace that night before going to bed; "but I fear it will be worse than I had supposed. The news is all over the county that I have inherited a fortune of many millions in gold. I am beginning to receive begging letters. People want to sell me blooded horses, claims against Congress, Confederate bonds, shares in undeveloped oil-lands, and I don't know what. It is amazing how swiftly a thing of the kind flashes abroad, and everybody tries to be first at me. Three men called this afternoon—one wanted me to allow him to use my name as candidate for Governor in the Convention; another was anxious to nominate me at some Railway Board as President; the last man had discovered a yellow root which is a sure cure for snake-bite, and he was eager to sell the secret. We must go abroad as soon as possible. I will be run to death. What amuses me is the cordiality with which I am congratulated by people who hardly knew me before, and who seem glad to do so, although I am sure they do not expect to be benefited by me in the remotest way. If I am in a crowd at the post-office, in a store, at the corner of the streets, the moment I begin to say anything a dead silence falls on the rest. As if I were any better worth hearing than before! If I had made a great speech, or written a famous book, there would be some sense in it."

"And yet I do not think," his wife said, smiling at him, "that Southern people worship money. I am sure that there are many things which we rate much higher."

"Of course, of course," Col. Dunwoddie replied; "but we have all been poor here in Clair County—*terribly* poor; and Alec's money has been so exaggerated that I do not wonder at the excitement. You have no idea what a power it seems—far greater here than in the North or East. Not that the people worship money, but that they are so dreadfully pressed. I believe I could

get out my revolver. You may shoot as many as you please."

"What a noise you made last night," Mrs. Dunwoddie said at breakfast next morning. "There must have been an army of cats. It was a long time before I could get to sleep afterwards. I hope you did not kill any of the poor things."

"We at least frightened them away," Horace said with a laugh.

"Cats! Why didn't you wake us?" George and Harry exclaimed in a breath. "We have so little fun, too."

But that afternoon May came home from school in a fever of excitement.

"Oh, ma," she said, hat in hand, her pretty face all in a glow as she tried to smooth down her hair, "did you know it? Those burglars we have been hearing so much about attacked our house last night. Everybody is talking about it. They say ever so many low whites and negroes with chalked faces tried to break in—into this very house — as they did in other places, with crowbars and knives and things. Only last night, ma, and you thinking it was cats! All the girls were telling me what a hero Horace was. How he crept down-stairs, and went out through the back-door, and stole around in front and began shooting at them on the front porch. There must have been nearly five hundred robbers. Only Horace by himself, and he ran them all off the place! All the girls are crazy about him," and the lively girl proceeded with the fullest details of a battle which, according to the version she had heard, should have been enrolled in history.

But Col. Dunwoddie and Horace only laughed, when they came to tea, at the exaggeration.

"I told our next neighbor this morning, when he inquired about the sound of shots," Col. Dunwoddie said, "and the great exploit has all grown out of that. You must all remember that whatever any of us say or do since that news came will be eagerly reported and greatly exaggerated—it is hu-

man nature. But, really and truly, Horace deserves much credit," he continued, in reply to the anxious questions of his wife and the rest. "It was a flank movement Horace executed. I was very wakeful, and stole quietly out on the other side of the house by way of reinforcement? There were a couple of rascals, and they were not much more dangerous than cats. It was all over before I could come into action. I am getting to be jealous of the way in which you are supplanting me as your superior officer, my boy. It was your first engagement, and that, what military men regard as very difficult, the repulse of a night attack. I wonder if they really believe we have money in the house? They will not trouble us again."

"Ha!" exclaimed George; "and you never even told me about the fun I missed. It was mean, Horace! I wouldn't have treated you so, not taking me with you." And George had tears in his eyes.

"What was the use of frightening mother," Horace laughed, "and about almost nothing at all? How people do exaggerate! You can take my place, Georgy, next time. Only I'm afraid you will not be troubled soon again. Those miserable cowards never try a place twice, and I am glad it happened before I got off. If you girls were worth a picayune," Horace went on, "you would help mother get those collars and neckties ready. I must go to-morrow. Mr. Middleton will not be back from his land trip till week after next. Give him my regards."

"Why, does he not know you are going?" said Alice with wondering eyes. "It is not right to treat him so. He is such a gentleman. And he knows all about business, too. Oh, Horace!"

Mrs. Dunwoddie, paler than usual from hearing of the attempted robbery, lifted her eyes to the face of her daughter. There was something painful to her in Alice's tones, in the interest she seemed to have in Mr. Middleton.

"Father's idea of things," said Horace, also surprised, "is to talk as little about family matters to those outside as possible. Mr. Middleton seems to see more of you than of any of us, Alice; I appoint you to give him my regards." But as Alice seemed somewhat vexed, and remained silent, her brother went on in a gayer tone. "I am going out into the wide world, only please don't tell anybody. I am going to bring everybody something when I come back: books for Harry, a ride for Georgy, a splendid silk—shall it be crimson?—for May, a set of jewelry for Alice, a magnificent Bible for mother, a dressing-gown for father, a silver cup for Charlie—and, anything else anybody wants? What is it? Let's begin with sober old Charlie. What will *you* have, Judge?"

It was a day or two after this that he walked to the depot, valise in hand, to set out upon his journey. The morning seemed created expressly for his going out under such circumstances into the world, it was so beautiful. Not often is it allowed even to young manhood to feel as he did. His father had easily secured cash from bank in anticipation of his wealth, and his son had a round sum in his money-belt, plenty of loose change in his pockets, with power to draw for all he might desire. And then he was his own master, free to go and to come as he pleased. With the kisses of his mother and of his sisters upon his lips, he had also the entire confidence of his father.

So full was he of overflowing life that it took a large part of his energy to keep the rest in due bounds. All his days he had been cooped up in the post-oak levels of Clair County, as well as in a still closer and severer school of monotonous care and hard work, for the absence of his father during the dark years of the war had made him a man before he ceased to be a boy. He had read more than is usual among boys, and had enjoyed the close companionship, interrupted only during the war,

of a thoroughly educated father, and, all the time, of his mother. He had learned much about the great world, the wide world of states, cities. It was almost as much to him in anticipation as is the universe beyond to a dying saint. He had everything he wished—

Except one thing. But that was more than all the world beside. As he thought he walked more slowly to the depot. Now, if iron filings are attracted to a magnet by a mysterious power, surely there must be a magnetism in a strong heart which draws to itself by irresistible force the object upon which it has fastened its affection, as in this case. Emmeline Anderson had been told that Horace was to leave in the night train of the day before; but he had been unexpectedly detained, and now he was conscious before he saw her of whom he should meet. Sure enough, as he walked along he saw her coming, for, supposing him to be gone, she was on her way to see his mother.

It was one of the most beautiful features of his deepening love for her, the effect upon him of the changes which had taken place in her as she had passed from a girl into a young lady. Her value to him increased as she seemed more removed from his reach. The alterations, as she grew, in her dress, in the arrangement of her hair, in the few articles of ornament she wore, most of all, the increasing reserve on her part as on his, her virgin seclusion from him even when nearest to him — all these had given greater depth to his love. And the more he loved her, that much more did he resolve to hide his love as the most sacred of his treasures.

"You looked down upon me so proudly when we were last together," he said to himself as he saw her approaching, "because you thought my father's money had intoxicated me. You forget whose son I am, apart from his money. And you are a queen? Well, I will be a king. I can be as proud as your majesty. Cold politeness will be sufficient as we pass. It is not necessary—is it?—that I should bid her good-by. Yes, Miss Anderson, you will find," he added to himself as the lady drew nigh, "that I am not a boy. You will learn that a man does not make a fool of himself twice."

The lady bowed in passing, her color coming and going, but her serious, unfaltering eyes were raised to his. True, it was but for an instant, but, alas, he could no more resist them than winter can resist the sun. Though he had congealed himself into an arctic coldness, her eyes were to him more than a tropical sun. Moreover, there was within him a traitor stronger than himself.

"Miss Anderson," he began, but the mightier self had, on the instant, its crimson color upon his face in proof of its mastery over the poor fellow—"Miss Anderson," he said, astonished at himself, in a voice so low as to make it all the worse, it seemed so determined, and, to his terror, he had taken her hand in his—"Miss Emmeline, I love you with all my soul. All my life I have loved you. I will love you as long as I live. I can't help it. And you can't. Good-by."

There was not another word, not a look even on either side. But the lover had a plenty to say to and of himself in the cars when the train rolled away with him soon after.

"You are no gentleman, sir," he said. "You are a villain, a blackguard, a ruffian, a perfect fool! You *are* intoxicated with your money, you very despicable fellow! The fact is," and he repeated it with cutting sarcasm, "you are *young !*"

He had thrust that stronger self back again into the basement where, like a servant, it belonged. It was having there, none the less, a riotous enjoyment at the mischief it had done.

———◆———

CHAPTER XVI.

MR. MIDDLETON AND THE "FOREMAN OF THE CROP."

"'The first of black men to the first of white,'
Thus to Napoleon did poor Toussaint write.
But spurned by white men and disowned by black,
Chains were his answer from his friend, alack !
Upon two Times he tried his foot to set
The Old not gone, the New not come as yet.
Too frail a footing for a man, I ween,
Who lifts a race across the gulf between."

SOME ten days after Horace Dunwoddie had, like a strong and eager swimmer, made his first plunge into the great ocean of the world, Mr. Middleton came back late one night to Clairsville from a search—armed with letters from Col. Dunwoddie—through the state for plantations which were worth everything and could be had for nothing. He arose late next morning, and looked out of his window in the third-story front. It was a dull prospect. The public square of the town lay beneath him, the red court-house in the centre. There were China-trees lining the streets, a row of them enclosing the towering and square-roofed structure in question; but they drooped their leaves under the coming heat of noon, coated with dust. During court week the well-gnawed horse-racks would be crowded with horses—the younger ones biting at and kicking each other with many a whinny, the older horses speculating as to why they had been created, their heads drooping, and disgusted with life. But it was not court week, and not a horse was to be seen. It was so sultry that Mr. Middleton languidly wondered as he brushed his hair at a glass in the window, to see a boy running through the square. Had he noticed he would have seen that it was a white boy whose bare feet could not otherwise stand the heat of the sandy street even at that hour. Immediately under his window was an old negro splitting kindling, as blissfully unconscious of the hot sand upon his naked feet as he was of the sun itself shining full upon his bald head. Mr. Middleton saw the patriarch pause to wipe his face and head with his dingy sleeve. Had he been nearer he would have heard him say, with a warmth as genuine as that of the sun—

"Bress de Lord for dis pleasant wedder!" It was his element; had it been hotter, he would have enjoyed it more.

Just then Mr. Middleton saw a white man stop, in passing, and shake hands with him. It was Hiddikel Queasy, and the looker-on considered him with profound interest, having heard how near he came to a beating at the hands of Tom Terrell, as well as of much else in regard to him. He was a stoop-shouldered, thin-visaged, lank, lean specimen of the Yankee, when, North as well as South, the name is used as a curse, his outer man corresponding closely to the typical Brother Jonathan as it is portrayed in caricatures and in the wooden images in front of cigar-shops, except that he was homelier, meaner, more cowering in appearance. Pitted with small-pox, which seemed, somehow, to have struck deeper than the skin, the lower part of his face was disfigured by a scanty beard of reddish hue. As has been said, his eyes were singularly small, of a watery blue, and set close together under a low forehead. His complexion was cadaverous, and there was a slimy writhe of the thin lips, the corners thereof answering to those of his cunning eyes. Underneath the film of his propitiatory demeanor there was a nature evidently as cold as it was stony. Poorly as he was dressed, Middleton knew that he was the most powerful man in that region—Col. Dunwoddie and Tom Terrell, had it been possible to combine the two, being as nothing to him. He had been in the employ of the Federal Government immediately after the war; had gone from that, by negro votes, to the Legislature. There he had been made Speaker of the House, and was known to be aspiring still higher. He knew every negro in the county; and there was not a secret league among the freedmen which he had not originated; not a document circulating among them which did not come through his hands. Unless greatly belied, he had made large sums while in office. Shrewd to the last degree, no man had a keener sense than he of the precariousness of his position; and he plundered as rapidly and as largely as possible, like a man rifling the dead on the night following a battle, knowing that his opportunity was short, and that it was his last for a lifetime.

As he looked down upon him talking in a low tone with the old negro, Tom Terrell rode slowly by, aware, in a contemptuous way, of the two men, and of the alliance between them.

"Curse you!" he heard him say, as he passed. "I let you off before, but if it wasn't, when it is once begun, such a *big* thing, I would ride you down. Just wait—!"

Middleton dressed himself, as the man rode away, in his best Southern suit of brown linen, with white vest, and went down to one of the two barber-shops between which he oscillated. The barber in each was a mulatto—very talkative—and between them he got, while under their hands, all that was going on in town, and a good deal more. It was a relief, after the innumerable house-flies of the hotel, its bar-room adorned with the highly colored chromos relating to bitters, fever-and-ague pills, and the most desirable blacking and sewing-machines. A poet in the rapture of composition is at the highest point of his being, but not more so than is a yellow man with a handsome white man in his barber's chair, and full permission to lather and shave and brush and perfume and talk to him at will. Between the two shops, with their array of colored-paper patterns, cut into lace, hanging from the ceiling, their shelves of bottles and cups, their rickety chairs and settees, filled, more or less, by idlers, Mr. Middleton was learning Clairsville by heart. All he had to do was to sit still and listen, turning the conversation as he desired by the merest hint of his lathered lips. On this occasion he went to Leonidas Dunwoddie to be shaved.

"Yes, sah; Col. Charles Dunwoddie, my old marster, is a high-toned gen'elman," he was speedily informed. "Nobody in dis city ob Clairsville stan' in a more exalted position. I was his property myself during previous days. His son Horace is a splendid gen'elman too, more decomposed dan his father — a stronger man. George, he cares for his fun. Harry, he loves readin'; he will write books like his father some day. De last occasion on which Col. Dunwoddie was here, I observed to him, 'Col. Dunwoddie, is dis essentially true what de county says? Hab you come into de possession ob billions through Mars Alec?' Hem!"—the barber coughed—"dat slipped out from de force ob habit. I call no man my marster now. He, Mr. Alec Allen, I mean, was corpulent, sah, an' lazy! Hcugh-cugh!" (expressing the unutterable). "All de Colonel observe was, 'Oh, Leonidas, you go on shaving.' Four weeks after, dis splendid chair you is sittin' in, sah, came all de way from de remote city for me, de first ob de species ebber seen in dis county. Dat fool—Yaller Jessamine—in de odder shop, is cursin' and dyin' about it. Better nebber trust yourself in his hands," he added, mysteriously. "He is a mighty powerful preacher—yes, sah—but I know things! But ob all de white ladies I ebber met, Mrs. Col. Dunwoddie—my Miss Eliza, I calls her, to dis present period—is de o⸺ Is de razor agreeable to your feelin's, sah⸺"

And so for half an hour, there being no one waiting his turn to be shaved, the white man has all the information he desires, the language of his tonsorial artist, as he styled himself, being more highly flavored, if possible, than his perfumes — his hands not more roundabout in their leisurely occupation than his tongue.

After going back to the hotel for a late breakfast, Middleton dropped in at the rival barber's also, to have a certain im-perceptible trimming done to his hair. As he took his seat in a chair much inferior to that of his rival, the mulatto looked at him with a mournful aspect, and remarked—

"You shaved yourself dis mornin', sah? Leonidas Dunwoddie did it? I didn't s'pose eben he could do it so bad. A fine chair can't make up for ebberything. Now his old marster is so rich, dat fool is swelled up like a bullfrog in a cypress-swamp. Col. Dunwoddie? Yes, sah. No one hab anything to say against de Colonel, 'cept dat he spoil his hands when he owned dem. Look at dat Leonidas. De Colonel is a mighty smart man, but he is not fitten to be a editor. Tom Terrell is de man for dat. You see you is 'bliged to cuss people in de paper, an' when dey come to 'quire about it you must be ready to shoot 'em down. Nobody in dese parts stood anywhere near Judge Anderson. Dat's where I was owned. Proud? Should think so!" And the loquacious man, as he combed and clipped, went into minute detail—there being no one else in the shop—of the glories of the Anderson family, the handsome sons, the grand dinings, the cupboards of silver and gold plate which had been melted for the necessities of soldiers' homes during the war; the diamonds and blooded horses which had been sold to fit out the regiment of the eldest son, the grandeur of Mrs. Anderson, the saucy beauty of little Miss Emmeline. Middleton had heard the long detail before, for he was endeavoring to obtain as thorough a knowledge as possible of the South of the past and the present. He now asked in a casual way as to Anderson Parker; he could not account to himself for the interest he took in the black Hercules. To his surprise, the barber seemed disinclined to talk upon the subject.

"Anderson Parker?" he said, clipping more slowly. "Yes, sah. He was a sort of head man among de field-hands before de war. I was a house-servant. Didn't know much about him, sah. Nobody did. Ebber see a man as black as dat, sah? Charcoal makes a white mark on him, dey say. An' he nebber talks. Silent as midnight, 'cept when he orders de hands in de field. Oh, but he's tight on dem! When he *does* preach, or make a speech—whew! But he keeps out ob dat when he can. Fact is, sah, colored people don't like him. He's too — too shet up, somehow. We sent him to de Legislature, an' he wouldn't hab any ob dat sort ob thing. Do you know, sah, dat man turn right round and headed straight for de cotton-patch again! An' you can't get him off dat plantation sence. He don't go wid us, somehow," the barber added, hesitatingly.

"Oh, he prefers to associate with white people," Mr. Middleton conjectured.

"Oh no, sah—not at all, sah," the other said, hastily. "Anderson Parker don't go wid anybody. He's big an' black, and holds his tongue; works like a brindle-ox all day, at his old books like a mule all night, dey say. Dat man nebber laughed out in his life—not sence de war. He's mighty powerful, but he always 'minds *me* ob a first-class fun'ral—dat's so!" and the voluble barber laughed at his own wit, but as if cautiously, and changed the subject. Middleton had noticed a number of highly colored and still more highly objectionable pictures on the walls of an inner room. From that, as well as from long observation among white men, he knew well what sort of a character this mulatto was. The snaky thinness of his body, the pallor of his yellow face, an indescribable way in which the man held his eyes half closed, these indicated the lewdness which made Yellow Jessamine, as he was called—his real name being Jessamine only—a proverb in the place. Middleton was no Puritan, and he had but slight ideas, at last, of the depths of pollution in which, like a maggot in carrion, this man habitually lived; but he preferred Leonidas Dunwoddie with all his grandiloquence, and he 'patronized his rival only to make his knowledge of Clairsville complete. So momentous was the matter he had in view that he could not be too thoroughly equipped.

"I have got the Colonel well in hand," he meditated, as he mounted a horse he had hired and rode slowly towards the Anderson place. "He may be a genius, but he is as simple as a child. As to Miss Alice—humph! If you were prettier, miss, I might think of it. Horace is the widest awake of all of them. And he had the start of me with *her*; but he is green—very green—and I will lose no time. Hang him! he is so much like his mother! There is the danger for me. She sits in her chair so quiet and pleasant, but ah, how clearly she sees with those steady eyes. *See!* I'm more afraid of her than of all the rest. I do not believe that woman ever winks or sleeps. She persists in living because she loves them so; she sees through everything with her *heart!* There's no trouble with sorrowful old Mrs. Anderson. She sees nothing except the past. One can see through her as through a pane of — ice. But her daughter! If I only understood her. One has to be as careful as if she were a princess royal. What an influence it has on these people — the very tradition of having owned slaves—it's in the blood. I must be slow and steady, and *very* careful; but I'm learning. And I am the soul of frankness. Besides, I'm already as much a Southerner as if I had been born here," and to all outer appearance, almost as to the tones of his voice, too, this was true. Middleton was being melted into the mould of those around him as by the heat of the season. So much so that, arrived at Mrs. Anderson's—having begged permission to do so—he sat on the steps of the front piazza quite at home, fanning himself with his Panama hat, while the ladies were seated in chairs near by. The visitor made himself quite entertaining. He gave an account of his trip. Everything was new and delightful to him. He dwelt with enthusiasm upon the hospitality of the people, the delicious buttermilk and clabber he had been feasted upon in the country. He was full of enthusiasm, too, as to the fertility of the lands. As soon as matters could settle down a little, cotton, sugar, tobacco, corn, pork, especially cotton, would be profitable in a way which would make the mines of Nevada barren in comparison; and he fortified all he advanced by statistics and anecdotes. And, finally, he had learned through Col. Dunwoddie that Mrs. Anderson had — and he apologized for talking business — some intention of selling her plantation and removing into Clairsville, where she could be freed from all care in regard to so large a place.

"I have often spoken of my sister Clara," he continued. "She has been teaching, but is, as the young ladies say, crazy to visit the South. I have some thought of buying a plantation and seeing what I can make of it. The idea has only come to me of late. The fact is, I am infatuated with the South. However, I believe all Northern people are, after visiting it. If you should at any time care to speak of the matter," he said, in the end, "Col. Dunwoddie will advise with you about it. He is our legal man; whatever he says we do. I am not able to buy, of course," he added frankly, "it is the company I represent," and he conversed upon other subjects.

An hour after this, Mrs. Anderson happened to see Anderson Parker passing in the distance through the yard, and sent Zady, the little negro-girl, to call him to her. "He is seeing to the dinner for the field-hands," she said, "but he can stop for a moment."

"Parker," she continued, as the man came and stood with his hat in his hand in front of the step upon which her visitor was seated, "this gentleman was speaking to me about buying the plantation. What do you think of it?"

The man turned his eyes with a certain deliberate movement from the lady to her visitor. He was, as has been said, powerfully built. His broad chest was well-matched by a large head—the brows not high, but uncommonly broad and prominent — and he certainly was exceedingly black. He wore a long handkerchief of blue silk looped about his sturdy neck in such a way that he could use it in wiping the perspiration from his face, and he slowly did so now as he looked at Middleton. So overpoweringly big and strong did he seem in comparison with his own dapper self, that this gentleman arose from his seat and stood up. It was a new experience to this man of the world. He had a queer consciousness of being a smaller man than he had supposed, as the giant in ebony gazed upon him without a particle of the deference he showed towards his former mistress and her daughter. Nothing could be more absurd. Mr. Middleton was a finished gentleman, and this creature, who knew nothing whatever, who had been a slave until lately, was regarding him as if he were an insect. The white man stepped upon the piazza beside Mrs. Anderson, and, although his head was now above the level of the other, it made no difference.

"Well, Parker?" Mrs. Anderson said at last.

The man looked at his mistress in silence for a moment, and then addressing her as he had done before the war—

"No, Miss Julia. No, miss." And then, very respectfully, "If you like, Miss Julia, I'll study over it. But," he added conclusively, "it'll be all no, jest de same."

"If you will allow me, madam," Middleton said, "I would like to say a word;" and he turned to the man: "I have consulted Col. Dunwoddie, and he tells me that our company can afford to do this with Mrs. Anderson."

Whereupon he stated at length the rate per acre he was willing to pay, the times of payment, and everything else connected with the matter, adding a good deal of what seemed to be clear proof of the advantage to the lady from such a sale. During all his remarks the other did not look at him once. He kept his eyes upon the face of his old mistress, and at the close of all that Mr. Middleton had to say he merely remarked as before—

"No, Miss Julia."

"Yes, but *why?*" the visitor urged. "Look at it, my man," and he went over once more the terms and the leading reasons for the sale. "People say," he ended, "that you have excellent sense. Now, *why* not?"

The other did not even glance at him, but only said—

"Miss Julia, no. I give you more dan dat myself, easy."

"*You?*" Mr. Middleton exclaimed with astonishment.

"Miss Julia, please, miss, I'd raver talk with you an Col. Dunwoddie;" and, accepting a nod from her in dismissal, the negro turned, and, without a glance at their guest, walked away.

"You must excuse Parker," Emmeline Anderson said with a smile to their visitor, "he is very odd. He does not like strangers. He has had experiences with a certain class of men from the North here and in the Legislature, which has made him almost venomous in regard to them. He is slow and sensible, but he is as dogged in his opinions as an ox or a mule," and the gentleman remembered that the barber had used the same illustration.

"He preaches to - morrow," she added. "If you want to understand Southern ways, since the war at least, you ought to go and hear him. But he will not want to see you there. His people don't like him at all, they're afraid of him, but they crowd to hear him. He is among them like an oak among saplings." .

"How does Mrs. Dunwoddie bear the absence of her son?" Mrs. Anderson interposed at this point, waiving the subject aside with dignity.

"Her son? Excuse me, I returned to town late last night and have not seen them," Middleton said.

"Horace Dunwoddie," Mrs. Anderson explained. As she spoke her daughter arose to adjust the curtains of a window behind them. "I supposed you knew of it," she continued. "Mrs. Dunwoddie tells me that he has gone to Nevada, and will come home by way of the East."

Mr. Middleton was too much astonished even to exclaim. The next moment he hastened to do away with any appearance of surprise, and conversed gayly upon his impressions in regard to the South.

"I have learned more in the last few weeks about it," he said, "than in all my life before. It is impossible to understand the South without visiting it, living in it for a time. Take the sudden coming on of summer, for instance. You are accused of indolence. With such a tidal wave of heat upon you, all at once, and to last so long, how can you help turning over all exertion to the blacks, who seem to enjoy it, seem to be the stronger for it?"

"But suppose we no longer own any blacks to turn it over to?" said the young lady. "I can imagine our young men, yes, and our young ladies too, determining not to yield to the heat or to anything else. If it is a wave, as you say, I hope they will come to rise upon it in some way, to be lifted up by it instead. We influenced the country, notwithstanding the heat, up to the war. If it had not been for a mere handful of weak and wicked men, North and South, my father used to say, we would have done so still, and had no war. We were overpowered by your numbers then, less than we were by the weakness of a few of our own leaders. Our day is coming again. As soon," she said, laughing, but meaning it all, "as we can understand things, can adjust ourselves to them. Wait until *we* are on the stage, we of the new generation. At least we intend to try," she added.

"I have not the least doubt of your success," their visitor remarked as he took his leave, and his manner in saying so brought yet more color to her cheeks. But it was not of her, beautiful as she was, that he reflected so seriously as he rode slowly back to Clairsville. Horace Dunwoddie? what was he trying to do?

CHAPTER XVII.

AN UNPOPULAR PREACHER.

"This world is like the player's ball;
  Smit by his oaken bat, it flies;
Then by some other in its fall
  Is struck again toward the skies;
All motion, since the earth began,
  It gets by sturdy blows from man.
Smit by some hero, it ascends,
  And makes an Era in the air;
To strike again as it descends
  A stronger still is waiting there.
Let other force be what you please,
Earth's grandest motion is from these."

AMONG many other things thought of by Gamaliel Middleton as he walked to his hotel in Clairsville was in what manner he could arrange to hear Anderson Parker preach next day. It was plain that this black Socrates held him in profound aversion. The negro's feeling towards him was worse than dislike—it was a deep-seated hate. The trouble with the white man was that he did not understand his enemy, and could not carry out his plans promptly from not being able to see clearly. He had that sagacity, however, which caused him to feel his ignorance and to be cautious accordingly.

"What can this black buffalo mean?" he demanded of himself as he walked. "And I wonder if it can be because this beauty is so dark, at least of eyes, that she, too, is so unfathomable. Mrs. Dunwoddie is a blonde, and she sees—*sees*—because she loves so utterly. Who would have supposed that a little town, sandy, level, dull, a million of miles from the world, could have produced such people? I must understand things better; but how to do it?"

This question had reference to his going to hear Anderson Parker. Mr. Middleton had once on a time been leader of a successful negro-minstrel troup, as he had once been a good many other things; and it flashed upon him, only for a moment however, to blacken his face as of old, and pass himself as a colored brother from a distance. But he had the slow eyes of Mrs. Anderson's manager upon him, in imagination, as he thought of it, and knew he would be detected. Very unwillingly he fell back upon the idea of learning more of the black from Leonidas Dunwoddie, or, and still better, from Yellow Jessamine.

Mr. Middleton had not put on his best clothing after his first Sunday in Clairsville. Before that day was ended he saw that the nearest approach to such style of apparel was on the part of the colored people, and it had hastened his adopting, instead, the plainer costume of the whites. The church of the "black folks" was the old warehouse, already mentioned, belonging to the Anderson estate, and upon the end of it, nearest Clairsville, in the suburbs of the town, indeed. The day following his visit to Mrs. Anderson was Sunday, and he stood in the door of his hotel watching the crowds of negroes on their way to preaching through the hot afternoon. The splendor of their attire had been a fresh astonishment to him every Sunday. On this day the disease of dress seemed to be raging with a fiercer fever than ever. The women, as they passed in all their shades of blood and color, from a blackness only less than that of Anderson Parker up to a fairness almost rivalling that of the purest Caucasian race, were alike in being almost superbly dressed. Middleton gasped at the sight of the silks, shawls, finely worked underskirts, gloves, and expensive parasols, which passed in procession before him. But the women were, if possible, outdone by the men. Rarely had the stranger seen a more perfectly dressed gentleman than was Leonidas Dunwoddie, who lifted the finest of silk hats to him in going by. All that broadcloth and white Marseilles, snowy linen and yellow kids, gold chain and highly polished boots could do to set off the person was done and overdone. He thought so at least until, a few moments after, Yellow Jessamine passed, with an expense and elaboration of attire which threw even his rival into the shade. A woman accompanied the highly perfumed gallant, and Middleton would have sworn to her, had he seen her on Broadway, as one of the most striking, and certainly the most expensively arrayed, of white women. As with many of the men, of whom he was but a leading specimen, Yellow Jessamine carried a silk umbrella with a handle of carved ivory to protect him from the sun. Small wonder, apart from the hard times, that the whites came to church dressed so plainly. The throngs of colored people poured along the dusty and dull streets like a pageant, the highly colored neckties of the men, the gay ribbons and amazing bonnets of the women, leaving more the impression of a circus than of Sunday; and Middleton regretted more than ever that he dared not go to their church.

The building used for worship had been whitewashed without and within. It was open to the shingles of the cavernous roof overhead, and was fitted up with rude benches. The house seated several hundred, and was densely crowded. The varieties of white and yellow and black in the faces of those present, the many-colored clothing, the multitudes of fans adding their hues as well as motion to the spectacle, made it as diversified as could be wished. Anderson Parker occupied the pulpit at the end. One patriarchal negro, with white hair, was with him in the place of honor, but there were quite a number of colored preachers in the congregation who made up for their exclusion from the pulpit by singing that much the more vigor-

ously. One voice would start a familiar hymn, but, with the second line, the whole audience would join in, and no sooner was one hymn ended than a voice in a different part of the room would begin another, in which all would follow. The singing was in keeping with the tropical hues of the people. There was the softness, sweetness, and the luscious richness, too, and ripeness, as of pineapple and banana, in the music. The accuracy of the various parts was beyond that which comes from instruction and practice, because it was as much an affair of natural gift as with the mocking-birds, and every line was colored, as it were, by the hearts of those that sang. Song after song; it seemed as if it would never end; as if it were impossible for any one to get himself out of the ever-renewed volume of melody. It was a voluptuous enjoyment which no one was willing should cease.

Even Anderson Parker, who had been for some time standing up in the pulpit, his Bible in one hand and motioning with the other, could not arrest it. Watching his opportunity at last, just before a chorus came to an end, he began to pray. His voice was so powerful from the first, although the words were slow in coming, that it gradually bore down all other sound like a strong wind against an inrolling sea. "Thou knowest, O God," he prayed, "dat song is good, an' thou knowest dat song is not always sense. In dis book is *thy* voice, an' we will shet up now an' hear God speak some;" and with a voice which more and more held every ear, he proceeded to ask for such a presence of their Maker as would keep everybody quiet. The man was undoubtedly addressing himself to one whose companionship was closer to him than that of his sable congregation. It was plain that there was a deep and sullen and defiant insurrection against their leader on the part of the people, and the effort of the one praying seemed to be to get into yet nearer relations to God in view of what he was about to do. In virtue of becoming absorbed himself, he absorbed the rest more and more in his supplication. The amens were becoming so frequent that his voice had to rise stronger and stronger, and as if from a reserve capable of anything. Suddenly, and with almost electric effect, a woman's shrill scream, "Glory! glory!" rang out upon the excitable congregation, and on the instant the preacher had done praying, and was reading aloud from the Bible. The change to the level of a slow and somewhat monotonous tone seemed to strike out all foundation for any enthusiasm, and there was a general silence. Throughout the South, when negroes are the hearers, no part of Scripture is quite so popular as the story of the leading of the Israelites out of Egypt; and Anderson Parker read it with increasing fluency, adding a word now and then of comment to identify the case of the Israelites with their own. He secured the unbroken attention of the people at last, with only an occasional "Bress de Lord," and "Yes, dat's so," from some one here and there, which but deepened the fervor. Carrying them up to the moment when, rescued from their oppressors, the Hebrews were standing in their greatest peril upon the edge of the Red Sea, the Egyptians pressing upon them from behind, the preacher read in full career—

"And de Lord said unto Moses, 'Wherefore criest thou unto me? Speak unto the children of Israel dat dey go forward,'" and then, shutting the book, he said with his utmost force—

"Go forward! The Lord says it to us— Go forward! Look here!" he continued rapidly, and so as to hold their strained interest. "See how it is," and he ran a rapid parallel yet once more, showing how often he had thought it over, between the Jews and themselves, depicting every point of slavery, plague, unbelief, deliverance, with graphic plainness up to the same point, and then rang his text upon their ears once more—

"Go forward! We are free! It was God did it. But we ain't out of Egypt yet. Canaan is right 'fore us. But we hain't got dere!"

"Bress de Lord, we soon will be dar," came from the old patriarch in the pulpit, beside the speaker.

"Yes, Farder Jones," he continued with increasing force, "dat is death. But dat is one thing. I'm talking about anudder. You can't keep from dyin' when dat comes. But de Jews wasn't dyin'. Dey was standin' still. 'Go forward' was to make 'em go. Go, when dey could go and didn't want to go. Some people likes to preach about dyin'—Brudder Erkle down dar, Brudder Poskins, Brudder Johnson, an' de like; Yellow Jessamine, he loves to preach about hebben. Dat is dere gift. But I hain't got dere gift. It's livin' I want to talk about. Look here! Most of us is got a good long time to live in dis world, please de Lord! Our people will be here hunders and hunders of years after we are gone. We must get ahead in dis world of where we now is. Must give our chillern such a start dat dey will give dere chillern such a bigger start along dat some day de Red Sea will be way behind. And how? Look here! I'll tell you what wont do it."

And the speaker earnestly proceeded, as against a counter sentiment of his hearers, to argue that singing was good, but that mere singing would not put them along.

"'Member," he said, "what corn-shuckin's we used to hab? Pile of corn almost as big as dis house, fifty black folks round it. We nebber sing now as we used to sing dose days! An' how dat corn would fly, ebbry ear shucked afore mornin'! De singin' was splendid — you could hear it miles an' miles. But it wasn't de singin' did it, it was de shuckin' goin' wid de singin'. Heh?" And the speaker wiped his forehead with his handkerchief hanging in a loop around his neck. "Go forward!" he exclaimed. "And it isn't readin' de blessed book only." Here he urged a thorough study of the Bible, in order to add, "Is dat all? God talks to you in dis book. S'pose you hear him, an' hear him, an' hear him, and keep sayin', 'Yes, sir,' an' 'Yes, sir,' an' 'Yes, sir?' What's de use of hearin' what he say unless you go and *do* it?"

Next he warned them, after fully urging the duty of prayer, against thinking that mere praying would do everything for them.

"Look dar at Moses!" he explained. "He was in a mighty tight place, sure. An' he stood dere cryin'. Yes, like a big baby, bress you, cryin' to de Lord. Best thing he could do, till de Lord said unto Moses, 'Wherefore criest thou unto me? Speak unto the chillern of Israel dat dey go forward! Start—march—get ahead— go on!' S'pose dey had just stopped dar cryin', cryin', cryin'; and dat is jest what you are doin'!" Which fact the speaker enforced with more power than politeness.

In the same way he proceeded to show that their class-meetings did no good, except as they helped them mutually onward. The bread and the wine of the sacrament was to give them heavenly help to go forward. In pathetic language he spoke of Christ, who had died to lead them further along. The man had evidently given himself up to one idea, and he wiped his face for a new onset, as, beginning afresh, he told them very definitely what held them back. As it appeared from the after-history of the Jews, it was the fish of Egypt, the cucumbers and the melons, the leeks, the onions, and the garlic; so with them.

There was the eloquence of fearless and personal application in all that followed. No one there could help being affected by this, as by the singing and fervent praying. Besides, there was the power in the speaker of being, perhaps, the largest man present; of having been in the Legislature, and, still more, of having despised and abandoned it. Moreover, all knew him to be by

far the richest colored man in all that region, if not in the whole state, and as generous as he was rich. His reputation for honesty, temperance, and good sense was universal. There was an elevation and breadth about him which separated him from them, and yet a force as of undeniable fact in all that he said, in virtue of which he was obeyed by his audience now as he was by his field-hands in the cotton-patch. Only a person born among such scenes can understand how much his homely garb, his language exactly their own, his exceeding blackness, gave him the leverage, so to speak, of being one of them himself.

At least for the moment every one present yielded himself to Anderson Parker, or Parker Anderson, as he was called indifferently, as to a natural leader, when he assured them now of his love for them, of his having no other object but to enable them to go forward, of his considering himself sent to them that day from God for this. It was old Bishop Latimer plying the flail in his sturdy way. There was such a passion of conviction that the most ignorant and debased there yielded to him and to their own conscience as he pressed home the history of the Hebrews.

"You hanker after de *fish*, do you? Dere is no white man here?" the orator continued. "An' do you want to know what *your* fish is?" There was an apprehensive silence; and, leaning over the pulpit, he said in a low whisper heard in the farthest corner—

"Bretherin an' sisters, your fish, de miserable catfish of Egypt, is—*chickins!*" Not an individual smiled, and the many exclamations of "*Dat's* so!" from various parts of the room seemed to express the general assent. It was a delicate subject. Leoidas Dunwoddie was also an occasional preacher, and the Colonel had urged upon him the duty of exhorting his hearers against the stealing which spared harc a poultry-yard in the county. This div had excused himself from doing so or very just plea, "Dat it would frow a cold-ness over de meetin;" and even the present speaker but touched upon it. "And do you know what *leeks* stands for?" he continued. "Help you to 'member—fish, F., stands for fowls. Well, leeks, L., stands for *laziness*."

Very graphic was the picture he went on to draw of that sinful yearning backward.

"An' cucumbers? It's *cow*-cumbers those people meant. What cowcumbers stand for? It begins," the speaker continued, "with a C. C? Canned fruit, sure's you live! It is amazin' to me you folks can spend your money dat way. Canned peaches, canned pears, canned oysters — what *you* got to do wid oysters? Some of you people buy canned corn, an' peas, an' sichike de Lord is sendin' you in your own patch, if you'd wait. An' C. stands for candy, as if we was babies; an' cranberries —ain't *our* berries good enough? The Hebrews longed for onions. My friends, dat was de sort of tobacco dey used in Egypt, it least may be so. Do you know how much money you pay out in a year for *dat?*" And the practical preacher told them the average sum, and how far it would go towards buying a home.

"Den dere is garlic. G. stands for gin, rum, whiskey," and the orator made a brief but forcible temperance address at this point.

"Dere is one more thing you hanker after," he continued, "leavin' out some things too bad to talk about in dis sacred place. It is—melons. It begins with an M. M? M? It means—what's de worst thing yet. All of you don't sin in de way I done mentioned, may be one or two don't, but you *all* do in dis. M? It stands for—*much*

their Maker. "Just take one good look at dem, O Lord," and he lifted and let fall, and lifted again, the people upon his muscular arms under the divine scrutiny in a way which was uncomfortable to the last degree to his hearers. Then, with sudden change into almost ferocity of rebuke—

"What you doin' wid dem handkerchers? Wipe off de sweat? What use dis bright Sabber-day you got for dem parasols and umborellas? Sun spile your skin? You mis'rable fools—I beg pardon, I mean dear bred'ren an' sisters—will you let me tell you de truf? One half of all de little you make you put in your belly. De odder half it goes on your back, you poor sinners, an' you know it."

But the man was sensible, and he was not so impassioned as not to feel that he had reached the utmost bounds of rhetoric.

"Sit down, Yaller Jessamine — you sit down," he said, as that individual had arisen to walk out or to reply. "You's a mighty big butterfly now, but you was only a grub a little ago. An' very soon you will be among de worms once more—yes, you an' all your fine fixins will lie a moulderin' in de silent tomb. An' den, whar will your soul be? Dat fool in de good book say to his soul, 'Soul, eat, drink, and be merry;' he talk to his soul as if it could eat an' drink, as if his *soul*, all de soul he knew of, was his—*belly!*"

"One las' thing, an' I is done," he added. "Dere is one thing not down here. De Jews wasn't tempted to it in Egypt. Dey went crazy about bread an' water in de wilderness, but not about dat. Dem people made wood gods to pray to in Canaan, but dey steer clear ob *one* thing."

There was a sensation through the audone before, the story of his own experiences at the Legislature and since. The mean white men, and the ignorant dupes among the negroes; the members openly paid for their votes; the champagne and cigars, and almost everything else, charged as stationery; the lying and perjury; the whole miserable story over again of corruption and gluttonous greed.

Somehow, and while yet an ignorant slave, he had vaguely imagined wonderful things in regard to freedom. Almost up to the day of emancipation it had been to him a sort of unutterable blessedness, as glorious and more out of reach than heaven. His reverence for Judge Anderson, the majestic old statesman, had given him, also, the most exalted ideas of the political working of freedom. Nature had cursed him, as it had Aristides the Just, with an excess of the instinct of honesty and truth. Moreover, he was so ignorant as to suppose that the fraud and falsehood he saw at the ballot-box and in the Legislature had never been 'nown among men before. He was so dis- 'hat he thought of little else; his . '- and politicians had become t.. ; of his large but uncultivated nature. i. would have grown into an insanity almost had not the tropical force of the semi-savage taken the direction of hard work with a view to owning a home for himself; and this he now urged upon the people as the duty, laying aside their foolish expenditure and attention to politics, of every one. He proved it by telling them about prices, wages, expenses, and then described the little farm every man might have, with its fields and cows and horses, swarms of children and hives of bees, its barns and orchards and poultry. It may not have been a sermon, but it was eloquent.

Then he told them of the advantages of samine was not the only one present who had been hit by his sharp personalities, and they yielded themselves to him as to a current too broad and strong to be resisted —never so powerful as when, in the end, he urged upon them to be Christians indeed. He closed, as negro preaching always does, with a rapturous description of heaven, leaving the people as tired as after a day's work when they stood up for prayer. This was put up by "ole Farder Jones," who was the chief authority in religious experience, and who now begged help from God that the people might do what the preacher had taught. The utterances of the patriarch, trembling at first, became more and more impassioned, and closed in universal amens. Before he was well ended a clear voice at the other end of the building struck up, all joining in—

> "When Israel was in Egypt land:
>   Let my people go!
> Oppressed so hard dey could not stand:
>   Let my people go!
> Go down Moses, way down in Egypt land:
>   Tell ole Pharaoh, let my people go!"

There were about twenty verses. Middleton, awakened by the singing from a nap in his room, nearly a mile away, thought the hymn never would end. But he agreed also that he had never heard genuine music before; there certainly was the plenty as well as the lusciousness of the Equator in it.

The preacher joined in, but he felt all along that the seed which he had tried to sow was being swept away by the sheer force of this freshet of song. And so the services ended with the setting sun. There was the usual and universal handshaking following upon this, but very few seemed disposed either to thank him or to shake hands with him. Alas for Anderson Parker, he did not know it, but he was in advance of his age.

"If Providence hath eyes for me,
  Providence hath hands to smite;
If Providence Good Shepherd be,
  Providence the wolf must fight;
If Providence hath heart to feel,
  Providence hath brain to know;
If Providence doth work my weal,
  Providence must work my woe;
If Providence be more than luck,
  Providence must wield the rod;
If Providence be more than Puck,
  Prov'dence is the mighty God."

GAMALIEL MIDDLETON had once been, as has been said, a negro - minstrel. But he had also been a school - teacher at one time, and a lawyer at another. As to that, he had been, at a variety of dates and places, an actor, a book-agent, a solicitor for more than one insurance company, a breeder and runner of race-horses, an eminent spiritual medium, a detective, and a hotel-keeper. It is to be feared that, in all instances, he was to the character represented what he was to the *bona-fide* negro when, with corked face and exaggerated collar, he personated him. But Middleton was not without his modesty. He would have disliked it if any citizen in Clairsville had recognized him as one he had heard lecture, with a stereopticon, upon the wonders of the microscope, in a Northern State. Since he did his best to forget it himself, it is less to be wondered at that he never revealed the fact, therefore, that he had once been a clergyman, and was, for a very brief period, a pastor, admired for his eloquence as well as for his social qualities. The truth is, Middleton had more reasons than the purchase of lands for sojourning in the South, which presented so wide and tempting a field for fresh experiments.

Not that he troubled himself except as to his own personal success. He had been as unfortunate as a boy could well be, in his parents and in his—it cannot be called home, for he had never had in all his life anything which was really a home. As an unusually bright and handsome child, he

had been tossed from hand to hand among people who became tired of him in proportion as they were struck with him at first. He had attended dozens of schools as he grew up, gathering a vast deal of knowledge very rapidly, and forgetting nothing. He had taken prizes at more than one college — had visited Europe. His movements through life had of necessity been rapid. Moreover, he had that freshness of complexion, as of manner, which made him seem many years younger than he really was. In addition to all, the character he assumed for any emergency, not merely cleaved to him while being worn, like the tights of a trapeze performer, but had the power of making him to *be* what, for the moment, he seemed.

At the bottom of his soul his creed consisted of two articles:

"First. I am the creature of circumstances.

"Second. Whatever happens, I must look out for myself."

The sole object of his sojourn in Clairsville was to accomplish certain exceedingly definite objects coming under the last head. Among these were two which he had immediately in hand—the two being, in fact, two ladies. One or the other of these he must marry, and, by marrying, put himself in a position beyond all he had hitherto dared to hope for. Once on a time he had been a conjurer at twenty-five cents admittance, and nothing was easier for him than to keep half-a-dozen balls in the air at the same moment. There were but two balls in this instance, but then they were balls which had wills, too, of their own. Moreover, the failing to catch one had to be so managed as not thereby to cause him to miss securing the other.

Mr. Middleton studied the situation as he had often done a problem in chess. There was Alice Dunwoddie, she would have her share in Alec's money, but she was homely, and had seen nothing of the world; she had come into her early womanhood through dark and trying times. Like her father in this respect, also, the poor girl had an amount of nervous energy too great either for her body or her environment. Full of aspiration as vague as it was ardent, Alice Dunwoddie was steady in but one thing, and that was, dissatisfaction with herself. She was a good Christian girl, and yet one night, in the excess of her misery, she told her mother that she was a wicked, wicked woman! Mrs. Dunwoddie was terrified at the confession, made as it was in an agony of tears; but was relieved to know, on tenderly questioning her daughter, that Alice had neither done nor said, thought nor felt anything in particular that was wrong. She was miserable, that was all, except that her misery took to her the hues of guilt.

Middleton was very careful in his intercourse with her. He knew that he could win her heart and hand with the greatest ease and at the shortest notice, if that should prove to be the best thing for him to do. While that was uncertain he could afford to be guarded, especially as he felt that the eyes of the mother were upon them both with a power of seeing only less than that of God.

He was like a knight of old who had so trained his hawk that he could send it after the farthest heron, or, at a whistle, recall it to alight on his wrist. So very often had he let loose his heart after some beauty and then recalled it to his hand, that he could love or not love, as he thought wisest; could love precisely so far and so long and then whistle back his heart, and ride merrily away to other fields. For sufficient reasons, the knightly huntsman, in this instance, regarded Miss Anderson as the most valuable game; but just now he must wait. Especially as he had his sister to bring into the field for an object equally important, he must do nothing, and that as carefully as possible.

A few days after Anderson Parker's sermon he dropped in upon Yellow Jessamine to be shaved, and obtained, during the process, a full and indignant outline of the doctrine thereof.

"As sure as you live, sah, dat unpopular Anderson, as people call him, will get himself into trouble," the mulatto remarked. The white man had heard of a war of races—say of white against black—but he learned, before Yellow Jessamine had got through with his soap and razor, towels and bay-rum, that the war between the half white and the black makes up often in venom for what it lacks in vigor. There was that in the exasperated barber which reminded Middleton of the yellow adders he had been terrified by once or twice since coming South; there was an oily horror about them which no mere snake could inspire. He knew by the vehemence with which the other attacked Parker, by a certain hurried motion — even trembl' of his hands — as he manipulated h... with comb and brush, that the mulatto was deeply excited; but, although he showed great interest in all that Jessamine said, he could induce him to say but little in regard to the black, and that guardedly.

"They tell me you are a preacher, too?" he said to him at last.

"Yes, sir, but I don't b'long to *his* 'nomination," the man said, with great contempt, and mentioned his own with pride. Both denominations stood on an equal footing with any in the land; and, remembering the queer pictures in Jessamine's back-room, as well as other things he had heard of the practices of the man, Middleton was perplexed. Evidently there were things in Clairsville he had yet to understand. He could see this much, however, that the black represented the original African—slow, sensible, faithful, capable of any amount of heat and work; the mulatto, quick in body and mind, smart—not sensible—treacherous, incapable in general of anything beyond the work of barber or waiter—the twilight, in a word, between the two races, and destined, as twilight invariably is, to perish.

From his barber Middleton went in the freshness of his personal adornment to call at Col. Dunwoddie's house. He found no one at home but Mrs. Dunwoddie.

"I am glad your son has gone," he said to her, after some conversation on other matters.

"He desired to go," Mrs. Dunwoddie replied, "and the Colonel and myself were entirely willing." She was seated in her usual chair, knitting. It was a pleasant afternoon, and the honeysuckles upon the piazza, where they were conversing, gave at once shade and fragrance.

"I know how carefully he has been trained, or I would fear for him," her visitor said, with engaging frankness. "Virginia City, for instance, is —" the gentleman closed his eyes for a moment to shut out sight, and opened them again to add— "is unspeakable."

"You told us so," the lady said. "But that is our happiness — in our children. Horace has an impulsive nature, but except that, he is all we could wish."

"Col. Dunwoddie told me," the other remarked, "that he could rely as implicitly upon him as upon yourself, and I cannot think of higher praise. He certainly seems to be a noble young man. There is more purpose in him, more energy of character, than seems to be common in—pardon me—this warm latitude."

"That is partly because the household was devolved upon him when he was a boy —when his father was in the army. But," he added, "we are foolish in regard to Horace, and in some points cannot fully understand him. Like Emmeline Anderson, he belongs to a different period. It is a broader and a grander period, I suppose," Mrs. Dunwoddie said; "but I am like Mrs. Anderson. My heart is in the past. That I know very well; but it is gone forever. Heaven so orders it, and I am content. The new world belongs to the young, and—" she paused a moment—"and to the strong. Have you heard from your sister lately, Mr. Middleton?"

The gentleman had received a letter that morning. He took it eagerly from his breast-pocket, and read parts of it. His sister gave a lively description of her school, of an opera she had attended the night before, of a church wedding, of the return of certain friends from Europe, as also a half-page in reference to a popular preacher, and devoted a whole one to the latest fashions both for gentlemen and ladies. It was a breath from a very different world than that of Clair County, and Mrs. Dunwoddie took a woman's pleasure in it.

"Clara is not pretty—that is, not very," her brother said, as he folded the letter, "but she is amiable, and she has all the accomplishments. You will know her — I hope will like her. As soon as I can arrange it she will join me here. We are alone in the world. I think she will be charmed with the South."

"Only for a while, I fear," Mrs. Dunwoddie said, after expressing her pleasure at the prospect of knowing the young lady. "Clairsville must be wearisome to one accustomed to a gayer life. Do you know, sir," she continued, "that there is no question which presses upon Southern parents more painfully than as to their daughters? Before the war everybody was prosperous; all that our girls had to do was to bloom as free from care as the flowers. It is all changed now. What can our young girls do as a means of living? They cannot all find schools to teach. If there were stores, factories, other businesses as elsewhere, it is not the custom for them to work in that way; they shrink from it, most of them, with horror."

"I understand, madam," Middleton said, "and there is a phase of the matter worse than all." He hesitated, but, determined to bring himself in closest relations to the other, he ventured to add, "Unless I mistake, madam, before your young men were devoured by the war, every young lady was, more or less, the centre of a circle of suitors. Young men, I would judge, esteemed themselves fortunate in winning a lady's love. Now I have been, madam, where it was too much the other way. I have known young ladies who have been trained to believe that it was their chief end in life to marry, and that marriage was not an easy thing to attain. It is disgusting, the way in which young men—the rascals—talk among themselves of the eagerness and hundred petty devices to secure a husband shown by such women. Men are conceited enough already. I mention it at all because with the Misses Dunwoddie it will, of course, be, and on every account"— with a bow—" so different. I hope," he added, in his sincerest manner, "that in the South they may never lose that deference for woman which is the highest mark of a gentleman;" and, beneath his respectful air, he congratulated himself that he was securing the esteem of good Mrs. Dunwoddie.

"These new times seem terrible to you, madam, on other grounds," he felt encouraged to proceed. "If I might say it, your sudden wealth seems to you like the coming almost of an enemy. Is it not so?"

The lady looked at her visitor more intently. She must understand him more thoroughly.

"I mention this," he said, aware of her thought, "because I can sympathize with you. Not that I have ever been rich myself. I refer to the suddenness with which events have befallen me. They come to me more rapidly—unexpectedly—I may say, abundantly—than is common to men. I certainly have had, madam, a remarkable life. Everything has been uncertain to me since I could remember. Many a time I have set my heart upon something—have worked and watched, and waited for it—for, oh, how long! It seemed as if the end never would come. When it did it was always unlike what I had expected. And that end was but the beginning of another, perhaps

still longer course of things yet more perplexing. May I ask, Mrs. Dunwoddie, you *do* believe, do you not, that there *is* a Providence?—a special Providence?"

Had he been the most ingenuous boy in her Sunday-school, when her health allowed her to have a class, he could not have looked up at her from the low stool upon which he had insisted upon seating himself, with a more innocent gaze.

"I do, sir," she replied, "and in a Providence which is special in more senses than one. Let me explain, for I think we often mistake. People generally mean by Providence a father fondly loving them, who will overrule matters in the end in their favor. Is it not so?"

What did this good woman mean? Was it possible she knew? Her eyes were full upon his, pushing him back like the soft palms of powerful hands into the past. He had been, not merely a clergyman, but, in his own estimation and that of others, a fervent believer. Long ago he had given all that up, because it had become very plain to him that, notwithstanding an inconceivable amount of praying, God, if there was a God, cared no more for him than if he were a mosquito.

"To some of us," the lady said, "Providence is—I speak deliberately—a superannuated grandmother, very great only in being very weak. I learned a lesson in regard to that from Judge Anderson. Shall I tell you?" she asked.

"If you please," the other said, but with less interest than apprehension.

"Judge Anderson," she continued, "was distinguished for his stern integrity and thorough, and, I am afraid, contemptuous knowledge of men. He attended church, but was not a Christian. The Colonel and myself were with him a good deal after the Confederacy began falling into ruin, as for many weeks before his death he did not leave his chair. The loss of his property, and of his sons in addition to all else, hastened his end. He had his peculiarities, and it was, I think, because he had been upon the Supreme Bench so long; but he wished to die sitting up, and as decorously as he had lived. I was knitting by his side one afternoon, no one else present, and he said to me, 'You have thought, madam, that I was an unbeliever. It is a subject upon which, like Washington, I never converse; but I wished to say to you that my unbelief has been in reference to the professors of religion. During this war I have come to a full faith in the one they so lightly style their Master. Wait, madam,' he added, as he saw that I was about to express my gratification, 'I believe in him in one way,' he said. 'I have watched the progress of our strife with the North from the beginning to the end. A vast variety of men, of interests, of terrible events have been mixed up in it; yet through, and by means of, and over them all, results have been reached that no man living ever imagined. From this, madam, I have come to know that there is a God—a God who controls the coolest plans as well as the stormiest passions of men to his own ends. According to the Bible, Christ is advancing to the dominion of the race, and his diplomacy is wonderful. And, madam,' he added, in his grave way, 'it is very terrible! You Christians fail to understand him in that. He is no longer the dying Saviour, madam. He is also a *king!* a dreadful sovereign! All the world lies dashed to pieces —to dust—around me, madam, by his hand, North as well as South, like a potter's vessel!' I can never forget," Mrs. Dunwoddie added, "how, his white head thrown back in his chair, his arms slowly lifted up with his great and serious eyes, he said, as if to one present before him, 'I love thee, O Son of God, because I respect thee. I adore thee, because I fear thee. Thy throne, O God, is for ever and ever. The sceptre of thy kingdom is a *right* sceptre. Thou lovest righteousness and hatest wickedness. *Therefore*, God, thy God hath anointed thee with the oil of gladness above thy fellows!'"

There was a pause, and the lady continued: "He died that night in peace, and his has become my idea of Providence, sir. God never ceases to be a Father who is also a *King*. Christ never orders matters for our happiness except as happiness comes to us from our being made better. He trod down his own life when it was in the way, and he never spares us."

"He certainly has not dealt with *me* with the pitiful tenderness that Sunday-school books babble about. I have had strong desires, madam, ardent—I may say impassioned—hopes, hopes, too, that were natural and proper, yet I have been invariably defeated. Often they were for things so small, so easily granted, and for which I had worked so long and so hard! Very little dandling on the knee *I* have had, I assure you!" Middleton said this bitterly, and regretted it the next moment. Why should he bother himself about the spectral illusions he had abandoned long ago? All he cared for was to ingratiate himself with a good woman, who was also extremely observant.

"You asked me about Providence," she added. "Yes, sir, you and I are watched over by one who loves us, and who therefore holds a drawn sword in his hand as he does it."

It was as if the man's conscience had taken flesh and was speaking to him through her lips. She was surprised at her own boldness, weak in health as she was, too.

"I wish I could have got a firmer hold upon her," Middleton said to himself, as he undressed for the night. "Instead of that, she took me in hand as if I were a naughty child. Which I am! But it is all nonsense. All I ever have I must *get*. The only person in the universe I care for, or am at all afraid of is — Gamaliel Middleton. Take exceeding care of yourself, my boy; you are the only providence there is, as far as you are concerned." And, his system being so simple, the philosopher went to bed and to sleep.

CHAPTER XIX.

HORACE DUNWODDIE GOES ABROAD.

"The eaglet in its eyrie curled,
Asleep or feeding, never saw
Beyond its realm of sticks and straw,
The rim of rocks which is its world:

"Till launched upon the boundless main
Of earth and sea, of air and skies,
Upon imperial wings it flies;
Nor is its nest its world again."

IF any one in the cars with Horace Dunwoddie had noticed him at all as the train ran out of the Clairsville Depot, it would have been to say, at best, "Hah! fine young fellow, that!" None the less was he, in the splendid realm of his own enjoyment, a crown-prince, if not an emperor. True, he could not swear that Emmeline Anderson loved him; there was an uncertainty as to that which gave charm and attraction to his imperial future. With humility the most abject he reasoned with himself.

"How is it possible that one such as I am can ever come into the ownership of this the most glorious woman Heaven ever made? It is madness to think of it. From this instant I cast it out of my mind forever!" All the time, like the steady drone of a bag-pipe under every variation of tune, ran arrogance, too, the most insolent:

"I am the one man in all the world for her, and she knows it. In the end she cannot help loving me, meanwhile I love her with all my soul, and that is next best, that is sufficient until then." From the hour he left Clairsville this love of his was the chariot in which he rode, out of which, wherever he went, he never descended.

It was from this rather than from his car that he noticed the change in things as the hours passed by. The post-oak levels gave place to a sandier region yet, whose only growth was pine-trees and sassafras, swine all snout, negroes all rags, poor whites seemingly all lice and laziness. He reminded himself that all this was to the South but as the husk is to the corn; and

as there was an abundance of things more pleasant to occupy him, he shut out the world with his hat drawn down over his eyes, and took to planning out his whole future that much the more vigorously. As night fell, the cars stopped for a while at the most deplorable of stations, while he ate a supper still more deplorable, paying a price for it, considering its quality, most deplorable of all. But the hot dough, fried cabbage, and black coffee were trifles to a digestion such as his. Coiling himself up in his berth in the sleeping-car, after feeling that his money-belt and purse were all right, he entered with fresh energy upon his plans for life, changing this, that, and the other, creating a new universe — enthroning Emmeline Anderson upon every height and turn — planning — planning — planning.

To wake up as in a moment to a brilliant morning, and to find himself in a city which appeared to him the summit of all civilization. Clair County was all at once merely a memory of his childhood, and he walked the crowded streets of what seemed a city of palaces with a feeling as if, for the first time in his life, he was getting into his own element. The world lay around him broader, brighter, more bracing; he rejoiced above all that he was no longer the young and inexperienced person he had been yesterday. Making his home at what was to him the most magnificent of hotels, the city and its splendors open before him, his chief enjoyment was in being completely master of himself. He had a sense of ownership in everything second only to that of Sardanapalus, in fact, when he made his discursive meals at a round table in the gorgeous dining-room, all to himself, the waiter behind his chair existing only for him. And what a pleasure it was to throw himself upon the busy life of the city. The shop windows, the rattle and crush of vehicles along the streets, the lines of granite buildings, the piles of merchandise blocking the sidewalks, the throngs of people—he was almost ashamed of the excess of pleasure he took in all this. His life had been such a sorrowful one so far, and the pressure had been as severe from either side as from above; his dungeon had been narrow as well as his burden heavy. Yes, he had looked forward to all this as the dying do to another world, and when one enters on the life after this it can be but the same feeling upon a grander scale. The gas-lighted streets, the gorgeous theatres, the very policemen with their stars and clubs—everything was a joy to him beyond expectation. Here was a volume of life, diversified, powerful, which would have smitten Clair County like a hurricane could it have been suddenly introduced along its sandy ways. How had he managed to exist away from it all these years! It was not until midnight that, after having walked many miles without weariness, he consented to go to bed. Hardly had he fallen asleep when, aroused by the bells, he dressed and hurried out again to a fire some two miles away. What enjoyment to him, freshened by his nap, the engines tearing along the streets, the vast crowds, their faces illumined by the glare of the burning buildings, the torrents of water, the red-shirted firemen periling their lives up the slender ladders and in the vortex of the roaring flames. He was drinking the wine of life sparkling and strong, and, used to the dull days of the past, how could he fail to be intoxicated!

Quickened by all he had seen during his stay into a greater eagerness to get on, he hurried away from the city a few days after his arrival. To do so he crossed the river dividing the South from the North, the steamers along the wharves being a fresh enjoyment to him.

"And this is the North of which I have heard all my life!" he said almost aloud as he stepped upon the farther bank. He had never seen a locomotive so large—he felt stronger himself at sight of it. In comparison with the narrow-gauge and dingy cars of the past, how sumptuous the train seemed, and it was so much longer too. The speed, also, after he had got aboard, was greater than he had ever known before; but how could he go slower, since a world so wide had to be crossed! Indeed, in his eagerness the most rapid rate seemed all too slow.

In the ardor of his enjoyment he congratulated himself upon making, soon after starting, the acquaintance—it would serve to sober him—of a clergyman who took a seat beside him. This gentleman wore a white cravat, which was in keeping with his pure face and silvery hair, his gentle tones and conciliating manners. He was well-informed in regard to the region through which they were travelling, and he told his young friend the names of the towns which followed upon each other with such astonishing frequency, the nature of the crops, the character of the manufactories whose towering smoke-stacks began at last to dot the landscape. Moreover, he gave him a great deal of admirable advice, from his own experience, as to the ways of the world. Nothing could have been more fortunate than the refined society of so estimable a person.

Upon their return to the cars, after taking supper at the wayside station, the pleasant-faced stranger took occasion to warn his young friend against the sharpers to whom he would be exposed, and, in the act of doing so, found to his own great distress that he had himself been robbed in the rush at the supper counter. He was left entirely without money; it was annoying to the last degree. It was absurd, he said at last, to ask such a thing of a stranger, but he had been so prepossessed with Horace Dunwoddie that he would do what otherwise nothing would force him to think of doing. If Mr. Dunwoddie would let him have his address, he would remit immediately on reaching the city where he was a pastor.

Now an intelligent companion is an excellent thing, but it is also good to have read books, to have associated much with men, although in a narrow circle, from childhood; above all, to have inherited from one's mother the faculty of looking steadily enough at an object to see it thoroughly—in fact, of seeing with the intuitions as well as with the eyes. So that the polished divine, in the very act of making his request, hesitated, stammered, changed countenance utterly, cursed his young friend with emphasis, and, passing into another car, the confidence man, for such he was, got off at the next station. Not that Horace Dunwoddie said a syllable, it was merely the smile upon his lips, the glance of amusement in his open and merry eyes.

But it was a good experience for him. As week followed upon week of perpetual change and excitement, over the prairies, among the cities, climbing the mountains, at last, of Nevada, he proved equal to his circumstances. Nothing could be more delightful than to throw himself open to all that was beautiful in river or factory, in museums or ranges of landscape, in mining operations or the breaking of morning upon the hills—nothing easier or more pleasant than this. And it rapidly became as easy, almost as pleasant, the not throwing himself open to men except as they presented themselves to him, like the landscape, in the mass. From the Colonel, his father, he had learned to sheathe himself in courtesy to all as in complete mail. Not going beyond a certain point himself in his intimacies with men, it was impossible for any one to get beyond the same limit in approaching him. In addition, he had from his mother the power of waiting, of letting people say, uninterrupted, all they had to say before replying, of quietly poising matters as in hands both strong and steady, until the moment of decision came. It was this, in connection with his otherwise frank and cordial manners, which made him a popular man from the hour of his arrival in

Nevada. There was a diversity of people there, every individual of whom had enjoyed a wonderful variety of experiences among men; but miners, hotel-keepers, gamblers, speculators, brokers, lawyers, loafers, and men who lived by hunting or prospecting, all, more or less, liked, and yet were puzzled by him. He abandoned himself utterly to the wild scenery which was so unlike that of Clair County—there was keen enjoyment in every breath of the air, in every change of the point of view, as well as in the food and the very quality of the sleep—but he did not abandon himself to anything else. Possibly the surrender was so complete towards nature that nothing was left in him for men. In a short time he had become known as the lucky "nephew" of the exceedingly lucky "Alec Allen Lode," and had plenty of warm friends. But they were all perplexed—they could not understand wherein the armor of the young fellow lay, he parried so adroitly as well as pleasantly the many offers to take a drink or an investment, to hold a hand at cards, as well as invitations other than these and worse. Even if his mother had not stood between him and the most seductive of the women of Virginia City, the most blooming and beautifully dressed of them vanished like a ghost to give place instead to the plainly dressed girl whose dark eyes were as much before him now as when he had seen them last. And so, like a white, if not a Black Prince, he kept his armor on until it became more natural to him than his clothing.

It did not take as long as he thought it would—his stay in Nevada. There were certain legal forms to be gone through; just so many letters of introduction to be delivered and honored by superintendents of mines and bank presidents; just such a verification by him in various ways of the inventory found in the money-belt, item by item. It took a good deal more time while this was being done, to toil up and down the mines, to make himself as familiar as he could with the workings of these as well as of the mills—cost, risk, loss, profit, and the like. People had much to say to him of the astounding luck of his Uncle Alec, but nothing whatever to say of his uncle himself, except as to the energy with which, amid all the pressure brought to bear upon him, he could eat and drink, smoke and sleep, and do nothing whatever besides. Then there was a good deal of hunting and fishing to be done, as well as hospitable dinners to partake of or to decline.

In one point he was signally disappointed. He had hoped to learn everything in regard to Gamaliel Middleton, and he learned nothing. It was not that everybody about Bigthing, Virginia City, and elsewhere did not know Middleton, and know him, according to their own phraseology, so well that they "didn't know anybody else." The trouble was that, on closer inquiry, the utmost that any one knew of him was, at last, very little more than of the external Middleton; about as much, and as little, as Horace Dunwoddie already knew of the man from the brief Clairsville acquaintance. When he called afterwards at the office—let it be recorded here—of the land company in the East which employed Middleton, they knew no more of him than that. They had taken such precautions that they did not care to know more. In fact, it had always been a peculiarity of that gentleman to come and go like a bird.

Horace Dunwoddie did not, however, go to the East direct from the mines. When he had finished his business in Nevada, he went for a few weeks to San Francisco. He flattered himself that, being merely the son of his father, he had managed matters, in virtue of having no power beyond that, even better than Col. Dunwoddie could himself have done. In any case, he went to California greatly relieved in mind. There was an inexpressible charm to him in the off-hand energy of the people of California, in their broad and breezy style of thought and deed as well as talk. Wherever he made himself known he was, in virtue of his father's wealth, a prince of course—that was becoming as natural to him as if he had been born to the purple. He could not realize at last that there was a time when he had not been the son of a millionaire. And yet, while Clair County lay immeasurably remote, among the earliest ages of antiquity, the whole world, future and past, still existed to him chiefly in the persons of those he loved; these never dwindled in his eyes—in fact, in comparison with these, all the race besides were but as flies and mice.

It was all very grand—the mountain ranges, the vast stretches of railway, the swarming cities, the broad Pacific, the vastness of the republic, in fact, of which he had before no conception; but even little Charlie of the sober face was more to him than all these. Distinguished men were often pointed out to him, but his only comment was, "What would these people think of such a man if they but knew my father?" The ladies who welcomed him so pleasantly to their fine houses were dressed more expensively than his mother and sisters — extravagantly, compared with Emmeline Anderson; but were these ladies to be considered superior to those he had left behind? Quite the reverse. It is amazing how bigoted a young man may be in regard to his own people; the broadening process he needed was in reference rather to persons than to places. At the outset, at least, of his experiences, it fared little better with the ladies he met than it did with the gaudily-clad images revolving with their unchanging smiles in the windows of millinery establishments, and which were melted like wax indeed in the contempt of his passing glance. It was a grander world than he had imagined, but he had adjusted himself so rapidly to it as to be fast forgetting that he had not been used to it all his life. In fact, he was becoming so far satiated with it that his chief pleasure, at last, was in writing home, and in anticipating the gratification it would be to those there to hear him tell about it.

Before leaving home he had marked out a plan of travel, and held to it. After seeing all that the West had to show to a rapid tourist, he went East and made a round of its cities. But he was not without his adventures. While walking one afternoon in the suburbs of San Francisco, he was accosted by a young widow in deep mourning, blooming although tearful, who endeavored to induce him, by a tale of children perishing for bread, to enter a house near by, which, notwithstanding her agonized entreaty, he declined to do. During his ride over the plains some one nearly succeeded in robbing him in the palatial sleeping-car. A masked thief broke into his hotel room at midnight, while in Chicago, and fled only after an exchange of shots. When he was seized upon one evening in an obscure corner of Fairmount Park, Philadelphia, by a vigorous ruffian, and nearly choked to death before he succeeded in leaving the villain with broken ribs upon the ground, he railed at the rascality of a world which so swarmed with scoundrels. Quite unjustly, since, widow and all, his assailants was the same professional, who, under a mistake as to the money he was supposed to have about his person, had followed him from Pacific to Atlantic. But these were the only adventures which he had thought best not to mention in his letters home.

As he completed his circuit through the Eastern cities, his experiences had reached a state of mere overflow, until at last, when visiting universities, navy yards, public libraries, his sole interest was, "If only my father could be with me here!" It was short work he made of art-galleries, parks, or concerts. His one feeling was, "How I *would* enjoy it if my mother were with me." He made a point of hearing popular preachers, as well as of visiting the largest dry-goods establishments in reach, for the purpose of wondering how "they" would like it. But, in all his travels, he had as yet seen nothing he considered of value sufficient for the one person of whom he thought most. Except for the necessary expenses, he had spent nothing upon himself, nor had he been extravagant in his purchases for the family.

One day he chanced to visit a celebrated jewelry-store in New York. As he leaned over a show-case he was, unconsciously to himself, under the close inspection of one of the clerks. This youth was rapidly advancing towards a junior partnership in the concern, in virtue of a twofold instinct which, in consequence of long practice, had become an almost infallible power. With miraculous certainty he could detect in the most plainly-dressed visitor the power to buy as well as to appreciate; and he saw in Horace an instance of this — the one exception out of many persons dropping in that day. With an accuracy still more unerring, the clerk could tell the precise article which such a person, however that individual might be ignorant of it, was certain to need. He now lounged up to the other side of the case, and said to him with the deference due to the very wealthy, and yet with the ease of one young man with another—

"If you will excuse the liberty, sir, I know what you are looking for. This," in a low voice, "is the only article in our establishment worthy of the young lady;" and he placed tenderly in the hand of the other a ring with one large diamond.

Young Dunwoddie was generally calm enough outside. There was an instant flame upon his cheek and forehead now, but it imperfectly expressed the conflagration kindled by the fire of the diamond within. We all know that the oxygen in the air would reduce the planet to ashes in an instant if it were not held in perpetual subjection by the nitrogen; and it was only the nitrogen in him of his mother's excellent sense which held down the fiery oxygen of his ardent nature. Had the clerk called him a liar by any chance instead, he would have struck him down with all the force he had. In this case, also, action followed as rapidly upon passion, for in a short time afterwards the young man had paid for the ring, and walked out with it in his breast-pocket. The price would have electrified Clair County, but it was all too little to express his feeling. It was but the culmination of an ever-increasing fever. He was astonished at himself; but that did not prevent his going to his hotel, packing his trunk, buying a ticket for the next train bound South, and asking for his bill while he sent out for a cab. It is true he had secured a seat for an entertainment that night which he had particularly wished to attend. He had also fully intended to visit, before going home, another city, which was really the one he had most desired to see. But he had rapidly come of late to be, in virtue of his wealth and liberty, quite a different person from the railway clerk of the Clairsville Depot. It was not only that he had become a crown-prince, but that he had suddenly come to belong to a dynasty, the wealth of which extended back beyond the memory of men. Should he not love also in a princely fashion? Especially such a woman? Who or what was to prevent his loving as heartily as he pleased? and his doing whatever his love should prompt? He would go home on the next train. He would—

As the clerk gave him his bill he handed him a telegram. He had arranged to hear from his mother very often; and, at least once a week since leaving home, had received a despatch from her. He tore it open and read—

"All as well as usual. Call at Lady Washington Institute, Fifth Avenue, and ask for Miss Clara Middleton. She will expect you. Arrange to escort her to Clairsville."

He read the telegram over and over again, especially the last line in addition to the above. What could she mean by it? But he felt her hand upon his, her kiss upon his brow, almost her voice in his ear as he read it once and again—

"Be prudent. You cannot be-too prudent.

"Your Mother."

————◆——

CHAPTER XX.

HORACE DUNWODDIE IS ACCOMPANIED BACK.

"The hardest quartz with gold is veined,
  The blackest sand with diamonds grained;
Through dryest plain some river flows,
On barest heath some blossom blows;
Through deepest woe some smile will run,
  The darkest day has bursts of sun;
To all from thorniest sheaths of sadness
There breaks some brilliant bloom of gladness."

ONE evening the Dunwoddie household were in the act of sitting down to supper, when a tall and bearded gentleman softly opened the door and, hat in hand, bowed to them, saying—

"Col. Dunwoddie, I believe? Good-evening, ladies and gentlemen."

There was a moment of astonishment, then a simultaneous outcry and a general rush upon the intruder on the part of the younger people. But he put them all aside with strong hands.

"No, George. Let go, Harry. Not yet, Alice. Go away, Miss May," and Horace Dunwoddie forced his way to his mother seated at the tea-tray. There are not many such moments in life. The long-absent son had not telegraphed, but he gave them more of a surprise than he had expected. Even little Charlie, looking on with undisturbed gravity, spoon in hand, would remember the event, photographed, as by the flash of the moment, upon his memory, as long as he lived.

"Why, mother, I believe you don't know your own son," Horace said, as he bent, quieting himself to do so, over her as she sat. She gazed up at him with her steady eyes, and yet as if in a dream. Could this man, this broad-shouldered, handsome man, this bearded gentleman with the pure fore-head and magnificent eyes, be really and truly her son? She could not realize it until he had seated himself on the low stool by her side, that she might look down upon him instead, as she was accustomed to do when he was a little child at her knee. Then her arms were around his neck and her kiss upon his brow. She merely said, "My boy!" and adjusted herself to the fact that her son was a man—fully grown.

"I have got to be so big and ugly even my mother don't like to acknowledge me," he said, as he rose to shake hands with his father and the boys, and to kiss and be very thoroughly kissed by Alice, and especially by May.

"Ugly? You are just perfectly splen-did," she said, expressing the unanimous opinion of all present. "Remember, Miss Alice," she said, "he walks with *me* to church next Sunday. And, oh, won't all the girls be dying in love with him." It was a long time before — seated for the fun of it on Charlie's high chair, and with Charlie himself in his arms—he could make a pretence, even, of eating any supper, all talking at once. May, George, and Harry insisted upon telling him, there and then, all the items of neighborhood news they could think of, and their brother did not let them see how small even the grandest events of Clair County had become to him. With quick glances he listened to each and all in turn, never failing in a single exclamation of due interest or aston-ishment. Then he gave ear to all that May had to tell him of the thrilling occurrences of school-life, wondering, however, that it was possible for his pretty sister to take such glowing interest in matters which seemed to him less than the bickering of bees in a flower.

When the young people had exhausted all their store of astonishments, the table was cleared away by the negro girls who, enjoying it as much as any, had expressed themselves as "Grad to see Mr. Horace again," although they would have felt bet-ter if they could have made it "Mars Hor-ace," as of old. Then Charlie remarked—

"Got what for Charlie?" to which point his knowledge of the language had ad-vanced.

"That's a fact, Judge—you are always the most sensible of us. I'd forgotten all about it," Horace exclaimed; and, zealously aid-ed by George and Harry and May, he drag-ged in his trunks from where the hack-man had deposited them upon the front porch, and seated himself upon the largest of them with a mournful aspect. "I did promise to bring a few things," he said in lachrymose tones, "but you have no idea how hard the times are. I was told on Wall Street that money is very tight. We all know that mother, there, can't bear to have us spend a cent. You mustn't be dis-appointed. But, economy—economy!"

It is not often one has such pure happi-ness. The younger members of the house-hold had admired everything about their brother. His very duster was of a pattern they had never seen before. So was his hat, his gloves. May fairly screamed over the carving of his umbrella-handle. She was delighted with his necktie and collar, boots, and shirt-studs—all were in advance of her previous experiences; and how could he fail to see that, in the estimation of his parents most of all, he was the noblest youth upon the planet. He had slipped a bundle into the hands of Alice, who had beckoned Charlie out unnoticed, and, as Horace was about to unlock the trunks, a little cherub walked into the room, clad in the purple of a velvet suit, with a lace collar, a plumed hat, scarlet stockings, and shoes with silver buckles. There was an outburst of admiration. The mother was weak enough to sob aloud. Charlie looked, with his fair hair and rosy cheeks, better than even she had imagined'; but it was the thoughtful love of her son which touched her most. And how could he know it was the one thing she had wished, when she had never breathed a word about it to any one?

But that was as nothing. There was a superb rifle for George, and a rosewood case with all the fishing appliances ever heard of, besides many other smaller matters. Horace piled into Harry's arms, as he stood, a London edition of his favorite Dickens, illustrated beyond his wildest hopes. May could only sob and hug, and hug her brother and sob, when she saw the dresses he had brought for her, already made, in virtue of a correspondence with Alice, who had supposed herself very confidential with her brother when he was away, until he produced others, still more handsome, for her, as the outcome of his correspondence with May; a beautiful set of jewelry included.

"Col. Dunwoddie," his son said at last, "don't be angry with me, but look at that;" and hastily writing down a certain amount on a leaf of his note-book, he tore it out and handed it to his father, whispering, as he did so, "You are worth that much more than we had supposed. I found it out at our banker's in New York since I last wrote to you. On the strength of it I got— Now I want to show you all what a wise judge Charlie is." As he said it he put upon the seat of a chair before that grave individual two watches. One was about as handsome a watch as he could find at the jewelry establishment where he had bought the diamond. In fact, the purchase of that article had been like the first glass to a toper, and the clerk again knew at a glance what he needed when he came the second time. Beside this he placed a toy-watch, gorgeous to behold.

"Now, old chap, which will you have?" he said to the child. "See what a splendid one this is," he added, holding up the gilt chain of the bauble. "Choose ahead, Judge."

The child looked at both soberly, but without a moment's hesitation took up the real watch, amid the applause of the others and their jeers at Horace.

"You will have to wear this one, sir," the eldest-born said, laughing, and handing the toy to his father. "I have no watch, you know, because I wanted you to let me have the one you've worn so long. Charlie is wiser than I thought."

"I will make it all right with Charlie," his mother said, kissing the child. "May we all judge as wisely, Horace."

"What to get for mother puzzled me," her son said. "She does not care for dresses or watches, nor for jewelry. Never mind, I brought something. But do, somebody, take this candy, here's enough for a wedding. And here are some things for the servants; Alice, suppose you take them to them."

It was not until very late that Horace could rest. When all except his parents were gone off to bed, at last, he sat down, with an exclamation—

"Bless their souls! I'm glad they're happy, and I am glad they are gone. For I love you two best."

"It is useless for your mother to lie down as yet," the Colonel said; "and now tell us something of your trip. You have written faithfully and fully, but we want to hear you, my son."

The young man paused a moment. His father had been greatly excited by his coming; but, now that the confusion was quieted down, Horace could not but notice that he was thinner and grayer than when he had left; there was an evident anxiety on his face, too, beyond all he had ever before observed. He hardly dared to do more than glance at his mother. Possibly he also felt the reaction from excitement, especially after the fatigue of travel. He gave them, none the less, a rapid but full and clear description of his tour from first to last.

"I will go over the documents with you to-morrow, sir," he said in the end. "There are some investments which should be changed, and very promptly. It will be well to make another agency in San Francisco, and a number of other matters need your attention. But I have made a thorough examination of the property, have seen every man connected with it, and I have had from people fifty urgent suggestions which I am going to beg you to disregard. As the result of all, however, you are, Col. Charles Dunwoddie, in actual money the richest man, I suppose, in the South. There is many a man worth a great deal more than you are outside the South. But, please Heaven, I do not see how, with your means, you can fail to become, some day, even with the heaviest of them. I know absolutely nothing about how easy it is to turn a large amount over, but I have found out. It is as easy, sir, as *that!*" and he turned his outstretched hand over as he said it. "Let me explain to you, sir;" and he did at length, illustrating his statements with many an anecdote he had heard in San Francisco and New York among business men.

"It is simpler than I had thought," he said at last. "There, for instance" — holding it out in his palm — "is a silver dollar. It represents one hundred cents. And there" — taking it from his purse—"is a hundred-dollar bill; instead of cents, its units are dollars, that is all. Or say the unit is a hundred dollars, or a thousand dollars; whatever it be, the unit is as easy to handle as if it were but a cent instead. You do your business by checks, and it is as easy to write the words hundred, thousand, hundred thousand, as it is to write anything less. It is merely a change of grade. Doubloons are as easily handled by a man as marbles are by a boy. A man soon forgets there is anything in it to be especially glad of. Isn't it so? The best thing about money is the freedom it gives. You don't have to bother yourself an instant as to what a thing costs—never even think of it. You are as free to go and come and do what you please as an angel."

It was very grand; but while the young man was absorbed in his narration, they were absorbed in him. They had not : posed it possible he could have improved so much. Did ever parents have such a son!

"I suppose I feel as to business," he said at last, "as my father feels in regard to a case at the bar, an editorial, a great poem. You know, mother, how I had to attend to everything when father was away fighting for the Confederacy. There are such splendid opportunities in business these days. Capital is to business what genius is to art, and I have got both from you, sir, only my genius is for business; and to think that we have been living so long in this little mousehole of a place!" But as the words escaped him he felt that he had made a mistake.

"Horace," his mother said, changing the subject, "you have told us nothing about Miss Middleton. She did come with you?"

"Come with me? Oh, yes. She kept me waiting for her a week first. I put her safe and sound in the hands of her brother at the hotel as soon as I arrived. It is the funniest idea calling a place like that a hotel."

"And what sort of a lady is she?" Mrs. Dunwoddie asked, her eyes on his.

"Well," her son replied, "she is as tall as our Alice, and as slight. Her complexion is very fair, so is her hair and eyes."

"Eyes?" his mother demanded.

"Yes, mother, why not? and she has the reddest cheeks I ever saw. Her lips are crimson, and she has beautiful teeth."

"Then she must be pretty; her brother said she was not," his mother remarked.

"Pretty? Oh, certainly. Yes, Miss Clara is pretty. I think I can say she is very pretty indeed. She could not help that, you know, and resemble her brother. Oh, yes, she is pretty," Horace added.

"How old is she?" Col. Dunwoddie demanded.

"Old? I declare, sir, I never once thought to ask her," his son said, with a light laugh. "I haven't the slightest idea. She has read all the books, has studied all the 'ologies, has seen all the pictures, attended the operas, has seen and heard, too, the great actors on the stage or in the pulpit, speaks the languages. I never felt so stupidly ignorant in my life. And, then, she plays and sings wonderfully well, and dances amazingly. You see I was at her Institute several times before we left. She has been — I would judge—all over Europe. How old? Who knows? I don't."

"She must be some years older than you are," his mother said.

"No, she isn't," her son answered warmly; "she is very young indeed. She is as girlish as you please. May is a grandmother to her in a good many things. She had a way of complaining, as we came, about little matters, like a child, getting into pets about — well, about anything. And she got angry two or three times, exactly as a spoiled child would. You see, I was her protector. I felt as if I were her venerable grandfather. Old? Not a bit of it. I had almost to pet her—to soothe her, I may say. She begged me like a child, you know, to buy candy for her, and picture papers. Once she took a violent fancy for some flowers she saw growing along the road, and almost cried—she is like a school-girl, you observe—because I wouldn't, at least, see if the conductor would not stop a moment for me to get her some. You see, we became so well acquainted before we started," he explained.

"And how does she like what she has seen of the South?" Col. Dunwoddie asked, somewhat dryly.

"She detests it, sir, the little she has seen," his son replied, as if in triumph. "It is the way I have told about her which makes you think her affected. She is not so at all. If she had wanted to seem amiable, she would have pretended to like us; but she don't, and she said so."

"Like us?" his mother asked.

"Well, the little she had seen of us," her son replied, with a blush. "She had heard so much, she said, as to Southern gentlemen, and she was sure she would be disappointed. I never saw such a mere child. But I tell you, she knows everything! At first, I hated dreadfully to bring her, mother. You see, I thought I would have to entertain her, and what do I know except about business? Entertain her? It was she who entertained me! If father was to put her in a poem, he would say that she had a mind like a diamond, with a thousand facets, whichever way she turned she sparkled; and, then, she was always turning. I will be glad when Alice and May can have the same advantages. People get to be so dull and slow living always in one place. But, you darling mother, it is time for me to take you up-stairs. Not a night while I was gone but I thought of it and wanted to do it."

His heart sank within him, however, as he did so. Either he had grown a great deal stronger, or she had become much lighter since he had last carried her up. He laid her upon her bed, went down-stairs again, took a heavy bag out of his trunk, came and knelt by her side as she lay, and emptied a pile of gold coin upon the bed-cover, while his father fastened up the house below-stairs.

"Father promised me," he said, "that I should have such and such a small percentage over and above my expenses—that is, and presents, too—and here it is, one thousand gold dollars. It was my fancy—we have been so very poor—and have seen so little gold. It is fresh from the mint — virgin money. Isn't it beautiful, mother?" and he thrust his hand under the heap, and lifted and let it fall, pouring it from hand to hand, washing his hands in it as if it were a precious liquid.

"Oh, you beauties!" he said, burying his face in the heap; "we have missed you so long, but here you are at last. And there are millions more of you—*millions!* Just to think—more than we can spend! I don't care for money myself, mother," he added. "Not to spend on myself, I mean.

But you have so many things to buy. Only this is all to go for yourself, mind. Uncle's money is yours — all yours — you know, mother; but please take this as a little present from *me*. Not a soul knows it is in the house, and I will put it under my pillow to-night for you; and father and I are ready for all the cats in Clair County."

"You have always been my own boy," his mother said, never once looking from his eager face to the gold, which he was pouring from hand to hand, "and I accept your gift; yes, and I will spend it, Horace—*spend* it! I know excellent ways in which it will give me real pleasure to do so. But there is another gift I want more, Horace. Will you give me that?"

The young man had never before heard such accents of eagerness from his mother.

"Why, mother!" he said; "*you* ask me such a question? I and all I am and have and can be, am already yours. You know it."

"That is all I want," she said; "I want you to give me yourself! Mind, you belong to me. You cannot dispose of yourself, sell yourself, give yourself, throw yourself away, keep yourself—without my consent! Remember, Horace, it is a promise—a sacrament! And now, dear, keep my gold for me to-night. Kiss me once more. I have something to tell you to-morrow."

CHAPTER XXI.

COL. DUNWODDIE AND HIS ELDEST SON GO
A-FISHING.

"'Tis but one form of suicide,
    The hermit's, who, within his cave,
    Anticipates with greed his grave,
Because by men too sorely tried.

"But 'tis the man most prospered with
    Men's love, who men the heartiest hates,
    Like Bonaparte, and abdicates
Imperial power, like Charles the Fifth.

"Yea, those on whom men most do smile
    From sweetness into sourness drift,
    Like Landor, Thackeray, and Swift,
Like Dickens, Ruskin, and Carlyle."

HORACE DUNWODDIE was toiling, in his dreams, with a pick-axe in the depths of a Nevada mine, the morning after his coming home. He had just struck into a vein of silver, already minted into dollars fresh and white. As he dropped his pick and stooped to gather them up, a strong hand was upon his shoulder. In the instant of awakening his first thought was of his mother's gold under his pillow, his next of the revolver beside it, his last that it was his father who was arousing him, and he burst into a joyous laugh as he sat up in bed. Col. Dunwoddie was not yet dressed, and Horace's mirth subsided when he saw how gray and gaunt he looked in the early dawn.

"I am sorry to disturb you, my boy," he said, untying the knot in his stocking, which had reminded him to do it, "but I want you to dress as quietly as you can and take an early breakfast with me. Bring your memoranda of the business which has to be immediately attended to, and we will go fishing. Your mother is sleeping, and we will not disturb her. Make haste."

His son dressed himself, locked the gold in a trunk, and went down to a hurried meal with his father, wondering at his sudden passion for the water. None of the family joined them, it was so early; and, taking a basket of lunch and fishing-tackle, and leaving word with the servants where they were going, the elder of the two, after looking up and down the deserted street, as if fearing some one even at that hour, led the way through the half-awakening town, across certain corn and cotton fields, to the river.

"I come here quite often with George or Harry," the Colonel said, as he unlocked a small skiff chained to a sycamore-tree; and getting in they pushed off, rowed down stream for some distance, and fastened their boat, at last, beside an island of rocks and willows near the other bank. It was delightfully cool at that early hour, and they were completely hidden from sight by the long and drooping branches of the willows, the leaves quivering green and white in the morning breeze which rippled the water.

"We can catch but few fish, and they are not good to eat at this season of the year," the father said, as they baited their hooks and cast them into the river; "but one has ɔ be doing something, you know. Very ften I do not bring the lines at all, only a ʘook, and lie down here all day in the boat and read, or bring May's little writing-desk and scribble whatever comes to mind. Anything to get away."

"To get away, sir?" his son said, with surprise.

"Certainly," his father replied. "Do you not remember how I was annoyed before you left? Of course you will not misunderstand me, Horace. There are no prouder people living than those in our state; nor any who would sooner disdain to ask, or to receive, a favor from a stranger. But I was born here; have lived here all my life. They have known me always. Do you see?"

"Certainly I do, sir. I ought to know my own people," his son said with pride, but with a sinking of heart as he looked at the other. While he was away enjoying himself elsewhere, and as long as he pleased, he had never done more than fear that it might not be as pleasant with those at home. He fished more thoughtfully as his father, rod in hand, continued—

"And, then, things are terribly changed by the war. It is not merely that people who were accustomed to wealth have lost everything, but that with everything else they have lost, almost, their faculty of hoping. The strain upon them during the war; the sudden shock with which it ended; the breaking-up of the whole system of labor; the death or maiming of the men —a thousand things made it impossible for them to go to work all at once.

"I care least for our men—they are able to work; hard labor will do them good. It is," added his father, "the women I care for. There are so many widows and orphan-girls left by men slain in battle; it is the women, old and young, who are struggling to live, that I am distressed about. They are the last people to let their wants be known. As colonel of a regiment that was cut to pieces during the war, as well as one who knows the whole state better, possibly, than any other man in it, from having been editor and lawyer so long, I cannot but be familiar with matters. People are continually applying to me in person or by letter in regard to cases of privation, when I happen to know, although they never allude to it, that they are themselves worse off than those they are so eager I should help. But it is our women, unfitted by their training, as well as by the climate, for work, even if they knew what to do; it is for these I feel most. The papers act as if, because I am an editor, I am their property; and they have made the South sure of three things in regard to me. First, that I have at least ten millions of dollars in hand for immediate spending. Second, that I am, or ought to be, eager to get rid of it. Third, that I am pretty sure to be made a rascal by it in the end. Such wealth cannot but intoxicate me. It is merely a question of how long I can keep my feet, and into what gutter I will tumble at last."

"You have a good many applications, then?" his son said.

"Applications!" The other laid down his fishing-rod, stood up in the boat, grasping an overhanging branch of the willow to steady himself. "Applications!" he exclaimed; "that is the reason we came here! If last night's mail is like the rest, my box at the post-office this morning is crammed with them. I have had to ask help from Harry and George in answering them."

"Rich men elsewhere told me that they had printed forms of refusal," Horace began.

"No, sir!" Col. Dunwoddie interrupted, with a violence which surprised his son. "It may do for them, but not for me. I am among my own people, sir! Every letter is read. I do what I can. When I can give nothing, I try to make up for it by explaining matters in the kindest way. As you know, I have abandoned, in large measure, my law practice, as well as the *Clarion.* From early in the morning until late at night I am occupied, one way or another, with affairs connected with your uncle's money. It is the most exhausting work I have ever done."

"I am glad I am back again to help," Horace said with energy. "I blame myself that I did not come back sooner."

"As your mother says, I suppose I *am* too nervous," the other continued. "The property came upon me in addition to severe troubles going before. I have been strained in every nerve. It is an excellent thing, Horace, that you do not have so sympathetic a temperament. I am glad that with all your impulse you have, I hope, something of your mother's calm and steady—shall I say sense?"

"I wish I had, if I could have your genius—your kind of excellence, I mean—with it. But," his son said, "it is because you do not know me. Impulsive?"

"For Heaven's sake, Horace, and while I think of it," his father broke in, "please do not make a fool of yourself by entangling your affections with anybody. Not just yet. We have trouble enough! Do you know, sir, Hiddikel Queasy dared to speak to me—had the audacity to stop me on the street and endeavor to engage me in conversation. The rascal!"

The incident was not in any apparent connection with Clara Middleton; but Horace could not help laughing aloud at his father's energy of disgust. "And what did you do, sir?" he asked, as the image of the crouching yet insolent demagogue rose before him.

"He wanted my name to some railroad, I believe; I did not wait to hear what. 'You should apply to Mr. Terrell,' was all I said. 'What do you mean, sir, by that?' somebody shouted behind me. It was Terrell, drunk, and eager for a difficulty."

"I ought not to have been away," his son said with flaming eyes.

"It did not matter. Major Clarke was with Terrell, and hastened to explain that I referred to Queasy's near escape from being cowhided by him. As soon as the drunken rascal understood, he was so delighted that he insisted upon shaking hands with me. I suppose he is glad, now, of any excuse to be on terms with one whom he has hated and abused for years. Of course," the father added, "I refused his advances. 'You are, sir,' I said to him, 'as great a disgrace to the South as this poor wretch is to the North.' My wonder is that he did not strike me. He is ten times my enemy since. But what I mean is, I have trouble enough, Horace. Don't inflict more upon us by any folly on your part. Had it not been for Emmeline Anderson, Hiddikel Queasy and Terrell would, between them, have given Clair County over to God knows what bloody scenes. That's why I have mentioned all this."

Horace had long been familiar with the conduct of Emmeline Anderson on the occasion referred to. But he did not know that she had sent Parker for young Clarke, and had compelled the reckless fellow to pledge himself not to quarrel further with Tom Terrell because of his conduct towards her, as well as to hold his tongue in reference to the whole affair. He was surprised, however, at his father's manner. He had never been so irritable; it distressed him.

"Applications!" Col. Dunwoddie resumed. "My office is crowded from morning till night by people wishing to see me for a moment, no two having the same errand, but the end is the same. I told you about all this before you left, but it has grown worse and worse. They come to me for a new railway; a factory of some sort, which is to be more of a mint than a factory, literally to coin money; mineral lands waiting the smallest of sums to yield the largest results; new inventions which are to revolutionize this, that, and the other; colleges needing help to be fountains of blessing to the world; plantations for sale for almost nothing, and the people refusing to be referred to Middleton, whose business it is. It is almost impossible for me to walk a square without being stopped. People want to make me trustee of a dozen different institutions; treasurer of all sorts of companies. I have ten times more law business thrust upon me than I can take. Do you know, Horace," the Colonel added with a laugh, which had little merriment in it, "I could make a fortune merely upon the reputation of being a millionaire, and without risking a cent? When I needed it I could not get it," he said with bitterness. "Gentlemen call on me for aid, and it is trying to me to refuse; but when ladies come," he said, recurring to what had distressed him most, "ladies closely veiled sometimes, it is worse. When little girls get Alice, or rather May, to bring them, or come by themselves, often in mourning, to the house or to my office, and begin to tell me their troubles, and break down and stand weeping instead, it is that which tries me. Would you like to know how much I have given away since you left?"

When his son declined with a laugh, he named an amount which caused Horace to exclaim aloud, draw in his line, wind it up on its bit of corn-cob, secure the hook, untie it all from the end of the pole, and put it in his basket. Here was business! Begging his father to go ashore upon the little island, the two sat down side by side, while Horace, producing a neatly kept note-book, went with him, and very carefully, over the many items demanding speedy attention. Large amounts were involved. Many investments were in a precarious condition requiring serious consideration. It was full noon before the two were able to pause for a time for lunch. In fact, neither had much appetite; they were worried, but from different causes.

"Even if I had known what you told me about last night, as to the income being more than I had supposed, I could not afford to give as I have done," the Colonel said at last. "I have mentioned the cash given. My subscription is out, and for large sums, to many excellent objects for which I will be called upon before long, and yet you have no idea, my son," he said with an air of weariness, "of the anger of many whom I refuse to help, or the disappointment of others at the amount when I do give. The word millions is so uncommon that people suppose it means infinitude. A millionaire is a man, they think, with the wealth of Jehovah. I have wondered myself why a God of unlimited resources—*unlimited*, mind—is so penurious in his giving, as if an ocean of pure water should grant of its unbounded and unfathomable self to those dying of thirst in the scantiest of occasional drops. It is bad, Horace, to have the discontents of so many against their Maker transferred to *me*," the Colonel added with a grim smile. "Ah, Horace, my boy, *venenum in auro bibitur*, which means, it is impossible to get anything but poison out of gold. By the by, you never can know what a bitter sorrow it has been to me that I could not, my son, give you a college course."

"I am heartily glad you did not," his son said with decision; "I prefer business."

"Ah, well," the Colonel went on, "I make it one condition of giving that it shall not be mentioned, and people think that I do far less than is the fact. And so I often have abuse from the very people I have tried to benefit, but they are exceptions, and I have heartfelt happiness, Horace, in the gratitude of others. Never, never fail, my boy, to do all you can; but I have learned more of the ingratitude, of the trickery, of the unreasonableness of people than before. As a lawyer I ought to have known, but I knew nothing! I am more tired, Horace—tired—*tired*—than you can know," the Colonel said, his hand resting heavily upon the shoulder of his son, his eyes upon the sand at his feet. "I *am* too nervous, I suppose," he added, "too emotional, too—anything you please to call it. The four years' campaigning shook me more than I knew, as well as all that came after it, even worse to bear. Do you know that I have been more violently attacked in the papers than ever?"

"No, sir, I did not," his son said in high wrath. "If any scoundrel has done it—"

"You poor boy," his father said, laying his hand again upon the shoulder of his son. "As if you could help it! It is partly because I have refused to go into the politics of the day. You know that I have hardly a thought apart from the South. I proved that by fighting four years. But I hated politics before the war, and I abhor them tenfold since. I cannot, of course, go with one party, and I cannot go to the extremes of the other. My tastes are different. Besides, I have read history. I often think of the followers of the Stuarts, and there was something sturdy in their detestation of their Hanover conquerors at the time and for generations afterward. We were shamefully wronged before, during, and, worse than all, since the war. I am no Christian, but I take your mother's view of it, however, that the grand purposes of Heaven are being wrought out in the South as everywhere. Why should I not look at matters now as you will look at them twenty years hence? Others may plunge into the petty bitternesses of the moment, but," he added with more than partisan violence, "I *won't!* Isn't it queer, Horace? Parker, Mrs. Anderson's foreman, you remember, and myself, are alike in our views, although he has, of course, never dared talk politics with me. The honest fellow hates not only the Tom Terrells, but, and more especially, the Hiddikel Queasys, worse than I do. Odd, isn't it, a negro should have so much sense?"

"It is indeed, sir."

"Don't misunderstand me, Horace," his father walked up and down the strip of sand under the willows as he said it, "the South is the best part of America, its people the noblest, its resources the greatest. It is wholly against nature that the rest of the country should have surpassed the South as in some things it has done. Mere science, invention, what is called energy and enterprise, may belong by natural laws to colder latitudes. It is so in Europe. But the government of this republic belongs to the South. It had it in large measure from the first, it would have held it still had it not been for the folly of a few when Lincoln was elected; it will assuredly come into possession of it again, to hold it henceforth. But that is not what I care for most. The South is the Italy of America. It should always have been the region of Art, of Song, as it has been of Eloquence. Don't mention it, Horace, but slavery paralyzed us. All that is past. Henceforth the South is to be all that Greece, that Italy has been. Not only to America, my boy—to the whole world! Mark what I say!" And Horace felt a thrill of pride in his father as the Colonel paused in front of him, erect, inspired.

"All these miserable little squabbles will perish with my generation. The next will revere us as a race of heroes, but will also smile at and pity us. Be broader than I am, my boy, but always be Southern. Don't make money your chief object. Never lie, cheat, or steal, when you are in Congress. Never be mean. Be energetic, but be honorable. Never let your honor be suspected, as when, for instance, any indebtedness is concerned. Treat women with all deference, but detest strong-minded females. Be a gentleman, Horace—a gentleman."

Fresh from his experiences when away, the other felt, but it was with indignation at himself, that there was something more old-fashioned and obsolete in his father than he had thought, and he loved him the more as with a tenderer respect and affection.

"I am glad you will soon escape from your annoyances, sir," he said.

"Escape!" his father replied. "Escape? When I was so poor I used to say, Oh, that I were rich. If I but had money—money—I could fly, as you said last night, upon the wings of an angel. How I would mount up," he said, his arms stretched out, his head thrown back, "above all the wretched annoyances. We would pay off every debt, help everybody that deserved help, bid every friend a hearty good-by, and fly, all of our brood, away to Europe, to Syria, around the world! When I craved wings, I had chains alone. The wings have come, but, do you know, sir," he added almost savagely, "that the wings make it that much the harder to endure the chains?"

"I don't understand you, sir," his son replied, with a sinking of the heart.

"She cannot help it," the other said, as if in anger at him. "Your mother is an angel, if, for the moment, her wings are broken. She will get well soon, and we will go. What I deplore is the way in which she allows herself to be prevented from getting well by her conscience."

"Her conscience!" Horace exclaimed.

"Yes, sir!" the other said with a bitterness which surprised his son afresh. "Your mother has paid off the debt upon her church, and I don't object to that, except that they don't deserve it. She has aided churches of all denominations in addition. It is small faith I have in them, but she is welcome to do so. She is making up the salaries of ministers all over the South, and that is all right, since she likes to do it. What I object to is the way in which she is allowing herself in her weak health to be murdered by incessant applications, wearied out, harassed—"

"I had not thought she was over-anxious as to anything," Horace said, knowing that, in contrast with his father, his mother was as the pure beach which at once embraces and quietly endures the restless sea.

"It is because you have been absent.

She is overwhelmed with letters, with callers, with trying to prevent people from annoying me. She endeavors to take upon herself all of their everlasting importunity. They got tired—the religious people I mean —of coming to me," he added with a grim smile. "Like Stuart Mill, the supreme argument with me, also, as to the Founder of Christianity, is his infinite superiority to his own followers. Look at the churches! They ought to be peacemakers between the South and North; and see how they hold themselves apart from and hate each other! But I care nothing for them. It is of your mother I am speaking. In spite of her sweet and smiling endurance, all this is surely killing her."

"It is a shame I should have been away so long from her when I was gone, and so long to-day; let us return to her," was all Horace replied.

When they got back in the boat to the place of landing, they found George waiting for them.

"Hi!" he said, "gone all day and not caught a fish! And oh, pa, such a lot of letters waiting for you. And there's an old, old gentleman, who stayed to dinner. He says he is our grand-uncle, our great-grandmother, or something. You have no notion, Horace, how many of our kin have hunted us up while you were gone, whole rafts of second-cousins and third-nephews and nieces. Oh, my, but we are a distinguished family, I tell you!"

When Horace stooped over his mother in bed that evening to bid her good-night, she detained him a moment.

"I had hoped to have seen more of you to-day," she said, "but I knew your father was wishing to talk to you, and I am glad you have spent the day together; he will feel relieved. But I cannot go to sleep, my boy, without telling you something, as I promised last night;" and she ceased a moment, smiling bravely, but with the tears flowing down her face. It was the more painful to her son, as she rarely wept in the presence of any of her household, not even of Horace, with whom her relations were really closer than with her own husband.

"I know it all, dear mother; you told me long ago," Horace said, kneeling by her side, "and it was because you compelled me to go away that I did so. You know how gladly I would have hurried back but that you kept me away with telegrams. Even you will have no power to separate us any more. Besides"—he tried to laugh as he said it—"people are losing their faith in doctors these days, as well as in everything else. What do *they* know?"

"It is not of myself I wanted to speak," she replied, restraining her tears. "We two have had no secret between us in regard to that for so long that we are used to it. More than ever, it is best your father should know nothing of it. I always make my doctors consent to *that;* and he is so absorbed in his other matters that he never dreams of it. I want to speak to you about something else."

"About poor Alice and Middleton?" Horace asked; and added, "Yes, it is about the bitterest pill I, for one, have ever had to take. He cares nothing for her—nothing whatever—poor girl. You and I have often talked of him; neither of us have any faith in him; but if he is a rascal, is it not strange that he prefers Emmeline to her, knowing how much wealthier Alice is? No, it is not strange!" he contradicted himself; "it is impossible for him to help it. For what I know, she will marry him; he is doing all he can towards it. I cannot—I will not be on my knees to her all the time. No man ever loved a woman more, but—"

"Hush, Horace!" his mother said, her finger upon his lips. "I was not going to speak of Alice, of Emmeline, or of Mr. Middleton. It is of something far more important than that. I want to speak to you of your father. Wait a moment, my son."

There was a long silence. Mrs. Dunwoddie lay still, her eyes closed, evidently a deavoring to gather strength for what she had to say. As to Horace, kneeling beside her, he felt his heart stand almost still for a moment, such a sudden horror had fallen upon him. The truth is, from the beginning of the war and ever since the household had been, and by the very circumstances of their case, detached from other people and thrown upon itself. What had been effected and confirmed into habit by common trouble long continued, had been deepened of late by common good-fortune. With Horace the case was peculiar. Cut off from his childhood from a good deal of that which attracts and interests the young outside of his own home, and possessed of an ardent nature, he admired as well as loved his father beyond measure. The conversation during the day had awakened vague fears within him. And now? He did not speak or stir until his mother said, "Summon all your strength, my boy, but see first, please, that the door is shut."

CHAPTER XXII.

CLARA MIDDLETON AND THE REST.

"Straws are not all that whirl and dance
    On varying winds of circumstance.
I am Chinese, with almond eyes,
    Or gypsy, I, with lice and lies;
A Spaniard in my pride and cloak,
    Or one of Norway's simple folk;
Prince, beggar, priest, or none of these,
    Scotch, Hindoo, Swede, or Portuguese.
Each man is what the babe did grow:
    I am because I happen so.
We are, earth round, but grains of dust,
    Our only law—As blows the gust."

MIDDLETON admired and sympathized with Blondin when he saw him walk a rope stretched over Niagara, for during his own life of diversified experiences he had never been able to doff his tights and spangles or to lay down his balancing - pole, much less to close for a moment his watchful eyes. The adroitness of the man was wonderful; but, then, it was the result of long and unceasing practice.

Never had he reached so dizzy a height as now. He was drawing towards an age greatly beyond his looks, which made him anxious to settle himself; after performances so long, and upon a rope beneath which some Niagara was always roaring, it was not in human nature that he should not be tired. Moreover he really loved his sister Clara only less than himself. Almost from the day their mother had abandoned them both for the vagrant minstrel and unlimited gin, the support of his sister had rested upon him. Compelled to scramble for existence himself, he had contrived as he grew up and prospered, but at the cost of self-sacrifice, to keep her at the best schools—even to take her upon a short trip to Europe during one of her vacations. His great desire now was to see her married, and, as chances went, the one man for her to marry was Horace Dunwoddie. True, his sister was older than that gentleman, but young Dunwoddie looked as many years older, as she did years younger than the actual age in either case. In addition to all this, the prize which Middleton now aimed at was all he could wish; and he was a man whose incessant exercise in life had, so far, done vastly more to whet than to satisfy appetite.

It was gambling, and he knew it. No man went forth from his chamber of a morning fresher in looks or, seemingly, freer from care, and yet it was often after he had handled the cards until late the night before. Not in a literal sense, for he was no more a gambler than he was a hard drinker. Even so far as smoking went, he would rather spend an hour in getting out of a communicative stranger all he had to impart than to smoke the best Havana. And so of cards and liquors, for stimulus and as things of wildest chance, they were insipid in comparison with men and women. The persons in whom he was most interested were, just now, not only his opponents in the game, but the cards and dice thereof. It was a matter of chance, but it was a game of chess also, and no piece, in his opinion, accomplished anything except as he moved it. There were three queens on the board—three queens? There were four—Clara, Alice, Emmeline, Mrs. Dunwoddie.

He could count upon his sister, and it was by his arrangement that she had accompanied Horace on his return. She had never met a person of his kind before. He knew less of dress, of the theatre, the opera, of city gossip, than other gentlemen; but there was a certain freshness of personal manhood, a country frankness about him, which had nothing to conceal and which was not without its charm for her, satiated as she was with life in the city, and having had no home since she could remember. He yielded to her from force of habit the deference he had shown his mother all his life; this of itself pleased her as no flattery could have done.

Middleton could count upon his sister. But could he count, in that connection, upon young Dunwoddie? He could not help knowing that Emmeline Anderson outweighed a boarding-school full of such women as she. He also knew that Horace was in love with Miss Anderson. Both upon his sister's account and his own he must supplant him and, at the earliest moment, marry her himself. Could he do it?

Another queen upon the board of which he made sure, in case he should wish to marry her, was Alice Dunwoddie. On her he could count as upon a safe reserve if he failed with Miss Anderson. Poor Alice! After a brief period of unwonted gladness she was sinking into a more sullen sadness than before. The sorrowful years had struck their stains of tears and blood too deeply into her nature. What good had her uncle's money done her? It had brought Mr. Middleton, in comparison with whom her father and brothers, sister and mother, had steadily become as nothing. Gladly would she have poured at his feet every penny thereof, even as, poor girl, she was coming to give him her every thought and emotion. Her silent passion partook of the obstinacy of her character; it was a current deep and strong, which was undermining her health, almost her reason.

"It is the bitterest mortification," her father said to his wife at last, "we have ever known. Middleton cares nothing for her. Very naturally he has fallen in love with Emmeline Anderson. It does him credit, knowing, as he does, how poor Emmeline is in comparison. Sharp and plausible as the man is, however, he is but a superior sort of Hiddikel Queasy. He will defeat Horace none the less. You never can know what to expect in regard to a girl of determined yet undeveloped character like Emmeline. But that a daughter of mine—!" and the Colonel walked the floor with mortification as incurable and bitter as if he had not been worth a penny. What could his wife say—despising poor Alice and yet sympathizing sincerely with her as she did? A keener grief she had never known.

Alice spent every hour she could with Clara, although there never were women more unlike than the volatile, fresh-colored, garrulous, carefully dressed Clara and her sad and homely companion.

And Middleton could calculate accurately as to himself, also. When the time came he could marry either Miss Anderson or Alice with equal alacrity; whatever might be the emergency, he was ready for it.

But there was Mrs. Dunwoddie. Now he had been in one of the lesser battles of the war, a brief but desperate fight, in which his side had been more than decimated by a battery perched high above them upon an inaccessible eminence near by. It was a small battery, but it was admirably served, and in the end decided the fortunes of the bloody hour. Middleton had not been cast so long and so intimately among his kind not to know, almost from the day of his introduction to Mrs. Dunwoddie, that she would be the person who would decide, next to Emmeline Anderson, matters in this instance also. On that account he was doing his best to gain her to his side. By reason of the elevated position of the guns during the fight spoken of, he had, all through the uproar of conflict, an odd sense as if heaven itself was warring upon him. So in regard to this good woman. Her eyes swept the field, and the only way to gain her was by getting above the world himself. He dared not play the hypocrite too much—she would see through that; but he would be, in a casual way, an inquirer after truth. On that account was it that he had asked her about Providence, as he did before and after, although always incidentally, in regard to kindred themes.

"I passed through all that," he would reassure himself in his room on nights after such a conversation, "when I was an eloquent divine. Oh, how I used to fast and weep and pray! It is all as utterly gone as Santa Claus and the rest of the childish beliefs. My religion — hell, heaven, God, and all—is, faith in myself and in nothing else. What does God, if there be a God, know or care about me? Oh, King Gamaliel, live forever!"

He was glad of Alice's intimacy with his sister. In Alice's estimation, apart from her being his sister, Clara was a most accomplished woman. What opportunity had she ever had in comparison? Clara was going to teach her French, German, music, how to do all sorts of fancy work. Compelled to be silent as to Middleton, Alice was never weary of praising Clara to her own household. "Such dresses as Clara wears! A new one—at least a charming variation of one," every time she entered the house. "And such jewelry!"

"Yes, she does make things as bright as you please," George acknowledged. "Oh, but can't she sing! She bangs away like thunder on the piano. I am so glad Horace ordered that one for you, and it *was* a surprise; you and May, though, never get half as much out of it as she does. But it is her singing I like. Those opera things is too grand for me, and I do like those rattling songs; ain't they bully? On Sunday afternoons, evenings along through the week, too, when she sings all those old hymns and prayer-meeting songs, doesn't mother enjoy it? You bet she does! If I was Horace I would marry her—that is, if I could, at half-past seven o'clock to-night. And then she makes herself so much at home."

"Yes, I dare say!" May interjected. "It is all very well to hear her talk history with pa—poetry, science, *and* art! She knows about everything! Did you ever hear anybody talk so fast? But the faster and more brilliantly she talks, it makes me feel that much more as if she was performing a fine piece of music on the piano; and *could* you imagine two such ladies in the same room at once?"

"Or two Miss Claras talking to each other," suggested Harry. "Whew! just think of it!" and they laughed at the idea even while they scolded him for saying so.

Miss Clara was sensible enough not to overdo it, however, with Mrs. Dunwoddie's eyes upon her. She had the best apartments at the hotel. The ladies of Clairsville had, out of respect for the Dunwoddies, called upon the new-comer; but she felt at home, she said, only at the Colonel's house. No one could help feeling so under that roof. It was an experience of hospitality wholly new to the homeless and city-raised girl, and she enjoyed it beyond measure. There was little for her to do beyond perpetually altering her dresses and being at the Dunwoddies. Harry loaned her his books and was studying Italian under her. George asked her in fun to go hunting with him, and she did, and came home helping him bring a string of squirrels. After that the young people went boating, fishing, picnicing together. The Colonel had bought horses and carriage, and Mrs. Dunwoddie took a short drive whenever she was strong enough, but the young people were on horseback every afternoon.

"The idea," May protested, "of learning how to ride from a city lady," for they were taking lessons of Clara.

"But they have riding-schools in the cities, you see," Alice explained. "And Clara rides better than any of us."

"And she understands cooking," May added. "She has made ever so many nice things for ma, but—but—" and May grew silent under her sister's frown. The truth is, May did not, after all, share Alice's admiration for their new companion.

"You like that way of dressing your hair because she showed you how," she said to Alice, "but I do not. It is perfectly awful. She is wonderfully pretty and bright and smart and all that, but—but—"

"But what?" Alice asked indignantly.

"But I don't like her, *there!*" May added, clearing for action, so to speak, by putting her abundant hair back from her forehead, first with one hand and then with the other. They were in their room undressing for the night, and quite a scene ensued.

"No, ma'am, I do not admire her—not one bit," May said at last. "She is very fine and she is very smart. I'll tell you what she is like. You know those shiny, showy silks that are so cheap and slimsy? Well, she is like one of them."

"She isn't!" Alice said in wrath. "You never saw such an accomplished lady. It is because she is superior to every girl you ever knew that you envy her. I didn't think you could be so mean," and Alice, to May's amazement, burst into tears. The older sister had been, during that day, and for a wonder, so bright and happy! Poor girl, she was nervous; her happiness was hysterical because it was merely an eager hope. Her life hitherto had been dull and empty in comparison, and her infatuation for Middleton was becoming an insanity. May was too utterly unlike Alice to understand.

"Superior?" she said. "Why, Alice, *you* are superior to her," and she tried, in her ignorance, to kiss her sister.

"Go away with you—I won't!" Alice exclaimed, throwing her off. "Clara Middleton is an angel compared to anything you ever saw. You can't appreciate her."

"Appreciate her?" May replied. "You know what you must have thought that day we returned Emmeline Anderson's call with her. Appreciate! Didn't you see them together in the parlor? Emmeline was a duchess in comparison. Clara had on her finest clothes, and her grandest airs and graces, but she felt her inferiority to Emmeline. How could she *help* feeling it? She talked and laughed and rattled on, but it did no good. When she played and sang so loud, she felt Emmeline Anderson's great eyes upon her; it was that which threw her out. It was like an artificial flower and a real one. The last time we went with Horace to call upon your Clara she actually offered to take his hat, insisted upon bringing him a chair! I can imagine Emmeline Anderson doing such a thing, or pressing him to call again, as Clara did! Appreciate! Emmeline is a real lady, and so is my mother; and—and," said May, wrought into unladylike fury, "she *sha'n't* marry Horace!"

"As if she would have him," Alice replied.

May opened her astonished eyes; her sister must be out of her head.

"You are a hateful thing," Alice continued, with tearless anger. "You are jealous of Clara because she is so graceful and you are—are—"

"What?" May demanded, as Alice paused.

"Are so *fat*," Alice added, driven to desperation.

"I ain't! Heaven knows you are—" *not*, May would have added, but it was too terrible a fact to state, and, being a warmhearted girl, she burst into tears instead. She dried them the next moment.

"I'll tell you what your Clara is," and she advanced upon her retreating sister, hissing the dreadful words through her teeth, "she is *old!*"

Language was useless before a slander so foul, and Alice fell weeping, and refusing to be conciliated, on her bed; and a sad night they had of it. But the elder of the two reserved her deadliest blow until the last. Just before entering the breakfast-room next morning, Alice turned upon May in triumph, and said—

"Horace likes her, he told me so himself!" and May had nothing to say in reply to that. "He *likes* her!" Alice repeated.

Ever since his coming back that gentleman had been very busy. His effort was to make up for his absence by helping his father day and night at the office. There was more to do than he had supposed, even from what his father had said. It was a relief to the Colonel. He felt as if it were his wife instead made young and strong again, made this time into a man vigorous and as full of sense as of affection, who was beside him. Business, in the strict sense, had always been distasteful to one of his poetic temperament; and business—business in the strictest meaning of the word—was what his son most delighted in. It was a natural inclination, confirmed by the habits of his life from his boyhood. His trip had given him that mastery of the details of their wealth which comes from personal knowledge; every day he assumed, and his father gladly yielded to him, a more complete management of affairs.

As Col. Dunwoddie walked up and down the porch of their home one night in the moonlight with his son, thought a more restless manner than ever, Horace said, "I am glad you have supplied yourself with the new books and magazines. You said you were sadly in arrears in your reading."

"So I was, so I was," the Colonel replied, "but I don't know if I am wise to heap so much fuel upon a fire which is too fierce already. *Quieta, quieta non movere!* You poor boy, why could I not have sent you to college? If you had been liberally educated, Horace, I might have told you something. I will say this much. You know—rather you cannot know—how the South has been sneered at as not having produced any great name in literature for, at least, many years. I have an idea, sir — a purpose! Poor Alec was stupidity itself, but his money will be a power beyond anything gold can do if it enables me to write — write! I will say no more now. I had hoped to enjoy books, to rest in them, luxuriate in them. No, sir; the more I read the more do they goad and drive me. I cannot explain now," he said in an excited way. "Good-night, Horace; go to bed, my dear boy. I want to be by myself and think. I have a great project on hand. I could not sleep if I were to go in. Many a time I walk up and down here half the night. It used to be hard for me to sleep, now it seems to be impossible! Good-night, good-night!"

Horace wondered, as he obeyed, what good the Nevada fortune had done his father so far. The Colonel was like a flame, always burning intensely, and varying merely as to the direction in which it was blown by the wind; a flame burning more fiercely every day. To judge by his sunken temples, hollow cheeks, excitable manner, it was a flame which was consuming him to ashes. This added to the anxieties of his son, and he was burdened as the days rolled by with an ever-increasing weight of hard work. Every night he came home very tired. He said nothing upon the subject, since it was impossible just yet, but how heartily he wished that they could break up and go abroad for a year or two! But even if his mother could have gone, would he have been willing to leave Emmeline Anderson? He had never forgotten the singular exclamation he had overheard from Middleton's lips in the hour of their first meeting at the depot; and Middleton would have been flattered had he known how sincerely his rival dreaded lest he should succeed.

"He is older and I dare say better-look-ing than I am," the poor fellow reasoned with himself; "and then he is so much more experienced in the world and in women—more polished and pleasing than I am. This wretched money of ours positively injures me with her, while his poverty is a help to him. Besides, he has time to devote himself to her, and what can I do?"

He was not so tired at night that he could not bear his mother up-stairs as well as down again in his arms every morning. She seemed to yield herself up to him more completely each time; and she parted from him so reluctantly when he left for the office after breakfast, and welcomed him so gladly when he came back at night, that he got into the habit of running into the house at unexpected hours during the day, if it was but to say a word and go again. He often found Miss Middleton there.

One night, as he laid his mother upon her bed, she said to him, "When did you see Emmeline last?"

"I have called several times since I returned," he said, "but it happened that she was never in. How badly Mrs. Anderson looks, mother. She seems to me to be getting whiter and colder every day."

"Mr. Middleton is often there," his mother said; "I dare say on some of the occasions of your calling he had taken Emmeline out riding on horseback or driving. It is natural she should like to get away from her gloomy home as often as she can, and he is a very agreeable companion. Good-night, my dear boy."

When Horace went down-stairs he found that Clara Middleton had just come in with Alice, who had been, as was often the case, on a visit to her. After a little conversation he lounged upon the sofa in the parlor, for he was unusually wearied, listening to the lively talk. It was a variety to him after the work and bother of the day. Clara's dress was as fresh as her face, and both seemed to be always as new as what she had to say. He had never known how much there could ' in a woman's dress which would remi... him of statues and 1 tures he had seen, as well as of poetry and flowers. It was not her fault if he had not thought of it. She gave a good deal of talent as well as attention to languages and music, but to dress she devoted her chief energy, since it was her highest talent. Horace listened to her laughing, singing at the piano, joking with George and Harry, with interest. Her voice was pitched upon a higher key than that of Emmeline Anderson, but it was pleasant to hear. Somehow it brought back to him to-night, all at once, his delightful trip with its varieties of novel experience.

"Alice begged me to come over," she said at last, "but I would not have done so but for one thing. I found something in one of the papers to-day, and I was so delighted with it I wanted to read it to somebody. Listen every soul of you!" and, standing near the lamp which was on the mantel, she produced a paper and proceeded to read a poem with great enthusiasm. The lines were excellent, and her reading was admirable. As she read she grew more erect, her color deepened, her soul was in her voice. No one there had heard such elocution before. "And, now, who wrote it?" she demanded, stilling their applause with her uplifted hand; and then —"Is it possible," she exclaimed, "that you do not know? No American poet, no English poet ever surpassed those lines. Oh, you stupid people! The man who wrote that will stand some day among the foremost men of his time. You know who wrote it, Mr. Horace; don't pretend you do not!"

Horace had been greatly interested, but he had to confess his ignorance.

"Not know your own father!" she exclaimed, for it was one of the Colonel's last poems of which none of them had heard. "I'm ashamed of you," she said. "If I had such a father, how proud I would be!"

Whereupon she compared what she had read with quite a variety of authors, praising some, ridiculing others, quoting from this and then from that.

"How accomplished she is—she knows everything," Alice, who was seated beside Horace upon the sofa, whispered, and then aloud—"Come here, Clara."

"Oh, yes," that lady replied, "I'll come, for I wish to ask your brother something. May is always telling us, Mr. Horace," she said, as she took her seat upon a low footstool in front of him, "that Miss Anderson is a pattern of propriety. She is the most beautiful brunette that ever lived; but must we be so—so reserved all the time? There's your mother, for instance, she is as open as day—as a bright, clear day—although she does not talk much. But then she is not a brunette. Mr. Horace," she added, not waiting for a reply, in graver tones. "You should be as proud of her as of your father. You do not seem any of you to appreciate them as they deserve. It is a shame," she added, laughingly, and looking up at him through her flaxen curls. She was not only a lady well-read in books, but, with eyes not large but lively, cheeks but a few shades less crimson than her lips, she was very pretty.

"Promise me you will love them both more than you ever did!" she added. It was like the coaxing of a child. Horace was so tired after his day's exertion, and it was very pleasant to be entreated by so charming a supplicant. Hidden in his bosom, a secret even from his mother, was the diamond ring he had bought, and this brilliant and versatile woman reminded him of it, she sparkled so—as he had told them when he first returned—in whatever light her incessant motion placed her. Would Emmeline Anderson ever consent to wear it? Why should he bother himself after all these years of privation? Small resistance he would meet in slipping the ring upon one of those fingers which were clasped, at the moment, in such pretty petition. And, then, she was familiar already with the great and glorious world into which he hoped soon to enter. Most of all, she appreciated his father as well as his mother.

"No," he said, when she rose to go, "I am not at all tired; I will accompany you with pleasure."

CHAPTER XXIII.

SUNSHINE AND SUDDEN CLOUD.

"The pressure of the fiery steed
  Which rears arrested in his speed
  Against the hand which doth control,
  Is measure of the charger's soul;
  For all the force which spurns the field
  Is that 'tis then constrained to yield.

"Thou who, some wall in act to vault,
  In mid career art made to halt,
  O man, thy halted vigor is
  The measure of thy strength with Ilis;
  Put into words its ounces run,
  'My will, not thine, O hand, be done!'"

"How do you suppose it is possible for us," Col. Dunwoddie remarked one day to his wife, "to know how Horace and Emmeline feel towards each other when, really, they do not know themselves?"

"Horace knows very well how he feels," Mrs. Dunwoddie replied. "He has told me everything that has interested him from the time he could talk at all; and he has concealed nothing from me in this case — at least, not until very lately. He is like you, my dear," she added, "a man of impulse — of noble, but of sudden and violent impulse."

"Perhaps so," the Colonel replied; "but he certainly is still more like you in concealing it under the calmest of exteriors. Horace belongs to a broader era than I do, Eliza. He will be as true to his state and to the South as I have been, but will be a citizen, as I have never been, of his great country, and, by business, by reading and by travel, a man of the world in the highest sense. I thank Heaven every day I live that he is not a bookish man. It frets me

at times that a youth of his superior intellect did not go to my old college so as to be able to read Virgil and Homer with me; but, after my own experience, I believe that I would rather catch him drinking whiskey or gambling than writing a poem. God forbid!" he added, with a shudder. "Not," he proceeded with energy, "that education is not a good thing, but what we need is to broaden the bases of society instead of trying to run up a few slender pinnacles into the clouds. What good has my education and genius, as people call it, done me? — made me nervous, sensitive, miserable. I detest books!"

"I thought, Charles, that you were hoping—" his wife began.

"And so I am," he broke in upon her with enthusiasm. "I have the grandest conceptions. You would not wonder that I cannot sleep if you knew. Listen." And, walking up and down the front porch, upon which they were enjoying behind the honeysuckles the rare seclusion of an afternoon free from company, her husband launched into details.

"My dear," his wife said an hour later, when he had exhausted himself, and her also, with his ardent intentions, "we were speaking of Horace. I said he was impulsive. Did you know? He has spoken to Emmeline. He told me of it because he tells me of everything;" and she related the two instances in which Horace had broken down in his efforts at self-control when with Miss Anderson.

"He has made several attempts to see her since his return," Mrs. Dunwoddie proceeded, "but has never found her in. Once he met her at our door. He was hurrying out to attend to some business as she came in. She is rarely here these days. You may imagine that he was embarrassed — remembering how headlong he had been at their parting. Of course she was more so, not knowing what he might do or say. As it was, nothing could be colder than their manner towards each other. Moreover," the mother said, with her placid smile, "Horace has been thrown a good deal of late with Clara Middleton, and Emmeline with Mr. Middleton; they are mutually aware of it, and that complicates matters. He has not confided to me of late."

"It is a miserable tangle," the Colonel said—"a wretched blunder like everything else in this particularly miserable world. Why do you not speak to Emmeline yourself?"

"Hardly," his wife said, with a smile. "Besides, Horace told me his woes only after an express promise of silence on my part. Moreover, things may have changed. Emmeline is pleased with Mr. Middleton. Horace seems to enjoy the society of Clara."

"Nonsense!" Col. Dunwoddie said. "Leave it all to me, Eliza. I will go over there this evening — to Mrs. Anderson's I mean. It is easy to arrange it. I will tell her—"

"Tell whom?" his wife interrupted, laughing.

"Tell whoever happens to be at home— Emmeline or her mother—that," he continued, "Horace did not approach her daughter in the flush of our wealth—that he has always loved her—that he loves her devotedly now. That—"

"Are you sure of that?" his wife said. "Horace has been so hurt by her supposing such a thing of him, so hurt, too, by her coldness as well, is ashamed of his boyish rashness in speaking to her as he did, that no one can tell how he feels, especially since he is with Miss Middleton every day. You must not say a word to Emmeline, Charles. Horace would be annoyed beyond measure if you should." Nor did she cease until her husband had promised that no impulse on his part should aggravate the mischief.

And here the mother fell into silent thought. Who was going to right matters in regard to Alice?

"It is amazing how keen the humiliations of life are," Col. Dunwoddie said to his wife at last; for, like all husbands and wives who are closely mated, they were very apt to be thinking at the same moment about the same thing. "That a daughter of ours should have so little spirit! and to know that Middleton's sister knows it. Of course he does. How does money help us in such a case as this? She is wasting to a shadow. Any one can see how forced her merriment is. This is the reason for her bitterness at Emmeline Anderson. Even Charlie could guess why her eyes look so swollen when she comes down in the morning. Poor, poor girl! Little wonder that she complains of headaches and sleepless nights. Life is an execrable chaos, Eliza," the Colonel said, with bitterness. "If we could but get out of this accursed Clairsville; could get Alice away—"

His wife winced almost as if he had struck her. The only thing detaining them there was her health. The best physicians had been called in, even from a distance, and they had agreed heretofore that, owing to some peculiarity of her case, her life would be endangered by travel until she had more strength to endure it. "Would that strength ever come?" No man could love his wife more than did her husband. He had grown into a habit, which had become a second nature, of depending utterly upon her judgment. His wealth was through her, and his chief desire had been to have her enjoy it, by travel and all other luxuries. Yet there she was in her easy-chair, an invalid still, weaker than before the fortune came. In her case a billion of dollars did no more good than a penny.

The annoyance of applications to him for money, the worry arising from the increasing political excitement of the state and the whole South were but the overflowings of a heart embittered by the illness of his wife. It was the one thing which held him to the same small spot when he was eager to get away; eager at times, almost to insanity; and it was the one thing against which he could not openly chafe.

As if she did not know his heart! Under her placid sweetness during the day ran the one thought:

"Oh, God, let me die. I can endure my terrible trial in silence. But how can I bear, as the days follow each other, to be the one thing which destroys all the pleasure the money brings! I may suffer thus as long as I live, and that may be for years. If it were God's will that I *could* die."

It is true that Col. Dunwoddie often took, sometimes his boys and then his girls to cities or watering-places near by; but the party always came back sooner than they had intended.

"Do you think," Alice or May, George, Harry, or Horace would reply to her, "that we can enjoy ourselves anywhere away from you? To think of you — a prisoner here and suffering — and we taking our pleasure. We can't do it! Besides, papa cannot live without you. He loves you so, depends upon you so, mother! And we are as bad as he is. You are the dearest woman in *this* world!" But the kisses and embraces lavished upon her could not make her well.

On this afternoon, however, she has a secret to tell her husband. Never did the fondest mother treasure up for a spoiled child every pleasant surprise in her power as did this wife whatever she imagined could gratify the Colonel. She searched the papers diligently for any favorable mention of his writings, his benefactions, himself. More frequently than she liked, unfavorable notices met her eye; but these were as the houseflies, cockroaches, spiders, which every housekeeper must expect, and she destroyed them before he could know of them, instantly, indignantly. From every source, through visitors or letters, she sifted out the bitter items and kept the sweet, and made them sweeter and all unconsciously more weighty in telling him of them.

"My dear," she said to him now, "the great doctor from the city who came in consultation saw me yesterday. He tells me—do you think you can hear with patience what he says?" she asked with a smile.

"Eliza," he said with violence, "the doctors are not a whit better than the politicians; they are ignorant rascals, most of them, the most distinguished ones are wretched charlatans. What does *he* know?" And her harassed husband looked down upon her gloomily.

"He *does* know this time," she replied steadily. "He says I will be able to go abroad with you in a few weeks."

"What!" the other exclaimed, his face lighting up.

"Yes, Charles"—his wife's face reflected the pleasure in his. "It is so, and I believe he is right. I have told no one, but I can arrange so that we can leave at almost a day's notice. Oh, Charles, I am so glad on your account!" the tears trickling down her cheeks as she spoke.

"You are a darling," her husband exclaimed like a boy, sitting down upon the piazza at her feet, and with a face from which it was as if years of anxiety had fled in an instant. "You always believe right. I am ashamed of myself! You can go in good earnest? Thank God! We will make a bridal trip of it, you darling wife!"

Tall and gray and gaunt as he was, the tears were in his eyes, he could say no more.

"I am glad, dear," she said, blushing and laughing like a bride indeed. "But we must take every child. If we could afford it," she added, with an arch look in memory of former poverty, "Charlie must have his nurse, too. It will be dreadfully expensive!"

"Dreadfully," the Colonel said, entering into the joke. "But we can pinch and screw, my dear. When shall we start? Say a week from to-day?"

The man seemed transformed with gladness, laughing, walking up and down the porch, rubbing his nose and his hands, stopping to kiss her.

"It was so good in you to get better. I haven't said anything about it, my dear," he continued, "but I have been exceedingly anxious to get out of this abominable political stew; the elections are coming on, you know, and I have been impatient to get away. In one month, with a change of air, you will bloom like a rose. It is the only thing for Alice! I tell you what we will do. We will take an easy trip through the Eastern cities, slowly, slowly as you can bear it. Then we will stop a while at some watering-place. Then," he continued with increasing eagerness, "we will run over to London and Paris and Rome, and all that. After we get tired we will go to some quiet place in Germany or Switzerland, and have teachers for the children. Then and there will be my time!" he said with rapture. "Escaped from all bother, among new scenes, with no interruption, don't you see, my dear? Then will be my opportunity. The thing I told you of has been fermenting in my brain for years. It has developed and ripened lately beyond my hopes. All that I have hoped so far is as nothing to it. Only give me a quiet opportunity, and I am sure of— But what is it, my dear?" he asked, for as he stood before her with his back to the steps of the porch, he saw her face suddenly grow pallid. She had heard the front gate close, and the rapid steps of her son coming up the front walk.

"Dear mother," he said, "I assure you it is nothing serious. You will believe me, won't you? It is a slight accident, a mere trifle. We will all laugh at it in a little while." And he smiled and kissed her as he said it; but his mother saw through all his precautions.

"An accident? I am strong enough to hear it, tell me at once." And she held her son with hands strong and steady from the experiences of years, her weakness forgotten.

"It is nothing at all but a little accident to Harry," Horace replied, less firm than she. "You see, George and he were out hunting. It was only a toy rifle that I brought him, and somehow it went off unexpectedly. But it was only through his leg. The ball broke the bone; but he will soon get over it. Harry bears it bravely, and doesn't suffer much. Don't be frightened, mother. It is only a trifle. Yonder they come now."

A woman of sense, even if she is a sick woman, is always stronger in an emergency than a battalion of men. Mrs. Dunwoddie rose to the need of the moment. It was, as so often before, the demand upon her of those she loved, and she was as equal to it as water is to thirst. Herself she had utterly forgotten, well or weak, and was gone, so to speak, to meet George, who was getting out of a wagon at the front gate, the doctor with him, while Harry was lying on a mattress within.

"Oh, money, money!" Col. Dunwoddie had said it during his deep poverty a thousand times, and as he went out to assist he said it himself now, "Oh, money, money!" But it was with a different inflection. He was as stern of visage as he was silent, but the fiercest swearing is that which is heard by none but God.

CHAPTER XXIV.

THE COMING OF THE KING.

"As is the lion, so its leap;
　As is the eagle, so its wings:
　Grade, rank, and fitness ruleth things,
Like orbits which the planets keep,
Like circles, which archangels sweep.

"When Philip's son the world subdued,
　The task was not more arduous
　Than when he mounts Bucephalus;
Each was to him like air and food,
He could no other, if he would!"

GAMALIEL MIDDLETON was careful to make his visits to Mrs. Anderson's neither too frequent nor too long, and at the hours most convenient to the ladies. No man was better informed than he, by this time, of the smallest details of Southern life and peculiarity. His talent as an actor was such that he had become almost in his dreams, so far at least as externals went, a Southern gentleman. He had modulated his briskness of speech even into those inflections and idioms of language, slow as well as soft, which are as inseparable to conversation in that latitude as are its curves and colors and sweetness to the orange or banana—the negroes held no monopoly of that. If need be, he could throw, at ten minutes' notice, all of this, Clair County, and Miss Anderson too, to the dogs. In case of failure, he could and would consign, and in a flash, the entire South and all it contained to a personage beyond the dogs. But there was to be no failure. He saw at this stage of his earthly pilgrimage an object before him beyond which was —empty abysm; if he failed to seize it, in giving other things and persons to the devil, he would hurl himself thither also.

"Will you allow me?" he said to Mrs. Anderson one evening in her parlor, when the conversation had been in reference to a certain speech by her husband. "You should know best, of course, but that speech of Judge Anderson was made in Congress the session *after* the one to which you refer."

"So it was," Mrs. Anderson said after reflecting; "but may I ask how you came to be so accurate?"

"Certainly, madam. Long before I thought I should have the pleasure of meeting you, I had taken Judge Anderson as the highest type of the Southern statesman of the Old School, and have made myself familiar with every point of his course and character."

For the moment the speaker really felt what he said, conscious how much the mother and daughter were .gratified. All these months he had done his utmost to interest this country-girl in himself. He had, during his many visits, as well as when they rode together, done all that man could do in describing to her everything he had seen which could give her pleasure. She had learned more about the great and brilliant world outside than in all her life up to that time. Places, persons, events, anecdotes of society, East, West, and in Europe, adventures in cities and in the Sierras, everything he could think of in literature, art, science even and invention, he had pressed, so far as he could do it without wearying her, into his service. And she had been interested, deeply interested. He had made her smile very often, had drawn the first laughter from her lips that she had indulged in for a long time, had brought the tears to her eyes, too, at some pathetic story, and more than once. Very naturally all he said had served to illustrate, without any apparent intention on his part, some new trait of his character— courage, generosity, abhorrence of meanness no less than of cruelty or falsehood. She had come to see him take his leave with evident regret, had felt the time hang heavier than ever on her hands when he was away, had welcomed him with pleasure upon his return. So far he had not made a false step. Nothing could be more certain than of her interest in, even liking for him. How far could he venture upon it?

"If I may allude for a moment to myself," he said now —"I have made it the law of my life to seek the best of everything. It is selfish, I dare say, but my object is to *be* the best I can. I began with nothing, beyond, at least, the influence of my mother, and few have had a more varied life. Sometimes I have failed, through trusting too much in others. At times I have succeeded. But I have all my fortunes yet to make, and upon two things I am determined— I weary you, I fear?"

"Not at all," Mrs. Anderson remarked.

I

No man could be more deferential to her, and he had interested her more than she thought it possible. "We will be glad to hear."

"One thing is, I will make the South my home. The other," he said, "is that I will aim at the highest possible ends here, and achieve them, if I can, by my own exertion."

There was the glow of an honest purpose upon his handsome face as he said it. Emmeline Anderson looked at him with fresh interest, to find so much meaning, respectful though it was, in his eyes fastened upon her face that she blushed.

"I can imagine," he continued in a lower tone, "some one object made known to a man, an object as much greater than anything he knew before as a star is greater than a bit of tin glittering in a gutter."

"A star?" the young girl asked, looking him as fully in the eyes as any Spanish belle of California might have done. "A star," she repeated gravely, "is out of your reach."

"That may be my misfortune," he said, "but I would rather die in trying for it than to succeed in the possession of anything less;" and he turned the conversation towards safer subjects.

"Take political affairs," he said at last. "Matters are in a terrible tangle here, Col. Dunwoddie tells me. He abhors the whole situation as much as your former slave, madam, Anderson Parker. What a remarkable man he is. I ascribe it to the unconscious influence upon him of Judge Anderson when alive. He is, Col. Dunwoddie says, a sort of Martin Luther, coarse and strong, and dreadfully set in his opinions. There is a kind of grandeur in the man, sturdy and slow, silent and burly, and black as he is. He has taken an aversion to me, I am sorry to say. But he hates me with his eyes shut, like a bison out West. The mulattoes have as sincere a horror of him, I find, as he has of them, except that *his* feeling is contempt. He is wrong.

Col. Dunwoddie is also wrong — wrong," Mr. Middleton said with honest energy.

"In what respect?" Emmeline Anderson asked. Absurd as it was, there was a certain power in the size and the blackness of her eyes upon his which reminded him of the sturdy strength of Anderson Parker. Young as she was, and unconsciously to herself, she was weighing the one who spoke very carefully, and he felt it.

"In this respect," he replied warmly: "I do not wish to flatter you, but the South is, in many respects, the most desirable part of America. By far the most fertile, better supplied with navigable rivers, having all mineral resources, its surface capable of railways and canals beyond any other portion of the country, its lands cheaper than any. You may smile at the notion, but I believe the day will come when the South will raise vast quantities of tea as well as of coffee — its climate and latitude is unequalled for it. My business is to understand all this. I made a report only last week to the land company I represent in regard to the manufacturing advantages here, the mills and the raw material side by side. It amazes me that the Colonel seems to have lost hope and has little faith in the future. Look at it, ladies;" and, taking a paper from his pocket, he demonstrated all he had said at some length.

"I understand you then," the younger of the ladies said, "that you think the South is before very long to be the most valued part of the country?"

"I do," he answered.

"Following on that, you believe that the controlling influence will pass into the hands of the South as it was—"

"As it was from the foundation of the Union up to the war," he interrupted her eagerly. "Yes, I certainly do."

"And therefore every man who can should go into politics as soon as possible?" she asked.

There was a meaning behind her words. He saw this in her eyes.

"If any man can hope to be to the state one tenth of what Judge Anderson was," he said boldly, "I think he is a coward if he does not try to do what he can. Would you believe it," he continued with a laugh, "some of these people want me to run for the Legislature. Of course, I should refuse."

The eyes were resting upon his face no longer, but Middleton trembled. A prize of such incalculable value had never been even proposed by the adventurer to himself as was this young girl. There she sat, simple, sedate, in easy reach. And yet? He could not understand her, that was his trouble! She could talk on any subject as lightly as he. No one seemed to put more of her soul into her singing when, at his request, she took her seat at the piano. But then her singing was by no means as if she were pouring out a song full of pleasure for him, as one pours water into a cup for another to drink; rather it was like the flowing of a river for its own sake. Somehow he stood, by permission, merely on the banks. It was that which perplexed him. He had seen an eagle once which had gone through thirty pitched battles. It was perched upon an ensign, and had a singular way of looking, as if miles away over the heads of the admiring crowd gathered about it, an expression as if it were upon a mountain-top, and alone. So of this woman. She was modest, beautiful; was attentive to all he said; no lady could have entertained a guest more politely. And yet?

How was it? Why was it? He felt that when such a woman loved, it would be with a devotion deep, unreserved, like the movement of nature. Certainly, boldness was his best policy.

"I think," he said as he arose to leave, "that in one respect I have the advantage of my friend, Horace Dunwoddie."

The young lady colored a little, and he felt as she looked at him that, for the instant at least, she had concentrated herself upon him.

"In this respect," he said, never flinch-ing, outwardly at least: "by wonderful good luck his family have come into the possession of an immense fortune, and Mr. Horace is," he continued, looking as closely at the young lady as he dared, "an excellent gentleman, making allowance, of course, for his inexperience, and for his—his natural elation, shall I call it?—over such sudden prosperity. But I do think," he added with great frankness, "I have the advantage of him. By reason of his money he can have all he takes a fancy to. He can buy anything and everything he may happen to like. In this sordid world I suppose there is nothing out of his reach. He is a splendid young fellow, and has improved by his travel, and since his father put his business into his hands. Do you know," said Middleton, conscious that, in the emergency, he was putting an almost magnetic power in his words—"Do you know, he reminds me of a young nobleman just come into estate and title. All men are at his feet, and, wherever he goes, all women will be eager for his notice, at least almost all. Is it not so? But I get nothing except by my own exertion. The highest object will be mine only by earning it against the whole world. And I must earn it by deserving it."

Never in his varied life had the man occupied so perilous a position. He could feel that the current of the times was drawing towards Niagara, quickening frightfully as it ran. In an instant, as it were, the critical opportunity would be gone, and forever gone. He was very cool, was perfectly aware of the crisis, was doing his utmost. He had enjoyed long practice upon what had been, so to word it, the trapeze as well as the stage, and, for the moment, he was what he personated. To his finger-ends he tingled with a sense of his sturdy independence.

He bowed to the ladies and left the parlor, for it was getting late. For the first time in his many visits Emmeline Anderson accompanied him into the hall to fast-on the outer door after him for the night. Evidently he had made an impression upon her nature, at once so proud and so reserved. An impression? In her case, once made, it would endure forever. Middleton never reflected so rapidly in his life. His attentions, if exceedingly cautious, had been long continued. His respectful admiration had been ardent and long suppressed, but in such a way as to show that it *was* suppressed. Was the moment ripe at last? If he could but have half a moment to consult his sister. Alas! he felt that she was, in comparison with this dark beauty, but as the gay-colored ribbon which fluttered about her throat in the draught from the front-door as he opened it to pass out. It was not merely that she was to him the woman most intrinsically valuable in herself, although he did not clearly know why, of any he had ever known. He saw her, through a medium known only to himself, arrayed in royal purple, imperial, magnificent, and would gladly have given his note for half a million, fully intending to pay it, too, if he could have known on the spot what to do in order to succeed.

So queerly is the brain constructed that, even in that rapid conjuncture, he remembered seeing in Paris a gymnast performing upon a bar suspended from a balloon far overhead. Boldness was *his* only course, also. According to the Southern custom, she gave him her hand in parting. He clung to it as to existence.

"Will you allow me, Miss Anderson?" he said; "I know it is a terrible risk I run. But I love you! I adore you! May I be allowed to hope —?" and the lover felt that he was pale as well as tremulous. "May I dare to trust that — that some day—?"

His back was towards the opened door as he spoke. On the instant her hand was withdrawn, and stretched out towards the darkness into which she looked, her face aglow with a sudden glare coming through the doorway. Middleton, at least, had heard no step upon the veranda outside; but Horace Dunwoddie had, on the instant, her outstretched hand in his, and was in the hall between the two.

"Don't be alarmed, Miss Emmeline," he said; "somebody has set the old warehouse on fire. Is that you, Mr. Middleton? Glad to see you. The negroes used it as a church. I have been fearing trouble there for a long time, and have been on the lookout. Let us go in and see that your mother is not alarmed."

The new-comer had held the lady's hand, and now drew her into the parlor, leaving Middleton alone. His first impulse was to curse, and with the sincerity of prayer from the devoutest of lips when death threatens; but what was the use? It was not merely the sudden arrival of the other; there was something in the coming of his rival like the rushing of air into a heated room; like the breaking of day upon the gas-lit stage of a theatre—it was the advent of nature, and who could oppose that? In spite of himself, Middleton felt as if he were a ragged tramp in the act of stealing something, and here was the owner down upon him in the very deed. It was not that this young millionaire was so tall, broad-shouldered, and bearded, but that he assumed as matter of course that he was lord and master. According to Middleton, a man's essential manhood lay in the abundance of things he possessed; had he been rich he would have been, in his own estimation, very strong; not being rich he was weakness itself. It was his desperate hope of becoming so which had made him bold; but this man came with the boldness of actual possession. No actor could personate a king better than Middleton; but, in this case, the king himself had arrived. All that was possible to him to say or do the dismayed lover had done; but here was—yes, a force like that of gravitation; could he grapple with that? He had all along acknowledged to himself that, in some subtle sense, although wholly apart from each other, Horace Dunwoddie and Emmeline Anderson were of royal blood, and, on the instant, here was the natural mating of the two; and he?—he was but the spectator in the press at the royal wedding. Perhaps so, but they were not married *yet!*

It did not come into Middleton's mind to return to the parlor. He must have time to think. The whole heaven was aglow with the blaze of the burning building, and he had to pass it on his way to his hotel. As he walked he observed continually increasing crowds of men thronging up the road from both directions—white men and black, on foot and on horseback, and not a man but was armed. It struck him as remarkable that there was no loud talking. As he passed along every person looked closely into his face. Drawing nearer to the flaming pile, he heard a black woman here and there break into a sudden wail over the destruction of the place of worship, and as suddenly cease. Dozens of boys, white and black, were laughing and calling to each other; some of them tumbling somersaults in the dust under the falling sparks, as he had seen them do in the excitement of a passing circus company. The sandy road looked as red as blood in the glare, and the trees on all sides seemed as if they had closed in and were crowding around to see. But that which he remembered best afterwards was seeing a group of black men beside the fire—not a mulatto near them—and, standing on the horse-block, was Anderson Parker. He was in his shirt-sleeves, his hairy blackness of bosom exposed, no hat on his head, and not looking at the fire; he was carefully scanning the road up and down, and the faces of the people as they came and went. He looked steadily at Middleton as he passed, but made no reply to his salutation of "How are you, Parker?"—did not even look at him again, although Middleton had paused a moment intending to engage him in conversation; but the man refused to be conversed with,

and he had to pass on with a sudden sense of being as thoroughly in a foreign country as if it were Spain instead. He was heartily glad the building was burning, and would have been more so if the crowd were perishing in it. Clair County and the South might go to ashes for what he cared, he wanted to get to his room and think—think! There was no doubt of the assumption of mastership upon the part of the young sultan his rival; but how about the lady? Would she allow it? Young Dunwoddie may have cast her by his insolence into his hands, who knows? Even in case she did not resent that proprietorship in her which the other assumed— Well, what? Once in his life Middleton had been compelled—unless reports greatly belied him at the time—to rid himself of a certain particularly inconvenient friend. It had been a desperate case for which really that was the only cure, especially as, camping out—those two by themselves alone—in a desolate part of Nevada, it had been a perfectly safe transaction. If he could have done so, in view of the unspeakable stake at issue, he would have tossed Horace Dunwoddie over the edge of a cañon as he would have done a bad cigar—that is, if it could be done with as little bodily risk. But one must be cool. Suppose he had lost the largest prize in the wheel? there was a lesser of which he was sure. He must think!

As he passed into the almost deserted hotel a hand was laid on his arm. It was Yellow Jessamine, and in a state of singular elation.

"It will all be right, sah," he whispered. "You take my word, it's done fixed—suah! Dose fool folks presist in having you," he added with a grin. "Been to de fire, sah? You don't catch me dar. No, sah, no fire for *me!* I wos burned when I wos a baby, an', you know, sah, 'a burnt child dreads de fire!'"

———◆———

CHAPTER XXV.

POLITICS IN CLAIR COUNTY.

"Like to a mustard-seed God's kingdom grows;
And high and higher yet this portion towers,
This province of his realm, this land of ours!
For think you to its North and West there flows
The sap of all God's purpose? Or suppose
The South shall, stayed from growth, forever wilt,
While West and North, bough-bent with fruit and
    flowers,
Shall flourish on its halted life upbuilt?
Not so; henceforth and purged its tropic blood
Shall flow as hot but with the health of law;
And so this many-petaled plant shall draw
East, West, South, North, an even masterhood;
In fruitfulness for all each state the chief;
Earth's grandest growth and green in every leaf."

HARRY's leg was broken in such a manner as to require the most careful nursing, the large arteries being so endangered that perilous loss of blood might take place at any moment. He was not without devoted attendants. When Alice was not with Clara Middleton she was with Harry, although she was good company for him only by a sort of enforced cheerfulness. George, by whose carelessness the accident happened, was very contrite, and did all he could to make things pleasant to his brother by reading to him, playing chess with him; most of all by being as funny as he dared to be without making Harry laugh too violently—that might bring on the bleeding. He had a vigorous ally in May, who brought a select assortment of her school-girl friends to visit him from time to time. And no one could have done more to amuse him than Clara. She laughed and talked with him; but once as she sat silently and alone by his bedside, supposing him to be asleep, Harry was amazed, looking at her through his half-closed eyes, to see how old she seemed to have suddenly become — her hands lying clasped in her lap, her head bent down in deep thought. At a slight sound in the hall, however, she started, and became, as in a moment, ten years younger, greeting Horace who came in with a bright smile and a merry remark.

It had become impossible for Horace to be with Harry, except of evenings, owing to the crowds thronging his father's office as election times drew on; and Emmeline Anderson must have known of this, for she was to see Harry quite often during the day, but always leaving before dusk. One afternoon she was seated upon a footstool beside him, her hair down over her face as she netted at a partridge-net she was making for the invalid, Mrs. Dunwoddie exchanging a word with her now and then, seated on the other side of the lounge which Harry occupied, when Charlie came into the room.

"Won't you give me a kiss, Charlie?" she said, lifting her glowing face as the child came and stood by her. He considered the proposition gravely, as became his judicial bearing, and, lifting his blue eyes to hers, he enunciated it as an opinion from the bench, "I don't love Alice's her."

"He means Miss Clara," Harry explained before his mother could stop him.

"But I love you. You," he said, with the eyes of truth upon Emmeline's face, "are Horace's her!"

"Charlie, Charlie!" his mother exclaimed, while Harry laughed in a way which was very imprudent, checking himself, however, as he saw that the color in the cheeks of their visitor was not altogether that either of confusion or pleasure.

After she was gone Mrs. Dunwoddie lay back in her chair in still deeper thought. While the dark-eyed beauty had been so busy among the meshes of Harry's net, she had wondered if it would ever be possible for her to forward the dearest wish of her motherly heart by saying anything to Emmeline. And it was strange that so kind-hearted a woman should have felt an aversion so deep towards Middleton—an aversion rising almost to terror in reference to Clara; or it would be strange were it not that such love to one's own awakens something almost of the tigress even in a heart as trained as was hers to watch first of all against herself. But she understood the high-spirited girl too well; and Emmeline and Horace being what they were, she left them to themselves.

The celebrated doctor from the city had reversed the decision of her rural physicians, and, as has been said, had urged, just before Harry's accident, a change of climate as essential to her life; but now the care of the wounded boy devolved, at last, upon her most of all. And she had never known her husband to be so disappointed; hide it as he might try to do, his defeated hopes recoiled upon him with disastrous effect—they had been so vast, so brilliant, he had been so certain of realizing them! In virtue of the necessities of his family, and as lawyer and editor, he had been compelled to be compliant with people, although it was always against the grain. Now that he had become independent of them, the old liking and disliking asserted itself as a steel spring of high temper and closely coiled would do when suddenly released. Mrs. Dunwoddie and Horace were kept in continual alarm, he was so reckless as to what he said and did. In addition to many lesser eruptions of impatience, there had been one or two bursts of hot indignation on his part that had terrified them. He did not know it, but the current of his life had quickened so of late that the intervention of Harry's accident was a sudden barrier against which it foamed with aggravated fury, although it was by no means upon Harry or upon his family that his impatience expended itself.

"I used, at least, to have steady occupation," he said to Horace at his office one morning; "now everything is utterly unsettled. It is impossible to read, much less write, with any fixedness of purpose. Never indulge your imagination, Horace. Don't read books. Never write a line except on business. Have no intimate relations with people. The vast majority of them are either rascals or fools—bores the best of them. What in the mischief is all this?"

It was a crowd who came at this moment to his office to demand that the Colonel should make a speech. They were led by old Major Clarke; and Horace saw among them Squire Stevens, who kept the best hotel in the town; Mr. Robinson, the keeper of a provision-store; Charlie Marston, who owned horses, and whose interest in the election was purely as of a race between the rival candidates; a doctor or so; a lawyer or two; the remainder were planters whose sons had been in the Colonel's regiment. The political excitement in the state, as throughout the South and the whole country, had reached its climax. The papers of that state, especially, were filled with violent appeals on the one side and the other. Secret organizations held midnight meetings, and people talked nothing but politics everywhere and in the bitterest way. From all this Col. Dunwoddie had held aloof, notwithstanding his well-known devotion to the interests of his state; and his son was alarmed now lest his father, in his violence of feeling, should give mortal offence to his visitors. But the Colonel was a gentleman still, although he had become, when not in a wrathful mood, a cold and acrid one, and he pleaded pressure of business and ill-health as a reason for refusing to speak.

The crowd went at last, very unwillingly.

"I am glad you declined," Horace said, with such energy that his father looked at him with a sudden suspicion in his eyes.

"What do you mean, sir?" he demanded, almost angrily, and his son remembered that an irritable doubtfulness as to others, because of itself first, is one of the surest proofs that an intellect is losing its balance. But, while he hesitated under the fierce gaze of his father, to the surprise of both Anderson Parker came into the office, hat in hand.

"*You* off the plantation to-day, Parker!" Colonel Dunwoddie said with energy. "I did think you had more sense. And *you* want to have a hand with the scallawags, to lie and to steal, do you? I had hoped there was one black man in the state who had judgment enough to work his way up by his own hands—"

"He isn't here about politics, father," his son said. "They hate him worse than they do you."

"Yes, sir, I is," the negro man replied. He had on his Sunday clothes, and both father and son thought they had never seen him look so big or so black. But he had a grave and even anxious look in his slow and serious eyes.

"I is afeared dere is goin' to be trouble," he said. "You has your party an' I has my party, but I want you to speak. Dere's a mighty heap of people, black an' white, out dere on de square. Dere's trouble in de air. We all know you. You must speak."

"Speak to them yourself," Col. Dunwoddie said roughly.

"I hab spoke. To de black people. An' even to de yellow ones. Not to de white. What for good can *I* do? You must speak, sir," he added, steadily.

"I *won't!*" Col. Dunwoddie said with energy.

"Dere's terrible trouble brewin'," urged the other.

"The town and the county, the South and the entire land may go to—!" The Colonel paused. These last few weeks, and more than once, he had startled Horace by coming very near swearing, and in the most violent form.

"You *fought* for de Souf," the burly black said, facing the nervous white man with his solid obstinacy. "Is you *afeared* to, sir?"

Horace laughed outright. His father stood looking steadily at the other for a moment. Then, without saying a word, he slowly put on his hat and went out into the crowded streets.

Tom Terrell had spoken for a tempestu-

ous hour when Col. Dunwoddie left his office. He was an able man, had a powerful voice, and he had not spared vituperation. But Terrell himself felt how hopeless it was, the people had been so long and so deeply exasperated at the horrible corruption in every department of the state government that it was simply impossible to excite them further. Hiddikel Queasy refused to mount the platform. Being pigeon-chested, his voice became a squeak when he tried to make himself heard in the open air; and he contented himself with moving about among the negroes, saying a word, shaking a hand, wherever he went—Yellow Jessamine circulating as actively as he and in the same interests.

When Terrell was through Major Clarke took the stand. He was an old gentleman with a white head and pendant red cheeks, who was corpulent in a way which is known as "pursy." Born and raised on a plantation he had never been outside the state. He read no books whatever, and only one paper. He had been the worst master in Clair County, in virtue, as all agreed, of ruining his negroes, as he had ruined his son, by over-indulgence. He cared nothing for politics except so far as they gave him opportunities, in addition to those of his home and the street-corners, of "pitching into the Yankees," as he phrased it. His anger at the "Federals" was a gale which blew due North without slackening; and that was the trouble with the Major's oratory, he began as now on the platform in such a whirlwind of denunciation that it was impossible to keep it up, especially as he was so very fat.

"Any woman that marries a Northern man"—he culminated in that now as always—"or Southern man that marries a Yankee girl, ought to be tarred and feathered; and, blast my garters, gentlemen, I'm the man to help do it!" But, having got so far, he was compelled to stop, panting and perspiring. And yet a more generous cr hospitable old man never lived than the Major.

When he got through there were loud cries for "Dunwoddie!" "Dunwoddie!" whose gray head, towering above the crowd, everybody had observed by this time. As soon as — in response to calls growing louder and louder—he was seen ascending the platform which was erected in front of the court-house, the news seemed to flash up and down all the streets, for every hotel and rum-shop, every store, confectionery establishment, office, and home even, poured its throngs towards the spot; and very soon the Colonel had before him the largest assembly he had ever addressed. It had been a long time since he had spoken in the open air, and his wealth had added greatly to the weight of his reputation meanwhile. There were as many colored people present as white, and every man had that keen edge of feeling which comes with the knowledge that, like himself, every person there was armed to the teeth. Horace, not without a deal of vague anxiety, got as near to his father as he could for the crowd, Anderson Parker being near him, the former in terror lest the excitement should drive the speaker into— He dared not define his fear.

Col. Dunwoddie had lost much sleep with Harry, and, in addition to all else, there was such an epidemic uneasiness of late in the very air that he, the most sensitive of men, could not but feel that also. He had left his office in wrath, intending, for the first and last time, to speak his whole mind. The instant he stood before his audience the old instinct of the orator was upon him. Former habit clothed him on the spot like a coat of mail. He was astonished at the courteous and conciliating way in which he began. There was deep attention as he reminded the people that he had been born in the South, had always lived among them, had fought through the whole war for the Confederacy. Then, repeating how sorely he had regretted being urged to do so, he entered, by force of his legal training, upon a consecutive line of argument, speaking to the point and more and more rapidly. First, he dwelt upon the natural resources of the South in general, and those of their own state in particular. Middleton, who was in the crowd, led the applause at this. Next he spoke of the people as being, upon the whole, superior to all other people as their region was, in natural advantages, superior to all other regions. There was a certain accepted exaggeration in all this. Not on the part of such present as had never been outside of the South, and whose reading was exclusively of papers published therein; to them this was gospel denied by none except wicked and prejudiced people. With Col. Dunwoddie and the class whom he represented the South was that portion of Christendom fully equal if not superior to any other, which had been, by some fatality, isolated from the rest, and, standing thus at bay, was bound to assert as well as to defend itself against the world. As an orator he spoke, and must speak, purely upon and from Southern grounds. It was as instinctive to the Colonel and to those who heard him as was the eloquence, and the kind of eloquence, of Antony with the dead Cæsar lying at his feet. The crowd was increasing, and the applause grew more enthusiastic.

On the strength of it the speaker drew a glowing picture of the day when the South would have resumed its ancient supremacy in the nation, and, standing firmly upon that assumption, he entered into a rapid detail of what they should do towards that glorious result. His blood was up by this time. Anecdote, illustration, poetry with ringing rhymes came freely to his lips. Now and then Horace trembled. Having got full mastery of his audience, the Colonel indulged, now and then, but always on purely Southern grounds, in scathing sarcasm and blasting invective. Master of others because master of himself, he held steadily to a few points. The state should have sole charge of its own affairs, of course. For what? To see that every man in it had justice; to see that every citizen, white and black, was educated; to see that every plundering office-holder was—*hung!* Last he urged that every man should own his own farm; work, or have it worked, under his own eyes; educate his own children; neither trench upon the right of any other man nor allow any other man to infringe upon his right. And so he made his closing words an importunate appeal to every individual present to do his best, assuring them that, white or black, all a man got, or deserved to get, was according to that; and all for the glory of the state and the South!

It was a genuine inspiration. Had he made elaborate preparation for the occasion he could not have done as well. For years he had thought, and very deeply, upon the subjects treated, and his speech was the outflashing of his inmost soul. Being as independent as he now was, he could, and did, speak as he never otherwise would have dared to do. It was the sweetest pleasure that Alec Allen's money had afforded him so far. The fact is, the speech, which was more than an hour long, was an event. Republished through the state and the South, it was the turning-point of a new era. Horace wondered at his father. It was almost impossible to believe that this impassioned orator was the gentleman whose fitful uncertainties had distressed him so of late; it was the transformation as of a mortal into a demigod. The excited son was eager to hasten home and recount it all to his mother. As he was turning away, the orator, stilling the applause with his long arm, said, in the mastership of his success—

"Friends, tell me, was I ever an abolitionist?" There was a peal of laughter at this; no reply was necessary. He continued.

"I speak to gallant men. Can you stand still and take a little bitter medicine to-day?"

"Go ahead, Colonel!"—"Out with it!"— "Ler 'er rip!" came in reply; the enthusiasm was such he might dare anything.

"I will now say," he added, "what has been a secret with two or three. You all knew Judge Anderson. You know what his plantation is. That splendid place has been sold. You know the—the man who has bought it. He has lived among you all his life—will live among you till he dies. You all respect him for his hard sense. No man has been such a help to Judge Anderson's family. He is honest, industrious, respectful in his bearing towards all, a generous giver, and hates scallawags, white and black, with all his soul. Gentlemen, gentlemen, *be* gentlemen," the Colonel pealed out with magnetic effect. "Remember, whatever else he may be, he is a *Southern* man! I introduce to you the owner of Judge Anderson's plantation, Anderson Parker!"

It was an undoubted sensation. As Col. Dunwoddie stepped to one side, the stalwart negro stood upon the platform before them. It was the first time that black and white had ever faced each other in that relation. The people were stupefied with astonishment, but the slightest thing would have changed their amazement into a howling tempest, a tempest in which every colored man present would be the object of assault, and with weapons other than words. The feelings and the conduct of the whites present would have been exactly that of any others of the race born, educated, situated under like circumstances. They held their breath ready for whatever came next.

Eloquence is the expression of magnetic feeling produced in the speaker by that of his audience, they being a thousand to his one. The first effect of that profoundly excited assembly upon the black man was to quiet him into a perfect control of himself. With the instinct of Col. Dunwoddie, as of Paul before Felix, he began by conciliating his hearers. Powerful as he physica⌐

was, his whole aspect breathed of that, his gesture of submission, his deprecating words.

"I is only Anderson Parker," he said at last; "everybody dun know me long ago. Plantation? Maybe so. But it ain't all paid for yet! Wish it was! Besides, it's de goodness ob de wife ob de man I was proud to call my marster, Judge Anderson! I guess de Judge was marster of good many folks in Clair County."

The audience had a memory, on the instant, of the stately ownership of them all, so to speak, on the part of the grand old Judge, and laughed.

"I own dat place," the man continued, "only because my Miss Julia *trusts* me! You see, she dun know me so long. But *I* ain't fitten to speak to white folks. All I can do is to say amen to what de Colonel says. Dis is de way I puts it up," he explained; and, making in his own way, a rapid restatement of the points of the speaker going before, he closed each with an amen, in which many of the negroes in the audience, as they got used to their novel position, joined with religious fervor.

"All dat you white folks hab got," he said, at last, "is what you or your farders earned. We black people will hab to do de same; we will hab to earn it—*earn* it by hard work! Dat's so! Dat's all I want; dat's all any man ought to hab."

"Who burned down dat preachin' place?" he added with the sudden change of the key in which he was speaking, as well as of subject, peculiar to his undisciplined race. It was a dangerous question. He stood on perilous ground, but he knew it. "Who burned down dat house? Mars Colonel," he said, turning suddenly upon the former speaker, still standing beside him, "I do wunner if *you* did it?"

There was something so comic in the manner of the Colonel at this, as well as of the one asking, that there were peals of laughter; and the black added, "No more did any odder respectable white man do it.

Ebbery man on dis ground who is a gen'elman like Col. Dunwoddie and Judge Anderson hates to hab it done worst of any. But yonder is de heap of ashes, an' "—his voice rising to the same pathetic key— "Who did it? Sometimes de young men do such things jest for fun. Dey want to hab some excitement—get into some debiltry, de young men do! I wunner," the man said, standing on the edge of the platform and looking among the people, "who? —who?" until his eye fell upon a young man crowded up upon the steps of the platform, his face towards the audience. "I do s'pect," the orator proceeded, pointing him out with his extended hand—"do s'pect *you* did it!"

There was a storm of laughter at this, for Horace Dunwoddie was the one indicated; and, if there was a person respected and esteemed in Clair County, one of whom the people were proud, it was Horace. His astonishment, too, and the way in which his face burned under the charge, increased the merriment.

"A fool kin see no decent man did it. But dere is de pile of ashes. It was de onny place we had to worship God in, an'," the speaker continued, with a wail of pathos in his tones, "till we get schools, dat is de *one* way we was learnin' to be good men, de *one* place an' way. Who burn dat church?" he went on, with a rapid change of manner, speaking swiftly and with a kind of ferocity which sent a shudder through his audience. "I know de man," the orator thundered, in a way Cicero might have envied when he assaulted Catiline or Verres, rising to his full height with denouncing arm. "I know him— know him well. People," he said, coming to the very edge of the platform again, bending over, lowering his voice to almost a whisper, which was heard in the hush by every one there, "I know dat mis'rable sinner. I know him—know him *well!* An' he isn't a white man. An' he isn't a black man. Gor Almighty an' I—we two know him! An' he is in dis berry crowd. An' his time is comin'!"

There was a death-like silence. But the speaker seemed to avoid looking in any special direction, much less indicating any one, and added—

"Dat is all I hab to say. I thank you for listening to me so long. Please 'member all de Colonel dun said. And oh, my marsters," he continued, using the disused term with great humility and pathos—"oh, my marsters! It is onny a little while. Berry soon we will all ob us, black an' white an'—an'—yaller—be standin' before de great Maker an' Marster ob us all. You colored folks, you stop rushin' away from your work into de towns; stop your laziness an' stealin' an' lyin' an' foolin' away your money. Vote if you want to, but you keep out of bein' voted for till you're fitten for it. You *earn* it, an' you'll get it. You think, now de Lord has made you free from de whites, it's all dun and ober. You fool niggers!" this blackest of them all said with the sadness of utter pity, "a nigger marster is thousand times worse, an ebb'ry colored man in de sound ob my voice is under jest dat! You got to break out ob your own ign'rant mis'rable hands 'fore you will stop bein' slaves, wus slaves dan ebber! But oh, marsters, my marsters," he added, with the pleading of his strong heart, "be marciful to us colored folks. You are higher than us. Then be dat much more like God. We didn't make ourselves black. We didn't put ourselves here. Was it *us* made ourselves free? Gib us a chance, marsters. Let de law touch us an' nothin' else. Be patient wid us—patient—patient—until we kin learn somethin'. De Yankees are a million ob miles away, an' we are in your hands under God. Onny gib us a chance, marsters—gib us a chance! I dun said all I know."

CHAPTER XXVI.

THE WRATH OF SOVEREIGNS.

"Proud wert thou, Pride, in heaven to dwell?
Too proud before thy God to bow?
Since then, say, Lucifer, art thou
Proud as of thy sufficient hell?"

AT the time these events were taking place there lived in the post-oak forests, a few miles beyond the Anderson plantation, the poor widow of a man named Pignelly, who had been killed in the Confederate service. She had an only daughter of eighteen years of age who lived in the log-cabin with her, and the two made a living by weaving rag-carpets, making butter, and selling such vegetables and fruit, poultry and eggs as they could raise upon the acre or two which made their home. Their place was so far away from any one else that, at Mrs. Dunwoddie's suggestion, the Colonel had bought and made them a present of a comfortable house and lot in Clairsville; and May, and even Alice, had gone with enthusiasm into the work of furnishing the house, while George, with the Judge to look on, had insisted, aided by some of his schoolmates, in whitewashing with his own hands, and very copiously, every square inch about the house, fence, and trees, in and out of reach. For some time the mother and daughter had refused, from motives of pride, to accept the gift, and it was not until George, May, and Charlie had gone out in the carriage and begged them to do so as a favor to their mother that they had consented. There was such an unwholesome uneasiness in the atmosphere as the election excitement deepened that Horace had ridden out one Tuesday afternoon to urge their immediate removal, and his father's wagon was to have gone for them on Thursday. Possibly this had hastened the catastrophe, for Wednesday morning Anderson Parker, riding by their home to see to the splitting of some rails for his decaying fences, had come upon such a scene of horror there that, abandoning his work-mule as too slow, he had set out upon a run to Clairsville, when he came upon Horace, riding out with a basket of luncheon from his mother, to save them the trouble of cooking while they were packing to move into town.

"You hurry back to Clairsville, an' bring out some white folks," he said, after he had told what he had seen to the horror-stricken young man, "while some ob my black people and me hunt down de scoundrels. We know who is de onny men in de county who could do dat. You be on the spot, but oh, Mars Horace," he added, "you all leab dem mulattoes to *me!*"

Col. Dunwoddie was out of Clairsville on business, but Horace managed, as he entered the town, to intercept George on his way to the house from the post-office, and gave him a charge against allowing the news to get to his mother's ears, and in an hour after was on his way back to the scene of the murder, accompanied by a few armed men. Chief among these was Ferdinand Clarke, in the highest of spirits, laughing and talking.

"Of course, I'm sorry," he said, "no fellow more so, but I'm so glad I happened to be in town, wouldn't have missed it for anything. Almost as glad as I am that Tom Terrell is off trying to bully your father, Horace, over some lawsuit somewhere in the circuit; won't he curse and tear around when he hears it! Because I know Anderson Parker will catch whoever did it. That man always does what he tries to do. Did you hear how near he came to killing me with a fence-rail? I have an account to settle with him for that yet. Hi-yah!" And, in the mere overflow of his exuberant spirits, the young dare-devil made the woods ring with the old battle-yell.

"Do hold your tongue, Ferdy!" Horace said impatiently. "You forget, man."

"That's a fact, old fel, so I did. But," he reasoned, "Clairsville is such a graveyard of a place, you never have any fun. I

was sure we would have a regular row of it the day your father made his speech, and I was horribly disappointed—not a man shot, nor nothing! Only once, Horry, old chap —Hi-hi-hi-*yah!*" And having relieved himself by another and more terrific yell, the dissolute companion subsided for the moment, especially as just then the scene of the tragedy came into view. "Don't faint, Mr. Middleton," he said, for that gentleman had joined the company uninvited as they rode past his hotel. "Better take a sniff at my smelling-bottle, sir!"

Middleton politely declined the whiskey-flask thus pressed upon him by the other. Years before, happening to be in a medical college, he had caught a glimpse, as he passed the half-opened door of a dissecting-room, of the dead bodies lying upon tables therein, and had shrunk back at the sight, sickened almost to fainting. The next instant, compelling himself to enter the room, he found that an odd revulsion of feeling had come over him, the corpses in all stages of dissection having become to him nothing more than so many images of wax or clay. Since then he had passed pretty much through all doors leading anywhere. Horace Dunwoddie was differently constituted, and seeing that the matter had passed into sufficient hands, he turned and rode homeward, meeting, as he did so, the crowds which were by this time hurrying to the spot, whites and blacks.

In an hour or two it seemed to Middleton as if the whole county was coming. And, wedged in among the excited multitude, he saw quite a number of the females of that peculiar type known as poor whites, as distinct a tribe of people as the Esquimaux. They all wore sun-bonnets and scanty calico dresses, and had the same cadaverous expression. Not a woman but had her jar of snuff and bit of dogwood stick, its ends frayed into a brush, with which she continually mopped her mouth. Their insatiable curiosity as to the details of the crime was one of the most curious things there to Middleton; none pressed in so near or listened so eagerly to the horrible details. But from the first there had been but one mulatto spectator on the ground—Leonidas Dunwoddie.

"Is you aware ob de circumstance, sah," he had remarked in Middleton's ear during a lull in the proceedings in relation to Anderson Parker, and with the swelling diction in which the mulatto delighted, "dat dis berry black individual is as much a slave to de Andersons as if he was dere peculiar property still? Ebber sence de Judge deceased, when de 'lections are comin' on at least, dat individual, dey tell me, sleeps ebb'ry night on de veranday. To watch ober de ladies, to preserve dem from danger, you observe. De ladies dey is not aware ob it, sah. But he does, dat man! Like an en-ormous black—black—quadruped!" the informant continued with disgust. "I believe," he added, "dat a human being is not a dog for anybody; he should be," he said with great dignity, and drawing himself up, "a gen'l'man!"

But Leonidas had not thought it prudent to stay. The man of whom he had spoken had taken occasion to whisper to him in the confusion and deadly excitement.

"You better get back to your shop, boy," and he had gone. Leonidas was, like many of his shade of color, an excellent, industrious, and deserving man. But people were, like Anderson Parker, prejudiced against mulattoes on the principle that, even in buying a cow or a horse, it is safest to rely upon one of some definite and decided color. A mere prejudice, of course.

The assemblage had given its highest proof of respect for Anderson Parker, who had himself captured the criminal after a severe chase and fight, when, infuriated as it was, they had turned over his captive to him and to a jury of black men selected by the whites. All the tables, barrels, washtubs had been brought together in front of the house, and upon these he sat as judge, and beside him the miserable wretch himself, a lank mulatto, with the face of a cat, the jurymen being grouped around. Crowded upon the roof of the house, perched upon ash-hoppers, clinging to the post and pole of the well, breaking down the palings and boughs of the orchard, clustering like bees upon all the fences and trees in reach, the whole region round about seemed to be there, looking eagerly on. Towering above them all, his face torn and bleeding from the hands of the mulatto, who had fought like a wild animal before he could be secured, the black judge had managed, as by the sheer force of his well-known character as well as his muscular might of voice and gesture, and a species of deadly calmness, to subdue the vast crowd into silence, of which he himself seemed to be the incarnation. Even Middleton acknowledged to himself that the black was master of the hour.

The criminal had confessed at last with frantic appeals for mercy. The jury had brought in their verdict. The black judge had said as little as possible. He now stood up, looked all about him, and said so as to be heard by every man clinging even to the farthest tree—

"I hope de day is comin' when dere will be onny two colors in dis land, white and black. People say I is too hard against de yaller people, dat dere is as many good yaller folks as dar is black. May be so. I is an ign'rant man myself. De blue is *blue* on de flag, de red is *red*, an' de white is *white*. Please God to bring dat day when it will be black or white! And de day is comin' when no man can do what dis poor sinner has done. Or, if he does, we can try him under a roof, wid walls around us, by de law. For all dat, and for him let us pray."

He had laid his powerful grasp upon the wretch when he began his supplications. It could not have been that he feared he would escape, for his own were the only eyes that were closed during prayer. In the agony of his entreaties his hand closed as if it would crush the yellow flesh to the bone, the lank felon swaying about in the fervors of his petition as if he were a straw. It seemed as if Anderson Parker had hold upon the very soul of the man whom he already regarded as dead, and was lifting it by sheer force to God for mercy. Perhaps it was the passionate pathos of the prayer which influenced the criminal. Whatever it was, as the prayer ended and people arose to follow to the dreadful execution, the doomed man whispered in the ear of the black—

"I hain't said so. But Yaller Jessamine was here wid me. He's arter you. You'd better be a prayin' for yourself!"

When Horace Dunwoddie was passing in front of Mrs. Anderson's place in returning home, he drew rein a moment and considered matters. He had not thought of calling, but ought he not to do so? If only to assure himself of their continued safety. He looked at the mansion in its environment of trees. Not a creature was in sight, not a sound could he hear. Surely it had been a base, an almost wicked thing, that Mrs. Anderson and her daughter should have been left to live by themselves in so lonely a place. True, his father and mother had done their utmost to induce them to remove to Clairsville. He would not speak of it to-day. Above all, they must see nothing in his manner to 'alarm them. He dismounted, fastened his horse, went in, and was admitted by little Zady into the parlor. Much encouraged by his last visit, as Emmeline Anderson entered the room he took her hand, and his excited feelings, reacting into an unspeakable affection for the lovely girl, he tried, for the first time in his life, to kiss her; but she repelled him with a coldness he could not understand.

"I hoped you had forgiven me," he said, "but you are so much more beautiful every time I see you that I despair of keeping up with you. Every time I see you, though, I love you so much more than I did before that my love lifts me to your level in an instant. When I was East, I thought this was worthy even of you," and as he said it he produced from his vest-pocket the ring he had bought. "To-day it does not seem worth your having. Will you let me put it on? I have been too impulsive, but you are such a frightful provocation. You are the one woman in all the world for me, and I do know," he said, standing up before her like a young Augustus, "that I am the one man on all this planet for you. Why, oh most merciful queen, why, oh, why do you not *say* you love me?—you know you do!"

The lady would not have been mortal if she had not glanced at the ring, nor mortal woman if it had not dazzled her for an instant. But she did not look at it twice. She had formed a purpose before she came into the room, and, alas for the lover, this but confirmed her in it. She had not seated herself, but stood looking at him with her great eyes, a certain poise in her person, a something new to him throbbing in her cheeks. It flashed upon him at the moment that, in comparison with this woman, Clara Middleton was like May's canary-bird, all chirp and twitter, all motion and feathers.

"You had better not be too certain, sir," she said, and paused. Little Zady had heard and told her of the dreadful event, and she was controlling herself by a strong effort.

Horace Dunwoddie looked at her a moment, perplexed beyond measure by her manner, and then said—

"I believe that the very soul of your father has passed into you. Do you know, you remind me now of one of your brothers, and then of the other? Miss Emmeline Anderson," he added gravely, "I admire and love you with all my soul, and, Heaven helping me, I intend to marry you."

"Would you have dared to say this before your money came?" she asked. "Did you earn it? Can you remember when you were merely a clerk at the depot? Your uncle's money has changed you more than you know, sir. We are poor, my mother and I, so poor that we were compelled to sell our place, to sell it for the pitiful sum things are rated at now, to sell it to one of our own slaves. And your father had the *heart*," she said, suddenly relaxing her control over herself, "to stand up in public and proclaim the fact! That Col. Dunwoddie should introduce him as the successor of Judge Anderson! Our black slave, taking his position as my father's successor by making a speech as he used to do! The boy would not have dared do it of his own mind. He was too respectful, too sensible. No one would have dreamed that he owned the place but for your father! You can understand why my mother does not come into the room. But why should I talk to you of this?—we are getting our small means together and are going away immediately."

"Miss Anderson—" the other began, moved more by her color coming and going, by the light in her eyes, by the tones of her voice, than by her words.

"—In one moment, sir. It was natural that money should intoxicate a youth like yourself." And the words hurt her, as she uttered them, far more than they did him.

"But," she continued with slow scorn, "I had not supposed even so sudden a fortune could have so disastrous an effect upon Col. Dunwoddie, a man I had heretofore regarded as a—gentleman."

The very lips of her lover whitened as she said it. His father! She was terrified by the effect on him of her words, but she continued none the less.

"Our slave has made money, earned it, sir, by hard work. Having made money, he can own our plantation. Because of your money you can own *me?* It never even occurs to you that we would object to what your father and yourself allowed Parker to do, compelled him to do, in public. And you are here to-day, assuming to have bought me also!"

She drew herself up and looked at him as an angered empress might have done. Even then the young man was blinded by a new measure of beauty in the scorn of her lip, in the wrath of her eyes, her very effort at self-control proving that which she reserved to be so much greater than what she expressed.

"Miss Clara Middleton will accept you eagerly," she said. "But you confound me with her."

"And you"—it flashed from him apart from any intention of his own—"will condescend to Mr. Gamaliel Middleton!"

"I will not at least be bought," she replied. "And now, sir, if you will excuse me—" and she made a movement to leave the room.

Neither of these young people had imagined that they could have become so enraged. Twice before something of the same kind had threatened, but this was such fulfilment of the threat as neither had even feared. The only adequate measure of their passion was—their power of loving.

"But one moment, if you please," her lover urged. His lips were so dry with sudden heat that it was difficult to speak. He continued, however, in a calm, and even cold manner, in singular contrast with the passions which raged within. "I only wanted to say that you have cruelly misunderstood me. You may be assured, however," he said with a deliberation which sent a chill through his own heart, for he knew it to be final, even as a dying man knows when his end is come, "that I will never trouble you again. What you have said of me is nothing, but what you have said of my father, the truest gentleman God ever made! is— I only ask that, under the circumstances," and here his voice faltered a little, "you will not revenge yourself upon my mother. I bid you good-by." And no man condemned to death ever bade a friend farewell forever with more certainty of the separation being for life than he, as he bowed and was gone.

When the girl reached her room she sat down to recover herself. Her home, the only one she had ever known, was gone as if from under her feet. Even then there remained an indebtedness, accumulating since long before the war, to importunate creditors, and so vast now that it was useless to try and grasp the amount. It was not merely a debt—it rested like a dark blot, a blot she could never hope to remove, upon the reputation of her father. Her mother had become indifferent to it as to all else, because she had whitened so rapidly towards the winter of death as to be benumbed to everything. Was a girl ever more absolutely alone in the world than herself? Of what use was it to her that she had within herself the strength, the soul for anything? What could she *do?* Her resolve had been, till life ended, to endure and try to fill worthily the place of all of those who were gone—but what could she *do?* That was the thing she must decide. Horace Dunwoddie was a master, born a master, but—and she ceased to think and began to weep. An iceberg may tower very high, sparkling brilliantly from every pinnacle; may have power to freeze and to crush whatever it smites; but it is merely frozen water at last; and, there being no exertion possible to her then, she relaxed into tears. She despised herself for it, but the mere woman in her was too strong for her, and she gave way, lying upon her bed, to a passion of weeping, blind, unreasoning, exhausting.

It is hardly to be supposed that a gentleman of Gamaliel Middleton's curiosity in crime, to say nothing of his delicate feelings in regard to other people, would allow himself to be torn away from the tragedy he had been witnessing by reason of any watch over the movements of his rival; however this may be, as soon as he missed Horace Dunwoddie from among the crowd he followed him. Thus it happened that as Horace mounted his horse at the gate of Mrs. Anderson's place, Middleton was riding homeward, and joined him. The man could have broken into a yell of delight only less hilarious than that of Ferdinand Clarke, the instant he saw the face of the other. He knew what had taken place almost as well as if he had been present, so wide and accurate had been his knowledge of men and women, and he could hardly keep his exhilaration in prudent bounds. And Horace had experience enough of the world also to know that his rival knew and rejoiced at his defeat, and this did not make that defeat any the less bitter. But his lifelong love was at an end, he would bury it now and forever, and he became more than composed, outwardly at least, as he listened to what his companion had to say.

"Outside the South they think it is horrible," Middleton remarked at last, "to lynch even as atrocious a wretch as that mulatto. They want the law to take its course. The law! When lawyers are well paid, and the natural horror has had time to cool, if the worst criminal does not escape conviction, his sentence is almost always far less than his desert, and even then he can count upon a pardon pretty soon. You people are right! But here we are in town. Call and see us. Good-day." And he went into his hotel in such a pleasant frame of mind that he kissed his sister tenderly, and asked her, since he was about writing to New York, if he couldn't order something for her in the way of millinery.

CHAPTER XXVII.

AN EDDY IN THE CURRENT.

"The fire that gladdens with its blaze
Your home, if it but disobeys,
And breaks the hearthstone's limit, lays
Your house in dust. Omnipotence
Itself is held by path and fence.
The highest talent yet is—sense
Which at the bound of reason stays
And grasps us, lest we stir from thence."

COL. DUNWODDIE's speech, followed as it was by that of Anderson Parker, was an event. Whatever part it had in producing the result, this at least was beyond doubt, it was the beginning of a new era.

"I see," Horace said to his father one Sunday afternoon, as the family were lingering about Harry's bedside, "that your speech is being republished in all the papers, South and North. I was sure it would be."

"So I have observed. But it is only," the Colonel replied, "because I have dared to say what the best men everywhere are thinking. People, South and North, feel that a more just as well as genial season is drawing near, and I am but the first robin which chirps a greeting to the coming spring and summer."

He spoke modestly enough, but he was greatly elated. The excitement attending the delivery of his speech seemed to have wrought a change throughout the whole man. There had always been a sufficient fire in his eyes, but now there was color in his cheeks, he stood erect again, appeared to be in more vigorous health; it was as if years had been suddenly stricken from his life. When he had first entered his home after delivering the address, he had gone to his wife and kissed her as if he were a bridegroom; and she, in her sympathy with, and pride in him, had received it with the smile and the mantling blush of a bride. Instead of diminishing, as the days rolled by, his excitement increased. He had said that new books were with him as fuel to the flame, but the letters he received, the visitors who crowded upon him, the abundant notices of the press, even the frantic hostility of Tom Terrell, were far more substantial food to the fires of an ambition which he had supposed to be lying dead within him in its ashes.

"I think," George said, as the family talked of the matter about Harry's bed, "that the least people can do is to make me a handsome present."

"You? What have you done?" May demanded.

"I shot Harry," her brother said. "If I hadn't been thoughtful enough to do it, we would all have left town long ago, and then, where would have been father's speech?"

"That is a fact," the Colonel broke in. "One of your providences, my dear."

"So it is," his wife said. "And the beauty of it was that we did not know you would be detained. Your speech would not have been so good if you had known even a day beforehand that you were going to make it. Heaven never tells us its secrets."

"Yes, it do," Charlie said very soberly; being the youngest, he was the smartest; and, having learned the verse that morning, he gravely repeated, "De secret ob de Lord is wid dem dat fear him."

"I wouldn't be a baby, and say *de* secret *ob*, and *dem* and *dat*," George remarked. "That's the way the negroes talk, Judge."

"Precisely!" his father exclaimed. "What are the blacks but children? It is astonishing how things work," he continued, getting to his feet. "First the slaves were freed. None of us wanted that, and none of us believe in the way it was done, of course; but, except Major Clarke, Tom Terrell, and a few like them, I hardly know a man but is glad of it. Next, by an astounding blunder, the ballot was put in their hands, while they are utterly unfitted for it. But look how it works! They would have been sullen, dissatisfied, forever clamoring for it if it had been withheld. Now they have had a surfeit of politics. The experiment has been tried, and they are getting as sick of it as the whites. And so they will be back on our hands again. Please God, we are coming to this that we will see to it every soul of them shall have as fair a chance as the rest of us to struggle up as fast as he can."

"Mother, Alice, May," Horace said, catching the enthusiasm of his father, although in a stronger because quieter form, "it is high time you ladies learned something about such things. Listen. Since you did not hear Col. Dunwoddie, I will make a very little part of his speech over again, and for Harry's benefit, too," and, assuming the attitude of an orator at the other end of the room, Horace began—

"Adam Smith, friends and fellow-citizens, made a discovery which revolutionized the opinions of the race. It was, in opposition to the universal belief before—that the success of one nation is the success of all, that the adversity of any one of them, even the weakest, is no advantage, but serious injury instead, to every other, even the largest. So with us. The prosperity of New York is essential to that of Alabama; if South Carolina languishes, Pennsylvania, California, sooner or later, are dragged down thereby. So of individuals. If Harry gets shot, the whole household suffers, and if the meanest negro, Yellow Jessamine say, is wronged, or left to his ignorance and wickedness, which is the same thing, every man in the county, the state, the South, the country, is more or less injured thereby. Please applaud, as they did in front of the court-house, for that is sound sense.

"And now," the orator continued, when the clapping had ceased, "listen to some more. I appeal to you who fought for the Confederacy," and he turned upon May. "Some of you will remember that glorious fifteenth of October, when we stormed the Federal battery in Virginia. In what you believed to be a good cause, in the face of death, forgetting wife and child, and all that is precious, even life itself, you took and held the position. I appeal to you to-day. You face this hour the redoubts of life-long prejudices, prejudices entrenched, so to speak, in your very blood and bones. Yield to your own excellent sense! Give up whatever prevents you! Storm them! For the sake of your children, of your state! Happy was I," Horace continued, personating his father still, "the day I led you to victory. Happier shall I be if to-day I lead you to this victory, more glorious by far!"

The applause was hearty. The father and mother were both thinking of the future of their boy, and enjoyed it greatly. But Mrs. Dunwoddie was somewhat disconcerted as the orator, continuing to quote from his father, pointed at her a finger of grave admonition.

"And you, who represent on this spot the Christian faith," he said, "do you know definitely what outsiders, men like myself everywhere, who are not, and never intend to be, professors of religion, think of religion? We at least hope that Christianity is the divine revelation of the supreme force which is in the end to revolutionize the world. For that we value it, by and for that alone! You urge us to believe. Why," the orator added, with such withering scorn as brought a color to his mother's cheek, "do not you set us the example by so believing in God as to submit heartily to his hand in the defeat of the South? You urge us to believe! Your Master declares that, seated in judgment at last, his decision for eternity upon every man is according to the way in which that man has or has not cared for the very least in our reach as for him. Are you, oh Christians," Horace demanded, in such tones as drew tears to the eyes of the Church there represented—"say, are *you* doing, trying to do, what you can for the ignorant negro at your feet? If you want us to go with you, prove to us first that you are going with your Master! Excuse me," said Horace, "it is my first attempt at oratory, and I promise it shall be my last," and took his seat, somewhat abashed at his own enthusiasm.

"You are a little too impassioned, my boy," the Colonel said, as even Harry joined in the applause, Charlie looking around with grave eyes and considerably mystified.

"You did it well, very well indeed, but," he continued, beginning to walk up and down the room, "that reminds me of one thing I deplore. Our people are full of a sort of tropical power. But it is wasted. There is sufficient energy wasted in sheer passion to develop all our resources, build up all our institutions. The eloquence now spent among us in raving against the inevitable, would, if rightly directed, create as glorious a literature as the world has ever known. We are too effusive, too demonstrative. We Southern people use too many adjectives, we exaggerate. I fear ours is the violence that goes with weakness. I hate to see a man too emotional. If there is a thing I admire," he said with increasing vehemence, "it is the repose of strong conviction, it is quietness which tells of depth of feeling. We are too gunpowdery to every wretched spark.

"But," he added, "I did not intend to speak of that. I have a grand conception in my mind. It has haunted me night and day. Thank Heaven, the day is at hand, at last, when I can go to some secluded spot, in Switzerland for instance, and concentrate myself steadily and peacefully upon the work I have always been anxious to do. I yearn for rest," he added with an increasing intensity which left the others in the rear, as it were. "I parch and perish to be freed from the eternal stress and strain of my shallow yet violent life. But we are soon to escape—soon, very soon! Thank God for that —thank God!" he continued, unconscious of the children; and Horace saw how wistfully his mother's eyes rested upon her excited husband as he walked up and down more rapidly.

"Politics? What do I care for politics?" he said. "You laugh at me for tying knots in my clothing at night, for staying out so late upon the front porch by myself. Wait! Poor Alec was but a grub. Who knows what may break with radiant wings from his nothingness? But I don't want to say anything unkind of your brother, my dear. By the by," he added, passing, as he always did, from one topic to another very rapid-

ly, "do you know what I think is the grandest theme an artist can handle, for it is part of the conception I spoke of?"

"You have told me, Charles," his wife said.

"Have I? Yes, it is woman I mean. There is," the husband added, "a blind instinct in regard to woman in every age. Look at the Virgin Mary. Nearly all of the Christian world, and for almost twenty centuries, have little conception of Christ except as a babe upon the bosom of his mother. They are a thousand times more sensible than those long-haired fools who are clamoring for woman's rights. The grand old instinct works in them, but they don't see that it is woman as distinctively *woman*—a wife, a mother—who holds the Christ in her hands because upon her bosom. Here's your mother, children, I believe she has had some baby in her hands to care for ever since she was born. First it was her doll, and then it was her father—"

"Her father! Oh, pa!" May exclaimed.

"Hush, Eliza, you know it. From the time you were a girl General Allen was as much in your hands, almost at least, as if he had been an infant. He depended, I mean, upon your loving good sense. A man of strong character, too, of violent prejudices—"

"Charles, I insist upon your saying no more," Mrs. Dunwoddie said, so earnestly that the children looked at her with surprise.

"Oh, well, I won't mention it. But there was Alec. If ever a woman had a troublesome baby upon her hands, he was one. It is your fate, my dear, you have had some fractious infant in your care all your life. Harry must needs get shot to keep you in practice. Get well, my boy, get well as soon as you can. We don't blame you. And George didn't intend it. It's all right. The doctor says you will be well enough to travel very soon. And when we do start we will give your mother a good rest. You deserve it, dear wife, if ever a woman did. Meanwhile I want you all to learn to be as quiet as possible. Look at Charlie."

But even Charlie felt as if his father had somehow struck a chord that was not wholly in unison with his mother or themselves. Horace had gone to the window, and was looking out. The night his mother had detained him by her bedside to speak to him in regard to his father, she had said that which had caused him to watch over every word, over almost every movement of his father, with new and painful interest.

"Yes, we are all too excitable," the Colonel continued. "As I said, we are like tinder to the meanest of sparks. If Tom Terrell had not gone off as soon as he had done speaking that day, I am satisfied"—Col. Dunwoddie reverted to the subject which interested him most—"we would have had a row. That is the trouble with us in the South. The vast body of the people, white and black, mean well; there are none equal to them, but one worthless scoundrel can upset a crowd of them in an instant. If Tom Terrell, Hiddikel Queasy, Ferdinand Clarke, any scamp on the ground, had hissed or yelled, or fired a revolver into the air, he could have turned that meeting into a massacre in five minutes. What we need is law, law of our own making, but law, when made, as relentless as fate. *Law* is what we need, prompt, impartial, supreme!" he added with great energy.

"And personal self-control, father?" Horace asked it as he turned carelessly away from the window and went out of the room. He had seen Leonidas standing at the front gate beckoning eagerly to him. There was enough of his father's quicksilver in his veins for him to know that some storm was impending. As quietly as he could he stepped up-stairs, belted his revolvers about him under his coat, and joined the mulatto at the gate.

CHAPTER XXVIII.

ANDERSON PARKER ONCE MORE.

"Yes, needs it must the Crucified
Not merely lived for men, but died—
All that he did were lost beside."

"I is seriously uneasy, sah," Leonidas said as the two walked away together. The mulatto was evidently in a state of alarm, but his grandiloquence was the habit of his life. "Ebber sence de date ob de 'lection begin, de people seem to me to hab lost dere insanity," he said. "Your father's great oration did a sight ob good. For de passin' period, you observe, sah. It had de effect of ventilatin' dem people, rustlin' dem up—you comprehend, sah?—mighty smart. De white con-stituency an' de black. But a numerous number ob dem is only dat much more excited—excited, you observe, sah—for good or debiltry, whichever comes handiest. Dat was a most misfortunate circumstance out dere," and the mulatto indicated, with a movement of his troubled head in that direction, the scene of the murders and their terrible avenging. "Dat has made matters worse. People's blood is hot and *coagulated!*" he added with emphasis. "On one side an' de odder. Dey are prepared to play de bery debbil!"

"Yes, I know that, but what is in the wind to-day?" Horace Dunwoddie asked impatiently, for he was not without vague fears for his father, and in more senses than one.

"Dere is two separate parties—" Leonidas began.

"Oh, I know that," the other said with some heat.

"Yes, but de one party an' de odder is like two bresh heaps in de post-oaks, all dead leaves an' dry sticks. An' de two am con-tiguous," urged the man. "A little spark sets one into a conflagration, an' dat inspires de odder. Now, dere is dat Anderson Parker! How dat man is hated! By bof sides, sah. You comprehend? He won't hab any individual ob any political complexion foolin' round *his* place. One party wanted to make speeches in dat ole warehouse whar he preached. Hiddikel Queasy went dere one night wid a brass band ob music, plenty ob ginger-bread—gingers you know, sah—an' whiskey. His notion was to hab mighty short speeches, but plenty ob music an' dancin'. Dey begged him for de use ob dat ole house. *No!* Den de odder party came tearin' in, certain sure to get it. *No* again! Den dey made a rush for Mrs. Judge Anderson. She wouldn't even go to de door to see 'em; sent 'em to Anderson Parker. You see," the mulatto explained, " he works a powerful sight ob hands. De county, an' de state dey say, is mighty close dis 'lection, an' de way de suffragings ob de hands on de Anderson plantation goes, fixes dis county, sah."

"That's the way, is it, the old house was burned down?" Horace Dunwoddie asked.

"Yes, sah, but not altogether. Dat Yaller Jessamine hates Anderson Parker wurst of all. Yaller Jessamine is—I tell you, sah —is—"

The man was on the point of saying something with energy, but stopped.

"Is what?" Horace demanded.

"Ahem! yes, sah, is a most a powerful preacher. I is a preacher myself 'casionally, an' consequently I is a jedge ob preachin'. Now dat man," Leonidas continued, evading the point, "is ahead ob me. When I am on de meracles I does pretty well, people say, considerin'. But when Yaller Jessamine gets to talkin' 'bout de bliss ob Par-'dise! De jasper an' de pearl, de gates an' curbstones ob gold an' diamons, de harps, de crowns, de bells ob hebben an' de chariots, de wings an'—an' de beatbetudes in gen'ral—! He beats me, dat brudder! He goes soarin' up out ob my reach. My! Brudder Jessamine can fly higher up dan any preacher I know, but," Leonidas added cautiously, "he can get lower down, too, when he wants to—an' dat is what he gen-

'rally wants—dan any gen'l'man of color *I* know."

"Well?" the other asked.

"You observe, sah," the mulatto continued, changing the subject with an anxious face, " it is de first 'casion in de biography ob de world a colored man ebber purchased a plantation. De Judge Anderson plantation, too! And to see dat colored individual, an' de bery blackest nigger Old Marster ever made, standin' on de flatform makin' a remarks as if he was Judge Anderson—"

"Take care what you say, sir," the other said, "it was my father's doing. He is responsible for it, and so am I. What were you going to say about Yellow Jessamine?"

"Well," the other added reluctantly, "Anderson Parker preaches about his wearin' fine clothes. I believe if a gen'l'man has got money, dere is no better use ob money dan to *be* a gen'l'man wid it. Now, I makes my money, an' *I*—"

"Never mind," the other broke in, "Yellow Jessamine?"

"He hates Anderson Parker for dat," the mulatto said. "He was to make de speech for a candy-date, too. An' dey do say Anderson Parker hustled him off de place wid his own hands when he came all dressed up an 'lectioneerin' around. Yaller Jessamine say he didn't hustle him, but"—the man added it in lower tones—"de warehouse was burned down! Den Anderson Parker's bein' boosted up on dat flatform —dat almost killed dat yaller man. And dey *do* say—;" but the mulatto paused, and looked carefully around.

"Out with it, Leonidas!" the other said impatiently.

"Do you know Yaller Jessamine?" Leonidas suddenly asked.

"Of course I do, he belonged to Judge Anderson; why do you ask?" the young man replied.

"Yes, an' dat is de peculiarity ob de circumstance. He was a likely house-servant, an' Anderson Parker was nothin' but a field-hand, an' de blackest on de place at dat. Dis is," Leonidas explained, "another corroboration why Jessamine hates him so, de black man is so ahead ob him, you see, sah. But you think you know de man? You know de *barber*—mighty poor one he is—but you don't know de man, de debbil, de—Yaller Jessamine!" Leonidas said, as if that alone could express his feelings.

"Look here, Leonidas, if you have got anything to say, say it," the other urged.

"To-rectly, sah. Do you know, dey do say Yaller Jessamine had a hand in—in—dat—dat—terrible comedy," the man said, nodding towards the scene of the tragedy. "And dat de miscreant dey—dey punished told Anderson Parker. Anyways, Yaller Jessamine he knows dat Anderson Parker knows it, an' is after him. He is endeavorin' to proticipate Parker, you see, sah."

"If you don't tell me now, right away, what you mean," Horace Dunwoddie said, stopping and looking sternly at the other, "I will leave you *now*, and," he added, "you will be held responsible for whatever happens."

"You had better listen, sah—dat Yaller Jessamine is—heugh-eugh!" It was only by this exclamation, with lips screwed up and eyes tightly shut, that the man could express the inexpressible in reference to one he abhorred so heartily. "Not dat I has any affection for Anderson Parker," he explained. "Fact is, I think a little castigiversation wid de raw-hide will do dat nigger good. He needs a bringin' down!"

So far Horace Dunwoddie had yielded himself, although very unwillingly, to the barber-like manipulations of Leonidas. He had known the mulatto all his life as well-meaning and indolent, and had indulged him in his roundabout ways as the only mode by which he could get at the man's errand to him. As Leonidas uttered the last words, however, the dreadful secret of it all flashed upon the other. There was not a moment to be lost.

"Leonidas," he said coolly, but in accents of command, sharp and strong, "get as many men as you can, right away. On good horses, mind, and armed. I don't care what color they are, nor to what party they belong, if you can rely on them. I will get as many white men as I need, and meet you where the old warehouse used to stand. Look here, boy," he added, laying a vigorous grasp upon the shoulder of the mulatto, "listen! if you are not there we will see if we can find you!"

There was not more than time for the young man to hasten to the house, get his father out without alarming any one, tell him the facts, obtain his reluctant consent, and then go upon a rapid recruiting service through the town.

And so it came to pass that Sunday evening that a score or so of men, white and black, of both parties, were riding through the post-oaks, several miles out from Clairsville, Horace Dunwoddie and Leonidas leading the way. As the party reached the descent which led into a swamp the mulatto said something to his companion, who halted his horse and beckoned for the rest to gather closer around him.

"You have been told," he said, "what brings us here to-night. We all know Yellow Jessamine, and we know Anderson Parker. We know, too, or ought to, what a disgrace these things bring upon the South. Vote as you please! What we all care for is right and justice and fair play, and that a handful of miserable scoundrels shall not be taken as representing Southern men. Don't kill anybody. Every man try to catch one, white or black. Are you ready?"

"Dey is down in dat hollow," Leonidas said, trembling in every joint. "You be so kind as to 'member, people, you dun promised you will nebber tell who conduc-ted you here. Yaller Jessamine knew whar Parker was haulin' rails. I ain't goin' any farther myself. It ain't in my line to fight—I shaves all who comes, an' cuts dere hair. Moreover, I done performed my portion ob all dis in revealin' de debiltry. 'Member, gen'l'men, you promised—"

"You coward!" Horace Dunwoddie said, "we will at least make you useful. Get off, men, tie your horses together and leave them with this man. We can creep up on foot. Make haste."

In a little time thereafter Horace was leading them towards a deep hollow in the woods, from which certain sounds as well as lights were growing more and more distinct as they drew near. The men paused at a word sent back to them from him, and repeated from lip to lip. They then crawled cautiously onward, and again were halted. One breathless instant, and then, rising to his feet, revolver in hand, their leader said—

"Now for it, men!"

There was a sudden rush, a confused waving of lights casting bewildering shadows from the trees, the incessant cracking of rifles and revolvers, yells and curses and shrieks of wounded men, and the fight was fairly begun.

In the centre of what had been a group of men stood Anderson Parker. He was naked to the waist, his hands tied together and held aloft by the rope which was fastened to the limb of a tree overhead. The limb had been bent down to do it, and when released the vigorous body was so suspended that the naked feet hardly rested upon the earth. He was being scourged when the rush was made, and there did not seem a palm's-breadth of his stalwart blackness that did not give evidence thereof.

Before cutting him down Horace Dunwoddie turned, as he stood by the side of the victim, and, with his hand shading his eyes, looked eagerly around. Sure enough, the man who held the cowhide had just dropped it, and was stealing off to one side into the darkness. The young man saw that it was Yellow Jessamine, saw that he turned and looked back upon his black victim as a yellow tiger disappointed of its prey might have done, saw him draw a revolver from his belt. On the instant Horace Dunwoddie, surprised at his own coolness, took deliberate aim for the knees of the man. There was nothing, so far as he could hear, but the crack of his own revolver, but he was thrown aside on the instant by a convulsive movement of Anderson Parker. The mulatto had fallen, but, as Horace was soon to see, not before he had put a ball into the black.

It was all over as in a moment. To judge from the volleys fired multitudes must have been killed, and yet, as is always the case even in regular battle, few were hit, and very few of these were killed. Several had been captured by powerful hands and were being securely tied, but many had escaped.

Anderson Parker had been set upon in the act of loading his wagon with rails, and he was now released, found to be badly wounded, and laid upon a heap of coats placed upon the rails in his wagon, the mules having not been unharnessed. As they did this, Horace Dunwoddie made a rapid note in his check-book of the enemy. There was Yellow Jessamine to begin with, a knee shattered, alternately cursing and praying in language horribly scriptural as he lay. Near him, wounded and tied, was Dick Ransom, who had been a deserter from the Federal army. There were Harry Chalmers and Tom Perkins, inseparable friends in billiards and sprees, as gallant young men as Clair County had until they came back from the war, unfitted for everything except gambling and all "cussedness;" these were hardly hurt. Next were three field-hands, Jake, Zekiel, Mike, only less black than Anderson Parker, and whom he had driven off his place for incurable stealing— the fact that each was known by only one name was an almost certain proof in that region of a worthless character; of these, Jake had been killed. To the surprise of the rescuers Yellow Jessamine was the only mulatto on the ground, but Leonidas explained that afterwards.

"It was owing to de circumstance ob dere bein' too sensible to stay," he said. "Like me, fightin' isn't in dere line. Dey prefers whitewashin', blackin' boots, an' waitin' at table, an' broke for de woods. Dat is dere peculiarity."

"I say, Horace, you come here and let me loose," some one called to him from the darkness on one side as he was making out his list. Taking a torch, and hastening in the direction of the well-known voice, there was Ferdinand Clarke. He had fought like a wild-cat instead of running away, and now lay bound, hand and foot, among the dead leaves. Horace knew that he had broken his mother's heart, and was doing all he could to beggar his father, the pursy old Major, but he was astonished to find him in such company.

"Why, Ferdy Clarke," he exclaimed, "*you* with such scoundrels? You were the first I thought of when I was rushing around to make up my company last night."

"Sorry you didn't find me, Horace," he said. "All I came for was the fun of the thing. Would rather have come on your side, of course. Anderson Parker tried to crack me over the head with a fence-rail the day Terrell and I wanted to cowhide Hiddikel Queasy. I swore I would whip him for that, and Terrell too; see if I don't. Yellow Jessamine begged me to come out and help lather Parker a little, and we have had so many coon-hunts together of nights, Jessamine and I, that I said I would. He is the grandest rascal living, and I had considerable hope of seeing Parker kill him. All I wanted was the fun of it, a little bit of deviltry. A fellow must have his fun! You let me loose. I'd a thousand times rather have been on your side. It's your fault. Why didn't you tell a fellow in time? Come, you let me go."

On one side of Ferdinand, shot through the head, was a degraded Irishman, Pat Ryan by name, who was always drunk and on the lookout for a fight. Near by, and badly wounded, was a man said to have been a bummer in the Federal army, Heze-

kiah Collins by name. Anderson Parker had more than once secured his indictment by the grand jury as the keeper of a place of vile resort, which was also a rum-shop and store for the sale of stolen goods. Jessamine was his chief patron, and had paid him well for coming, furnished, as the wretch was, with the whiskey which fired the men for their work. Besides these there were two or three men who had always been the lowest of the low, and one or two who had once stood well, but who had fallen through indolence and its kindred vices.

The leader of the rescuing party had brought out with him, to kill or to heal, as events might determine, a surgeon, Dr. Peters, who had enjoyed extensive opportunities of practice during the war, and who now entered, with pleasant memories of old times, upon the work of caring for the wounded. A guard was left over the prisoners and the dead until Clair County could learn of the facts and arrive on the spot, which would not take very long. As the wagon was being slowly driven homeward with its wounded owner, Horace Dunwoddie galloped before it, as the openings in the midnight forest allowed, until he struck into the highway, and so made as rapid a ride as possible to town and to his father's house.

Checking his horse into a walk as he drew near, for fear of disturbing his mother, he dismounted at the gate, and was joined there, in the darkness, by his father, to whom he related the whole affair, receiving his cordial approval.

"You know I cannot sleep," the Colonel said. "I was naturally anxious about you; but I am accustomed, as you know, to walking up and down here, thinking and planning until very late. I wish I could sleep, for your mother's sake. I am tired to death of these miserable brawls. What we all need is rest, rest," his father added, with his hand upon his head. "Yes, you had better ride back and see that the wounded man is cared for. Don't disturb Mrs. Anderson or her daughter."

Perhaps it was the excitement, or the desolate appearance of the town at that dead hour of the night, or his own wrecked hopes, but to Horace his father looked, in the struggling light of the clouded moon, almost as ghastly as a ghost. Money was a grand thing to have, at least it would be when they could begin to use it, but it was not as powerful a lever as he had supposed. That is, so far. With it all, he had failed of the one thing he had set his heart upon. In fact, it was his money had lost him the woman he loved, and more money would but make matters worse. It was a sorrowful ride he had of it over the deep and silent sands, lying so white in the dim light, of the road to the Anderson place.

When he got to the cabin near the ashes of the old warehouse, which was Anderson Parker's home, the wagon had just driven up, and he helped the surgeon bear the wounded man into the house. By his command, when he had taken his horse from him after the fight, Leonidas had ridden back with the wagon. He had done so most unwillingly, but, as he helped with the disabled man, his feelings became interested, and, as they placed Anderson Parker on his bed, with the sudden changes of the mulatto character, Leonidas was the most voluble and excited person there.

"He has no wife nor offspring, sah," he said to Horace Dunwoddie. "Dey tell me if he had he wouldn't be such a—a individual. He would hab got in de habit ob purchasin' candy an' dresses, canned oysters an' jewelry, an de like, for dem. He suffered, dat man did, for de civilizin' an' refinin' influence ob de female sect. None ob us all had as much currency. De plantation, *dat* was his wife an' child. You needn't shake your head at me, sah," he continued, " *he* don't mind what I say. He doesn't take any notice—lies like a log."

"What he says is true," Dr. Peters, the surgeon, remarked coolly. "I am sur-

prised. Men hit that way in the war were always calling for water, groaning, cursing, praying, or something. He might almost have been killed for anything he says. Except that he said, as we drove up here just now, 'I hab done de best I know how, oh Lord'"—and at this point the medical man whispered something to his white companion, who made an exclamation, and, drawing closer to the bedside, looked with new interest at the wounded black, giving him water as he did so.

"Please get out ob my way, sah," Leonidas, who was busily at work, remarked; "fightin' is not in my line, but dis is. If you will hold de basin, sah, an' de odder parfernalia," for the mulatto had searched out water and towels, and was engaged in washing the lacerated nakedness of the burly negro. The light yellow of the barber, his narrow chest, thin, long arms, and rapid hand, now that he was of important use, contrasted as much with the sturdy blackness of the one he tended as did his unceasing tongue with the silence of the other.

"You keep a good heart in your big bosom," he said to the one he cared for. "'Member how much money you hab possession ob. By de time dey is prepared to hang Yaller Jessamine you will be well enough to be dar. A man like you will recuperate bery soon." And he talked on in the same strain, having the white men help him to turn his patient as he needed, until Anderson Parker lay at last clean, and covered to the chin by the quilt. He was conscious, acknowledged the attentions of the others by the assent of his eyes, but refused to say anything, looking steadily before him out at the door which had been left open. In answer to all questions he would nod his head or shake it a little, but he would not speak. "Please don't ask me to talk," he had said.

"He was that sort," Dr. Peters remarked when the three men stepped out for a moment into the fresh air. "Ferdinand Clarke told me that he killed the negro Jake with his axe before they could master him. It took every man they had to tie him, but, they say, after he was tied, he never said a word. They did all they could to provoke him to say something, but they could not get even a groan out of him. "Look here," the Doctor said suddenly to the mulatto, whom he had beckoned to follow them out, "ain't you a member of his church, boy?"

"Yes, sah, we b'long to de same communion. But," Leonidas added, "Yaller Jessamine don't. People say Brudder Jessamine is de best preacher ob de two. He hab de holy tones in de pulpit far de best. I jest want you to see dat man when a camp-meetin' is agoin'! He ain't a good barber, an' he's a mighty bad man, but for a powerful preacher—heugh-eugh! dar is no words for it!"

"He is, is he?" said Dr. Peters, who was not by any means a believer. "Well, sir, you'd better get that excellent divine to visit him, if his broken leg permits. Go and bring the Right Rev. Yellow Jessamine to pray and talk with him, he hasn't long to live. Don't *you* preach?"

"Yes, sah, in camp-meetin's, not regular. Not long to live? Anderson Parker? You is jokin', sah. Anderson Parker? An' him ownin' a plantation?" and the mulatto looked at the one who spoke, and then in and at the wounded black with breathless astonishment, his hands dropped to his side, his eyes and his mouth wide open.

It seemed impossible! The black man had come to be looked upon, even by those who hated him most, so much as the very foundation and chief support of all the colored interest in that section, that it was long before the barber could be made to realize the fact that Anderson Parker was really dying. When he did, his feelings, according to the nature of his race, took a new and ardent direction. Hastening back with them to the side of the dying man, he told him of his approaching death, and then

began to talk to him religiously, exhorting, praying, singing, with astonishing volubility and fervor.

"Had you not better get down his Bible and read to him?" Horace Dunwoddie suggested; "that is better than anything you can tell him."

"May be so, sah, but it is too slow an' cold like. Religion is a circumstance ob de heart, ob de feelin's. You devolve it upon me, sah?" Leonidas said with clerical dignity. "Brudder Parker, you jine in as you can," he added, turning to the wounded man and beginning again to pray and to sing.

There was an abundance of genuine feeling, of heartfelt eloquence in the man, and his singing was exceedingly pathetic; but through it all the black lay as silent and unmoved as before. Long ago had he learned how much value to attach to exercises which began and, alas, ended in mere rhapsody and enthusiasm. With his lips set, he merely looked steadily out of the open door towards the east, which was slowly getting gray as dawn drew near.

Meanwhile the whole plantation had been aroused. Negroes, male and female, came crowding in. The white men noticed that the situation of the black sufferer seemed to strike every one of them, at first, in the same way. It was impossible that Anderson Parker was to die! He had been so much to them, and for so long, that it was as if the very substance and basis of nature was endangered. Generally they would have indulged in outcries, now they seemed stupefied, weeping, if at all, silently. The man had impressed his own nature, too, upon his own people; there was marked contrast between them and the excited barber, who never ceased from his religious exercises.

In the midst of it all there was a sudden movement, and Emmeline Anderson came into the cabin, little Zady having wakened her in her eagerness to make known the great disaster. Horace Dunwoddie and Dr.

Peters arose as she came in and placed herself beside the wounded man with an exclamation of grief, and a burst of silent weeping as she did so. Her lover grew cold and stern as he looked upon her, and as by an effort against the inexpressible pity which filled his heart. Her mother was slowly dying, and upon whom could she lean, now that Parker was cut down? There was, as if under her dignity of bearing, an utter desolation in the droop of her head, of her eyelids, as she restrained herself from her tears, which inspired Horace with a kind of blind rage, but against everything in the world except her. He made no sign, however, and Leonidas, with great officiousness, waved the negroes out of the cabin, which was crowded to excess. Yellow Jessamine had been his most formidable rival in the pulpit, and he had a not unpleasing sense of his added importance now that the other was disabled.

"I'll hab a prar-meetin' wid dem poor sinful people outside," he said, for he had now got his camp-meeting garments, so to speak, fairly on. "It is my bounden duty an' privilege, 'specially as Brudder Jessamine is hurt, to improve dis solemn circumstance. Soon's I get dem to singin' an' shoutin' I'll come back to-rectly."

But, to his surprise, the mulatto found it required more effort to do this than he had ever known before, and the white people were left almost alone for some time with the dying man.

"Have you nothing to say to me, Parker?" the young lady asked at last, weeping once more and very bitterly, for she had known the black all her life.

"No, Miss Emmeline," he said; "'cept to ask, please gib my sarvice to Miss Julia. I dun de best I know how."

That was all. The man, with his eyes upon the east, was conscious, was suppressing all sign of the severe pain he endured, was thinking. He was not so absorbed, however, that he did not turn his eyes eagerly towards Horace Dunwoddie when

Dr. Peters suddenly exclaimed, "Why, Dunwoddie, you are shot! why didn't you tell me, man? You are as pale as death. Come out here into the air."

"No, sir!" the young man said, almost roughly. "It is merely a slight wound in my arm, and I had forgotten all about it. I have lost almost no blood at all. Wait."

The young woman had merely acknowledged his bow when she entered. Now she started towards him with a sudden movement of both hands, the tears gone from her eyes, the color from her face. But Horace Dunwoddie held up his hand in an attitude of attention. Leonidas was praying very fervently outside; the windows and door were crowded with colored people. The east had been growing brighter and brighter. Suddenly the first ray of the rising sun, striking through the post-oaks, and over the heads of the people in the doorway, lighted up the broad, black, silent brows of the wounded man. His eye kindled. It was as if some one had asked him a question—

"Yes, Marster, my Marster," he said in his slow and steady voice. "Yes, Marster, I dun de best I know how."

The next moment a great hush had fallen upon the people outside, subduing even the fervent barber—they all knew that Anderson Parker was dead.

The heart of Horace Dunwoddie was very bitter. His money had availed him less than nothing. Nor had his love for this woman, pure and lifelong as it had been. Here was this black man. No Paul or Socrates, no Huss or Luther, had ever striven to benefit men with a steadier purpose, a more unselfish heart, or with greater practical sense. Yet there he lay—dead!

"My father will be over to see to all that is necessary," he said, as he bowed to the lady as to an utter stranger, and left with Dr. Peters.

As he walked away the words sounded in his heart with the shrillness of a hiss. "Let her go. I am rich; the money *shall* avail. All I will care for henceforth is for that!" and an oath came to his lips, the first in his life. But, in the same breath, he cursed the serpent instead, and crushed its head under his heel. His blood was hot and bitter, but the milk of his mother in him was too sweet and strong even for his embittering experiences.

The funeral services took place two days later in Mrs. Anderson's parlors. The Rev. Gen. Atchison, as he was called in memory of his military history during the war, conducted the exercises with sincere solemnity, all of the leading white men of the region being present. Mrs. Anderson, her daughter by her side, sat at the head of the coffin almost as frigid and still as the black who lay, his calm brow exposed to view, like the fallen statue of an heroic age. The porch and lawn were crowded with colored people. A reaction had followed with them upon the stunning blow of his death; and, the services in the house ended, they wept aloud when the body was given over to the many colored preachers present, Leonidas Dunwoddie taking the lead. Horace was glad when the exhortations at the grave, the ardent prayers, the weeping, the singing, and, at last, the shouting, was ended, it was in such discord with the character of the dead.

CHAPTER XXIX.

GAMBLING FOR HEAVY STAKES.

"'All this wide world is but a stage,' he said;
'We are but actors here.' Yes, for our bread.
'Each man his several part.' But who, I say,
Doth cast my part? and who doth write the play?'"

WITHIN ten days after the death of Anderson Parker, Horace Dunwoddie took the hotel in his way home from the office, having promised to meet his sister Alice at Miss Middleton's parlor and escort her home. He did not want to do it, but such a horror had fallen of late upon the women of Clairsville that they shrank from going out alone, even in daylight. Besides this,

the young man was keenly grieved for h..., sister, she was so pitifully unhappy, her only consolation seeming to lie in the society of the sister of the man she loved.

"Alice will be in directly," Clara said, as she came into the parlor; "she is with her dress-maker, who lives next door, and begged me to ask you to wait a few moments."

The young man seated himself, and entered into a lively conversation with the lady, whom he had not seen for some time. Alice had told of his intended call for her. She knew that she was pretty, and had left no art untried that could render her more fresh and engaging. Her dress conveyed to him the idea of a new variety of flower which had just blossomed, and she herself seemed to be, even more than usual, in keeping with it.

She did her best to please her visitor, recalling to him what they had seen together in the East, singing for him at the piano her most sparkling songs, telling him of her laughable mistakes in her inexperience as to Southern life. It was not in human nature not to relax. Not because her curls were so fair, her lips so red, her complexion so much like the inner surface of a shell, her eyes so bright, but that she knew such a wonderful variety of interesting things and told them so charmingly. He was hot and tired, and he felt as if the dust of the streets had entered his very heart and soul. Moreover, he was wearied of the crowds of people he had been among all day, and of the one eternal subject—money. Politics had held it in abeyance for a while, but the political excitement had suddenly ceased with the elections, and now the dull, unceasing grind of the mill—money, money, money—was heard again, louder and stronger than before. He was tired of planning and dreading, of being disappointed and disgusted; and now all he had to do in Miss Clara's beautifully arranged parlor was to sit and look and listen, as if upon the bank of a brook sparkling and rippling at his

...eet, making light and music for him without an exertion of his own. He was so tired that he enjoyed it greatly.

There was his father—he thought it over even while seeming to listen to the lady with a smile upon his lips. He was not merely a man of genius, but thoroughly educated; not only unwearyingly industrious, but honest, good, true, self-sacrificing, devoted to every noble object as well as to his family. And yet, after a life spent in hard work, what was the result of it all? True, money had come, but it was not in consequence of energy or character, it was pure luck with his lazy uncle, while his father had earned only weariness and poverty. Now that the money had come, what good did it do him? There had never lived a woman like his mother, and she was an invalid; her life-long endurance and excellence availed her as much, and as little, as her wealth. Why should he try any more? "Why not let things *slide?*"

"What folly," he continued to himself, "to cherish any hope in regard to one so cold and self-contained as Emmeline. If Middleton had not already won her she could never have treated me so. That is ended. Let him have her. I will never go to her again. And," with a bitter smile at the idea, "she will never come to me. She has been my life-long object, and what have I accomplished?" and he would have been angry but that he sank as with the weariness of his useless toil into a sense of disgust instead, with Emmeline Anderson, as of the whole world.

"Here," he said to himself still, as Clara sang at her instrument, "is this woman. She is lovely and accomplished. She does not need to be toiled for. No fear she will throw back into my face as pure and honest a heart as a man can offer. Why cannot I ask her and have her, and be done with it?"

The man had a strong nature, but he was overtaxed, and the lady knew, almost as well as he, what was passing in the mind of her silent visitor. It was the crisis of her life, and she was more wearied out with it than he with his. All the soul in her came to her help. She had once hoped, but had learned of his infatuation for another, and had tried to give him up. But that proud and dark beauty had driven him off in some mysterious way. Here he was again, and evidently on the point of yielding. If he could be led to say the words that would hold him and all he had for life! The power as of another Cleopatra came upon her. By no means a bad girl, all she wanted was to escape from her unsettled life, her eternal economies, to be married to this splendid-looking man, to be rich, to go with him to the East and triumph over those who had despised her there. But this Herod was of a sort whom his Herodias might frighten away in an instant. In the excitement of the crisis the girl became electric with a certain charming life in eye and cheek and tongue, laughing and talking as for dear life, her manner all innocent gayety, the most agonizing anxiety gnawing at her heart.

As he sat listening, Horace Dunwoddie had already said everything to her she wished, so far as his eyes could speak. He was too much like his father not to have done that, and the girl read it in his eyes, knew it as well as he did. But he had not, as yet, said a syllable of it aloud—he was too much like his mother to do that; so far, the mother in him had been too calmly strong for the father. Slowly, and with an art which had come to her with her knowledge of music, she allowed the cadence of the conversation to slacken and soften and change.

Yes, everything, she said, was new to her in this great and glorious South. She wondered she could be so cheerful, she was so lonely. Mr. Horace had heard the story of her life at boarding-schools. Her brother had been very good to her, but it was a wretched sort of life for a young girl at best. She had no special fondness for general society. A very few friends, in some secluded spot, was all she cared for. They did the best they could for her at the hotel; the ladies of Clairsville had been very kind in calling; May and especially Alice had been sisters to her; but, but it was very, very — she hardly knew what to call it! The eager and voluble girl was gone. Here was a gentle and loving woman in her stead. A woman who could be the slave of the man she might love, radiant for his hours of gladness, sympathetic for his times of gloom, living only for him. The mother in the bosom of the young man began to go over to the side of the father. He had waited long and worked hard but hopelessly elsewhere. A word would decide matters here. Why not?

He was seated on the sofa. She had been speaking in a very modest way, quietly, sadly. The tears had come into her eyes. She had risen, gone to the window, looked out a moment, then came and sat down near him, her hands lying relaxed in her lap. She could do no more. Nor could he resist any longer. Why should he? Besides, Alice might return any moment. He was his own master, and could do as he pleased. He said the few syllables over to himself, clearly, distinctly. His lips were opening to put them into imperishable words—

The lives of both were balanced as upon the razor-like edge of that instant. Her eyes lifted to his said it, the words trembled within her parted lips, "Oh, if you who are so calm and strong and good would but open your arms and take me to your bosom! How I would rest there, for the first time in my life—rest, *rest!* I would be a so much better woman. I would make you the most devoted wife that ever breathed—"

It is impossible that the soul can utter such impassioned cries, and the soul to which they are addressed, and in less than arm's-length, can fail to hear. Another woman had said to him, "Remember, my son, you have given yourself to me;" but this woman was nearer. He was strong, but he was also very weak. It was all over. He surrendered, but he would do it too with energy, with decision, as from his heart—

"Miss Clara—" he began.

But at that instant the door opened and Mr. Middleton came into the room. That was his everlasting misfortune! No man could be more intelligent, more energetic or adroit; assuredly no man could have a more vigorous reference to himself; and yet it was always Gamaliel Middleton who ruined Gamaliel Middleton's best plans. He had done so a thousand times. The culmination was always suicide in some form, the climax of his adroitness lay in that; the stupidest fool on earth could not have blundered so invariably. After describing so vast a circle towards an object, and for so many months, if on this occasion he could but have stayed away one minute longer!

And yet Middleton had excellent reason for coming in so abruptly. He had gone out upon a visit to the Andersons, for he had been of late a more and more frequent visitor there. The death of Anderson Parker had given him opportunity to offer assistance. Middleton was far from being officious, and adapted himself as subtly to circumstances as a serpent does to the angularities and undulations of its path over rock and through bramble. Horace Dunwoddie was, as he well knew, no longer a suitor for the hand of the young lady, and Col. Dunwoddie was naturally estranged from the Andersons also. The death of Parker had thrown things into such confusion that the hand of some business man was essential, and Middleton seized the opportunity eagerly. The power of young Dunwoddie had lain, he reasoned, in his almost insolent self-assertion—nothing was to be gained by whimpering at the feet of a woman of this sort; and Middleton clothed himself, before he went to the plantation that day, with assurance as with a garment. He had often worn the suit elsewhere, and flattered himself that it fitted him perfectly.

At the very moment his sister was, if such a thing may be said, pressing her suit upon her visitor, her brother was doing the same with Miss Anderson.

"I am a poor man," he said to the lady, at last; "all I ever get must be by my own hands, and I don't think I am a bad business man, if I might say such a thing. More than any woman I ever knew I admire and respect and love you. You will find me a devoted friend as well as a lover, whose delight it will be to relieve your mother and yourself from all care. May I venture to hope?"

The young girl sat in the parlor, the dingy old parlor which had not been refurnished since before the war. She had endured so many years of unceasing anxiety alone. Her mother growing colder to her as she grew feebler, what, after all, was there to live for?

Since Horace Dunwoddie had left her forever, she had, at last, realized her love for him; looking back, she could not remember when she had not loved him, so slow and imperceptible had been the growth of the feeling — and now it was with all the intensity of her nature. But that was all over. At last she knew herself and him—and knowing him, she knew he would never seek her again. Her black dress and extreme pallor deepened the expression of utter weariness that rested upon her face, and the fatigue as of her soul, too, was evident even in the position in which she sat—her hands relaxed and motionless in her lap, as were Clara Middleton's at the same instant. Against the inevitable her strength availed no more than did Clara's weakness. Why should she struggle any longer? The world had mastered her father, her brothers, her mother; it had seized upon and mastered Horace Dunwoddie, the one man whom she had supposed strong

enough, young as he was, to rise against and resist it—why should she, a mere girl, alone in the world, try any longer to stand against it? Here was this experienced man of the world, he was handsome, pleasing, he had said he loved her, why not marry him? He could be nothing to her, except as she sided with him against herself. Why not?

Mr. Middleton had exhausted the language of admiration and love. He had said and done to the utmost all he knew, and the reticent beauty seemed almost persuaded—but not quite! If he only knew what to say to secure the one little word from her, from which she would never recede, never, come what might! He sat for a moment as silent as herself. The room was so still that he could hear the ticking of the clock on the mantel, the purring of a cat on the window-sill near him, the stirring of the clematis on the porch in the breeze, almost the beating of her heart, certainly of his own. The silence grew intolerable. How could he induce her to lift to his in assent those large eyes, so dark, so deep, so hard to gain?

If Middleton could only have remained quiet! But that was not his nature. "Whatever I am to have I must *get*," was his profoundest conviction. Yes, he was an acrobat, and to stop upon the tight rope was to fall.

"Miss Anderson," he said at last, weighing every word before uttering it, as if it were a coin of gold which needed testing, "like your distinguished father you love the South. Through you I have learned to love it too. It has a great future. It is awakening from the shock of its defeat. Very soon the Government will come to its help. Its rivers will be improved, subsidies will be given to its European steamers, railways will be built through it to the Pacific. Who knows but compensation may be made for its slaves, even if its other and just claims are not acknowledged. It may be strange to tell you this, but I am a practical man, and I would like to live here and devote myself to helping towards all this certain and glorious future of the South. It is a noble career, but I will not attempt it without you. With you to inspire me I can do more than you imagine. Will you not speak?"

Emmeline Anderson heard every word he said and understood it, but she was saying to herself, "How stupid and sleepy I am. And everybody about me, in my old castle, is dead instead of asleep. Is this the fated Fairy Prince? Then I must awake." But she merely sat still, her eyes upon the floor, like one in a dream.

Middleton grew desperate. Some one might come. Who knows but young Dunwoddie might break in and end things at any moment! Putting it off would do no good. He had his last card, he would play it, for the desperation of the gambler came upon him.

"Miss Anderson," he said, "I hoped to have won you without saying it. But I must risk telling you. I hold in my possession a secret of the highest possible importance in regard to you. It is in my sole possession. No man living has the least idea there is such a—such a fact as I have in my keeping. Nothing that I can say can move you. Grant me one word, and this secret is as much yours as I am. It is of inconceivable value to you, as you will say when I tell you. One word? Will you not let me have that?"

As he ceased speaking her eyes were raised to his with the troubled look of a serious child. But, as they rested in his, the thought came to her slowly and piecemeal, as if still in a dream—

"The slaves are to be paid for some day. He knows how many we have lost. As he says, we will be rich again. He says he is very poor. Why," and the truth dawned upon her slowly and steadily, "this man is an adventurer! He is speculating. He wants to speculate in—me."

He wanted her eyes. He had them. But he shrank from what came in them, as

they fastened upon his. Without removing them, she arose from her seat, all her weariness and stupor gone. He felt at such a disadvantage seated that he also arose and stood. But it did no good. That was why Clara Middleton had not been sure of Horace Dunwoddie. Men may all be free, but Jefferson lied when he said that they are equal. It was not a question of North or of South, it was a matter of natural rank in creation, as God confers rank, a matter of grade, an affair of essential degree in the ascending scale, from the ape to the angel. He did not belong to her species. She felt it dimly all along, but not as clearly as did he. In his very marrow he felt it, he was as a mouse and she was— And he cursed and struck at her in his heart of hearts as she stood.

"Do I understand you to say, sir, that having failed to win me to be your wife, you intend to bribe me?"

"Bribe you? by no means. But it is a secret of tremendous importance. It is in my sole and exclusive possession. Only my desperation lest you would not—" he began.

The man saw his disastrous mistake as clearly as she did now; for, at last, he was not of another species, but only lower down in the line of development. Great Heavens, yes! He had been trying to dicker with her for herself as if she were a hogshead of sugar, a diamond, a claim in the Comstock Lode. He now cursed himself.

"In other words, you also intend to buy me. I am in demand. You think, too, that I am worth quite a large price."

To his wonder her face cleared of all anger as she said it, and became as bright as morning. "No, sir," she added, with a merriment worse to him than her darkest anger could have been; "if you are in the South, you forget that the auction-block is abolished. I, at least, am not for sale."

There was a reaction in the girl which resembled insanity. She was sincerely relieved, was glad, she knew not why—was full of joyous feeling; Mr. Middleton had suddenly become as much and as little to her as a fly is to the sunshine. Possibly heaven never seemed so brilliant to the archangel as when that potentate was in the act of falling from it, under the pursuing thunderbolt of the knowledge that he had destroyed himself. The adventurer had not dreamed that any woman could be as beautiful as she was in this last moment. His secret—of enormous value, as heavy, as solid, as imperishable as gold—which he had cherished so long, had failed to secure her; and, so far as his uses of it were concerned, it had crumbled into dust in his hands. Like many another, he also was learning that even millions will not secure everything. He was hardly aware of Mrs. Anderson's entrance into the room.

"Mr. Middleton," she was saying, "is this true that I hear from my servants?" She seemed taller, colder, whiter than ever, her eyes too bright for one so weak.

"Madam?" Mr. Middleton stammered. That was why he had tried to hurry matters to a conclusion. If he could only have won the word from the daughter which would have committed her to him! After that Mrs. Anderson's news could have been explained away.

"I am told, Emmeline," the mother said, turning to her daughter, "that this person has been elected to the Legislature by the negroes, and that the infamous Jessamine was his chief agent!"

"It will open wonderful opportunities to you, sir. I think *opportunities* was the word you once used in speaking of it," her daughter said, the merriment brighter in her eyes. "Was that your great secret, Mr. Middleton?" she asked.

"No, miss — to your sorrow," he said, and left the room, he scarcely knew how.

Afterwards he explained to Col. Dunwoddie—

"When I was approached, I positively refused to accept the nomination. I had

no more hand in it—upon my word and honor—than yourself, sir!"

But the newly made legislator did not, upon the spot, refuse to serve. Possibly because he had other and far more important work in progress, work which the defeat of his plans in reference to Miss Anderson made it the more necessary he should push to instant conclusion.

———

CHAPTER XXX.

LINES OF LATITUDE.

"*Pickens.* From the dark deeps of our abundant South,
Which hangs on your horizon like a cloud,
Weighed to the earth with ripe beneficence—
"*Lawrence.* And not without its thunder even now,
Following upon its dreadful lightning flash—
"*Pickens.* We snow on you our fleecy wealth.
"*Lawrence.*   Aye, and
We weave it into use and send it back;
And so would we with *you*—would mill, refine,
Would work you into shape—
"*Pickens.*   We thank you, sir!"

UPON the third day after the events last recorded Alice Dunwoddie made another visit at the rooms of her friend. It had been raining steadily all day, and the restless girl had been more miserable than ever, walking up and down like her father, looking out first of one window and then another, as if in hopeless expectation of the coming of that for which she was perishing. Her mother had done all she could, now as so often before, to divert her daughter's mind, but in vain. There was an ever-increasing wretchedness in the obstinate girl which was like a cancer feeding upon her body, and yet having its malignant roots beyond all cure, because in her very soul. Immediately after dinner, under the plea of business with her dressmaker, she persisted in going out through the rain.

Strange to say, Clara Middleton, when she had reached her rooms, seemed to be as little disposed to talk as herself. The brightest days could not enliven Alice, and the darkest days could not depress Clara, and yet she seemed to be as dull as her friend on this occasion. Neither had hinted to the other of the one consuming hope of her life, but no measure of confidence could have made them understand each other better than they did.

To the astonishment of Alice, Clara broke out at last, and suddenly, into a kind of perverse and reckless gayety, which was more bitter than tears.

"What a charming gentleman old Major Clarke is," she said. "He is as handsome as he is gallant. Do you know, Alice, he has fallen in love with me. He has been boarding in this house, dear, especially to make love to me."

"Horrible old wretch," her friend replied; "he is eighty years old, I suppose. All he cares for is to eat and drink, and to talk about his lands. He always says the same thing about you Northern people—"

"That any man ought to be shot, or something, who marries a Yankee girl," interrupted the other. "Oh, yes, I know. I told you, Alice, how his son Ferdinand fell in love with me; he is a wild, handsome young fellow. He grew so pressing at last that I reminded him of what his father said. The poor fellow was almost beside himself. He swore that he would shoot his venerable parent if I said so. I do not know how long it would have lasted, but he did love me; really and truly, he does love me, Alice."

There was a sudden going back to nature in the tones of the lady as she said it, for although Miss Clara laughed and talked a good deal, and wore colors in her face even brighter than those of her dresses and ribbons, it was not always of nature that she reminded one.

"Not many ladies"—she resumed her old manner as she said it—"have a father and son among her lovers at the same time. I do wish," she added, possessed of some devil of perversity, "that my brother would marry Emmeline Anderson, and be done with it," but she refrained from looking at her friend.

Alice Dunwoddie's strength usually took the form of a sullen obstinacy, but now, controlling her sickness at heart, she was able to ask with a kind of calmness, which a woman of a truer heart than Clara Middleton would have trembled at, "But how do you know that Emmeline will consent? Besides," returning stab for stab, "Horace loves her."

"Does he? Well, dear, I happen to know that matters are such—affairs are so arranged, I mean—that Gamaliel will beat him in the race!"

Her brother had always assumed, in conversation with his sister, that he would succeed, and he had not cared as yet to tell her of his defeat. When his plans were developed he would let her know, but he had been too much staggered as yet—stunned, in fact, to a degree which astonished him—to inform her what was next to be done.

There was the intensest bitterness in the words, but the speaker was frightened at having spoken them, and, changing the conversation to old Major Clarke, she spent half an hour in ridiculing him. Strange that a woman should not have known a woman better. Not that Alice seemed other than she had always been—a little gentler, even in her manner, sharing, too, the fun of the other. Nor was there anything unusual in her as she kissed her friend and bade her good-by. Her brother George, who passed her on the stairs with a joke after she had returned home, saw nothing peculiar in her. She laughed as she went on up, but when she reached her room she sat down, her walking-gear still on, her soul steeping itself in the despair to which it had been habituating itself for so many months. Once she got up, laid off her wrappings, turned to her bedside, at which she had been trained to kneel from her infancy, sank down with clasped hands, to arise in the same instant. With a cold, set face she unlocked a costly writing-desk her brother had brought her from the East, and took out a silken cord.

The tassels showed that it had once been part of a dress, but it had been coiled closely and hidden under the papers. She had indulged one hope in life, but one; that was destroyed; what was there in the future for her.

At this instant May burst into the room, overflowing, as she always was, with high spirits. It was pitiful to mark the contrast of the face of the younger girl — bright, open, blooming — with that of the other; it was as of a brilliant morning in comparison with a wintry night. The happy girl, her hair all about her face, was full of their approaching journey — for Harry was almost well enough now to go, her father had announced to them over and over again — and in the midst of her joyous talk she seized her sister about the waist and endeavored to whirl her around the room, kissing her, and singing as she did so. It was some time before Alice could get her to go by pleading a severe headache, but she kissed her sister on her radiant cheek, a thing she rarely did.

As soon as the door was closed she drew the cord from under the bed where she had thrown it. Then she drooped her head in thought. Was there one thing on earth to live for? — one single thing? May was beautiful, and was growing more so every day; but she? In her desperation she stood and studied her face steadily in her looking-glass. Her hair was not silken like her sister's, not soft and curling. Who could blame Mr. Middleton for preferring the large eyes of Emmeline, deep and dark as they were, to hers, which were so small and hard and dull? May was fair of complexion, Clara had an exquisite color of cheek and lips, Emmeline had, more lovely still, the olive hue through which the blood came and went, more eloquently expressive than language — and how pallid and sallow her face in comparison! And her outer person was but, she knew, a true expression of her inner self, dull, uninteresting, weak. *He* could have transformed her,

within and without! There was nothing to do but to rid herself of herself. No one could loathe her more heartily than she herself did.

The door was not locked (she thought of that), and, the last ray of light gone out in her soul, she laid her hand upon the key to turn it, when the door was pushed open and her mother came in, for the first time, on account of her sickness, for many weeks. It was a blind intuition which had driven her there, but, with one glance at her daughter, there was no longer any blindness. Mrs. Dunwoddie had endured much, but this was as if the suffering of a life had been brought into the supreme agony of an instant; it was, as with the Christ on his cross, the blending in the same moment of unspeakable love for its object and yet of a horror as unspeakable. But an angel remains an angel — it is its nature — although on an errand through the smoke of hell. Mrs. Dunwoddie turned without an exclamation, locked the door, took her daughter to her bosom, bore her down beside her upon her knees at the bed, and no one — not even Horace or her husband — ever knew what passed between them. An hour had gone by before the mother was back again in her own room, lying upon her bed utterly exhausted.

Among other peculiarities of the Dunwoddies was that they could not live apart from each other, and it happened now as it had done very often before. Coming into the room, May crept to her mother's side, "just for a moment," to see if she was sick.

"Only a little more tired than usual," her mother replied; and, as she sat down to kiss and comfort her, little Charlie oozed in through a crack in the door and perched himself upon the foot of the bed. Then Harry came in, on his crutch, to remonstrate with Charlie and May for disturbing his mother when they know how much she needed to be quiet. Next George came to rebuke Harry, for the same reason, for staying there. By this time Col. Dun-woddie arrived from his office, and hast-ened to the room to see how his wife and Harry were. When, half an hour later, Horace returned from down town, he also went, as usual, to wherever his mother was to be found. His father was standing at the window looking out upon the dreary scene; and, as usual, the rest of the family, except Alice, were seated upon Mrs. Dun-woddie's bed or standing near it, laughing, talking, arguing, loving each other very much, and their mother, whom they were seriously injuring, most of all. But she lay unusually still to-day.

On this occasion the discussion, when Horace entered, was upon the points where-in the natives of the South were most su-perior to those of the North—the superior-ity itself being assumed, as a matter of course. A vast deal was said, in which the names of Mr. Middleton and his sister, of Hiddikel Queasy, and the Federals before, during, and since the war, were used in one way or another. Col. Dunwoddie had been unusually moody—affected, possibly, by the weather—and had said nothing.

"I am so glad," May summed matters up at last, "that we are Southerners! I was afraid when Uncle Alec went away that he would marry some Yankee girl out West. Wouldn't it have been awful! Horrid thing! I never would have owned her as *my* aunt!"

"Yes, but suppose Horace had brought a Yankee bride when he came back," Harry urged. "You'd have *had* to love her! Now, then! A Yankee sister, Miss May! *she* would have made you mind!"

"I wouldn't! You ought to be ashamed of disturbing mother by saying such dread-ful things. She shouldn't have kissed me," said May. "I would make myself so dis-agreeable she couldn't love me! The idea! I hate the Yankees," said the excited young lady.

"Why, May," her father said, listening at last, "your mother's mother was a Yankee."

"My dear Charles, some other time!" his wife exclaimed. She was weaker than she knew—far weaker than her husband im-agined. But as the Colonel had said it, there was an unfeigned burst of surprise from the lips of George, Harry, and May.

"Oh, pa, how can you distress ma by joking in that way?" May said, when she could recover herself.

"Charles! Charles!" Mrs. Dunwoddie said with her utmost strength, "not now;" but the mood was upon her husband, and, without even looking around, he said—

"It was an insane mistake upon the part of your father, Eliza, to try and hide it. You foolish children! Your mother was born in New England! Horace and Alice know it, and the rest of you should have been told long ago."

It was too dreadful for a joke! There was an outcry, and then a silence more signifi-cant still, for they had never dreamed of such a thing. Mrs. Dunwoddie lay, with her eyes closed, in utter exhaustion, and Charlie looked first at her and then at every other with amazement. Something had befallen too terrible for him to under-stand. It was worse than if a wintry gust from the bleakest of Massachusetts hills had suddenly howled through the room. The children had instinctively drawn away from their mother, and now stood looking at her with alien eyes.

"I never could understand," Horace said, "how Gen. Allen could be such a—singular person."

"As to try and hide it? It is easy to explain. Gen. Allen, your mother's father, was married to a Northern lady, an ex-cellent woman, I happen to know, when he was at college in New England. His father was so exasperated with him that he would not allow him on the plantation after it, and your mother, her mother hav-ing died, was nearly ten years old before your grandfather Allen could bring her, when his father died, to the South. And, meanwhile he was so enraged by what was said about the South and slavery while he was compelled to live in the North, that," Col. Dunwoddie said, "it became a mania with him. When his wife died he sold his father's plantation, and forbade your mother to mention it when he bought his place here. And then the coming-on of the war embittered him still more. Your mother is not a woman who talks, and that is the whole story."

"And Uncle Alec—?" George began.

"—Was a born Yankee, too. And he was regarded as a specimen of a lazy Southern man! I am afraid he used to lie about it; certainly he fought for the Confederacy the more willingly on that account. It is the most abominable nonsense!" Col. Dunwoddie continued. "I am a Southern man in every drop of my blood, and yet some of the most rascally Yankees I ever knew were born here, and were never out of the South in their life."

"And I met in the North some men— men born there," said Horace—"who were almost my ideal of Southern gentlemen."

"It is all folly! The American of the future," his father said, "will have the breadth and bone of the West, the force of the East, and, warming and controlling it all, the heart of the South. My dear, I wouldn't have mentioned it if I had supposed you cared. I am surprised," the husband added, as, for the first time, he saw how exhausted his wife seemed. "Children, you must *not* disturb your mother," he said, for a reaction had come by this time with them.

"Oh, you darling, darling mother!" May was saying on her knees by her, and kissing her. "I love you just as much as ever! You darling mother," she added, with streaming eyes, "it isn't your fault. You didn't go to do it. You couldn't have helped it, to save your life! And you have been such a good, good, darling, darling mother ever since! We won't tell a soul about it! Please don't look so pale and tired. You precious mother! We *do* love you still!"

But at this moment Horace interposed, with a firmness which impressed his father almost as much as the children, and insisted upon his mother being left to herself. In a few moments afterwards, leaving her in the care of Alice, whom he had sought for the purpose, he hastened to bring the family physician.

"Oh that it had been possible," he said as he went, "that Emmeline could have been a daughter to her! It must be because she knows that I have lost Emmeline forever, it must be that which has prostrated her so!"

———————

CHAPTER XXXI.

EVENTS CROWD TOWARDS A CLOSE.

"The Hand which did my being make
Doth strive my utmost strength to break;
Ulysses-like He bends His bow,
And tests my utmost fibre so:
'Tis thus He learns if I will do
To send His arrows strong and true."

THE day following upon these events was Sunday. As Clara Middleton passed Horace Dunwoddie in leaving church in the morning, she contrived to say in his ear, "Please call on me a moment this afternoon. It is business which cannot wait."

"You must have thought it strange, sir," she said to him when he came to her parlor after dinner; "but I will explain in a moment," and she seated herself beside him.

She had laid aside the bright colors of the morning, was dressed simply, almost sadly, and her whole tone and bearing was in accordance. It was as if a woman of fashion had transformed herself into a nun.

"I never was situated as I now am," she said with a modest gravity. "It is impossible for me to consult with any one; strange to say, with my brother least of all. Only yesterday I made a discovery, when I was cleaning out a trunk of his, which is a very important one, and I spoke to you to-day because I can see you without interruption, and it must be attended to promptly. I have had no mother, Mr. Dunwoddie, to advise with since I was quite young," she said sadly, "which has compelled me to act for myself, for I have been separated from my brother also most of the time. I know that you good people here regard me, all of you, as frivolous. Perhaps I am. But I can act with decision when it is necessary. I know my first thought to see you was best, for I slept sweetly upon it all night, and have never doubted."

"Would it not be better to consult my father, Miss Middleton?" Horace asked gravely.

"I would have gone direct to your mother if her health had allowed," the young lady said. "Your father then occurred to me. There are reasons why I should not speak to him. You will learn that—I fear," she added with a species of reluctance which awoke vague apprehensions, while it increased his interest.

There was a clear purpose in her eyes which pleased him, anxious as he was, and he felt more at ease with her than he had hoped. Evidently there were to be no sentimentalities on this occasion.

"I know it is an unusual thing for a young lady to do," she said with a slight color, "but my course will justify itself. The best plan is to come direct to the point. I have a terrible surprise for you, sir. Do you think you can endure it?"

There was such meaning in her words, such pity in her eyes, that Horace Dunwoddie felt his face turn pale, his lips grow dry.

"I think so," he said, "and perhaps better than you imagine," looking her steadily in the eyes.

"Mr. Dunwoddie," she said, "there has been a dreadful mistake about that property of Mr. Allen."

"Hardly," he replied; "he died without a will, and left no relatives besides ourselves, you know. I have seen to it myself, in Nevada, San Francisco, and in New York."

"Yes, sir," she said slowly, the pity deepening in her eyes; "but it does not belong to your mother, nor your father, nor yourself. Please read that; it was what I found in the trunk."

As she said it she placed a large brown envelope in his hand. On the outside was engrossed, in round, lawyer-like writing, a statement in due legal form, underlined with red ink, that it was the Last Will and Testament of Alexander Allen, Esq., of such and such a township, county, and state, made at such a date, before certain specified witnesses, at such a place in Nevada. Hardly conscious of what he did, Horace Dunwoddie opened the envelope, which was unsealed, and came upon a sheet or two of heavy law paper, endorsed upon the back in the same way. Unfolding this, he saw that it was a clear statement of the bequest of his uncle's possessions, with every item of which he was familiar, to Emmeline Anderson, daughter of Judge Pickney Anderson, of such a township, county, and state. There were bequests of large amounts to his mother, but the bulk of the property was thus bequeathed, and all was attested by the witnesses, certified to by Gamaliel Middleton, Esq., Notary Public, with Alec Allen's rambling but well-known signature at the bottom.

As the young man read the document, all of his uncle's well-known attachment to Emmeline Anderson came to his mind. As long as he could remember, it had been the topic of the family, but always as a matter of amusement. It was like the blind devotion of a dog to its mistress; it was an infatuation, an insanity of the slow-witted fellow, all of whose brains, so to speak, had run into that one mania. The very depth and power of the girl, as well as her beauty, had produced this effect upon poor Alec Allen, in virtue, probably, of being himself so unlike and inferior to her. Horace remembered how he had been almost ashamed of his own affection for her, and how he had so carefully concealed it because of this standing joke in regard to his lazy uncle. This will was in strict accordance with all he knew of his uncle, as well as with things he had said and which had been laughed at and forgotten. It was a genuine document, and, in the light of these memories, nothing could seem more natural.

Both of the young people arose from their seats. The lady reached out her hand for the paper; but the young man, cold and white, put it back into the envelope, put the envelope into his inner breast-pocket, buttoned his coat over it, and took his hat.

"Mr. Dunwoddie," she said, "I am only a poor, inexperienced girl. Perhaps I have made a terrible mistake. It seemed to me to be the right thing, the true thing, the only thing to do. You are the one person in all the world— Will you only say I did right?"

She was weeping now. He took her hand in his.

"My brother may be dreadfully angry with me," she added, looking up at her visitor through her tears. "I cannot imagine why he did not tell you all. He has been a good brother to me. Oh, I wonder," she said, as if the thought had struck her for the first time, "if your uncle did not make another will after he got back here from Nevada! I had not thought of that. Of course he did. I am so glad! I am merely a child in such matters. I only wanted to do right. Have I done anything wrong?"

She looked at him pleadingly. Could he have thought of her at the moment, the result, in one sense at least, would have been decided. Possibly she had made sure of this. Not for a moment, however, had he thought of himself, certainly not of her: he was thinking of his sisters, of his mother; but, strange to say, most of all of his father.

"I know I could not have had the courage to tell you," she added, "but I have always thought that you cared as little for

wealth as I do. And I am sometimes afraid," she said, hesitating, "that my brother has been so thrown about among all sorts of people that he might not always—always do exactly—what other people might think right. He would think it was right, you know, and he is the kindest brother that ever lived."

Horace Dunwoddie was deeply moved, even now when the globe itself seemed gone from beneath his feet, as he looked at her. He thoroughly appreciated her course, felt honored by her confidence, was deeply touched by the utterness with which she seemed to throw herself upon him in her emergency. But other considerations claimed him first. For the instant, she was but as a rosy mist through which he fastened his eyes upon his father—his father! He pressed her hand in his, he lifted it to his lips, and then, with a white, set face, he was gone.

He passed out of the hotel and along the streets as in a dream, bowing to acquaintances, lifting his hand to his hat to ladies as he met them on their way to Sunday-school, but all in a mechanical way.

"Why has Middleton hidden this from us?" he asked of himself. "What has been his motive in hiding it from Emmeline Anderson? No need to ask that: he wants to secure the hand of the heiress first—that was plain enough. Had he succeeded? Was it not probable that, in any case, he had told her of the will long ago?"

He found himself, and as if he had been walking in a fog, at the gate of his home. He would go direct to his mother's room. It was as much his instinct to avoid his father until he had seen his mother as if he were a bee instead on the way to the hive wherein was the queen bee.

"But no!"—he halted on the stairs, unconscious that he had taken little Charlie in his arms and was talking with him meanwhile—"she is too feeble for such news. And surely there is no need I should consult her, when I already know what to do."

His father, he was told, had been called for after dinner by Mr. Middleton; they had gone in the direction leading to the river, and he followed them rapidly, asking himself, "What could Middleton want with my father? Who could say what Middleton was or would do? Outwardly we are friends, so far as rivals can be friends; inwardly we are as far apart as the poles. My mother, she does not know why, distrusts him. We will soon see if she is right or wrong. But what does he want with my father?"

Hastening more speedily along, he struck across the fields, at last, to the point where the boat was usually chained. It was gone. Evidently the two had rowed to the island where he had been with his father the day after his return; but there was no other boat, and there was nothing for him to do but wait. He sat upon a fallen log and tried to think. But the tide which had poured through his brain was merely an excess of blood; he would wait a little.

"There is, of course, but one thing to be done, and to be done instantly."

At last one thought came around, upon the whirl of things in his mind, again and again so persistently, that it arrested his attention and insisted upon being considered.

And it was the question—"What can Middleton want with my father? Supposing, for instance, that he is scoundrel enough to wish to do anything wrong, would he dare to propose it to him? Evidently he has held this paper as a secret for his own purposes."

And then he remembered how keen he had been to every sight and sound the memorable morning he had told the household of the inventory he had found in the belt; but now he was dull, stupid. Everything was to him as if it were in a hazy picture—the leaden river flowing slowly and without noise at his feet, the willows and poplars turning their leaves, alternately green and silver, to the breeze. He was barely conscious of a cat-bird scolding him vociferously from a bough overhead. The sun was beginning to sink in the west, as he was vaguely aware, without looking up, by the reflection in the water, which was turning, at last, from lead to gold. A moccason snake came swimming to where he sat, and paused in the water almost in reach of the stick he held in his hand; and as he looked at the head and bright eyes of the reptile he said, almost aloud—

"You vermin! You are not as venomous as you are loathsome! Who fears you?" and at the lifting of his stick it had sunk into the muddy stream. "But, my father —my father! He has set his heart upon what this money alone can enable him to do! And he has been so severely shaken of late! I do not know him, but "—as he thought it, he cast aside his stick, arose and stood—"I know myself."

The shades of evening were falling when he heard the distant sound of oars, and soon the boat appeared in sight, Middleton steering, while Col. Dunwoddie rowed, but (his son thought) in a languid way. Middleton hailed him in a joyous tone, but did not attempt to shake hands with him when they landed.

"Mr. Middleton will take tea with us," the Colonel said as, after fastening the boat, the three moved away; but his father did not look at him as he said it. When they had reached the old field on their way home, the young man said to Middleton—

"Will you be good enough, Mr. Middleton, to excuse us for a little while? I wanted to see my father a moment; we will join you at the house." The person addressed hesitated for an instant, turned as if he would say something. It might have been the aspect of Horace Dunwoddie in the dying light, but he merely said, "Certainly, sir," and passed on.

"What is it, Horace?" the Colonel asked impatiently.

"Let us sit down on this log for a moment," said his son. All around them were trees, stripped of their bark and leaves. They had been girdled years before, and, although still standing, were dead and dry. Many summers and winters had bleached their towering trunks and extended boughs, and they stood white and ghastly, the ghosts of what they had been. But Col. Dunwoddie seemed more stricken than any of them as with the whiteness of death. As Horace looked upon his father there came upon him a passion of respect, of affection for him, of love which had in it the tenderness of a woman for an ailing child.

"What do you want, Horace?" his father asked more impatiently, and refusing to sit down. "Horace," he continued, not waiting for a reply or looking at him, "Mr. Middleton came to ask me for Alice. He is not the son-in-law I would like, but your poor sister loves him. I cannot imagine where she gets her ardent nature. And such a shy and silent girl as she is, too. What do you say?"

The other stopped to ponder. What could be Middleton's reason for this? The man had sufficient reason, he knew: what could it be?

"Mr. Middleton is a scoundrel, sir," he replied without heat, "the coolest and most consummate scoundrel I have ever known."

"That is what I feared," the father said. "What is the sense of being so impulsive?"

"Has he told you all, sir?" his son asked.

"All what? What do you mean, Horace?" But he saw, by a glance at his father's averted eyes, that Middleton had anticipated him, had told him everything. It was only too evident that the wily adventurer had not spent the whole afternoon with Col. Dunwoddie in idleness; and it was singular that Clara Middleton should have taken that precise hour to unbosom herself to him. As rapidly as possible, however, Horace detailed the story of the will

and its contents, without taking it from his pocket.

"Your Uncle Alec was an ass, an infatuated idiot! I could establish in any court of law that he was too great a fool to make a will," the Colonel said with violence. "How can we ever pay back what we have spent, sir? Do you know, it will kill your mother, sir? And what can that girl do with such a fortune? Have you actually broken with her?" he asked.

Horace Dunwoddie had hidden nothing from his mother as to that, and she, with his consent, had told her husband of this long before.

"I have, sir," he said.

"Well, the only thing to do is to make it up with her instantly. Don't you see, sir," his father added angrily, "that she has rejected this man Middleton. He is not in your way."

"He concealed the will from her like a rascal," Horace answered, "until he could marry her. She must have seen that he was without principle, even if she did not know in what sense."

"But he has not told her yet," the father exclaimed eagerly. "Besides, the witnesses are dead; one was shot, the other was killed in an explosion in the mines. Your uncle had forgotten the will—it was just like him, the fool!—and Middleton was bringing it with him to record in this office. That was the paper he spoke of in his letter. He told me, you remember, when I pressed him at the time about it, that it was merely a copy of verses, some of Alec's nonsense—miserable joke!—and which he had destroyed. She knows no more of that will—"

"—Than we did, sir. But we have found it out," interrupted Horace, "and so must she."

"You must make it up with her immediately, my son," the Colonel began again.

"That scoundrel, Middleton, actually supposes," the son remarked, as if he did not hear his father, "that we will keep this concealed, and that by marrying Alice he will share the stealings with us. If there were no other reasons, the knowledge of this will would prevent my further suit to Miss Anderson. That matter is settled."

"It is not stealing, sir," the overwrought father replied. "She rejected Mr. Middleton because, or largely because, she loves you. Your mother knows her better than she does herself. The curse of the Anderson stock has been its abominable pride. Judge Anderson was too proud, sir, to bow even to his Maker; not, at least, until he had been stripped of everything, and was actually dying. She is the incarnation of the pride of her whole race, but she loves with the same—"

"My dear father," the son said respectfully, "once, twice, I have had occasion to ask the lady's forgiveness. I asked and I received it because I was in the wrong. In this last case she was in the wrong, and—"

"There is nothing in the world to hinder," Col. Dunwoddie broke in with sudden energy; "Harry will be well enough for us to go very soon. So will your mother. We will let Alice marry this man. She sincerely loves him. He wants to buy the Anderson plantation and go into politics. Hang him, let him do so! We will leave for Europe. As you know, her mother died this morning, and she will be glad to get away. Your mother will persuade her into being sensible. We can make a bridal trip of it, Horace."

"I have no hope of it, sir. But that is not the question," his son replied. "This paper must be put in her hands immediately, let what will follow. Of course you agree with me in that?"

"As I have just said, her mother died this morning," his father broke in querulously, "and it would be grossly improper to speak to her on such a subject. And she is such a determined, such an undeveloped woman, who can tell what she might do? I will not throw myself into her power—will not risk it, sir. I mean,

until things are settled. We will think it over. Give me that paper."

"You must excuse me, father; but I should like to keep it."

Col. Dunwoddie looked at him with a strange light in his eyes as he said, "Do you dare, sir? Do you know what I have suffered? Do you suppose I will allow myself to be robbed without examining the matter? Give it to me instantly!"

"You will excuse me, father," Horace said; "but I cannot."

"Excuse you, sir! What do you mean, sir?" and, for the first time in his life, Horace Dunwoddie heard his father swear and add—

"Your uncle was a slobbering idiot. The idea of placing such wealth in the hands of a girl, to make her the prey of any fortune-hunter!"

Horace listened as one in a dream, not daring to speak lest he should increase his father's fearful excitement. He realized now, for the first time, and fully, the truth of what his mother had told him. He had resolutely refused to see or believe it before. How his heart yearned over his father—his *father!* as the Colonel suddenly changed his imperious tone to that of entreaty, too pitiful to hear.

"I am old before my time," he said; "and I have great plans in view — great plans, glorious plans! I only wish to examine it, my boy," and he laid a hand upon his son. Before Horace could frame a soothing reply—his cheek wet with tears—his hesitation had again aroused the demon, and with another oath, and "Take *that*, sir!" his father, no longer master of himself, struck his son in the forehead with his utmost force, and strode away through the night.

When Col. Dunwoddie reached his house, he went around it to the well and washed his face and hands, wiping them upon his handkerchief, for he was tremulous—hardly knew where he was. Then he walked stealthily back to the field where he had parted from Horace. It was very dark. He could see nothing. Once or twice he called, and there was a reply at last.

"Yes, father!"

When his father had struck him, for the first time in his life, Horace fell, but it was not from the force of the blow. He lay still. He had no desire ever to rise again. The night was rainy now. He felt the driving drops, but he was so cold and dull of heart that he scarcely noticed them, and could not reply at first; although he had heard his father call once—twice—gently and naturally now. Slowly he arose, and, having answered, came to the fence on the other side of which Col. Dunwoddie stood.

"It is all right, father," he said, anticipating anything the other could say. "No, no, please! If you love me, do not say anything. I ought to have been more respectful. I beg your pardon. It is all right now. Please go on home. I will come directly."

But when his father had gone at last, he sank down on the earth again.

When the miserable man reached his house, May was waiting for him.

"Oh, pa! guess what has happened," she said, too absorbed in her news to notice him more closely. "Mr. Middleton has been here. He asked to see Alice, and was talking to her in the parlor for ever so long. We asked him to stay to supper, but he said he would come again very soon and stay next time. When he was gone, Alice came out and gathered me up in her arms, crying and kissing me, kissing and crying. And she is so happy she will eat you up when she knows you have come. Ma went soon after dinner to see poor, poor Emmeline. The doctor was here and made a dreadful fuss about it, and said he never would have consented to it had he known it."

"And the doctor told us," George broke in, "that he had been looking for Mrs. Anderson to die for a long time."

"I don't think having money makes any difference," George said to May, as their father went slowly up-stairs. "Pa looks like a ghost."

"That's a fact. If," added the lively girl, throwing her hair back, first with one hand and then the other, "there is a thing I hate, it is being sorrowful. Don't you, Judge? I hope Alice will keep on being happy. And I am so sorry for poor, poor Emmeline! What a pity ma had to go there, though! Oh, yes! don't forget, all of you, to tell Horace, when he comes in, that mother said he must come for her just as soon as he has had his supper."

CHAPTER XXXII.

MRS. DUNWODDIE SLEEPS SWEETLY.

"'I once of all this world was lord,
    Decreeing from its central throne:
    'My sovereign will is Law alone;
    Ye shall, all things, with me accord.'

"With calm continuance instead,
    A mightier Monarch smote me down.
    I rose to give to Him my crown:
    'Rule Thou what Thou hast made,' I said."

BEFORE sitting down to the table, after coming in at last, Horace went to his room and wrote a brief letter to Miss Anderson, explaining, in a purely business way, the fact that the existence of the will had come to the knowledge of his father only that day. He added that his father would meet with her, or any one she might appoint, at the earliest moment, to make all the arrangements necessary to fulfil the terms of the will enclosed; and, with merely a word of regret for intruding on her at such a moment, he signed for his father. Then he enclosed the will, with his letter, in an envelope and directed it to her, adding the words "*Important. In haste.*" And, putting the document in his breast-pocket, he ate his supper, hardly aware of the wonderings and sorrowings going on at the table among his brothers and sisters over the death of Mrs. Anderson. When he had first come in, Alice had embraced and kissed him, and told him everything. She was almost hysterical in her happiness, it was, poor girl, so unexpected; and the heart of her brother melted with that kind of pitying affection for her which is so nearly allied to contempt. She knew so little of the man she loved, and yet had accepted his tardy response to her devotion eagerly and gratefully. George enjoyed the transformation in his sister, and tried to lead an assault of raillery upon her; but his father's silence gave him no encouragement. Col. Dunwoddie was indeed unconscious of any of them, except Horace, to whose face he did not once lift his eyes. As soon as supper was over Horace went out and found that his mother had sent back the carriage for him, and he left immediately for the Anderson plantation. It was pitch-dark; the rain was falling steadily; and he felt as if he were moving upon iron rails, and under the driving of a force more powerful than the pulsation of his own heart. Whatever lay across his track would be crushed, as he had himself been crushed, under this higher force which impelled him.

When he reached the place the trees in the yard seemed to be holding a whispered conference among themselves in the darkness, and he sent the driver in for his mother, while he remained with the carriage at the front porch. The hush upon the house was deeper than the darkness, and he was glad to find a refuge in it as a hermit does in his cave. His inmost soul was bruised, and he found a balm, not in the silence and the darkness only, but in the sense of being under the very wings of death. The servant returned with a request from his mother that he should come to her in the parlor, where, according to the custom of the country, the body lay already prepared for the burial. As he entered the door he saw the daughter withdrawing at another, weeping but silent. His mother was seated in the dim light beside her dead friend.

"She was many years older than myself," she whispered as her son stood beside her,

"but I was her little bridesmaid. We had just come to live here when she was married. I know I ought not to have left home on such a night. The doctor has been here to upbraid me. But how could I stay away? I want you to see her."

As she said it she removed the covering, and the young man looked upon the face which had been of late so hard and stern and cold, but which now seemed so peaceful. Rest was the one thing pictured there—rest.

As his mother was leaving the room to prepare for going home, he gave her the bundle of papers for the daughter.

"Please tell her," he whispered, "to pardon my troubling her at such a time, but I could not help it. The papers are exceedingly important. Beg her to lock them up safely, and to look at them as soon as she can."

When Mrs. Dunwoddie came in again, her son took her, notwithstanding her protest, in his arms and bore her to the carriage. He found Emmeline Anderson standing on the porch, and, for a moment after Mrs. Dunwoddie was placed in the carriage, the two wept silently in each other's arms.

"Your mother ought not to have come," she said to Horace at last; "but I am very grateful." And so, kissing her again and again, she allowed her to depart.

"She is silent and strong," said Mrs. Dunwoddie as the carriage rolled slowly home along the road showing white through the darkness, "and her depths of power are depths also of sweetness. It is for such persons that heaven reserves its severest trials. May God help her! She is alone in the world. It is the crisis of her young life. She will harden into something sterner and prouder henceforth than her parents even, or melt into something more womanly than ever. Her mother was the coldest and most reserved woman I ever knew, except to a very few whom she accepted fully as friends. Until of late she was as gentle with me, and as loving, as a child. But she had begun to class your father and myself with this new state of things, and I cannot say I am sorry that she is gone with the things that were. She is at rest now, because she understands now. Or, what is better, she loves and trusts now, it may be, without understanding. Your papers," she added, "must have been very important."

"They could not wait," her son replied with a sense of relief. He had a feeling also that what he had done was in singular keeping with this death. Never could he enter that house again. All that he had done was as inevitable as death, as final and as sacred.

When they reached their own door, Horace carried his mother up-stairs to her room, where Alice and May were waiting to prepare her for the night. While Alice was clinging to her, weeping and telling her of Mr. Middleton's eventful visit, May went to the head of the stairs and called her father and brother up to the room.

"I want to show you the nicest lady you ever saw in your life," she said. "Doesn't ma look just lovely to night?" she added, opening the door for them to come in. "I wish I was half as pretty."

Horace went up, followed by his father, the rest of the household, as was always the case, gathering sooner or later into the room. There was entire unanimity with May in her opinion. For delicate color of complexion, clear sweetness of the loving eyes, the gentle wisdom of the forehead, the fascination of the smile, there was none to compare with her as she lay in bed, protesting against their foolish flattery.

"Oh, but you are a darling," exclaimed May, "if you *were* born in New England! And it wasn't your fault; you would have helped it if you could."

"She looks young enough to be your granddaughter, pa," George remarked. "She is every bit as pretty as Clara Middleton, and I know," he added, "that she is twenty years younger."

"As pretty as Clara Middleton!" said May indignantly. "She is as handsome as Emmeline Anderson, and nobody could say more than that; is 't she, Horace?"

"I am delighted to see you looking so well, my dear," her husband said, "and feeling so well as y u say. In a month or so from this time, children," he continued, glancing at Horace, "we will all of us be in London or Naples. As I said, my dear, we will make it our bridal trip. We did not take one, you know, and you look younger than you did when we were married. I am sure you are a thousand times sweeter and more sensible. You see, children," he said to them, smiling, "I married her when she was young, and have moulded her with my own hands into the most perfect woman living. But," he added, stilling their instant denials with a gesture, "I can't stay. Major Clarke wants me to defend Ferdinand, his son. Your prisoners, Horace, are to be tried soon. All the county will be present. The case will be reported throughout the state. It will interest the whole country, in fact. I never had such a grand opportunity; and just at this critical time, you observe."

"What my father intends," George added gravely, "is to get himself before the country for the Presidency. He wants to let the world see one person in the White House who is a genuine specimen of a Southern—lady; for," he added stubbornly, "I don't believe, myself, one word about her not being born South!"

"Hush, George," his father said, "you are too noisy, and all of you too impulsive. Go away, and let your mother sleep. I am compelled to defend those rascals, for Major Clarke says that great offence has been taken at my putting Anderson Parker forward on the platform."

"He knew that you would have gone in on the other side, sir, and he retained you for Ferdinand to forestall that," Horace said, to reassure his father. But Col. Dunwoddie answered in a hasty manner, not looking at him.

"Perhaps so; in any case, he pays me the largest fee (in land, of course) ever paid a lawyer in the state, and I am glad to *earn* a little money. It tangles matters terribly my being on that side, but I think I can arrange that also. I am going now out on the front porch to study it all over, as the negroes say. Go to bed, every soul of you. No, Alice, my dear, I won't have you say one word more to your mother to-night. You can talk to her all day to-morrow, or listen to what she says, which will be better still. Good-night, and go to sleep, my dear wife." And, driving the others before him, he left the room. Horace lingered behind, for his mother held him by a look.

"Horace," she said, drawing him down to a seat by the bedside, "something has happened, and I will sleep the better when you have told me. You need not try to hide it. I can read you and your father like open books. What is it?"

"To-morrow—not to-night, mother," her son said, rising. "I ought not to keep you awake one moment. It is all right. If I had known of any other way of getting those papers into her hand, I would have done so; but I am so stupid. Good-night," and he stooped to kiss her, laughing lightly.

"Sit down," she said, drawing him into his seat with the hand which had controlled him since he was born. "I know something very serious has happened, as much by your father's manner as by your silence. Your papers did not make me think so."

"I really do not think," Horace said to her gravely, "that I should talk to you to-night. It is all right."

"Yes, it *is* all right, and therefore I must hear everything," she said as steadily as he. "I may not be as ignorant as you think. Tell me."

The young man had never disobeyed her, and there was a command in her eyes which he could not resist. He told her of his interview with Clara Middleton. His mother listened to him without betraying any surprise—much calmer than himself.

"Clara Middleton acted with the genuine impulses of a child. I sincerely sympathize with her," he began. "Any one can see that she is—"

His mother had not said a syllable. There was nothing in her eyes but a smile, which was first a flash of pity for him, and then good-humor. He looked at her a moment and flushed. But he was an older man by a good deal, in experience, at least, when he proceeded with his story. Not one syllable did he utter as to his father's apparent hesitation in reference to the course to be pursued: he merely mentioned Middleton's asking for Alice, and how he had enclosed the papers and given them to Emmeline Anderson through her.

"That is all," he said. "I did not wait to consult you, knowing perfectly what you would say and what I ought to do."

"You have done what was the only thing to be done, my son. I thank God," she added afterwards, and in a sentence to itself.

"It is impossible to imagine a more terrible blow," she continued, after a long silence, during which she had been thinking, but without a shadow upon her brow. "I tell you frankly, I cannot imagine a more terrible disaster to your father—and just at this time." And she remained silent.

"It is entirely natural," she began again at last, "that your father should confidently count upon making it all good by your marrying Emmeline. And you, my son—you love her, that is sufficient. It does not excite me, Horace; tell me over again your whole conversation with her the last time."

Every word of it was graved too deeply to be forgotten, and Horace Dunwoddie repeated it in the smallest particular.

"I understand it all perfectly," his mother said, when he was through; "but I must tell you, my son, that I cannot even conjecture what she will do. She has relations also, who, of course, will use their utmost influence with her. They are coming to her mother's funeral, and she intends going with them to Europe. They leave immediately. Do you know, Horace," she added, "I have never spoken to her of you. It seemed strange to me not to do so, and it may have seemed very much so to her. But I could not. Perhaps it was my knowledge of her, of you—my pride. All my life I have tried never to violate my clear convictions. They have always been very strong, and I have grown to be very obedient to them; nor have I ever regretted it afterwards. All my judgment has been against speaking to her of you."

"I would not have had you do so," he replied. "I greatly prefer to stand upon my own feet, apart even from you and my father."

"It takes a strong man, or woman, to have millions and not be crushed under so much gold," his mother said; "and to handle it wisely for others, and without harm to one's self, one must be able to act with as much coolness, as much ease and self-possession always, as if it were instead a handful of pennies."

"I can imagine," said her son, "that a man is most like his Maker when, possessed of vast power and of ardent love, he remains calm and wise. My father is a man of splendid genius, but I know that he could do more, as well as be a happier man, if he could be—calmer."

"He told me so himself, yesterday," Mrs. Dunwoddie said with a smile. "At least, he said that the reason why men of talent at the South do not achieve more general and lasting distinction is that, like tropical flowers and fruits, they ripen too swiftly."

"And that," her son continued for her, "when the breadth of the West and the persistence of the East get into the blood of the South by immigration here, we will be the noblest people living—yes, he has told me so a hundred times. Dear mother, go to sleep."

"I cannot say," Mrs. Dunwoddie added slowly, "what effect her vast and sudden wealth may have upon Emmeline. I know people in general," Mrs. Dunwoddie said, with a smile.

"Miss Clara Middleton, for instance," suggested her son, ruefully.

"But I must confess Emmeline Anderson puzzles me. Her mother did not know her," she continued; "she does not know herself. Good-night, my dear boy. Go to bed and go to sleep. As I have so often said, you, as well as Emmeline Anderson belong to a different time. Good-night," for her son stooped to kiss her again.

"I wish I were more like you," he said wistfully.

"I am only a weak woman, but listen to me, Horace," she said, keeping his hand in hers; "I believe in God, that he holds us and all things in his hands, and that he does all things well, although almost always against our ideas of what is best. He is closer to me than any other person, and I try to live near to him, to do what he seems to direct, to submit to him absolutely. That is all; but there is no strength or peace, my son, apart from that. In regard to all these matters, we have done what we can, and we are in his hands; and now good-night in good earnest."

But as Horace was leaving the room, his father came in.

"You here yet!" he said. "It was wrong in you to keep your mother awake—very wrong. But," he added, "I may as well say that I have got my line of defence. It and all my plans for the future lie before me to-night with singular clearness. Mrs. Anderson's death seems to break the last tie that holds us here, and we will leave as soon as this trial is over. We will not talk about it now; it is a shame you kept your mother awake. We will soon have her upon the ocean, so broad and blue, so deep and strong. I enjoy it most for its perpetual motion. It will be a glorious change for us all." He glanced wistfully at his son as he talked. Evidently the approaching trial was a new cause of excitement, and he took more than a lawyer's interest in it as the greatest opportunity of his life. "Yes," he continued, as he untied his neckcloth, "I have been, like Samson, grinding at the mill long enough. We will take one good wide sweep over the whole world, and then, as I told you before, we will buy a *chalet* over Lake Geneva, say; and I will see if I cannot condense into a book a little of—of what has been fermenting in my brain so long, of— I sincerely think," he interrupted himself, all his youth in his eyes, "that I can write a book which will make one more name for the South, God bless it! You know how ambitious I used to be, my dear. Don't tell anybody I said so, Horace; but I begin to hope that I may possess more than talent — genius, perhaps. *Vita*," he declaimed, in his shirt-sleeves—"*vita sine literis mors est!* which means, I must write or die. Go to bed, Horace; you poor boy! I am sorry you have learned no Latin. Never mind, you can take all my business off my hands; for, besides writing, I am going to give George, Harry, Charlie, May too, the best education Europe affords. It will be a delightful recreation to me to see to that. Thank God the end has come at last—the end of our bother, and the old inspiration is all back again. 'Oh, I see,'" he said in mock earnest, and striking an attitude, a night-shirt thrown over his outstretched arm—

"'Oh, I see the ancient promise of my spirit hath not set;
Ancient founts of inspiration well thro' all my being yet!'"

"Dear father," said his son, standing at the door, "ought we to keep her awake?"

"It is a shame you have not let her go to sleep long ago. Why are you smiling, my dear?" he added to his wife.

"I was listening to you, Charles," she said as her son left the room, "but I was thinking of Mrs. Anderson too. She is gone on a grander journey, through all the worlds, dear husband—to eternal peace and

rest. Good-night, Charles. I am going to sleep now. I have not felt so well for years."

"You have not looked so well for a long, long time, Eliza. You are beautiful, as May says. Good-night; sleep sweetly," and her husband kissed her, and, taking the light, left the room for the next, which he had long occupied for fear of disturbing her.

Yes, she slept very sweetly.

When her husband stole quietly into her room next morning she was still sleeping, her cheek in the palm of her hand, like a little child. The Colonel paused a moment to admire her peaceful aspect. Then he reached out a hand to touch her forehead, his face growing as white as hers. The next moment a dreadful cry rang through the house, and he fell insensible upon the floor. It was as her physicians had long feared. She was dead.

CHAPTER XXXIII.

COL. DUNWODDIE DEFENDS HIS CLIENTS.

"The river's loitering length fatigues,
Yet some day all its miles are past;
Th' Atlantic rolls a thousand leagues,
To break upon some shore at last.
And yet the weariest one who dies
To wake in heaven's eternal noon,
Though long his road, awak'ning, cries,
'O God, and am I here so soon?'"

MANY weeks had passed since the death of Mrs. Dunwoddie. Although the most domestic of wives and mothers, she had been like a rose-tree which breathes its fragrance beyond its own garden; and, long before her wealth came, no woman in the state was more universally beloved. The money had not changed her at all, either in dress or manner; and she had given of that which she had supposed hers in secret, separate, manifold sums, amounting to a total which would have paralyzed Clair County could it have known it. Her generous heart was felt in its pulsations to the

M

remotest parts of the South, as well as of her own state. Clairsville had never seen such a funeral—not even in the case of Judge Anderson—as that which followed her to the grave beside her brother Alec; and the negroes were as largely represented as the whites.

Col. Dunwoddie and Horace were highly esteemed, yet there was something of a consolation even to good friends of theirs in the disaster which had befallen them.

"Ah, yes," many such said with a shake of the head, "even millions cannot keep off affliction. They have their troubles like the rest of us—worse, perhaps!"

For it had crept abroad that Mr. Middleton was to marry Alice Dunwoddie against the wishes of her family, and that Emmeline Anderson had rejected Horace, and was about leaving for Europe with some distant relatives who had, since her mother's death, made their home with her until she could settle the estate.

Since the night on which he brought his mother home from the Anderson place, Horace Dunwoddie had not spoken to or heard from her. And he, almost unaided, had to sustain the weight of the whole household. Col. Dunwoddie had lain seriously ill, his son despairing for a time as much for his reason as for his life. Alice, like her father, in this, also, had been utterly prostrated; but when she did revive, it was suddenly, and, at last, into more vigorous health than before. But she was changed. To her Middleton had become almost the only person in existence. Not that she was demonstrative, but that henceforth, whatever her lover said was the law of her life: as he had calculated, she gave herself to him with an unquestioning faith and love which were a fanaticism. Carefully as Horace Dunwoddie hid it, there was a bitterness in this which made him turn to May more than ever; and she had, as in a moment, developed a womanly strength which made her almost cheerful as she strove to aid her brother in the management of affairs: it was as if the good sense of her mother had been added to her bloom.

Amid all his anxieties, Horace Dunwoddie had no feeling as of being separated from his mother, although she was dead. "But from Emmeline I am parted forever," he said to himself. "My mother's judgment never failed, and she knew that my life-long hope in that direction was ended forever. Yes, failure—absolute, invariable failure—sooner or later, is the law of this world. Only the young hope, and they hope because they do not know."

But he grew impatient, at last, to hear from the heiress. He had received no word from her so far, and he had not as yet told his father that the will had passed into her hands. Although his mother's funeral took place a few days after that of Mrs. Anderson, Emmeline had been present, dressed in black and deeply veiled. He knew that she was there, knew that she was weeping within her shroud of crape; but his father had, for the time, become almost his sole thought, and until the trial was over he would say nothing to him as to what he had done.

He had urged his father to continue his connection with the case. The fee would be of importance in the altered state of their affairs; and it would divert the mind of the Colonel (he thought chiefly of that) from his affliction.

The day of the trial had been put off again and again on account of his father's illness, but it came at last. Intense interest had been excited in the case. Correspondents were present from almost every leading paper in the country: the old anger of South against North had given place to the hotter heat of a strife at home within party lines, and the proverbial ferocity of feeling in the case of quarrels between closest relatives was more than fulfilled. The entire state almost seemed to have taken possession of Clairsville, multitudes being unable to get near the court-house, which was packed to suffocation; the very windows crowded with eager spectators; every one aware that every other man was armed as well as himself.

The trial of the prisoners for the assault upon Anderson Parker was duly begun. With a full sense of the fact that every incident of the day would be published throughout the land, the usual processes of law were carefully observed. All of the prisoners had been bailed out from the beginning except Yellow Jessamine, who had lain in jail since the assault, lamed for life by his shattered knee. The mulatto was in terror lest things worse than the attack upon Parker should come to light, knowing well that, if they did, the forms of law would be swept away like chaff and he would be hanged to the nearest tree. He lay upon a bench in court, perishing with fright, like a viper which had received its death-blow and was dying in the dust. Not so with Ferdinand Clarke—dressed in a "nobby suit," and, when court was not actually in session, with his felt hat very much to one side upon his head—he was by no means averse to the notoriety he had attained, and, since he had not intended the death of Parker, he rather enjoyed the affair as the best joke of his life; as ready to appreciate whatever might be pathetic or funny in the proceedings as any man there.

Emmeline Anderson had endeavored to aid the prosecution, which had been placed, as was usual, in the hands of young lawyers, by a promise of larger fees to others to assist them. Even if her mother, in dying, had not urged this upon her as a duty to the foreman[?] their crop in former days, she wo[ ]l have done so if it had taken her last cent. But the prosecution were oppressed by the weight of the occasion; and the more they exerted themselves to win a reputation, that much the more sophomorical they became. So much so that, in the highest flight of the most eloquent of them, Col. Dunwoddie arose

and, with ill-concealed disgust upon his face, went out of court on plea of illness.

Leonidas Dunwoddie gave in his testimony gorgeously arrayed. During his examination and cross-examination he kept the crowd in good-humor by his grandiloquence. It was the supreme occasion of his life, and he made the most of it. But the heart of the honest mulatto was touched at beholding his prostrate rival, and he made a point always to refer to him as "Brudder Jessamine," insisting, as often as he could slip it in, that, whatever might be charged against the prisoner, "Brudder Jessamine is a most a powerful preacher!"

There was breathless silence when Horace Dunwoddie, worn and pale, but composed in manner, underwent his examination. This completed, with the evidence of the men who had aided him in rescuing Parker, the first day, and the vast assembly dispersed for the night.

"For my part, gentlemen," Major Clarke said, in the presence of a number of friends who had dropped in at Mr. Robinson's provision-store on the corner of Court-house Square, after supper, "I had no idea that Parker was such a strong character. We all knew that he was honest, industrious, respectful, saving, and all that. He always took off his hat to me. And if he was only a negro, he was a loss to the country, gentlemen. Fact!"

The Major was over sixty, as has been said, very fat, very red in the face, and very rich in land. He had so little to do these dull times that he passed a good deal of his leisure in Mr. Robinson's store—a good article of Bourbon whiskey constituting part of the provisions of the establishment; and (land, alas! not being money just yet) he was deeply in debt to Mr. Robinson, who could, in consequence, take liberties.

"You see, gentlemen," he explained, "Anderson Parker had also become a holder of real estate; the Major has a fellow-feeling for him."

"Well, yes," the other assented; "that

boy is the first negro I ever knew to own land. It is a curious fact, isn't it? That's my idea of a man. No man is a man until he can stand on his own acres! As sure as you live, gentlemen, Anderson Parker was right, insisting, as he always did, that his people never would be worth shucks until they paid taxes on land of their own. They would respect themselves, and we would respect them then, and not till then. I hope I may be shot if I ever thought so before, but that negro was—yes—a great man, by jingo! That son and scamp of mine was at the whipping only from deviltry; *he* had no feeling against Parker."

"Ferdinand ought to have a mother to manage him, Major," Mr. Robinson remarked. "Get a wife, Major, get a wife!"

There was a general laugh at this, for it had recently become known that the old man was to marry Miss Clara Middleton, and had already gone into partnership with her brother in the land business. There were rumors, too, of a new railroad in contemplation by them, Mr. Middleton having "facilities," as a member of the Legislature, in reference thereto, and, altogether, the two men were considered to have in hand a pretty large and very good job. As for the marriage, so far as the Major was concerned, nothing was more natural. The lady was very pretty; he boarded at the same hotel, and had seen her every day for a long time. Gossips had urged his age as a possible objection, but Miss Clara felt that his broad acres, encumbered with but the one scapegrace son, were an ample compensation therefor.

"You mind your own business, Robinson," the Major said now with great good-humor. "What I was going to say, gentlemen," he continued, "is, that some of these days, as sure as you live, people will put up statues to just such men as that boy; Anderson Parker, I mean. See if they don't! The way the war ended has killed my power of being surprised at anything. Yes, a statue—"

"Want to bring your coal quarry into market, don't you, Major?" Mr. Robinson remarked, for he had not merely a reputation for intimacy with the rich old Major to keep up, but also that of a wit. "Ah, Major," he added, shaking his head, "you forget Washington's farewell advice. Better beware, sir, of entangling alliances with foreign powers."

There was such cordial appreciation of this joke in reference to the union of the Major with a lady from the North that Mr. Robinson, standing on his scales as upon a platform, and imitating the Major as far as he dared, exclaimed—

"Any man that marries a Yankee woman ought to be hung! And, blast my garters, gentlemen, but I will help do it!" Which was received with roars of laughter.

At the same moment Col. Dunwoddie was pacing his front porch in the darkness. He supposed that Horace was asleep with the rest of the household, but he was mistaken; for now that his mother was dead, her unsleeping watchfulness over her husband had come to Horace as her chief bequest. The love he had felt for his mother was centred upon his father; for, besides the children, whom did he have to love but his father. As to the Colonel's violence towards him, that had not for an instant awakened in him any other feeling than a deeper love and more tender anxiety.

Like Col. Dunwoddie in that, the excitement, also, of the trial sustained him, and he sat within the house, listening to every foot-fall as the lawyer paced up and down, sometimes speaking aloud as if he were rehearsing his argument for the morrow. Suddenly he stopped, came into the hall for his hat, passed out and down the front walk, closing the gate softly behind him. In another moment his son was following him, filled with terrible fears. He felt that his father was utterly reckless of life, and dreaded to see him turn down the street leading to the river. But no, he walked the other way, and, keeping him in view through the darkness, Horace knew that he was going to the grave of his wife. He followed him none the less, repressing his own emotion.

It was a long walk, but he hoped the fatigue might weary out the unnatural strain upon his father and enable him to sleep; and at last he saw him enter the gate of the cemetery. Continuing after him as near as he dared, he saw him throw himself upon the freshly heaped earth where his wife slept. Horace recalled the night—ages ago it seemed—before the money came, when he had seen him prostrate upon the ground in such bitter distress. Well, what had the money brought but sorrow and disappointment? But his thoughts were less bitter when he heard, as he stood, the weeping of his father—the simple weeping, like that of a child, of the strong but broken man. No fear now lest he should take his own life. The husband was too near his wife again, was too completely under her influence once more, for that. If he had cursed more and more fiercely since the money came, he had meant every oath of it that much the more because it had been uttered when alone or under his breath. Men were less to him than mosquitoes, and he now knew that God had heard him, and that it was God he had really cursed, and God alone. Horace turned to go, then paused as he saw through the darkness that his father had knelt beside the grave in prayer. He heard the first importunate supplications for help, and then stole away; the spot was sacred, and he was relieved of all anxiety for the time.

"When I was in the North," Horace said to himself as he walked back, "I was thrown with more than one set of people who ridiculed the class my father represents. And yet, does not that class embrace Washington, as well as John Randolph of Roanoke? Was it not the highest flower of its time? an order, in fact, of nobility—and of nobility in the truest sense of the word? People laugh at the defects, extravagance, absurdity, of men like my father—laugh, when every paper they read is filled with the rascality of men in politics and business, of men who hold the highest rank in these days. For my part, inexperienced as I am, partial as I must be, I prefer the old idea of a gentleman, if it is perishing from the earth, to the new." And knowing how, as his mother had warned him, his father's reason threatened to give way beneath the long-continued strain, he thought of him with a reverence and love stronger than ever.

"It was I who should not have resisted him," he said to himself. "No wonder a man of his intense character was enraged by what seemed my obstinacy. It was merely as a lawyer that he wished to examine the will. It was a discovery too sudden, too terrible to a man already tried beyond his strength. Besides, that scoundrel Middleton had been with him, and had urged, who can say what? Not unless his reason had given way utterly would he have destroyed or concealed the will. No!" Horace added to himself. "Even in death or in a mad-house my father could not be any other than he is and always has been—the truest gentleman that ever lived!"

At breakfast next morning Col. Dunwoddie seemed wearied and said little, and Horace accompanied him soon after to the court-house.

As they went out of the gate they were met by Mr. Middleton.

"I was dropping in," he said in an offhand manner, conscious of a new dignity in the aspect of Col. Dunwoddie, "to get that paper, if you please. I should have asked for it before, but I did not wish to trouble you during your—"

"Do you mean the will?" the Colonel asked, with something more serene and steady in his bearing than his son had observed for a long time before.

"Yes, if you please," Middleton replied in a lower tone, and glancing around, lest he should be overheard.

"My son placed it, sir, the day he received it, I presume, in the hands of Miss Anderson, to whom it belonged. If you supposed, sir, that we would be capable of doing anything else in regard to it, you are mistaken," and, without another word or glance, the two passed on, to find the court-house packed, if possible, more closely than the day before, the crowd increasing the heat almost to suffocation.

Against his will, Col. Dunwoddie had been compelled to see Tom Terrell associated with him for the defence, and he had left to him the examination of the witnesses, as well as all other details of their common duty.

But the moment came at last when he must speak; and when he arose to begin his argument, the tallest man in the assembly, the excitement reached its highest pitch.

"Blast my garters," Major Clarke whispered to Mr. Robinson, who sat beside him, "if he don't seem ten years older since that day he put Anderson Parker forward to speak!"

"So he does," Mr. Robinson replied. "See how white his hair is. His face is shrunken somehow. There isn't a bit of the old fire in his eyes. You made a mistake, Major, giving him that big fee. He can't speak worth a cent, and Ferdy would have got off easy any way."

"Hush!" said the old Major, "I can't hear what he says."

For the lawyer had begun in such a low tone, and with such a tired manner, that Horace, seated near him, felt sorry he had urged him to accept the case; but he had trembled when his father mounted the platform the last time he had spoken: that had seemed to do him good; perhaps this effort might also.

As the speaker proceeded he seemed to gather strength. In a few words he summed up the evidence, so far as it had been at all favorable to his clients. Then he stated the law of the case, dwelling as little upon Federal law as possible. Next he urged every extenuating circumstance—the ignorance of the men who had seized upon Parker, their not intending to do more than to frighten him. Then he took up Ferdinand Clarke, as illustrating matters. Here was a young man (and Ferdinand stood more erect, conscious with pleasure that the eyes of the crowd were upon him) who, too rich to toil for his bread, overflowing with high spirits, eager for excitement, apt to increase it by drink, had gone into whatever offered, not from malice, purely for the deviltry of the affair. Unlike others who had made much noise since the war, but who had evaded fighting, this youth had fought gallantly. The crowd relished this hit at Tom Terrell, who loomed large, and red of face, on one side. "Yes, this youth," the Colonel continued, "stood ready still to fight—and, if need be, die—for his state and the South."

It may have been his life-long disgust for the burly lawyer associated with him, but he began to speak more rapidly as his eye turned from Terrell and Ferdinand Clarke, from the jury even, to the dense crowd.

"But let us listen," he said at last, "to what people may say on the other side. They may demand why we do not educate our youth, control them, compel them to engage in some honorable business." And he became more excited as he continued to dwell, in the person of some objector outside of the South, upon all that might be said in regard to allowing ignorant, reckless, irresponsible persons to take the law into their own hands. From that, with a passing eulogy upon what slavery had been, he proceeded into the arguments people elsewhere used in reference to the folly of not submitting to its abolition as an accomplished fact, and as to the misery as well as absurdity of trying to continue to live in a dead past, while a future so much more glorious opened before them!

He became more impassioned as he proceeded. His previous speech had for its object conciliation, and had been but the unsealing of fountains of feeling. Since then he had thought and read more earnestly upon the subject; and this was the unimpeded gushing-forth of the utmost he had to say. Utterly reckless since the death of his wife, his intellect shaken to its very foundation, who can tell what may have been his half-conscious purpose in abandoning himself now to the tide of his feelings? Possibly he was indifferent, or had a blind hope even as to the cataract towards which the current was hastening him. Still urging what men outside the South might say, he spoke with increasing force, his eye grew brilliant, his gestures more frequent, his tones more thrilling.

"I'll be shot," old Major Clarke said to his friend beside him, "if he hasn't forgot that he is only trying to say what other people think! It sounds mightily like he was saying what *he* thinks!"

"The old race-horse has got the bit in his teeth," Charlie Marston, the jockey—standing behind the two—stooped down to whisper to the Major. "His blood is up; you'll have to let 'er rip, Major."

"Oh, Ferdy's safe, anyway. Who cares?" the Major replied. "It *was* a big fee I paid, but he's welcome to it. Blast my garters, but it's worth the money, don't matter what side he is on!"

The blood of the man *was* up—up into his overtaxed brain. He had utterly forgotten that he was for the defence, that he had begun merely to say what others might urge.

"In every place," he thundered at last, "there are dangerous classes — wretches who are the scum and refuse, the offal and excrement, of society, the ruffianism and disgrace of humanity. Do not we have them also? We have our Hiddikel Queasys! Detestable reptiles!" he said with such loathing as to bring down an uproar of applause, drowning the protestation of the judge and the outcry of the sheriff. "Hiddikel Queasys?" he continued. "They

are not natives to our soil. Locusts they are, which come from the hand of offended Heaven to devour, during their brief moment, and then depart. Hiddikel Queasys! Very soon will they fly before the vengeance of the people they have plundered; fly, pursued, wherever they seek to hide themselves, by the vengeance of man and of God! But shall *we* escape who sin and remain? Because a man is born here; because he adds to the infernal fires of alcohol the fury of an insane patriotism, shall he escape?"

The audience shrank terrified before him. The sudden alternations in his experience of joy and grief had been too violent: his reason was giving way.

"You," he said, at last, turning upon some of the Clairsville pastors who stood to one side of him—"you preach the gospel of the Son of God! You tell us of that Saviour who, becoming himself a poor man, stooped from heaven to save the lowest. Are you—you who South and North represent Christ—are you doing, and persuading us to do—compelling us to do—what you can to save the lowest among us by saving them from themselves?" There was solemn attention through the audience as he continued, turning to the judge, in the same strain. "And you, sir, who represent the awful majesty of the law—that law which is the voice of God! Men are failing of faith in religion, and what is left but law? Ministers preach, but you are the executive agent of the Almighty. Do you always shield the wronged? Do you always smite as with an unsheathed sword the oppressor?

"There can be but one result, when," he added in deeper tones, "our conflict is not with man, but with God. However right or wrong we may have been about it, slavery has perished before Him! Who but knows that the Turk, that intemperance as an institution, shall be struck down also? And so shall perish everything among us, ignorance and prejudice, whatsoever is hostile to Him still; as everywhere else, here, too, it shall add its ruins to those His victorious footsteps have left behind Him. You or I, sir, like many a shattered institution, may be suffered to engage in hand-to-hand conflict with the terrible King, to learn submission through disastrous defeat!"

His words were a torrent which he seemed unable to check. The people sat as if they could not move. Horace had arisen, and had, at first, laid his hand upon his father's shoulder, then his arm, as he stood behind him, around his person; but he was ignorant of it.

"And shall this our glorious South be forever given over to lag in the rear of the land and of the whole world?" he continued, his eyes dry and terrible to behold; "the helpless victim of the unjust rule of the North and the apathy or passion of its own children as well? I appeal to you, O world," he added, his hands extended as if to the race assembled before him, "to put yourself in our place. Only give us time, and we will prove to you what we are! But as to *us!*" he exclaimed, with flaming eyes, "there is war here, and there shall be war henceforth! War, no longer of section or of color! Henceforth"—and it seemed as if the soul as well as blood of the man had gone to his face—"henceforth there shall be war here upon ignorance and passion! War upon the lawless, and their father the devil! *War* upon these by all true men of the South, and God—God—!"

He staggered, his hands still uplifted, and the son reeled under the sudden burden as his father fell into his arms. Horace's watchfulness and the physician's warning had been in vain. A blood-vessel had burst in his brain, and, although he lingered unconscious for days, he never spoke again.

———————

CHAPTER XXXIV.

A QUEEN ABDICATES.

"Strike, sword !
    If thou dost lay me dead outright,
    I go to God and walk in light.
Strike, sword !
    If thou but wound, not lay me dead,
    God comes and brings me light instead."

IT was some weeks after his father's death before Horace Dunwoddie could look his situation steadily in the face.

One dark December afternoon he was seated in the parlor of his desolate home trying to think and plan for the future. The rain was falling steadily, as if to rain always had been and forever would be the ordinance of nature, except that the cloudy sky was closing in upon the earth more and more darkly, as if to bring its long and weary history to an end. Harry was in his room up-stairs, trying, notwithstanding his grief, in a stealthy way, to write for the press—his ambition being to see himself, if possible, in the print of the town paper —more fearful of detection in his attempt than a criminal. Alice was getting ready in her room to visit Clara Middleton; for old Major Clarke was more troublesome in urging on his marriage than a younger lover could have been, and the bride elect (not diverted from it by any interest in him) had given herself exclusively to the subject of dress. As Alice was to be married before very long to Middleton, she devoted herself wholly to his sister, and to the silks, ribbons, laces, jewelry, and dressmakers, to which Clara Middleton had now surrendered herself entirely.

George had taken his gun and gone out, when it first began to rain, hunting partridges. May had been driven in the carriage immediately after dinner to see Emmeline Anderson, notwithstanding the rain; and Horace, not having heard from the heiress as yet, had merely sent word by May that he would wait upon her "in reference to business"—he carefully repeated the words —whenever she would be ready to see him.

Poor little Charlie, more sober than ever, had clung to May and to Horace of late, for Alice was too much absorbed in her own matters to show him any attention, and, May being away, he had climbed into his brother's lap. He sat there now looking out on the rain and meditating upon the wholly unlooked-for vanishing from his life of his father, and especially his mother; the mystery was too great for him.

"I hope," Horace said to himself as he sat, "that Alice will be happy with Middleton, provided he does marry her, especially as he will be taken up with his land business, his railroad, and his politics. She worships him too blindly ever to find him out."

At this moment Alice came in, seeming remarkably well in her black dress and crape veil.

"Dear brother," she said, as Horace looked up, and tried to smile, "don't be so sad. It is a dreadful affliction, but try to think how happy *I* am. You don't know Mr. Middleton, Horace. He is the best and noblest of men. He is so practical and sensible; see if he does not come to be to us all that papa was. He will be a brother for you to lean upon and be proud of. I grieve as much as you do, but I am so happy! Good-by," and she forgot to kiss little Charlie in her haste to be gone.

"I am glad," Horace said as she closed the door behind her, "that with the doctor's help I contrived to hide my having been wounded from my mother and father. And I will hide things from Alice. If the rascal should marry her, I will have to watch him closely. He will be a curse to us. But he will not marry her. He knows she has nothing, and is only watching his chance to give you the slip, you poor, poor girl! Scoundrel! If I can hide this, I may come to bear and to hide the loss of the woman I loved."

"I will wait no longer," he added after a while. "To-morrow I will apply for the place they wanted me to take at the railroad, and go steadily to work. I am not sorry I had an experience of money: I know now what it can do, and I know, too, what it cannot do. Perhaps I have learned not to be so blind in my enthusiasm. How much of my father's fiery energy was wasted in resistance to the inevitable! I will try to submit myself to that. It will take years of hard work and severe economy to make good to Miss Anderson the money which, over and above what Alec Allen bequeathed to them, my father and mother have given away. But I will do it to the last cent. It is the inevitable, and I accept it;" and there flowed in upon him the pleasure which, to men like himself, always accompanied the entering upon new and hard work.

"I see," he added to himself, as the head of his little brother fell upon his bosom at last, "that poor little Charlie has given up bothering himself about things and gone to sleep. Perhaps"—but he did not say it to himself even; the thought was too deep to be more than a silent resolve— "if, like my mother, I too could rest upon the bosom which made and manages the world, I would have more strength left for work."

There was the sound of wheels at the gate, but he would not disturb Charlie, who was sleeping so peacefully, and sat still, merely saying, "I hope Miss Anderson and her relatives will allow me to see them and be done with it. Hard as it was to hide from the public the news, when it came, of uncle's money, it will be harder still to let it be known that it was not ours. But it will be a relief to have it said and done. If she has sent me no word by May, I will make a secret of the matter no longer. To-morrow I will call upon her relations and insist upon a hearing. Glad to see you back, May," he said aloud, as his sister came into the room. She had changed, as in a month, into a blooming young woman, energetic and full of housewifely virtues.

"Oh but it is pouring down!" she said,

"and I am glad to get back. I don't like Emmeline's kin at all—her grand uncle and aunt, or something of the sort—they are so grim and suspicious. Poor thing! she has to travel with them, you know. Let me have the Judge, for your wounded arm must ache," she added, taking her sleeping brother with a kiss into her arms. "Miss Anderson insisted upon riding back with me, and has gone up-stairs to take off her wrappings."

"Give her my respects, and say that I will call upon her uncle and herself to-morrow at any hour that may suit her. Upon business," Horace added as he went into the hall, took his umbrella, and put on his hat. "I have something to attend to at the office, May, and will not be home until very late. Good-by."

"Please wait one moment, brother," May said. "She wanted to see you to-day; she will be down in a minute."

Horace Dunwoddie, holding his hat and umbrella in his hands, went silently back into the parlor, and stood at the window looking out upon the gloomy weather.

It is said that our planet is but a shell enclosing an ocean of liquid fire. The surface is heaved thereby at times, occasionally the hot blood of the world forces its way out at some volcanic opening; but, as a general rule, the crust of the globe has hardened enough through the ages to resist any such injurious eruptions. Horace had been impulsive once. But that was when he was young and happy, ages—it seemed to him—upon ages ago. He had no fear of himself now. His experiences had been such that he had hardened down and down into the very centre. More than that: the last spark, he thought, had been extinguished within him.

He was as calm as he could wish as the lady came into the doorway. When he had seen her last it was as a proud and angry woman. She had endured severe experiences since then, as well as himself. Had death smitten her, as it had done her

father, her brothers, her mother, she could no more have resisted than these had done. Anderson Parker had been like a wall of stone, rough and remote from her as he might be, and death had struck him down also. Death had subdued Col. Dunwoddie, Mrs. Dunwoddie too—all she had cared for. It was not possible for destruction to come so near her upon every side, and that she should not have felt in herself its awful might. But she stood in the doorway as calm as he, although worn and pale.

"I am sorry to trouble you, sir," she said timidly, as he advanced to meet her. She lifted her eyes as she said it, and met his, stern and cold.

"Do not mention it, Miss Anderson," he said; "my regret is that you should have to trouble yourself to come to me. I would have waited upon you and your relatives with pleasure instead. The weather, too—"

"The rain makes no difference," she replied; "I sent for May that I might be sure you were at home. I did not want you to come to me. I wanted to come to you."

In her dark eyes, raised to his, was the same purpose as of old. They were softer, but steadier, more resolved than ever. "After what has passed," she added slowly, lowering her eyes, the color suffusing her cheeks, "it was my place to come to you."

She said it standing humbly before him. He could not believe his eyes, his ears, his heart. The fire was not gone out within him. It was even rising in rebellion against the rock enclosing it. But he was under some delusion. It was not she, it was his own foolish emotion which confused him. He would make no more boyish mistakes. There had been impetuosity enough, and more than enough. He held himself still and silent for a moment, and then said, as any business man might do, and to any one—

"I expected to hear from you in reference to the papers my mother gave you the night your mother— Excuse me."

"The night my mother lay dead. Yes, your mother gave me a package," she said simply, still waiting upon the threshold of the room like a child, almost like a servant, before him. It was a new aspect of her power—a power over him in comparison with which her sovereign beauty, in days gone by, was as weakness itself.

"I beg your pardon, Miss Anderson," he said more coldly than before; "as I said, I hoped to have heard from you—"

"I wanted to come, sir, long ago," she interrupted him, like a child which seeks to excuse itself, "but I did not know how —when—I did not know if you could see me. I was afraid—"

Her embarrassment was painful to see; she seemed to droop in her lowliness, her hand lifted to the doorway for support. Horace Dunwoddie was becoming desperate, resisting her and resisting himself.

"Miss Anderson," he said, "it was necessary to act at once. As soon as we knew what my uncle had done I sent the papers to you, on behalf of my father. I sent them to you immediately. You should have let me hear from you sooner. I could wait no longer. I had intended to-morrow to let it be known that the property never was ours. I have not done so before merely because I hoped every hour almost to hear from you. Your silence has placed me in a false position. I have been surprised—"

"To hear? Property?" she asked, looking at him with eyes which were filling with tears.

"Can it be possible that you do not know?" the other asked, glad to find some escape into astonishment. "Have you not read the papers?"

"No, sir," she answered simply. "I saw that the envelope contained a letter from you. It seemed to be a remarkably long one," and she smiled as she said it, "but I did not want to read it. That would be for you to come to me, as you did once or twice

before. I am very determined, you know," and the smile and the color came to her face again, "and I wanted to come to you instead."

"This is too painful to endure!" the young man exclaimed hastily. "Miss Anderson, it was all a mistake about my uncle's fortune. At least, it never was ours. He left it to you. That was what the letter was about."

"Was it?" she said, with deep mortification. "Is that all? I hoped that you had —that is—I thought—" and her eyes overflowed with bitter tears as she turned to leave the room.

Horace Dunwoddie was now wholly beside himself. "For Heaven's sake, Miss Emmeline," he exclaimed, trying to stop her, but not daring to touch her, "please understand. You are an heiress! You are the owner of a vast fortune! I don't want to take advantage! How *can* you treat me so?" he said at last, like a boy again in his desperation.

"And how can you have the heart to treat *me* so?" she said, weeping as if she were a mere girl. "What do you suppose I care for the fortune? And when I came to you because we had known each other all our lives—came to you trusting—trusting—that you loved me and would forgive me—"

There was nothing of the rock left now, not the least particle. The insurgent heart as of the world itself had overmastered him also.

"I hope you will excuse me," May remarked when she hurried into the parlor half an hour after, "but Charlie had slept so long in your arms, Horace, that he *wouldn't* go to sleep again. I had to tell him all the Bible stories I could think of. The trouble is, ma has told them all to him already so often —" and her voice broke.

"Did you tell him about Ruth in the barley-field of Boaz?" Emmeline Anderson asked, her eyes soft and smiling. "And there is the story of the Queen of Sheba coming to Solomon. It is a beautiful story, May."

"Yes," said Horace, who was standing very close to their visitor, "but Charlie is like me, he wants to hear about things that have happened since then. Tell Charlie next time, May, about how a goddess came to King Numa, and how he was a king at all only because the goddess took pity upon him and visited him."

"I don't understand—" his sister answered, bewildered by the radiant looks as well as the words of the others, and turning with wondering eyes from the bright face of her brother to that of their visitor, who seemed literally as happy as a queen.

"What do you mean?" repeated May, who had never had a love affair, so far, of her own. "I don't understand you— Yes, I do," she exclaimed, with a sudden rapture, in the same breath. "Oh, yes, I do understand—you darlings!" and she flew into the arms of her brother only to break from them and to embrace her new sister. To May's astonishment, the girl she had thought so proud clung weeping to her, as if she, May, were the woman instead, and herself only a little child.

<hr>

CHAPTER XXXV.

A LANDING UPON THE STAIRWAY.

"As we climb our Alps and Andes,
    There are level ledges, where—
    As on landings of a stair—
'Halt, and breathe here!' the command is,
    'Ere you toil to higher air:
Utmost resting is at length
    Your to-morrow's utmost strength.'"

A vast deal took place during the weeks which followed. But the day came at last when all the household, Mrs. Alice Middleton excepted, stood together upon the deck of a steamer which was entering the Bay of Naples. Even little Charlie was with them.

The beauty of the scene which unrolled itself in panoramic loveliness as they advanced upon the right hand and the left as well as before them, has been too often described to be dwelt upon here; but to them it possessed a charm which was unspeakable. Now one and then the other of the party would call the attention of the rest to some feature in the glorious landscape more beautiful than anything seen before, breaking out in expressions of amazement and rapture. But to those looking on from another world, the men and women in any spot on earth are of far greater interest than any landscape in which they may for the moment be acting their part: it was so when the dull scenery of Clair County was around these, and so, to us also, in regard to them now.

"Was it not strange," May said, as Charlie insisted at last upon being held up in her arms, that he might make a more judicial investigation of the scenery, "that Alice did not insist more strongly upon the Judge's being left with her? We all used to cling together so that I was certain she would not give him up. He is the wisest of us all, and we couldn't have enjoyed one thing if he had stayed behind; but it is strange."

"Not at all," George replied. I don't believe Alice cares for anybody or anything in the world but Mr. Middleton. She was glad to have us go, so that she could have him all to herself. But I'm glad the Judge came," he added. "You can't astonish him, you bet. Whatever he sees, he looks as grave as an owl. Hi, old Solemn! Yonder's a volcano. See the smoke? What do you think of *that?*"

"George is right about Alice," Horace said when he and his wife were left alone for a moment. "Did you ever see such blind devotion? But she will need to believe in him. He is going headlong into all sorts of experiments. I say nothing about it, but, sooner or later, he will wreck himself in some way."

"I am sorry, for her sake and for yours, for it is what I have feared," Mrs. Dunwoddie said. "He will be a great trouble to you, dear; but as to Alice, he can do nothing to shake her faith in him. She will believe in him, whatever he does."

"I confess he is a terrible affliction to me already," said Horace. "But we will need some severe trouble, such as he is sure to be, to keep us—to keep me at least—in due bounds."

"Look at May and the boys yonder. Is it possible," his wife exclaimed, "for human beings to be happier? And yet, what do they know of *my* happiness? The greater the suffering, the greater the gladness."

"Because," her husband added, "the greater the capacity, the character. The one question as to pain or pleasure, poverty or wealth, is, how much character one gets out of it. I believe my mother was a nobler woman by reason of her life of trial. If she was born in the North, she ripened in the South; but, next to her religion, it was her sorrows which made her what she was. My father used to speak of breaking out some day from his troubles like an angel. Into some heaven of freedom, of poetry, of fame, he meant. Who doubts that he has done so, but into a very different and more glorious heaven than he imagined. And Uncle Alec did not live in vain. You have never let me say a word about his will to anybody. When will you, Emmeline?" the young husband asked fondly.

"Never, Horace," she added, with serious eyes. "When Mr. Middleton spoke to me of his secret that day, I thought at first he meant compensation for our slaves. I knew better after he left, and I had time to think; for the day your poor uncle called upon me from the depot, on his first coming home, he told me he had made a great fortune, and had willed it to me; so you see I knew it all the time, and I knew, too, there was some reason why I heard no more of it after his death. Dear husband," she added, her loving eyes in his, "I never doubted you or your father one instant. After Mr. Middleton was gone I understood his secret, and why and how and by whom it had been concealed. But you should never have known, dear. Don't, Horace; people are looking! I want to be serious. Listen. We are to live for ever and ever, dear, and all together, and I am glad our Creator has ordered our lives with reference to that. George *is* right, Horace—that is the volcano. Look!"

Yes, it was Vesuvius. There are many mountains and hills, great and small, but the molten heart of the world does not break through all of them, not even through Vesuvius except now and then.

There is no such molten heat as there is in the hearts of men; and, as in the case of some whose story has been here attempted, it is well that there should be a Vesuvius now and then among men also: it helps to show what is going on in the heart, flaming out or not, of the world everywhere and always.

THE END.

www.ingramcontent.com/pod-product-compliance
Lightning Source LLC
Chambersburg PA
CBHW030610040726
47497CB00008B/2917